Unfollowers

Unfollowers

Leigh Ann Ruggiero

University of Massachusetts Press

Amherst and Boston

ISBN 978-1-62534-640-7 (paper)

Designed by Deste Roosa

Set in Perpetua and Miss Lankfort

Printed and bound by Books International, Inc.

Cover design by Deste Roosa

Cover art by Sara Tafere Barnes, *Dreamscape,* 20"x16" acrylic on canvas painting,

© 2020. Courtesy of the artist.

Library of Congress Cataloging-in-Publication Data

Names: Ruggiero, Leigh Ann, 1983– author.

Title: Unfollowers / Leigh Ann Ruggiero.

Description: Amherst : University of Massachusetts Press, [2022] | Series:

Juniper prize for fiction

Identifiers: LCCN 2021054331 (print) | LCCN 2021054332 (ebook) | ISBN

9781625346407 (paperback) | ISBN 9781613769157 (ebook) | ISBN

9781613769164 (ebook)

Subjects: LCGFT: Psychological fiction. | Novels.

Classification: LCC PS3618.U436 U94 2022 (print) | LCC PS3618.U436

(ebook) | DDC 813/.6—dc23/eng/20211116

LC record available at https://lccn.loc.gov/2021054331

LC ebook record available at https://lccn.loc.gov/2021054332

British Library Cataloguing-in-Publication Data

A catalog record for this book is available from the British Library.

Excerpts from the first Welete section appeared in *The Write Launch* 21 (January

2019), https://thewritelaunch.com/2019/01/unfollowers-chapter-one/.

for my heart-grain

Contents

Unfollowers

One

It is the easiest thing in the world
for a man to look as if he had a great secret in him.

Herman Melville, Moby-Dick, *chapter 19*

KALDI AND THE
DANCING GOATS

I T'S NO SURPRISE WHEN YOU'RE CHOSEN TO CARE FOR THE goats. As a child you spent days chasing their tails as they grazed the hills. You spent nights bedded down not with your family but with the herd.

You have always held yourself apart, as a herder should.

The years pass, you marry, and the goats start to stumble over rocks, tears streaming from their eyes, until the day you lead them south. They graze and you grow hungry, eat the *injera* from your satchel, and sleep. Your dreams shift among familiar landscapes and faces, among the hills you roam, among goats and humans, among beings that are a mixture of the two—these images always umbral, always in shadow.

You wake suddenly to the bleating of the herd. It sounds like fear, and the goats are nowhere in sight. You follow the noise until you find them, butting heads and nipping tails, looking to all the world as if they're kids again. They circle a tree you don't recognize and nibble its purple-red berries from the ground.

You lift one sweet berry to your mouth, chew, and spit out the pit. Something unnamable creeps along your body and seeps through your skin.

Perhaps the berries are magic, firelight by which to read your dreams.

You fold them into your satchel to take home—to your family, to the village, or to the monastery, depending on who's telling the story.

———

WELETE

Barb · May 1978

BARB EKLUND DIDN'T CHOOSE WHERE SHE WAS BORN—NO one could—but she still regretted the way America sat lodged between her ribs like the pain of a torn intercostal. Her parents brought her from Maryland to Welete, Ethiopia, when she was four. Barb didn't understand what she was leaving behind when she boarded the plane: Oscar the stuffed cat, the season of winter, or the red bike with training wheels she rode when winter was in abeyance.

Any sadness was short-lived. The scenery around the Welete mission—hills upon hills of vibrant red soil, the steep banks of the Omo River, the groves of unfamiliar trees and flocks of peculiar birds—extinguished her guttering homesickness. There were too many buildings to explore. The gatehouse. The office. The refectory. The schoolhouse that doubled as the church, its mud walls and tin roof just like homes in the village. The hangar and its Cessna, that magnificent growling machine that popped in and out of the clouds like magic. The missionaries' bungalows, larger than her parents' cramped apartment in Baltimore, and with raised foundations, shingled roofs, and plastered walls. They had no kitchen or running water, just three rooms. Everyone relied on kerosene lamps, and that was part of the fun.

It was the middle of the Red Terror. Ethiopia was ruled by the Derg and led by Mengistu Haile Mariam, deposer of Haile Selassie. Barb pictured Mengistu angry and brooding atop a throne in Addis Ababa, a five-hour drive, but a world away to her in 1978. The villagers preferred the *Gadaa* system to the chairman's rules, and Barb was more concerned with being alone. It took a year to find a friend among the village children. Makeda was the only other five-year-old girl and the only girl of any age who didn't call Barb *ferengi* to her face.

They met during morning lessons. Barb sat in the last row behind a barricade of books. She kept her head down, her pencil moving while Marty, her mother, spoke in a tangle of English, Amharic, and Oromo. (Simeon, her father, taught boys in the other classroom.)

Makeda's hair was plaited in rows along her scalp, and one of her bottom teeth was chipped. She sat directly in front of Barb, turned around, and said, "Hello. How *are* you?" The question felt like a prelude to more ridicule, but Barb answered anyway.

"*Dehna negn.* I'm fine."

Makeda pulled a bean from her dress pocket. "We play!" She mimed what looked like feeding chickens. Barb nodded without understanding, and Makeda, pleased, turned back around, grinning over her shoulder whenever Marty wrote on the board.

From that day on, Makeda would tug Barb away from lunch and lead her to the grove of eucalyptus and coffee trees on the mission. There she taught Barb how to spot and flush mole vipers, to feed the ibises, and, most importantly, to play *mancala* with beans stolen from the mission's provisions. The player who collected the most beans at the end of the game won. That player was invariably Barb until Makeda started bringing extra beans and sitting on them. When the game was over, she slipped them into her stash.

Barb argued she wasn't playing by the rules, and Makeda laughed. Barb suddenly wondered if she'd been wrong—about her insistence on fairness and that cheating was a "sin"—but Makeda was already on to something else.

They didn't trade pieces of glass like the other children, but languages—flower for *abeba,* mountain for *terara,* coffee tree for *buna-zaf.* Sometimes Barb told Bible stories, but she'd rather listen to Makeda's tales stolen from the village healer—about the brothers Borana and Barentu, about the Rat King's Son and the man who grew feathers, about *budas* who wielded the power of the evil eye.

Barb's favorite story was of Kaldi's dancing goats. It made her hold the coffee berries in reverence. They were smooth and dense like her mother's pearls—the Eklunds hadn't brought much with them, two suitcases of clothes and books, pocket Bibles stuffed into every crevice, but the thing of most value was the necklace. Marty had tucked it in her bra to clear customs and had carved out a place to stash it in the plaster of the Eklunds' bungalow. Now the hole was covered by a beaded wall-hanging that depicted images from the Twenty-Third Psalm: a shepherd's crook, a stream, a valley, a chalice.

When the sun reached its peak, Barb crushed the berries between her fingers and elbowed Makeda. The girls raced back to the schoolhouse, hands sticky and uniforms stained. Her mother would hiss out a sigh, but Barb's need for friendship eclipsed her impulse to lead by example.

Makeda and the other children vanished after the mission gates closed, leaving Barb to wander the grounds alone, looking for scenes to draw in the sketchpad she got from the Bjornstads, the couple who tended the chickens. Barb made a game of turning over rocks. Some undersides bore the imprints of pinnules: tiny encoded messages that had taken millennia to reach her.

Sent from where? she wondered and squinted at the sky.

These aimless evenings disappeared when she was nine and a half. The mission pilot transferred, and Barb considered this an open invitation to explore the hangar. Inside she found a wall lined with an alphabet of tools: clamps in the shape of *c*s, iron tubes bent into *l*s, a hinged device like a *w*. She gazed at *o*s and *u*s and *i*s, trying to translate their uses as Daniel had the message in Belshazzar's dining hall. She wondered if the tools were as threatening as the writing on the wall: MENE, MENE, TEKEL, UPHARSIN. *God has numbered the days of your kingdom.*

Behind an unlocked door in the back sat a room with a bed and a dresser. She didn't search the dresser—it felt too much like trespassing—but turned her attention to that growling glory, the Cessna. The plane delivered food, something Marty called *pro-fill-ack-ticks,* and the Good News to nearby towns, roaming the hills like the hyenas that scavenged them. The plane felt just as wild. Barb peeled up the dust cover and slid inside the cockpit to examine its profusion of dials and levers. She often returned with a book and her sketchpad.

The book, usually an L. M. Montgomery from her mother's collection, she read with her legs stretched across the seats, careful not to disturb the throttle. The sketchpad she filled with animals—trout slipping through the currents of the Omo; a viper swallowing one of its babies under the lettuce patch; two hooded vultures fighting over a lifeless jackal, their wings casting sickly shadows along the grass—and portraits of the missionaries. She tried to pin down the puckered expression of Reverend Nilsson or Mrs. Bjornstad's smile between a set of dimples. Barb conserved paper by confining these drawings to corners, as if they had retreated to their own cockpits for privacy.

Her secret evenings ended after she turned ten and the replacement pilot arrived. Declan Kline wore a wrinkled button-down and a pair of Wranglers to his welcome dinner, a traditional spread of *wats,* or stews, served atop the sour flatbread *injera.* He nodded as those around the table offered their names—the Eklunds, the Nilssons, the Bjornstads—and was silent until Marty asked his age (twenty) and where he'd grown up.

"Outside Atlanta, ma'am." He glanced up from his food.

"Just call me Marty." Her voice was cheerful, but Barb noticed her lips tighten.

Dinners continued this way for the rest of the week. Barb sipped her *atmit,* a creamy drink no other missionary seemed to enjoy, and divvied up her time between stealing looks at Declan and avoiding his eyes. Marty seemed suspicious of his silence, but Barb saw it as an indication he hadn't been happy for a long time. Perhaps it was why his shoulders sagged—*hanger shoulders,* her mother called them, though Barb heard *hangar.* The skin pinched between his brows as if he were working out a problem. Barb felt an instant kinship and wondered if she could fix whatever had broken.

One evening he cleared his throat and asked whether the old pilot had left any paperwork in the Cessna.

"What do you mean?" Simeon asked.

"I checked the cockpit today. Found some personal papers under the seats." He looked about to go on but thought better of it. Barb suddenly remembered the two drawings that had come loose from the sketchpad: one of Makeda climbing a eucalyptus and the other of the mission's Leghorn rooster, its eye never accurate enough. The pages must have slipped out as she scrambled from the cockpit one night.

Reverend Nilsson assured Declan, "Jeff didn't leave anything behind."

"No one's touched the hangar since," Simeon added with a wry grin, an expression he usually reserved for chickens and children. "I should probably apologize for the dust."

Declan searched the faces at the table until his gaze settled on Barb. She trained her eyes on her last ort of *injera*. Red broth from her stew seeped across the crumb like blood from a fresh wound.

"If you need a copilot," the reverend said, "I'm willing and able."

"Might take you up on that."

Marty clutched her napkin, and the Bjornstads changed the subject to the state of the runway—just a swath of unkempt grass now.

"Get the villagers to bring in their goats," Simeon suggested, but Barb had stopped listening.

After dinner, she felt a tug at her sleeve. It was Declan, who nodded in the direction of the porch. She suddenly felt the way Anne Shirley must have when Gilbert asked her to marry him (the second time, after the typhus). *Happiness broke over her like a wave.* Wasn't that it?

When they were out of earshot, he asked, "You know about those drawings?"

Her guilt tempered the thrill of a clandestine meeting. She looked at her dirty toes on the porch's weathered slats. Marty fought with her about going barefoot and getting hookworm but—with Simeon's encouragement—had come to a compromise: bare feet indoors only. Here on the porch, a meter from the scrub grass, the rule's threat materialized as suddenly as thunderclouds in the wet season. God was always watching, after all.

"Just want to know how you got in." Declan rubbed his hands in a way that reminded her of the vendors at the *mercato,* as though his livelihood depended on her.

"I wiggled the doors apart." She wasn't sure if Declan would approve, but her body mutinied at falsehood: her eyes, voice, and posture always gave her away. Besides, lying was wrong.

He stood silent long enough that she wondered if the conversation was over. Then he said, "Well, the doors are open now."

She looked up to find him smiling. The sight pleased her so much she felt embarrassed.

But his face was suddenly in shadow, the light from the doorway blocked by Reverend Nilsson and her father.

"How'd she fly today?" the reverend asked while Simeon ushered her inside, his grip on her arm surprisingly tight, so unlike the ethereal tug Declan had given her sleeve.

"You know what your mother says about shoes, even on the porch," Simeon warned, but his eyes betrayed him. Barb was being rescued, not reprimanded.

She visited the hangar the next evening, happy she no longer had to sneak in. (The guilt was fun only for a moment.) She found Declan at the worktable newly littered with parts, his eyes on a wallet-sized photo that disappeared when she knocked. He smiled at her again, a slight twitching at the corners of his mouth, before reaching into a drawer to retrieve the sketches.

"Next time sign your work."

"Thanks, sir." She grasped the pages, disappointed their hands didn't brush like those of the protagonists in her favorite books. The rooster leered at her with its lopsided eye.

"You're awful polite for someone who creeps into cockpits." He scratched his chin where a five o'clock shadow had formed. She couldn't tell if he, too, was disappointed or just bemused.

"Sit?" He gestured to the wall, where the Cessna's back seat stood anticipating an audience.

For better or worse, an audience was what Barb became. She sat and studied Declan's hands as he tuned the plane's engine or unloaded its cargo. She would draw in her sketchpad or, with her big toe, write names in the dust on the floor. Once she asked, "How do you spell 'Declan'?" and, "What does it mean?"

"Beats me. Extreme screw-up?" He smiled at the ball bearing he was wiping.

"Know what Barb means?"

"I have my guesses." He tossed her the rag, which she dodged. He didn't elaborate.

"It means 'foreign.'"

"Really?"

"Like *ferengi*. I hate it." She crossed her arms.

"Huh. Thought it was short for Barb Wire."

"You're joking." His face gave nothing away. She pictured the stuff on the fences that surrounded the mission, along with the birds small enough to land on it.

"This is gonna be loud, Barb Wire."

She reached for the headphones next to her as he slipped into the pilot's seat. A moment later the engine and propeller roared to life. He always warned her of loud noises, not wanting to startle her as the ibises did when they took flight. Their wattles hung limp from their beaks, one appendage a parody of the other. If one of the birds gave its brusque cry—*crrk-haa-haa*—Declan, startled himself, would swallow a curse.

"Y'all look like the goddamn devil," she once heard him mutter.

Barb had grown used to his curses and proud she was the only one privy to them. She wasn't even sure God minded. Still, she worried someone would hear and put an end to their rendezvous, so she argued. "The ibises are *nice*. I've fed them."

"Anything you feed will be nice to you, Barb. Don't you know that?"

She paused, picking at a frayed seam on the row of seats. "That doesn't make sense."

"Why?" He sat next to her.

She suddenly felt warm. "You're nice to me. I don't feed you."

"You're twisting what I said." He half-smiled. "People are different. 'Times you feed them as much as you want, they still hate you."

He held her gaze, and she ripped through the seam.

The mission required that he keep his hair trimmed. The longer he let it grow, the more it stuck out, black tufts with two cowlicks in the back. His skin, like Marty's and Barb's, was darker than the other missionaries'. Sometimes Barb held her arm against his to compare. He laughed the first time she did it.

"We're better suited to the sun than the Bjornstads, yeah?"

"Is that a *thing?*"

He kept smiling. "Where the others burn, we just toast."

She liked that.

Declan never told her parents she'd snuck into the hangar when it was empty—she would have heard about it if he had. She wasn't sure if he acted out of loyalty to her (she hoped so) or out of distrust of the other missionaries. She noticed he had two voices: one that made jokes when they were alone and another that held a quiet rage when he was with the adults.

"He has a chip on his shoulder," Marty complained to Simeon, who shrugged.

"Most men his age do. Remember me in the Coast Guard?"

Marty appeared about to argue but looked at her daughter and reconsidered. Barb wasn't surprised. All adults kept secrets. Declan spoke to her as an equal, but only ten years separated them, half of what separated her and her parents.

One evening he looked particularly thoughtful as he joined her on the back seat.

"Must be hard here, Barb Wire. No other kids around."

She set aside her project of arranging ears of corn to hang from his door. "There's Makeda during the day. I don't need anyone else."

His eyes fixed on a distant point, and she knew he was about to reveal one of his own secrets.

"I had a friend like that once. Rod Granger. Called him the Man of Steel, like Superman."

"Who's Superman?"

"Big, tough, good guy. Rod had these intense arms." Declan flexed his biceps and scrunched his mouth. Barb smiled, too nervous to laugh. "His name was already *Rod*. I don't know why we belabored the point."

"So the other kids—they weren't . . ." She searched for the word. "Nice?"

He hesitated. "I wasn't in a good place. Before I got here I was lost no matter who I followed." He clasped his hands behind his head. "You ever feel that?"

Barb wanted to say, *yes, always,* to confirm their solidarity, but it wasn't true. She always had something to follow—her lessons, her parents, God, even circuitous paths into the cockpit. Maybe later it would be true. Maybe in Declan's posture now—head thrown back, eyes closed—she was seeing her future.

"I don't feel lost with Makeda or with my sketches and books." She paused. "And I don't feel lost here—in the hangar."

He opened his eyes. His gaze felt like a warm breeze wrapping around her shoulders in the grove.

"Good. That's good." He stood and slapped his knees, on to something else.

Sometimes he took breaks to show her some wonder he'd made out of spare parts. He used rubber bands, a set of washers, a dowel rod, and an empty coffee can to build a wind-up toy that sped along the floor when placed on its side. He explained the can's torque and steering (the dowel rod worked like a rudder) as Barb watched him put the contraption together. During lunch the next day she dragged Makeda to the hangar to see the coffee-can car. Declan, surprised by the visit, disappeared into his room and returned with a small hyena, carved from wood. He placed it in Makeda's hands. She kept the toy close for a month, until one of her brothers stole it. Barb was more than a little jealous, but two weeks later he presented her with a finished model of the Cessna, six inches, with a working propeller. She wondered if the hyena, too, had been meant for her, but never asked.

———

Makeda · September 1979

One day long ago the white people came. First the Portuguese, then the Italians, then the missionaries.

I never questioned their presence, and at age five I attached myself to the lone girl on the mission. We met each other under the trees and watched the skies for clouds. We could talk of them forever. There was a mission Jeep. There was a scarab like the one crawling on my arm. There was the pack of hyenas that kept me awake at night with their laughter.

It was hard not to think of myself as American, of her as Ethiopian, as long as we were looking up.

My parents weren't friends with anyone on the mission. They kept their distance. I didn't understand why until the famine, when the missionaries were the only ones with food for months at a time. I heard the way they spoke of us, with pity in their voices. They thought everyone—the healer, my brothers, me—was ignorant.

They were the ignorant ones. They didn't know that long before the mission, before the Derg, before time itself, the god *Igziabeher* blessed the land.

Some in the village seemed to have forgotten, like Dahnay, who spit on the healer whenever he passed.

I didn't fault my parents for taking advantage of the mission's stores. We were a proud family. (I was named for the Queen of Sheba.) And I didn't fault the girl for being a part of the mission.

She believed in me so deeply I wanted to take advantage of her. It was the smart thing, even if it didn't feel right. Instead I defended her to my brothers. They called me a traitor, but never around Mother. (I hid in her bright skirts until she kicked me out the door.)

One day Gabra, a girl two years older, called me *ferengi*. A fire roared in the pit of my stomach. I laughed and pushed her to the ground. It was a mistake. I had no allies in that fight. The other children piled on my chest, and I sucked air until someone knocked me out.

When I got home, Mother kicked me hard and clutched me to her chest. What had gotten into me? She blamed the fight on the weather, and I felt safe again.

The next day the girl held my hand and asked if my face hurt. I lied—why did I lie? So she would tell me how brave I was? She could never do what I did.

"Did your mother get angry?" she asked. Her mother would have.

I shrugged, and she hugged me, a hug that felt so different from Mother's. It was like the warmth of the sun or the rush of the river.

It was like power.

———

Barb · April 1984

Famine hit during the first year Declan was on the mission. Barb wondered if his movement across the Atlantic had upset some cosmic balance. The last famine struck the year she was born, and she couldn't keep herself from ascribing meaning. Why, in God's Plan, were her life and Declan's connected to the starvation of a country?

Makeda spoke of the famine as a purging. "The healer warns us not to attend your services, says, 'A bird perched on two branches will get bitten on both wings.'"

"The famine's a punishment for the mission?" Barb was just scared enough to believe it.

Makeda shook her head. "For those who come here for help."

Barb felt the pain in her ribs. "Will you stop coming to school?" She knew what a drop in attendance could mean.

Makeda laughed. "Mother says, 'Only the man who isn't hungry says the coconut has a hard shell.'"

Barb's relief lasted only a moment. "But the famine is—"

"It's bad, Bar-bra. Of course. It's punishment for the Derg." Makeda stopped herself. Barb knew why. Mengistu—like God—seemed to have eyes everywhere. "*Ethiopia tikdem,*" Makeda whispered. It was what the Derg made them chant at lessons.

"Ethiopia first," Barb repeated, and meant it.

Second only to the Derg in inciting fear was her mother. But Marty, for all her distrust of Declan, seemed unthreatened by Barb's hangar visits. Maybe because he always got her to dinner on time. Sometimes Barb trailed behind and stared at the hat he wore backward. The Atlanta Hawk fixed her with its beady stare. She had been near Atlanta once—at a homestay in Decatur during her family's first furlough, one of the sabbaticals that punctuated their lives on the mission every three years, when Svenska missionaries returned home to reunite with family and friends and to solicit money from churches. Barb dreaded these furloughs as much as her parents welcomed them. She wished she could be like Declan, who skipped them for a bonus. She feared that anyone left in Welete would be lost when she returned from the States. This had been true of Desta, the aide at the school, and Berhanu, the *zebunya* at the mission's gatehouse.

On her second furlough, she turned twelve and counted down every day until she was on the plane headed back, anxious to lay eyes on both Makeda and Declan. She burst from the Jeep as it pulled up to the mission office and ran to the hangar, ignoring her mother's admonition not to bother Mr. Kline.

The doors were still open. As Declan came into view, he smiled and crouched. She ran to his arms, stopping just short of hugging him. She squeezed her eyes shut, trying not to cry with relief. When she opened them again, his smile had disappeared.

"Don't worry. Be happy," she said, still breathless. "That's a song in America."

His hand was on her shoulder, his eyes searching her face. Maybe her tears were confusing him. "Have you heard?"

Her first thought was that he was going to surprise her with wonderful news—she didn't dare imagine what—but his expression said something was wrong. She shrugged off his hand, hating the sudden feeling of powerlessness.

"Tell me!" She'd gone from ecstatic to wary to angry so quickly she felt guilty.

"I thought your parents already had. It's your friend."

Makeda had moved to Nekemte, a four-and-a-half-hour drive northwest, to live with an aunt. Declan pulled *Anne of Green Gables* from the drawer of his worktable. She had lent it to Makeda before the furlough. Now Barb wondered if she had even read it. Her ribs ached. Maybe her ties to Welete had only ever been ties to Makeda.

Declan had stopped talking. Even this close to him Barb felt scared. "She was my sister."

"I know."

How could he know? She wondered if he, too, had a sister who'd been plucked away, but that seemed impossible. She looked at him hard. "Don't ever disappear." She wasn't a demanding child, but she demanded this. "Promise."

His nod was barely there.

Maybe Ethiopia was a catalyst for disappearance. Even the Derg disappeared when Barb was fourteen (though Mengistu didn't), but Declan's promise held. While other mission workers came and went, he remained as though nailed to the wall between the metallic alphabet and the Cessna's spare propeller.

The Eklunds' third furlough was even more unbearable. Barb turned sixteen, and the furlough coordinators had arranged homestays with other teenagers, teenagers who did little more than sneak time in front of MTV or on their new Game Boys. They excluded her and then delighted in her ignorance, so she made herself scarce. In each new town, she prayed to be placed with empty nesters, but it never happened. She would have written to Declan about it, but why should he care about these problems while he was busy doing God's work? Her parents just told her to make friends. She tried, even telling one girl, Julie, about Declan. Julie had cooed and accused Barb of having a crush, only to grow suspicious when she learned Declan's age. In that moment Barb wasn't just uncomfortable in America. She hated what it did to people without their knowing, its seeming perversion of their humanity.

Part of the furlough was spent at her parents' college reunion, and Marty started dropping hints about Barb attending Trinity—hints she ignored. Back on the mission, she cloistered herself in her room to avoid the subject and read from Marty's box of classics. She avoided Declan, too. Something inside her wanted him close, but Julie's voice told her it was hopeless—that he only thought of her as a kid.

One hot afternoon in May, when Barb was just starting *Moby-Dick,* he appeared in her doorway.

"Today's the Obi trip. Wanna come?"

She marked her sentence before looking up. Stains collected on his once-white undershirt, but the black that streaked his neck and cheeks was faint, as if he had tried rubbing the oil off with a rag.

"What did my parents say?"

"Your dad thinks it's a great idea." He didn't mention Marty.

"You don't need a copilot with a license?" Reverend Nilsson had held that position until three years ago.

"You're company enough."

It was all she needed to clap her book shut and follow him outside. The invitation meant she would get a bird's-eye view of the countryside, all the towns she prayed for on Sundays but had never seen. "Do you go to Nekemte?"

He looked at her long enough to make clear he knew why she asked. "Too far north." He pointed up, as though the city were in the clouds. She tried to hide her disappointment.

She was used to flying in the back when she and her parents were being taxied to Addis. Being in front she learned that flying was less about freedom and more about approved altitudes. Declan prided himself on applying for permits well in advance. It was his purpose on the mission, after all, to provide the clans of Oromia with provisions and tracts, even if those tracts went unread. "Kindness is more important," he explained with a shrug.

Their weekly flights suspended the inevitability of college somewhere between the ground and the sky. Her thoughts filled with drag and lift, flaps and ailerons, call signs and manifests as she watched the Omo River glissade through the hills. When Declan wasn't on the radio, she read aloud from *Moby-Dick* and studied him in her periphery.

"Your parents ever mention me?" he once asked. "The Nilssons?" He glanced at her but then fixed his eyes on the mountains.

"They wouldn't be caught dead gossiping." But Barb wasn't sure: gossiping within earshot of the only kid on the mission was one thing, in private another.

"They don't like me."

"How do you know?" she asked, though she'd sensed the same thing since Marty had shied from him at dinner that first night.

"My file."

He immediately regretted saying it. It was true that the missionaries' medical records and intake interviews were housed in the office, but no one read them.

"Sometimes," he went on, "it feels like we just brought America with us."

Barb straightened in her seat. "Don't say that."

"Yeah, yeah. You and America don't get along."

"It makes me sick! I've thrown up in every rental car, I swear."

"You shouldn't swear." He smirked. "You told me about the ice cream in Lubbock."

"Because that was *the worst* time."

"Why? Did a cute boy see you?"

The comment stalled her. She looked away.

"My parents want me to leave sooner now. Stay with a cousin in Idaho to finish high school." She squeezed her eyes shut and blinked them open. "I don't remember Idaho."

"It's Mengistu. People are rising up." His face tensed as he worked the throttle. "They're just worried."

She knew he was right. Lingering famine had led to insurrections that threatened Mengistu's power, and a takeover would lead to war. She was irked to fall victim to her parents' superior knowledge: of God's Plan, of Ethiopian politics, of her future. She'd hoped Declan would defend her because, of course, he would miss her.

"I won't leave," she tested him.

"We all go back eventually."

"Not you."

He half-laughed. "I don't have a reason."

She almost believed him. He never mentioned his family, never made a point of writing to them, not even at Christmas. "Well, I don't have a reason either."

"You don't know if you do. You're too young."

"Blaming my age. Hardly fair." But he had confirmed her fears—she was a child to him.

He sighed. The crease on his forehead fell away, but the tight line of his mouth remained.

Their flights in the Cessna continued, as did Barb's avoidance of her parents. When her mother dared bring up college—in front of the schoolhouse, over meals in the refectory, on trips to the *mercato*—Barb was reduced to shouting. But it was useless. Her parents had decided against Idaho, but not against Trinity; she would leave for America in the August of her eighteenth year.

———

She spent her last morning in the hangar. Declan was readying the Cessna to fly her family to Addis, where she would board her first of three flights to O'Hare: more than twenty hours aloft and alone. Declan had received permission to fly five weeks ago, five weeks that felt like a forced march to a cliff's edge, a bayonet arching her back. Mengistu himself had fled to Zimbabwe in May, leaving Ethiopia to its squabbling factions, which meant an uncertain future for the mission.

"You're getting out just in time, Barb Wire." Declan loaded her suitcase while she stared at the tools on the wall. They had lost their allure once she'd seen Declan's mastery over them.

She helped him return the back seat to the Cessna. The significance of packing away her old vantage point wasn't lost on her.

"God will go with you," he said in Oromo, which only made it hurt more.

"Yeah, sure." She hugged herself, as though they were already in the air and he'd dipped the plane without warning.

"Come on. America won't kill you."

She sneered but remembered this might be their last meeting. "Can we write letters?"

He didn't answer, just wiped the collar of his shirt across his mouth. She sighed.

"You know I never read your file."

"Because you're kind like that."

"I thought you'd just tell me. I was waiting, logging all those hours in the air." His eyes were trained on a washer on the ground, probably from one of the coffee-can cars they'd made when she was eleven. "I thought you'd trust me."

"I do."

She straightened her shoulders. "Then tell me."

Instead, he crushed her against the fuselage and kissed her.

They parted moments later at the sound of voices outside the hangar, but, for Barb, the kiss continued for hours. On the quick flight to the airport, Marty asked if she was excited to be going. "You seem strange."

"Nervous."

She could remember nothing past Declan's salty mouth on hers, his hand on her neck, and what he'd whispered as they parted: *I shot someone, Barb Wire.* The confession started a humming in her stomach that disappeared only when she was halfway across the Atlantic.

———

She wrote Declan from her parents' alma mater and signed her initials with Amharic for love. By the time his response came months later, she had sloughed off the desire to fit in at Trinity, avoiding her suitemates with their teased hair, their tied-off shirts, their Friday-night floor parties. She wore a sweatshirt from the bookstore over denim jumpers donated by her family's sponsors. Her only other purchases were a fanny pack and a pair of tennis shoes that looked like they had been designed by NASA.

Classes here started on time. It took both an aggressive note from a TA and a phone call from an advisor for her to notice. She noticed the weather instead. Storms came year round, not seasonally, and the wind was so sharp against her skin that it felt as if it might pluck flesh from bone. Her refusal to buy a coat (in Welete it would have languished on its hook) resulted in a chronic runny nose. This, coupled with the throbbing in her ribs, made her wonder if there was something worse happening inside her.

The school was an hour from Chicago, a city that was less than half white, but on campus white was all she saw. She sought out everyone else, the students who were called in to photoshoots to showcase the school's commitment to diversity. Because most of these students had grown up in the States, Barb never quite caught the tide of their conversation. They called her the *Norwegian,* though she was a quarter

Lakota on Marty's side (not that her mother spoke of it). The nickname was short for Norwegian Elkhound, a dog that someone had once owned and a play on *Eklund*. It made her smile, but when she tried to explain the nickname to her suitemates, they were offended for her. It was like telling Julie about Declan all over again.

She spent Christmas break with her art history professor, a kind, introverted woman who let her be. Barb had no stories to tell when the other students returned, no breathless excitement with which to describe the Christmas dinner she had attended with other undergrads from overseas. She returned to her studies, used them as a barricade as she always had. Two months later Haile Selassie's remains were found buried under the toilet in Mengistu's former palace. To learn this news from the *Tribune* felt wrong. As a child, the Derg and Mengistu had been cause for fear. Now they felt like her only links to home.

Her evenings were overtaken by her work-study job at the library and reading for class (she couldn't bring herself to sketch), but between Odysseus's stay on Circe's island and Young Goodman Brown's meeting with the devil she searched Declan's letters for the cipher to his feelings. He mentioned nothing of his past. His silence forced her to guess how and why he had shot someone—in self-defense or in cold blood. She justified every possible scenario (even one remarkably like "Folsom Prison Blues") so the details he confessed later wouldn't faze her. The news in his letters was banal by comparison, about his itineraries or what he'd eaten that day. He never used the word *love*, not even about food: *enjoyed, savored,* but never *loved*. Sometimes a compliment appeared that made her hold her breath—a non sequitur preceded by lines vigorously scratched-out—and with the kiss fixed in her mind, she purchased tickets for home.

———

He met her at the airport that summer. The tension in Ethiopia unnerved her; it was like the sinister vamp of an orchestra.

"Everyone's eyes are bloodshot," she whispered as he loaded her suitcase.

"Not here. Get in."

She kept quiet during their long taxi on the runway and studied him discreetly. He was thinner, paler, and had stopped shaving despite the mission's hygiene code. As the Cessna drew even with the clouds, she touched his shoulder. Her hope for a lovers' reunion wilted upon seeing his face.

"It's best we forget." His gaze shifted from the dash to the sky. "So much has changed."

"Oh." She faced out the window, where the mountain peaks pointed at her like spearheads.

Her parents and the Bjornstads were the only families left on the mission, the Nilssons having fled like Mengistu. At dinner they apologized for not killing a chicken.

"With the looting we're lucky to keep the eggs." Simeon winked and Barb felt lost.

Later her parents made her promise to stay in the States.

"Until all this is over." Marty worried Barb's hands in her own. Barb couldn't remember ever seeing her mother frightened before.

Declan avoided her. From doorways she watched his tight circuit between the hangar and the outhouse. She never saw him at meals. At night she reread his letters and cried into her mattress. She didn't pray—prayers had been required so often at school, both in chapel or class (professors shoehorned them in), that they had started to feel unreal, like fables the campus told to justify its existence. Besides, praying for Declan's attention felt like performing a love spell, and weren't those always against the rules? One night she doused her light and stood topless at the window. The hangar's kerosene lamp watched her. Thrilled and ashamed, she threw herself on the mattress and rolled under the mosquito net, hugging her knees to her breasts. She was thankful for the days there were supplies to unload or weeds to pull. Those nights, she kicked off her NASA sneakers bestrewn with red dirt, drew the mosquito net closed, and fell asleep without trying.

She used to think of the pearls as a string of small worlds safe in Marty's hands, and one evening, desperate for something familiar, she lifted up the beaded wall hanging only to find the cache empty.

Simeon found her frozen, staring into the hole, and explained that her mother and the pearls had caught a ride to the *mercato* in Jimma the day the mission's two-way radio had died. Marty had returned with a month's supply of oil and a replacement. Barb couldn't name how she felt—betrayed? diminished? The only thing that hadn't changed on the mission was the flock of ibises. She still fed them with worms unearthed in the garden or with mice caught in traps, and admired the violent jerk of their heads as they ripped their prey apart.

Her last night in Welete, she refused to cry. The old pain returned, prodding like a spur at her ribs. She whipped back the mosquito net, jammed on her reddened sneakers, and made for the hangar.

She found Declan under the Cessna with a flashlight shining between his teeth, legs lolling from the dolly.

"I know it's me." She still felt like a child drawing in the dust with her toe. "Something in me that's wrong." Julie, her suitemates, her TAs, even her mother had confirmed the feeling.

Declan's flashlight clattered to the floor as he slid out from under the plane. She lost momentum at the sight of his hollow cheeks.

He stood and wiped a rag across his face. He wore his old Hawks cap. "You should find someone else, Barb Wire."

She didn't know how to respond, so she waited. He held out his hand, the movement enough to let her mind run with possibilities—what she would say yes to, what would cause her to tremble. Their fingers touched and she wondered how his beard would feel against her skin.

He kissed her so differently from last time—her *only* time. She had imagined this scene so often: her hopes and worries, her clammy hands and shortened breaths. Here he was, finally touching the back of her neck and kissing her mouth open. It was nothing like in the books she had read.

He pulled away. "What brought you here?"

The question had so many answers—nearly a decade of shared history, a year of correspondence at college, and these were just the most obvious. Was it the pain in her ribs? The dwindling time she had here? The need to draw close to someone who had seen all of her?

Declan was a mystery on his best days—all inscrutable truths and bone-crushing gravity. She could handle mysteries. She could mend broken things or people.

The corner of her lips twitched. "What do you think?"

He smiled. She'd never seen his face so open, so she kissed him again, this time walking him back to the Cessna, pressing him against its metal skin—a perfect mirror of their first kiss, a symmetry that made her proud even as she orchestrated it.

It was the bravest thing she'd ever done.

That bravery dried up as Declan's hands found her waist. There was an end to this kiss—an inevitable end that she longed for—but she hesitated at the revelation that he actually hadn't seen all of her. His hand burned along the hem of her shirt and the skin underneath. She wanted more than anything to believe this wasn't a sin.

His hands dropped away, as though he sensed her thoughts. "Do you want . . . ?"

He didn't finish, as if he expected her to say no. The surprise was her wanting him at all.

She pressed a cheek to his chest. Because she could be brave, just not while he was looking at her like that.

"I want anything with you. I don't have a name for it." She reached for his hand and moved it to her breast. He tensed before he understood.

They moved to the Cessna's cargo hold. Its floor was cold, one of many new sensations.

It wasn't how she'd imagined it—more intense, more uncomfortable, more ineffable. She was inside her body for the first time, not just wearing it—being filled to the edges with color or light or both because in that moment words stopped and there was only her, pulsing, tightening, alive.

———

Marty · September 1992

Marty watched the hangar from the porch of their bungalow, staring daggers at the building that had been home to too many mysteries nearly a decade ago, when Reverend Nilsson's affair upset the mission's equilibrium. Svenska Ministries didn't transfer the reverend but the pilot, whom Marty had thought was the victim. Nils Nilsson was a hard man to say no to, after all. His sermons struck her with a blunt force and took no prisoners.

She had worried as the plane sat untouched in the hangar. The Cessna was the main reason the Derg let the mission get by with the occasional threatening visit. Each visit ended in a shared meal between the soldiers and the Bjornstads, who kept the soldiers happy with an ease that made Marty think they should be canonized. She always let herself hope, for a moment, that the Derg would shut down the mission anyway. Then she could recross the ocean, drag her family back to Standing Rock, and find her father and brothers.

But Marty had changed too much for that, even her name.

She didn't know how to feel when the new pilot arrived. He didn't smile as easily as the other missionaries, as if he'd forgotten God could conquer all. In his sloped shoulders and pinched brow she saw he was lost. It was the way she had felt on her first day at the primary school in Bismarck.

She remembered a time before that, on the rez: when summers were spent on the earth between houses rather than on the floors inside them. Who needed a roof when the air was warm and inviting against Marty's skin? She remembered watching her father emerge from a sweat, smelling of sage and animal skins. She hadn't known what went on in the lodge, only that her father sometimes stayed for days at a time, then reappeared skinnier and sun-kissed, despite having been shut up.

As if he'd seen the face of God.

Her father turned divine while she played in the dirt with her brothers. Her mother frowned at her—her mother who had been taken in by the Standing Rock Lakota when she married Marty's father. Once a week she hunted Marty down and dragged her inside to scrub the backs of her arms, knees, and ears raw. Her brothers received no such treatment. Her mother said, "They wash in the river." She meant the Cannonball—home to walleye and pike and catfish that Marty could catch, clean, and cook all on her own. Her mother was wrong. Her brothers never paused in the river to rub a rag or a handful of leaves against their skin. Marty knew this because she was always with them, except for now, when her mother spirited her into the tub.

She scowled. Her mother ignored it.

Her parents talked about land when they were alone. Marty eavesdropped, accidentally at first, but then she found excuses. She shucked corn or peas or worked on her beading nearby. She didn't know they were talking about leaving Standing Rock, but each time her mother brought up the ranch she'd inherited outside Bismarck, dread pooled in Marty's stomach. It was only a matter of time until they headed north to that ranch. Her father would still disappear for days, sometimes for weeks, on pilgrimages back to the rez. He took her brothers, but never Marty. She knew why without asking.

When school came, she was bused into town with kids who looked like her mother—so blond Marty didn't know what to do with them. Her own hair and skin were darker than the other girls'. She thought of it as a gift: the sun stayed with her year round, as if Marty and her brothers were anointed. They were rougher around the edges, too. The things she saw on the ranch—didn't even flinch at—made the girls in her class twist their mouths: rattlesnakes sheltered under rocks, prairie dogs caught in traps, not to mention the manure she and her brothers waded through while taking care of the cows.

Marty's mother feared this roughness. When her lectures on poise and propriety didn't sink in, she tugged her daughter in front of the mirror as if it were time for Marty's bath. On the counter sat a jewelry box whose drawers opened and expanded like a closet of tiny secrets.

Her mother pulled out the pearl necklace that she wore to church and pressed it into Marty's hands.

"Be a woman worthy of these."

No other explanation was needed: Marty should be more like the blond girls in class and less like her brothers. Her mother wouldn't have given up the pearls if that hadn't been important.

So, on the bus to and from school, Marty taught herself how to transform. She became two people—Marty in Bismarck, who over-enunciated and dressed up dolls, and Marty on the ranch, who spoke in the cadence of her brothers and trussed up chickens. At fifteen, she started working at Woolworth's downtown and something shifted: Bismarck Marty slowly rewrote ranch Marty.

She remembered sitting on the back porch one day, the breeze disrupting her updo, when her oldest brother handed her an apple and said, "That's you."

Her brothers laughed. Marty knew what the symbol meant: *white on the inside.* For the first time she mourned the loss of the dirt between her toes and the earthy smell of her armpits.

The mourning soon turned to indignation. "You're just jealous I can pass!"

Her middle brother snorted. She decided not to care.

Marty started attending church with her mother. The hymns were sung straight, unlike her father's vocables that filliped and wavered, dancing around the pitch. She'd never imagined it before—a life without wavering, without the need to clean coops and haul water and dig in the dirt until her hands were dark. Sure, she wanted that life, but she wanted this one too. She started to sing with less contour and found beauty in the steadiness.

She applied to a Bible college in Illinois, where her mother hoped Marty might meet her future husband. She did, of course. Simeon asked her to study, one of the few tolerated interactions between the sexes. She hesitated to say yes, afraid her veneer would rub off if a person got too close, but she'd noticed Simeon's easy smiles around campus, his warm laughs. These particulars—and his broad shoulders, it was true—told her to say *yes* to studying, *yes* to holding hands, *yes* to kissing out of sight (but only for a moment), and *yes* to the ring he offered on their one-year anniversary, two months before he enlisted in the Coast Guard.

They married and moved to Baltimore before he reported to basic training. Those two months alone didn't bother her. She checked out books from the library—classics, like *Moby-Dick,* that she'd missed at school—and found a kinship with the Brontës, especially Anne's book *Agnes Grey.*

Losing herself in *Agnes* made missing Simeon easier. Agnes would never be subdued; she swore to always fulfill her threats and promises; and she believed "habitual associates" could lead a person anywhere against their will. Marty's mother agreed—hadn't she moved Marty from the rez to the ranch just to break her habits?

There was something sinister in the thought. Marty ignored it.

Simeon returned a changed man. Melancholy nestled in the turn of his mouth, and his movements contracted with new anger. Marty didn't tell him about *Agnes.* She read from the script of a supportive spouse for three weeks. Then she smashed a plate in the sink.

Simeon pushed back his chair, a harsh scrape along the tile, but didn't say a word.

"What's wrong with you?" she cried. "The man I married would rush to my side."

His jaw worked back and forth. *More anger,* she thought, but when he spoke, his voice was thick with something else.

"Divorce me, Marty. Just do it."

The words opened the ground below her. One wrong step and she'd fall into the abyss. Simeon. Her Simeon, who was everything her mother wanted for her—and he was giving up.

Marty had been ready to pounce, but his gaze, submissive and expectant, stopped her. He looked lost, like he couldn't remember who he was. Marty knew the feeling. A week ago she woke to thoughts of her father and the rez. They made her dust off one of her beadings, a depiction of the Twenty-Third Psalm; the solid feel of it under her fingers let her breathe again.

She grasped Simeon's shoulders. "The Lord is my shepherd; I shall not want."

Her voice soared, finding clarity as she recited the entire psalm—from the pastures to the valley to the table—and promised to fix him.

"And I don't break promises," she said, thinking of Agnes. "Especially when you're going to be a father."

It was probably true. More importantly, it brought him back to her. They couldn't both be wandering around, torn from the ground like weeds, roots dangling.

Besides, Barb arrived ten months later, and Simeon never did the math.

After his service was up, they were called to Ethiopia, where Marty had to face the world she'd left behind: cleaning coops, hauling water, digging in dirt. This time the land wasn't her own. She was an interloper who carried that irony in her chest. There were days when she felt suddenly, intensely the way she'd painted herself into a corner. She ignored it, like always.

One Sunday Reverend Nilsson preached about the forty years the Israelites spent in the desert in search of the Promised Land, a search that Moses started and Joshua finished. Marty sat in the schoolroom-turned-nave and understood she was in the middle of those forty years, in danger of dying in the desert like Moses. She looked at Barb next to her in the pew and thought, *My daughter will never know her homeland.* On her other side Simeon asked if she was all right.

"Fine." She inhaled, trying to expand time with it, but she felt herself starting to fall, and fall she did, right into the opening in the ground, hell come to greet her.

She remained in hell for five days, lying under the mosquito net, humming songs from the rez that she thought she'd forgotten. Simeon told everyone she'd had a malaria scare. The excuse would fall apart if anyone bothered to test it. Barb believed him, which was all she cared about. (Because to have Barb in her arms after hours of labor, Marty delirious from the loss of blood, had been the most beautiful moment of her life.)

She didn't know how to live with the truth: that she was the colonizer now.

She hummed and sank deeper, deeper. It wasn't until Simeon climbed under the net, held her close, and sobbed, "Come back, come back," that she did as she was told.

She had made her peace. Like Moses, she would never leave the desert.

If she was Moses, then Barb was Joshua. Marty started plotting her daughter's return, and the tension didn't leave her shoulders until she watched Barb's plane leave the tarmac.

She read her daughter's letters from college, hoping something would settle for her, but found no proof. Barb was more likely to write these things to Declan anyway. For every letter Marty received, the pilot received two. She had been so busy engineering Barb's return she'd missed her daughter's fervent gazes at him across the refectory table. If Declan wooed Barb, he would bring her right back to Welete.

She had to put an end to it. Like her own mother, she must banish the "habitual associates" that led Barb to her dissatisfaction.

Marty descended the porch's wooden steps and went to face him.

"Mrs. Eklund." Declan stood at the hangar door. He always had a look about him, like he was searching for his own white whale. "Something broken?"

It was a reference to the day he'd taken her to sell the pearls. She had made the sacrifice without looking back. God asking for her most prized possession had biblical precedent, and she refused to become a pillar of salt. She still had the beading of the psalm, at least.

She stared hard at Declan. Persuasion was her spiritual gift. (It had worked on Simeon.) All she needed was to palpate Declan's tenderest bruise.

"I know what you're planning."

"Ma'am?"

"Don't pretend." He blinked, a crack for her words to shimmy through. "God is loving, but that's not what some of us need."

Some of us need to be told what to do, but even as she had the thought she wavered. The sweat. Her father skinny, sun-kissed, and anointed—he had never lived by the rules.

Perhaps there was a balance, one Barb could find—a space between the vocables of the tribe and the straight tones of the church. The only way to know was to push Declan away.

"That's why I'm here," he said, remorse on his face. "To make amends."

She grimaced and pressed harder. "You haven't served your time."

Her words seemed to release a catch inside him. He slumped against the doorway like a book with worn binding. The movement gave her pause, but she had already spoken her truth.

A month later her prayers were answered. The pilot disappeared.

———

Barb · December 1992

When Declan's letters stopped arriving during Barb's sophomore year, she blamed the international mail, but in December, when she was getting ready for another Christmas dinner with her fellow out-landers, Marty wrote that Declan had driven a Jeep to the capital and never returned. Barb suddenly remembered the model of the Cessna he had given her—its lacquer smelled of ripe papaya. She had lost it to a customs officer at Bole.

She reread Marty's letter, Declan's absence nothing more than a footnote. The anti-American sentiment in Ethiopia hadn't changed since Mengistu left; it was still possible that a *ferengi* could be viewed as a threat. Barb thought she would know if he was alive—wasn't that how it worked?—but the pain in her ribs was always there now, drowning out all other signals and chasing her from the dorm. She loitered outside the chapel or in cubicles at the library and smoked menthols at off-campus diners. The cigarettes smelled like eucalyptus. She reached for each one as though for Declan's hand.

She tried to forget him the way she had everyone else who disappeared from the mission.

It didn't work.

He was equal parts dead and alive, like Schrödinger's cat, and there was nowhere for her imagination to take root. God had started to feel just as muddled. She remembered days as a child when God was as concrete as the berries of the *buna-zaf*. She dreaded losing them both.

Then, a month later, she woke, resolute. She wound Declan's letters with a rubber band, took the Metra into Chicago, and dropped the bundle into Buckingham Fountain when no one was looking.

She met Ross, a seminary student, in her African history survey that semester. He listened as she protested the scant space the class gave Ethiopia—the one chapter it shared with Eritrea. Ross asked her to fill in the gaps, beyond the origins of coffee and the early church. He was Italian on his mother's side and hungry for details of the Italian occupations—"the sins of my people," he called them, which surprised her. They spoke over pizza at his favorite dive.

"It's myopic to leave out Somalia," she said. "Italy invaded all three. Somalia and Eritrea both attacked during the Red Terror. The fighting never stops—"

"It goes in and out, like the tide," Ross offered.

He surprised her again because—why? He'd been listening? No, he hadn't just listened. He'd understood something beyond the words she'd spoken. This wasn't something she expected from an American. "The Eritreans have their independence," she continued. "Now they're fighting Ethiopia over Badme, this sliver of land. I bet we don't even mention it in class."

Ross wanted to know about life on the mission, too. She touched on everything except for Declan and Makeda. These relationships felt like secrets—more theirs than hers. Ross called it their first date. All she knew was that he tolerated her smoking and chronic lateness.

He had no end of his own stories and rants—how broccoli as a pizza topping was underrated, how the phrase "made out" was grotesque, how a life-sized Barbie couldn't even support her own weight. The only subject he skirted was his brother, Jason, who had died in a car accident when Ross was ten. Sometimes Barb found Ross staring out the window or looking away from a scene in a movie, and she imagined these were the moments he remembered what he wouldn't say. She was used to this—Declan had secrets—and, at first glance, Ross was Declan: thick dark hair, olive skin, brown eyes. They checked all the same boxes, but the details of Ross's face, the animation of it, dismissed any comparison. There was a spark in Ross's eyes, even behind his glasses, and when an opportunity for something new presented itself—Bulls tickets, stargazing invites, a trip to Canada or the dunes—he agreed so quickly it was almost as if he'd foreseen these events. One day she had the thought that if Declan were the moon, Ross would be the sun, then hated herself for it. A sentiment so clichéd undermined its accuracy, even if it was sort of true.

A month after they started dating, Ross confessed he had been called to Africa in the seventh grade after seeing a commercial for the Children's Fund. She rankled at his use of *Africa,* as though the continent could be folded up and neatly placed in his pocket, but this was the way in the States—Africa, like Canada, like Mexico, like Russia.

"The look in their eyes." He sat cross-legged on her bunk. "Desperate for something."

Barb tried to remember Makeda's eyes, but saw only the intensity as they taught each other words in the grove. When he spoke of "Africa" Ross's eyes burned with the same intensity, and she thought, *Here's the one who'll take me back.*

That summer she stayed on campus, worked in the library, and lived in the dorms alone, determined to shake herself free from the memories of her previous summer in Welete. Ross helped. He had been an undergrad acting major; and once he started taking her downtown to see shows, she noticed the overlap between the performances onstage and those extended rants he fell into: about the beauty of Rothko, about the pronunciation of the word *blessed* (the adjective had two syllables), about prayer chains at churches, and, again, about Barbies. Barb expressed the same horror when first faced with a row of them at Toys "R" Us. Ross had taken her there looking for Hungry Hungry Hippos, which she'd never heard of. They spent the rest of the evening slamming the hippos' mouths open and retrieving marbles from under couches in the student union.

"Why is there so much pink?" Ross continued between games. "They all wear variations of pink!"

"I think the real question is why they're all the same color," she said.

"Others exist, just not at that store. You haven't even held one! They make this horrible cracking noise when you bend their legs."

Suddenly she did remember holding one—at a homestay on furlough—and eliciting those same cracks. How had she forgotten?

Later, when she teased Ross about a five-game losing streak, he threatened to start calling her Barbie Doll.

"You wouldn't dare."

"Wouldn't I?" His laugh made her feel safe.

She never got used to the way Ross's hair fell over his eyes or how a passing compliment from him made her feel warm, even in the awful air conditioning. By the end of summer, her evenings were full of him showing her "what she had missed" in Ethiopia. Sometimes he even convinced her she *had* missed something, though she wondered if she had just missed knowing him.

The pain between her ribs began to fade. Classes started and they both got busy, but Ross would be there, at the library while she worked, at her door on the nights when her dorm was open to members of the opposite sex. Fall break, the first cold snap of the year, they held a movie marathon. He rented a trilogy of Apocalypse films from the '70s about a group of freedom fighters who'd converted after the Rapture.

"These terrified me as a kid," Ross confided, brandishing the VHS box set. "And tonight is revenge, Barbie Doll."

"Seriously with the 'Barbie Doll'?"

"I'm never serious. Promise."

They spent the night eating candy from the grocery store checkout line and laughing at bad special effects. Barb was still sucked in by scenes of freedom fighters being tortured by the Antichrist's minions: the too-vibrant blood reminded her of the bodies she'd seen suspended from trees on trips to neighboring villages, casualties first of the Derg and later of infighting. Simeon had clapped a hand over her eyes as they drove past, but she'd seen the bodies in the rearview mirror, nothing more than red pulp left of their faces.

Ross broke her concentration. "Are they using corn syrup or Heinz for blood? Think the effects guys ever tried it on their sandwiches?"

By the third film, Ross's commentary and a box of Junior Mints had taught her that neither Mengistu's soldiers nor the Four Horsemen were coming for her. As the credits rolled, she felt Ross watching her. He closed the space between them on the couch and threaded his fingers through her hair. Their noses touched and he sighed.

"Is this okay?"

She waited too long to answer and felt his hand go limp against her neck. In that moment she saw what it would be like to let Ross slip away. Her life had already started to form around his, his around hers, in a way that comforted them both. She let out the breath she'd been holding.

"I love you." It was something she never said to Declan.

He smiled, took off his glasses, and kissed her.

Later he offered to walk her back to the dorm. As she reached for her sweatshirt, he said he loved her too and laughed. "You *need* a coat."

He reached into his closet and pulled out an orange parka with a hole in the right armpit. She accepted it without hesitation.

He proposed over Christmas break. They were on the couch in his parents' basement, alone except for the yellow lab nestled between them and some holiday movie playing in the background, when Ross asked if she ever thought about getting married.

She smirked and scratched Olly under his collar. "Why not? You're as good as anybody."

"Thanks. So much." He smiled back and kissed her over the dog. "You first said *I love you* on a couch like this."

She trailed a finger along his jaw. "It was secondhand, wasn't it?"

"I hope you mean the couch." He kissed her again. "Olly hates that collar. Give him a breather."

When she reached to unclip it, she noticed the ring clinking against Olly's license. These delicate touches from Ross always surprised her. Here was something she hadn't even imagined until the ring sat in her palm. It felt like proof that America could push a person downstream so fast that they forgot to hop out. She found herself wondering if the slowness had died with Declan. (Was he dead? Would she ever know?) Maybe after a loss like that everything moved more quickly—once you knew death was ongoing and inevitable.

They held the wedding that June while her parents were on furlough. Her guests needed only the first three rows while Ross's filled even the balcony.

She never got around to seeing his beloved Children's Fund commercial until he sat her down in front of the TV in their first apartment. She was met with a sea of brown faces and distended bellies. The onscreen spokesman, nearly as white as his wrinkle-free buttondown, described the children as if they weren't there.

Ross made a face. "Things are never as good as you remember."

Declan, Makeda—the commercial was just another thing she didn't discuss.

AFTER WELETE

$\mathcal{B}arb$ · $\mathcal{J}uly$ 2004

I T'S ANOTHER JULY IN WESTERN PENNSYLVANIA. TODAY
Barb turns thirty-one; tomorrow she leaves for the missionary
conference without Ross.

She's learned that America doesn't just speed time up. It can also,
as at this moment, slow time to a stop. She sets the oven timer and
stares at the clutter on the granite counter: a receipt pike stuck with
expired coupons; two bunches of not-quite-ripe bananas in a wicker
bowl; and the waffle iron, cardinal reminder of her infidelity, perched
at the edge as though threatening to jump.

She splays her fingers and looks at her wedding ring. The skin
beneath it is pale and macerated, but she only removes the ring at
the conference: four days, over too quickly, in the nation's capital.
This year, with the ultimatum looming, she looks forward to the
conference with equal parts excitement and dread.

She first removed the ring five years ago and left it on her lover's
alarm clock. She was back in her own hotel room, on the phone with
Ross when she noticed its absence. He was saying, "Routine goes
out the window without you. I'm eating cold pizza for breakfast."
The comment made her pause the way she would pause to examine
the undersides of rocks as a kid. In it seemed hidden the fact that he
missed her.

She stopped at a Walmart on her way to Dulles, wedding band
secure, and stuffed the new waffle iron and three boxes of waffle mix
in her carry-on with the hope that they would be her surrogates each
July when she returned to the conference. She presented Ross with
these gifts at the baggage claim in Pittsburgh. (When had lying turned

easy?) That evening he volunteered to whisk the batter and poured first too much, then too little. The iron hissed and spat in protest, and Barb braced herself for catastrophe until certain of having escaped it.

Each year when she leaves for DC, Ross upholds his ritual of cold pizza as faithfully as his weekly duties as head pastor of Mount Olive Baptist. The possibility of his missing her has dissolved. He prefers leftovers for breakfast, the scarcely used iron and passed-date waffle mix evidence enough.

His alarm bleats from upstairs. She listens to him move from bedroom to bathroom and starts the coffee, wondering if it's her last morning to drain yesterday's dregs, separate filters, and eyeball the water and grounds; her last morning to arrive at the church office, answer calls from distraught congregants and disgruntled deacons, document prayer requests, and balance the books at her desk. Locked inside her center drawer are her flight confirmation and a sheaf of divorce papers.

She's given herself until the flight to serve Ross the sheaf or shred it.

He descends the stairs and shuffles bare-chested into the kitchen, gradually advancing on Barb's position at the counter. Her mouth, a rigid grimace, checks him at the refrigerator.

"No run this morning?" she asks.

"Late night."

"I noticed."

He tugs on an undershirt and squints at the calendar featuring Mount Olive–sponsored missionaries. This month it's Barb's parents. Simeon swims in an oversized sport coat while Marty attempts elegance in a borrowed pillbox hat. A floating outline of northeastern Africa is photoshopped behind their heads, along with a terse description of their mission: *Education and Conversion of Rural Ethiopia.* Ross scans the calendar and frowns.

"House visits today." He shoots her a look. "You usually warn me."

"Lot on my mind."

"The conference?"

"Trusting Raji to run things while I'm at the conference."

Ross met Raji in Mumbai a year ago, during one of the ten-day trips he organizes for the "Followers of Christ" every other summer. The group returns with inspiring stories of God's work in the Dominican Republic or Russia or India—stories packaged into a PowerPoint and presented at a special Wednesday-evening service, much like the stories Barb's parents shilled on their furloughs. Without fail, Ross's slides display a conversion story: Carlos Reyes, the construction foreman who spoke in tongues at his first prayer meeting; Olya Popov, the street vendor who painted watercolors of Saint Basil's but had never been inside; and Raji Amin, the barista who muttered his Hindu mantra while slinging espresso. Barb doesn't know what happened to Carlos or Olya, but Raji started at Edinboro University last fall and was hired as the church intern a month ago, the internship being Ross's brainchild and Barb's annoyance.

Ross pours his coffee and makes their breakfast. Lately she's been unable to stomach shredded wheat, so he prepares two bowls of yogurt with delicately sliced peaches. His persistent acts of kindness prod her to confess her sins. She thanks him instead—a politeness that, given the length of their marriage, feels more like an impoliteness.

They take their places in the breakfast nook. Ross stretches his body along his chair, jostling the table legs with his own.

"Have you thought of what to get your parents?"

Simeon and Marty had weathered famine, civil war, and five presidents in Ethiopia, but last week, just as the boundary conflict with Eritrea was heating up again, they called to announce their retirement. Next May they'll move to a community of retired missionaries in North Carolina, a ten-hour drive from Bethel, which worries Barb. She's acclimated to—even likes—their living an ocean away. Their faces hang from her fridge, but their personalities have simmered so long in her memory that they've been reduced to only their most obvious traits. She pictures Simeon relaxed, welcoming guests to the mission, taking communion with Americans, Ethiopians, and Scandinavians, and Marty vexed, disciplining her students with a wooden paddle. Their quick visits on furloughs have only solidified these pictures. Every so often a memory resurfaces that contradicts these roles—her father punching a wall in the refectory, her mother laughing as a house snake wriggles along her palms—but the dichotomy sticks. And when Marty's monthly letters (not emails, never emails) arrive, Barb sees instead of the words themselves the spaces between the words. Ross reads them to her in one of the accents he collected as an actor. The Russian one is her favorite, a vestige of a Chekov play. Only her husband, as a bumbling New Yorker or British aristocrat, gives Barb permission to laugh at the seriousness of her mother.

She tells him she has no idea what to get, but suggests a nice bottle of wine, a gift Simeon would appreciate more than Marty would. Ross picks up a *National Geographic* from the pile of lapsed subscriptions on the table—more clutter Barb has never adjusted to—and smiles. "We could always give them the waffle iron."

Her response is to fidget and glance everywhere but at him. It's the same way she watches the evening news, unable to look the anchors in the eye. Viewing reports of disasters, everything from vandalized local homes to earthquakes overseas, ignites her sense of doom. While Ross scours these accounts for sermon illustrations, she receives them like prophecies of greater devastation to come.

He rests a hand on her knee by way of apology. She scrapes the bottom of her bowl with a spoon, the only sound between them until the oven timer reminds them they'll be late.

———

Ross pulls into the Mount Olive parking lot, alongside the forsaken box office. The church used to be a Cineplex—concessions were sold in what is now the narthex, and summer blockbusters were projected onto a wall that reads *Rejoice Always!* The building's insides were gutted—arcade games yanked from the floor, projection booths cleared of film reels, gaudy carpets peeled back from cement—but the remodeling stalled at the façade. The funds have run dry, which so embarrasses the deacons that they've planted a row of elms to hide the marquee lights. Barb once watched them reprimand the youth group for playing with one of the pinball machines in the storage closet.

"Got the cards?" Ross asks, and she jumps. He rests a hand on her shoulder, gives it a quick squeeze.

The index cards are from a Rolodex of housebound church members. Today Ross will attend a tea party with Delia Torrez's stuffed animals, taste test Mrs. Moreno's new granola recipe, and weed Mr. Meeker's rhododendrons. His day ends with a grocery run for Ralph Wheaton's painkillers and frozen potpies. Ross will line the chest freezer in Ralph's doublewide with every available flavor: beef, turkey, and endless variations on chicken—creamy parmesan chicken, creamy mushroom chicken, even cheesy chicken and bacon for good measure. This thoroughness in her husband once endeared him to Barb. Now it makes her shoulders sag.

She reaches into her pocket and hands over the cards. As he thumbs through them, she slips a nearly empty pack of cigarettes from the glove compartment and into her cardigan. He raises his eyebrows. It's no secret she only smokes when something's weighing on her. She can feel his urge to ask what's wrong, but he looks at the clock on the dashboard. There's no time.

"I'll take 89 home so I can fill up at the cheap Sunoco." He hesitates. "I'm sorry about your birthday."

It's the first time he's mentioned it, and Barb knows why. If he'd had something planned, any excitement had evaporated the moment he realized the day had fallen on house visits.

"We can celebrate when I get back from the conference," she says, without knowing if she'll be back. "I'll get a ride home with Joan. Maybe she and I can go out to eat."

He hides his disappointment with a wry smile. "Think of me, laden with frozen dinners."

"Save your receipts," she says, though he will claim to forget. She surrenders a kiss before escaping to the office.

Everything boots up: the copier whirs, the printer shifts its weight, and Barb's computer tower roars to life. She counts her remaining cigarettes—three—and peeks into her desk drawer. The pages of her flight confirmation and the divorce papers have threaded together overnight, mixing in ways that defy chance. *The contents of drawers shift,* she tells herself, and shuts it quickly, as if Raji might suddenly materialize, though he never arrives before 9:15.

She welcomes his late arrivals. They prolong the calm before his dressing-downs about Ethiopia—the Red Terror, the famine of the '80s, the civil war. Barb had grown so used to the congregation's repertoire—"Did you get malaria?" "Did you go hungry?" "Did you see lions?"—that at first the precision of Raji's questions startled her. Now she just tries to ignore the way in which they grow more personal each week, like a noose drawing taut.

He arrives later than usual, characteristically overdressed in a pressed shirt and silk tie. Ross wears nothing nicer than polos to the office, and Barb prefers plain blouses and garish skirts purchased from thrift stores. This morning she's wearing her favorite, the color of sand populated with a rainbow of Egyptian symbols: all ankhs and eyes and asps. She greets Raji and trains her gaze on her monitor, hoping to update the budget before tomorrow. She wants to leave the office in order.

He starts a pot of coffee. "Know what I found last night?"

He's been googling (again). "No idea. Remind me when Joan's coming in?"

This time he's discovered that Italian soldiers first encountered espresso during their deployment in Ethiopia and brought the drink home with them. "Hate Starbucks? Blame Ethiopia!"

"I think she said 11."

"And! The first Christians were from there."

"The first set of *organized churches*." The correction is knee-jerk.

He leans back in his chair, victorious. "Coffee and churches. This is your entire life!"

She scoffs but can't argue—out of the grove and into the pew. She wonders if their proximity on weekdays has allowed Raji insight into what Ross, sequestered behind his Head Pastor's door, remains ignorant of.

When Raji speaks again, an hour has passed; she's almost forgotten him—the yogurt, it turns out, is just as hard on her stomach as the shredded wheat.

"Do you miss Ethiopia?" It's his most personal question yet.

She follows his gaze to the office building across the street, home of the largest law practice in Bethel. Raji is pre-law, the building a symbol of his future. The sun's reflection off its skylights reminds Barb of the tin roofs in Welete. "You don't miss India?"

He shrugs, giving up on something. A Black woman in a miniskirt exits the law practice, someone Barb recognizes because the sea of white in Bethel is almost as pronounced as it was at Trinity. Raji averts his gaze.

She remembers being his age, a newlywed trying to convince herself she didn't miss Welete. That changed when she stumbled on a recording of "Bohemian Rhapsody" at Live Aid. The lyrics reminded her of child soldiers, not *Wayne's World*; neither the plastic Pepsi cups littering the piano nor Freddie Mercury blowing kisses to the crowd kept her from the realization that she would never truly leave Ethiopia behind.

Raji's still in denial, still has "favorite things" about America, like fried Oreos at the fair. In time he'll see how his habits betray him—his distaste for miniskirts and red meat, his insistence on removing his shoes in the church as though it were a temple.

Today he prepares a leftover Gujarat curry for lunch. He clicks the microwave door open and the rich sauce sizzles. Its smell—cumin and fennel—reminds Barb of her favorite *wats*.

"A man called while you were letting Joan into the sound booth."

"Yeah?"

"No name. Wanted to know when your flight gets in tomorrow."

She can see where his story's headed: how Raji looked for the answer in her desk and what did she mean by *the marriage is irretrievably broken*? "What did you say?"

"That I didn't know. He hung up on me."

She wonders if Raji is Ross's spy, but nothing in the drawer looks out of place.

"It's better not to think about it." Raji's returned to their previous conversation. "I've changed too much for India."

He stirs his curry into a bed of basmati as if his words are unimportant, yet he's spoken one of her greatest fears: that she's changed so much she won't recognize Welete or, worse, that it won't recognize her.

Then there's the phone call. Other than one letter apiece, she and Declan have avoided correspondence. The call, placed to a number she didn't even know he had, must be about the ultimatum. Maybe he thinks she's made her decision, that it's as obvious as their unspoken rule against keeping in touch.

Five years ago it would have been.

———

Barb · July 1999

She was at the conference's opening reception waiting for Ann, a missionary kid from Nigeria and one of the few college friends she still spoke to. Barb was on her first bite of crab Rangoon when she saw him speaking to a volunteer. The hair at his temples was gray and his shoulders no longer slouched. She wondered if his hands still smelled of sap and iron.

As soon as he was alone Barb touched his arm. "Are you Declan Kline?"

He turned and stared; the age lines at his mouth were what she noticed.

"Declan?" He nodded. She pointed at herself like an accusation. "Barb. From Welete." She remembered the feeling of standing bare-chested and breathless before her window.

"Oh. Yes." He smiled in the same circumspect way he had for the volunteer.

"How are you here?" It was a question she had often imagined asking him while brushing her teeth in front of the bathroom mirror: the first week she had learned of his disappearance, the week before her wedding, and (though she tried to stop) nearly every week since.

"I'm speaking." He unrolled his program and pointed at one of the next day's sessions: *Harrowing Tales from the Mission Field.*

"Not the best title."

"It was last-minute." He paused long enough so that she felt the silence like a draft on her neck. "Need to prepare. Excuse me."

"Of course." She envied his ability to erase their past with a tone.

But then he was leaning in, and was that his old smirk? "You should come."

"Okay." She hid a grin with her fingers and, without meaning to, flashed the ring Ross had just inscribed for their fifth anniversary.

The next morning she made dinner reservations for her birthday—herself and Ann at Nora Pouillon's restaurant. She attended two sessions without listening and smoked to calm her nerves. She arrived late to Declan's talk and sat in the back as he stood onstage answering questions that had haunted her since college. After the power vacuum left by Mengistu, the EPRDF had stepped in. She already knew this, but not that they had detained Declan's Jeep in Addis and taken him into custody. His guards were Sudanese and had immediately noticed his Atlanta Hawks hat. They followed the NBA on account of their countryman Manute Bol. "We knew him!" they said. "We beat him in *fútbol!*" The audience laughed. To Barb the story seemed censored for people who needed the gristle cut from their meat.

Declan played poker with the guards while other prisoners marched past his cell to the firing squad. After six months a guard took pity on him—"You still here?"—and unlocked his door. God had answered his prayers, just like that. The audience stood and applauded, some descending the aisle toward the stage. Barb was far from first in the receiving line. She gave up her spot to sneak another smoke in the stairwell. Why had she come?

The stairwell door swung open as she stubbed out her cigarette. "Barb?"

She steadied herself on the rail.

"Not what you expected?" He gestured to the auditorium. She couldn't tell if he was ashamed or proud.

"I didn't have expectations." He hesitated. It was possible she made him nervous. "First you find Rod Granger, then that guard who let you out."

He was impressed by her memory and met the challenge. "Let me take you out for your birthday."

She pursed her lips, pleased, then remembered Ann. "I'm meeting a friend at seven."

He nodded like it was nothing.

"Come along?"

They exchanged room numbers. Both were at the Renaissance.

"My friend's nice," she promised.

———

Barb wore a light blouse and gauzy skirt to stave off the muggy DC evening. She told Ann she was waiting for an old friend from Welete, but seven came and went and Ann sighed.

"Just because we used to show up six hours late to everything doesn't mean we still should." She led them out the door.

At the restaurant Barb ordered three glasses of wine and still couldn't mention Declan. When Ann took her back to the hotel, Barb announced she was going for a walk.

"Honey." Ann used the same tone when her four-year-old picked up the scissors sharp-end first.

"I'll call you." She grasped Ann's arm to reassure her. Then she bolted.

On the elevator to his floor, her head thick with sauvignon, she thought of Ross. He deserved better. Why had he bothered with her of all people? Why hadn't she warned him?

The elevator dinged open and she was suddenly in front of Declan's door, knocking. His silhouette darkened the light under it. She held her breath as the knob turned.

"Barb?"

"Declan." His name felt new in her mouth.

"Sorry. I ran out of time."

She knew he was lying. He disappeared inside the room. It was the reverse of hers. She crossed the threshold and started to cry.

She hated the pity in his eyes as she took off her wedding ring, squeezing it until she felt its shape in the fascia of her palm, and asked the one question she would never outgrow: "How can I go back?"

His hands answered: one at her neck, the other untucking her blouse.

———

Her first night with Ross had been a comedy of errors. Intent on getting it right, he ended up all angles and calculations, their bodies hitting marks called out by an invisible director. They'd grown familiar since.

Ross silently reached across the no man's land of their queen, held her hand, and waited. One night (after house visits) he slid next to her and asked the ceiling, "It would be easier if God existed, right?"

The question didn't surprise her in the way it should have. Perhaps Ross had seen the same doubt in her that she had seen in him: the way his face sagged on Saturday evenings when the pulpit loomed, the way she sneaked through the backdoor to avoid the painting of Golgotha hanging in the foyer (a gift from Ross's mother). When they made love that night, the attentiveness of his fingers and his mouth surprised her. It was as if he were shining light into her corners.

She calmed her breath. "That was new." She felt his embarrassment in the dark.

"Good?" She kissed his hand in answer.

But the brilliance of that night was an anomaly. He took time with her, and in that time she imagined Declan in his place.

There had been too many things she wanted to do with Declan, scenes that had played in her mind during those first years at college. They were old enough now that some seemed foolish—her somehow surprising him with her pilot's license, his argument with her parents as he asked for her hand. There was no end to her imagination then.

Declan's weight against her felt right. She pulled his shirt above his head and saw the chain of scars along his torso, new since their night in the hangar. These he'd omitted from his "harrowing tale."

"Sorry." She withdrew her hand.

He kissed her. "They don't hurt."

Something in her suddenly went limp. *I'll let him do anything to me,* she thought.

Later she touched the scars carefully, examining the warped skin by the bedside light. A teardrop wound on his left oblique was larger than the rest. It seemed a manifestation of the old pain between her ribs.

Declan had been a lucky American, his country responsible for funding the EPRDF, but an unlucky opponent of the guards. "For when I lost." He placed a hand lightly on hers.

"They cheated," she said matter-of-factly, remembering the beans in Makeda's tight fist.

"For when I won, too." He shook his head. "They said they asked the mission for a ransom."

"Oh" was all Barb could say. They fell asleep shortly after.

When she woke the next morning he was gone. Her chest seized: had she somehow lost him again? But his clothes were there. Her wedding band watched her from the alarm clock. She took a breath and looked out the window. The room had a view of the United Methodist Church across the street. *Churches always within spitting distance,* she thought. Then the door opened and Declan appeared, carrying a plate from the continental breakfast.

"Eat and we'll go, Barb Wire." She stared and he shifted his weight. "Having second thoughts?"

"No." She reached for her underwear.

They walked to the National Mall. Barb spent most of her time at the African Art Museum, staring into the red eyes of a *Male figure* about a foot tall. Declan had to touch her wrist to get her attention.

"Do you still draw?"

"Not as much as I'd like to."

For dinner they found an Ethiopian restaurant on U Street. He ordered beer and a platter of *wats,* ladled onto a circle of *injera.* Declan thanked the server in Amharic, and she replied in Oromo. He asked if she knew Welete.

"I had cousins in Jimma."

"Did you know a Makeda?" Barb asked. Something in her snagged at speaking Amharic again, as though the language had outgrown her. The server shrugged. "Thank you anyway. *Ameseginalehu.*"

She nodded and left.

"She probably knows a dozen Makedas. How stupid." Barb stared at her hands.

"When were you last there?"

"When I was with you." She didn't meet his eyes. He touched her face so she would. She wondered what the other patrons saw, if they could tell the two of them were lovers. She unfolded a piece of *injera,* holding it to her nose like the wine from the night before. They took their first bites of *doro wat* and he asked, "What does your husband do?"

To Barb, he looked too calm, evenly tearing a wedge of *injera* and wrapping it around a bite of chicken; she tensed without thinking.

"We met when I thought you were dead."

He didn't ask about Ross again.

Declan currently worked in Svenska's Florida office; Barb remembered it from the furloughs. "It feels a little too close to home, if you can believe that."

She mentioned that she, too, had an office job, but not how far from home it felt.

When he pulled out his wallet to pay, he gazed into its contents long enough for her to wonder what was inside. He'd always had secrets. It was hard to believe she was now one of them.

Each year they met like this: Barb attended enough sessions to report back, met Ann for lunch, and spent evening till morning with him. She avoided talk of Bethel, just as he avoided talk of Florida. They spoke of what they shared—and he recounted what had happened on the mission after she left. The situation was worse than her parents had told her. Soldiers routinely stole from the refectory and sometimes performed inspections of the school, taking with them children who never returned. Most of the missionaries assumed the worst.

"Your mother seemed unfazed," Declan admitted, "like she had it on good authority she would be just fine."

It sounded like Marty, whose faith often struck Barb as a kind of arrogance. She grew sullen in the wake of this old news, unsure why her parents had kept it from her, but unsurprised they had. "Just think if I had never left. We could have been just like this."

He propped his head on the pillow. "You never told your parents about us. You know what they would have said."

She paused. "So this was our only chance."

"No such thing as coincidence."

God's Plan, he meant. How to explain she hadn't just stopped searching for a plan, but had stopped believing there was one? At least not one she could divine from her corner of earth.

She wondered about those parts of Declan's past he was leaving out. Barb at seventeen was willing to wait, but not Barb at twenty-seven. The next night she pressed him. "You've known me my whole life. There's nothing embarrassing you haven't seen. We're lopsided."

His brow furrowed, a sign he was at least considering her request. "I wasn't the same back then." It was the language of conversion stories, testimonies of Christians who felt so drastically changed they were unrecognizable to their former selves. She once envied these tales—Christianity stuck to her like the coffee berries' pulp—but with experience came skepticism.

"Lopsided," she repeated.

He pressed her close, held her so tightly she dared not move. He placed his mouth to her ear, whispering this secret as he had the one from the hangar: "It was my father." She was scared for a moment, more from the force of his arms than from his confession.

"Why?" She scanned his face for a readable emotion. None appeared. Instead his hand moved between her legs, teaching her to forgive him before she knew the need.

There was more he wasn't saying, which left her to theorize about the circumstances of the shooting as she had at college, an endless soundtrack of thoughts.

Months later she woke beside Ross from a nightmare that featured Declan and his father without faces, images of a hunting accident or of Declan protecting himself from abuse (perhaps this was why he never spoke of his family). The dream sank into her chest. Over the next week, it shook loose without warning, pervading her thoughts when she was shaving in the shower or when the doorbell rang. It happened once at the church office. She was staring at a spreadsheet on her computer when Ross rubbed her shoulder.

"Okay?" he asked.

She blinked. "Just tired."

"Michael's for lunch?"

She nodded and grabbed their coats. They walked five blocks to the Italian place, and he kept bumping her shoulder. She smiled and told him to quit. He tucked his arm around her and kissed her cheek.

"Good mood?"

"Just distracting you." He held the door open. "Last thing on my to-do list."

She frowned on purpose. Ross smiled like he'd already won.

They took menus from the host, and Ross held out her chair. As he pushed her in, he leaned down and whispered something that made her blush and forget. But when the sun set, she was lying in bed, worrying the dream would repeat on her like garlicky pasta. Ross slept silently beside her while she stayed up searching for the thing that would put an end to her worry. What if she wrote Declan a letter—was that allowed?

Not knowing seemed the greater risk, and she was surprised how easy it was to put into writing what she dreaded saying. If a return letter came, she would tell Ross part of the truth: she'd reconnected with a Welete missionary. But he tossed the envelope containing Declan's secrets across the coffee table without comment.

———

Declan · May 1981

He had been paranoid for as long as he could remember, resolutely searching for meaning in small things, whether in the whirling of his cowlicks each morning or in the rebuilding of a '68 Mustang at the vo-tech. As graduation loomed, he changed out the alternator and saw his future in the used-up part. He knew suddenly that blue-collar work wouldn't be enough to please his old man, who was the boss of a boss of a boss at the Coke plant, someone for whom the hum of conveyer belts was a gentle backdrop to paperwork.

So he enrolled in flight school at the first opportunity. He preferred moving around anyway, among towns or girls who never seemed to stick. Even when he sat, his leg jogged up and down of its own volition.

He was nineteen when it happened, celebrating his pilot certification and three Yuenglings in at his parents' kitchen table.

His father pulled up a chair and cleared his throat. The man had the voice of Zeus. Declan had trained himself to remain calm at the sound. (The Yuenglings helped.)

"It's time that you know," his father boomed. There was a pause long enough for Declan's thoughts to drift where they so often did—to his sister, Ellie, cold in the ground for thirteen years—but his father was plowing ahead, a businessman closing a deal. He said, "Your mother and I aren't your parents," and Declan's world changed.

The kids had come to them as wards of the state—Declan at eighteen months, his sister at age four. He never forgot the frown in his father's brow as he spoke, nor the way his mother trained her eyes on the teakettle.

He pushed away from the table so suddenly that his mother gasped. Of course, she wasn't his mother anymore. He had only just discovered the calm of rising above the clouds, the turbulence required to get high enough. But here he was, not calm at all, his life some cosmic joke.

Declan retreated to the den, where he was confronted by the shrine of artifacts Zeus had held on to after retiring from active duty: his army dress hat, a set of engraved bullets, and a Beretta to match. Zeus had once made a speech: "These bullets are named for fallen soldiers." Ellie had been standing beside him, alive and pulsing. The children had taken turns feeling the weight of the gun. Declan, barely five, lifted it as though to shoot. Ellie stopped him before Zeus noticed.

The adoption pressed into his shoulders; he was—had always been—a thing cast aside.

No. It was more than that. The revelation made too much sense. He had always felt like a blot on the blond-haired, blue-eyed suburban landscape. He never spoke of it—not even to himself—but the thought lay just out of sight, waiting. News of the adoption didn't give him peace. It confirmed his displacement.

He fished the keys out of Zeus' desk. He needed to open the cabinet, to feel the weight of the gun in his hand again, to load it with one of the bullets (the one that read *Cpl. Thomas Hayes*), to hold it to his head and pray that he belonged here.

He heard footsteps and turned to meet them, the gun sagging in his hand. Zeus caught sight of the barrel. Declan saw only contempt as the man wrestled him against the wall. "Jesus Christ!" One of Zeus' hands was at his windpipe, the other at his wrist, pulling. Then he shot.

The woman—Hera—ran to her husband as Declan crumpled against the wall. Their faces went slack with shock.

There was nothing left to do but call an ambulance.

The bullet had ruptured Zeus' subclavian vein. Under different circumstances—his parents being real parents and not pursuing a verdict—Declan could have gotten off. The shooting was an accident. He pled guilty and was sentenced to a year.

He knew he should be angry—that's what others said—but he felt nothing.

Rod Granger was a fellow inmate at Fulton County Jail and old enough to be Declan's real father. Declan hoped that he was. It was a stupid fantasy, but it helped lull him to sleep on his slippery mattress.

At lunch one day Rod pointed at his face. "Those eyes," he told the whole table. "Dead eyes."

Rod had a theory that Declan was too clever, that he had wound up in jail on purpose. Declan knew the deadness in his eyes was just despair, nothing quite so interesting.

"I'm no mastermind," he promised.

"You're one of them." Rod nodded across the cafeteria at a group of Hispanic inmates.

Declan hesitated. What did Rod mean by *one of them*? He shook his head. "Course not."

Rod didn't believe that either.

Hera wrote letters, but no one visited. Declan didn't write back. (He wasn't supposed to contact the victims in his case.) Instead, he relived the shooting: being pinned to the wall, crying out, feeling the gun kick. When missionary recruiters arrived at the jail, they found him muttering "Jesus Christ" over and over, his trigger finger tapping his thigh. They showed him a picture of a white man with glowing skin and luxuriant hair, an image that threw Declan's curses into relief.

"We're all Christ's children," the recruiters told him. "He takes us when no one else will."

He didn't question it. He had seen the church spires of Baptists, Methodists, and Presbyterians downtown. *Sanctuaries,* he thought. How had he not made the connection before?

The missionaries needed a pilot—they always did—so Declan read a Gideon Bible in the commons and bided his time.

He was out after nine months and paroled for the remaining three. His old teacher at the vo-tech got him a part-time job in an auto-body shop. Declan learned languages and applied for his passport and visa. There was more paperwork (re: suspicion) for an ex-con, but his crime had nothing to do with drug running. Keeping his pilot's license was the harder task, but he jumped through every hoop, unwilling to lose his ticket out.

Two weeks before he left, he wrote to Hera to let her know. He never got a response. It didn't matter; he planned to remain on the mission without furlough.

He landed in Welete the fall before he turned twenty-one. How strange it was meeting Barb as a child, feeling drawn to her as a teenager. Their attachment felt primordial, out of their control. He felt certain of little, not even of his own humanity, but he was certain of her. It was the same way he thought of God. They would come together, no words necessary.

She was asking for words now, so he wrote the abridged version, telling her about the shooting but not his sister. Only one person knew about that, and Tilde was too many time zones away to count.

Barb · October 2000

It was his first letter to her in seven years. Barb took the trash out as an excuse to read it, so the tears, if they came, would stay hidden.

Mrs. Matheson, here are the details you requested:
No, he didn't die. He's still alive, in fact. But he isn't my real father. They told me I was adopted the day it happened and I don't know why, but I went to look at his guns—old war souvenirs—and when I took one out of the case, it was a jumble of things, all too fast, before the shot fired.
It was an accident, so I was paroled after 9 mos. I came to Christ in jail. As you know, my understanding of this relationship is different from most people's. The rules of it don't always stick.
But I try.

No tears came, just a solace settling in her chest. She'd finally gotten what she wanted: a peek inside his file. His account was cryptic, yes, but she accepted that he would always leave things out. The letter explained at least some of the darkness around Declan's edges.

She dropped the letter into the dumpster behind the house.

At the conference that year the letter went unmentioned. Instead she kept thinking of two years ago and their trip to the African Art Museum. She asked if he remembered the *Male figure*.

"Half-man, half-hyena? Red eyes?"

She rested her head on his bare shoulder. "It was beautiful, yeah, but the others—the tourists—they stared at it without even a tingle."

"Okay."

She tried again. "It was out of place."

"You talk like it's alive."

"In Welete, people believed in it."

He scoffed. "Did you?"

"Things like that scared me as a kid." Sometimes they still did.

He took her hand, which reminded her of Ross at his neediest. "What's worth believing?"

She sensed what he meant: was *he* worth believing in? were *they*? "You're the best man I know. To overcome what you did . . ."

He rolled onto his back. She listened to his breath and worried she'd said too much.

"We have till Monday?" he finally asked.

The question invited her guilt. She tried to think of her pilot only in DC, of her husband only in Bethel, but Declan's tone illuminated the selfishness of her annual pilgrimages. She wondered who else she'd betrayed without knowing. Makeda jumped to mind, her deictic finger indicating a viper's head in the grove's undergrowth. She was somewhere in the hills between Nekemte and Welete now. Hopefully alive.

Declan touched her jaw. "Where'd you go?"

She hesitated, ashamed of forgetting him. "Makeda."

He shifted closer, the movement too deliberate. "I saw her in Addis before I left."

She thought of Makeda's options in the capital: secretary at a foreign-aid organization, maid for a government official, retailer at a local shop.

"Was she well?"

"She wore her hair the same way."

"Dec?"

He kissed her so gently that Barb knew Makeda's position was more complicated than she'd imagined. Worry settled deep in her stomach.

The next year Barb's parents were on furlough and therefore at the conference. She had envisioned a chase sequence of opening and closing doors from *The Benny Hill Show,* which Ross had shown her in college, but none of them were even staying on the same floor. She attended sessions with her parents to avoid suspicion. Still, Marty had knocked on her door one morning when she was with Declan.

"I was in the gym," Barb said later, a plausible excuse. Marty was more impressed than suspicious. But that evening she spotted Barb in the lobby with a man who'd already disappeared from their lives once.

Barb went rigid. Declan noticed. As Marty headed over to greet them, he stepped forward and took the lead. Barb loved him so completely in that moment she surprised herself.

There was a horrible tension in Marty's face. Simeon showed no unusual emotion, clapping Declan on the shoulder as they spoke. Barb faked her way through the interaction, unable to recall what anyone had said.

Her last morning with Declan, when her parents were finally on their way to their next fundraising stop, he pressed his lips to her bare stomach. "Let's make a family."

She'd never let herself imagine a family with Ross. She laughed if he brought it up and reminded him of the complications of her own birth: "You know my mother barely survived. That stuff's genetic." Though she was twenty-nine, her parents' introductions of her still began "This is Barb, our miracle child." But with Declan, she saw their children immediately: two boys with his sloped shoulders—one with her passion for drawing, the other for reading.

Declan took her silence as a reproach. "I've been tracking missionary openings. Nothing serious, but you should know."

The boys disappeared; in their place Barb saw herself growing smaller, stuck on the runway as Declan took off.

"I'd want you with me."

She shut her eyes to the possibility, it being precisely what she had once wanted.

He watched her. "You haven't done anything wrong."

She tried to ignore the feeling that she had.

A year later and Barb had already grown too familiar with her secrets. She attended the conference only to check in. She didn't call Ann. If Ross asked about her trip when he got back from India, she would secure an alibi from the catalog on her flight home. She and Declan sequestered themselves in his hotel room. That morning he'd been particular in their lovemaking. She could feel the seriousness of his thoughts as they moved together. Then he turned his back to her, a posture she'd learned to dread.

"The Welete pilot's retiring. They need someone in two Christmases."

Barb wondered if she'd sensed this coming. Was everything that had gone wrong that year—Mount Olive's membership dropping, their mailbox being vandalized, gas prices rising—a subtle portent of the ultimatum? On her flight, had the turbulence over West Virginia been a wind shear or a warning?

He stared at her over his shoulder. "I want to raise our children in Welete. I want you to teach at the school and be free."

This future that he wanted, perhaps had wanted ever since their first time in the hangar, rang hollow after eleven years—because now there was Ross, who had never hurt her on purpose. Of course neither had Declan.

She asked for time and watched his fingers flex.

"A year." He touched her face like nothing had changed. "You know this isn't enough."

"Oh?"

"I can't feel God anymore."

When they'd started, he'd held her waist and said God had never felt closer. She'd envied this closeness—with God or with people. For her whole life she had sat at the back of a classroom behind piles of books while everyone else had formed connections. It took some otherworldly force to break through the barrier: Makeda's curiosity, Declan's mystery, Ross's attention.

"Hey." She smiled so the truth might appear kind. "I haven't felt God since college."

———

Ross · September 1988

Ross didn't study acting at college to be the center of attention, as so many of his classmates did. He did it because he liked stories.

Eight hours from Pennsylvania, he made a new home for himself in the odea of movie houses and the open mics at local bars. He often took the train downtown, walked across the river, and wandered into one of the glittering theaters that studded Chicago. Each performance transformed its space so completely that he felt disoriented when the lights came back on. But this transformation, he understood, was exactly what good stories did: made something unfamiliar into a metonym for your life.

When onstage himself, Ross excelled at commanding the audience's attention, but he got stuck smoldering in silence. The plays were more serious than anything he'd done in high school, and between lines he found himself suddenly thinking of his dead brother. "You're too in your head" was the note from his senior advisor. At the time, the comment struck Ross as a copout. Hadn't this phrase been used to describe mediocre performances throughout history—from failed spiritual quests to bad rounds of golf—and wasn't the phrase itself an obvious choice, something the theater had taught him to reject? Besides, who could *stop thinking*? It was as essential as breathing.

Ross had since accepted the critique, one that was as applicable to his acting career as to the careers of promising college athletes who struggled in the pros. To be great, one had to achieve effortlessness; an instinct had to take hold, leaving your head to idle like a car whose driver had forgotten something on the kitchen counter. Some would call this idling the hand of God. Ross wasn't so presumptuous.

So he performed his own monologues each Sunday morning. The Mount Olive job came with an added bonus: he was preaching in an old theater. Each Monday he collected a ladder and box of vinyl letters from the utility closet, climbed within reach of the marquee, and replaced last week's message (NOW SHOWING: KING DAVID AND OEDIPUS REX) with this one's (COMING SOON: PORTABLE

RADIOS AND PRODIGAL SONS). If he ran out of letters, he used 5s for *s*s and inverted 3s for *e*s; he made anything else with a Sharpie, scissors, and discarded plastic packaging. The deacons hoped to replace the marquee, but their remodeling campaign foundered, perhaps because Ross deadened his voice each week when soliciting funds from the congregation.

His sermons blended narratives from history, the news, and his life with those from the Bible. The tale of the Good Samaritan became Ross's first Little League at-bat; an international Ponzi scheme became an allegory for Jacob's theft of Esau's birthright. Ross's finished sermons read like linked parables. That these parables rarely included a moral aggravated the deacons.

It was Barb's job to proof his sermons with the deacons' objections in mind. Ross rarely cried except when she gave him these notes. The first time it happened, she held him and said, "You were made for Welete. Their stories—" But he pulled away.

The rest of her notes were given at arm's length, no matter how many tears were shed.

He had caught on lately. His sermons minced words. He stole absolutes from Calvin and Luther. He snuck in Mamet without the hope that anyone in the congregation would notice. Barb might have noticed, but she said nothing. When he handed her the draft of a sermon now, he offered an instrument of surrender. His eyes grew dull behind the pulpit, his words lining up like the boxes of expired waffle mix in the pantry.

———

Barb · July 2004

If Barb dreams, more and more it's of her eleventh birthday, when her parents took her on a picnic to the Omo River. She remembers running to the hangar that morning, bursting to tell Declan the news and invite him along. His face was already oil-stained when she found him at the worktable. She wondered if he'd stayed there all night.

"Look what Mom let me wear!"

He startled and turned to see her holding the string of pearls out from her neck. "They look good."

"It's just for today." Her expression fell for a moment. "There'll be peanut butter sandwiches. You *have* to come."

Now it was his expression that fell. "Not today, Barb Wire."

The sadness in his eyes was more pronounced than usual.

She said, "You don't like peanut butter."

"Who doesn't like peanut butter?"

"*I know.* But some people in America are allergic."

"It's the water," he said suddenly, and leaned against the Cessna's tail.

"Oh." Some kids from the village hated water, too.

"Rivers have *mouths,*" he offered.

"I learned that in school." She paused. "Not *those* mouths."

He shrugged and pulled something from his back pocket. Then he surprised her with a hug. He smelled like earth and something sour. When they pulled away, she saw the gift laid out in her palm: a set of pencils.

"To add color," he said, though he didn't need to. The rainbow in her hand was all the evidence she needed.

But Barb's dream starts later: after the picnic, when she walked to the river's edge and leaned over. There was a fifteen-foot drop to the water. Exposed tree roots reached from the bank like weathered hands.

Marty shouted as Barb fell, rolling down the bank, desperate for something to hold on to.

At thirty-one she still scrambles for a foothold.

Three months ago, an elderly woman approached her in the produce aisle. Skin dripped from her face like molasses—the way Dahnay, the mission's oldest convert, had looked before he died. When the woman in the store spoke, her voice shook with the effort. "I'm constipated. Will this help?" She held up a package of iceberg lettuce.

Barb smiled and shrugged, prepared to leave, until the woman gripped her arm too firmly.

"Wh-what do you eat w-with it?"

Barb remembered the tasks she didn't have time for: zucchini bread to bake, paychecks to submit, Ross's sermon to proof. Her life carbonized under the pressure of these tasks, like a fossil under rock.

"I don't work here," she said, louder than she meant to.

The woman squinted and pain throbbed in Barb's arm. She remembered Makeda's stories of *budas* who cursed their victims with the evil eye and wished she'd never known the convenience of grocery stores. She felt as displaced as imported fruit sold out of season.

She was asleep when Ross came to her that night. His fingers found hers, and their bodies rolled together. She bit at his ear, his shoulder, before letting herself be kissed. She sensed his hesitancy—he hadn't known she was angry. It wasn't until his legs slipped between hers that the fear bloomed between her shoulder blades. Even then, she knew. She never used the pill—her mother discouraged it, but she also hadn't needed to. Her calendar keeping was meticulous.

It felt right, being punished in this way: legs bent open as a pain more acute than her first time slid along her spine. She yelped when Ross came, which surprised them both.

In the bathroom afterward she watched her stomach in the mirror and dared it to make the first move.

Remembering that night now in the church office makes her want to call Ross and reveal enough detail of her affair to make him fall apart. Instead, she tucks the divorce papers into her cardigan and leaves Raji to sort pew envelopes at his desk.

She escapes to the roof and hangs her feet over the edge, arranging the papers and three cigarettes next to her on the hot cement. This is her own version of the ultimatum: sign or shred once the cigarettes are gone.

Footsteps ring in the stairwell. She covers the papers with her sweater just as the door crashes shut behind Raji.

He looks nervous. Barb softens as a result.

"You smoke?" She holds up a cigarette and the lighter.

"Only *bidis*." He walks to the roof's edge, leans over, and waves to someone down below.

Barb flicks the thumbwheel. She takes a drag of the first cigarette and sets the lighter between them. "These are my last three." It's strange Ross isn't the first to know.

Raji clears his throat and she's afraid to look at him. "You were always Christian?"

She taps the ashes over the roof's edge, unsure, as always, if they make it to the sidewalk or get caught in the elms' branches. "It's always been there. Ross is the same."

"My family, too, but Hindu." He folds his hands behind his back, reminding her of Declan, who hid his dirty fingernails this way. "You don't miss your Mum and Dad?"

"Sure I do," she says, though she wonders if it's them or the mission.

"Would you do something even if you knew it would hurt them?"

Again she worries he's found the papers in her desk or—in a spectacular fluke—her pregnancy test in the garbage outside the Kwik Mart. "No," she says, a falsehood made true (for now) by the breadth of the Atlantic.

She finishes her cigarette, starts the second, and hands it to Raji. He takes it without a word, staring across the street at the law office again.

"There's something I want." His tongue probes his cheek. "But it means risking my parents and sisters."

He feels too close, the desperate look in his eyes what Ross must have seen in the Children's Fund commercial. She finally understands why, of all the converts, Raji ended up at her husband's church. She wonders if she had the same look when Ross met her.

"What do you want?"

"A date after work." Raji indicates his tie. "With a beautiful Black woman."

Barb remembers the woman who exited the law office this morning. It wasn't the miniskirt Raji was unable to look at. Without thinking, Barb had let her own doubts at twenty-one palimpsest his.

All she sees now—in his endless questions and the way in which he cradles his cigarette—is loneliness.

The last person to ask her advice was the woman who cursed her, so Barb says what she should as the pastor's wife: that family is more important. She wants to say *America changes everything*, but she swings her legs back onto the roof, solid beneath her feet, and stands to light the final cigarette. Raji follows her, and for a moment in their shared smoke she wonders if he's not the spy she thought—if he's a friend instead.

"I'm pregnant."

He smiles. "Congratulations!"

The pregnancy's always been a curse. She forgot his is the proper response. He opens his arms to her and Barb laughs. She clutches her elbows and shivers.

Raji reaches for her sweater. She lunges forward—the papers.

The moment expands. Raji's gaze catches on her face. What he sees is this: an unhappy pregnant woman sucking down cigarettes, laughing too loudly, and bolting for the roof's edge.

He clutches her arm. The momentum throws her sideways, her skirt splays—a burst of color against the drab cement, like a dance number in a tedious play. She lands on her stomach, her arm on the cigarette.

She opens her eyes to Raji's shoes in front of her on the ground.

"I- I thought you were." He can't say it. Her arm burns, whether from the cigarette or the *buda*'s evil eye, she isn't sure. By the time she catches her breath, he's scampered to the stairwell and disappeared.

She rolls onto her back. How stupid of her to tell him anything. The papers, at least, are safe. She remembers how, after tumbling down the riverbank, her dress snagged on the exposed tree roots and she grabbed hold. She had wished to turn into a stone like one of the heroes in Makeda's stories. Puff adders and crocodiles paid no mind to stones; even the current purled around them.

Then Simeon was there, scrambling down the bank and climbing back up with her. Marty had touched the pearls at Barb's throat and hugged her fiercely. Were there tears in her eyes or had Barb imagined them? They were gone by the time Marty smeared her raw palms with iodine.

The stairwell door slams behind Raji, now carrying damp paper towels and a first-aid kit. He crouches and dabs her arm with hydrogen peroxide instead of iodine.

Barb's wounds hiss. "You'll be fine," he answers.

"Did you call him?"

Raji nods.

For three months she's tried to stow away the memories of Declan as her mother did the pearls, to stash them in some hidden crevice of herself, but the string has snapped and sent them spinning. She suffers every moment with Declan at once—in the hangar, his rough hands on her arms, his beard burning her skin; at the hotel, his fingers inside her, his teeth on her collarbone. But other scenes force their way in: a customs officer frisks her family; Makeda slaps her hand while they play *mancala;* her college suitemates critique her wardrobe in the mirror; Ross tugs on her hair while they watch reruns. Each scene flips past like a drawing in her lost sketchpad. Barb's whole life clamors inside her, converging on the child, whom she will certainly have.

She's eleven again on the edge of the Omo, leaning over and tumbling down. This time she doesn't reach for help. She transforms into a stone. Under the water her memories wash away one by one. She forgets even the present—the bankrupt cineplex below and Raji above. He touches a trembling paper towel to her cheek. She's not a stone after all, and he could be anyone, gathering the pearls one by one and placing them back on the string.

—————

BEFORE WELETE

Barb · July 2004

I'M WORRIED ABOUT THIS."
Raji's voice came to her as if from a different plane as he cleaned the burn on her arm. He helped her up, and pain shot through her calf. She balanced on one foot as he retrieved her cardigan, revealing the divorce papers.

"What are these?" he asked, though of course he knew. He was pre-law, after all.

She leaned against him as they turned toward the stairwell. "I need you to shred them before—" The pain cut her off.

"You're not leaving?"

She didn't answer, just kept staring at the elastic webbing on his shoes. What were they—boat shoes? deck shoes?

They didn't speak again until she was lying on the floor of the office, her ankle propped on a cushion from Ross's couch. Raji was shredding the papers. He felt like family. She stared at the ceiling tiles, waiting.

"You should be with her," she said, "if you make each other happy."

His smile was so kind she was suddenly sorry for everything: her bad advice, her affair, her disposition for the past three months—no, the past five years—all at once.

"You don't want to go to hospital?"

"Let me see Ross." She remembered the baby inside her. "Then the hospital."

"I'll get some ice."

She was alone when Ross entered. He took her in: ankle elevated, arm bandaged, cheek scraped. Remorse crept into his eyes: he hadn't been the one to clean her wounds or prevent them in the first place. *The marriage is irretrievably broken*—what a lie. It was her. It had always been her. He knelt and adjusted the cushion under her calf. The change relieved a pain she had presumed was unavoidable.

He wiped the hair from her forehead, his smile sad. "Happy birthday?"

She almost laughed, but tears were suddenly in her eyes—in his, too. "I'm pregnant."

"Raji told me. Looks like we found that retirement gift for your parents."

"House visits?"

"Left Delia mid-tea party. We should get you out of here." She nodded. Something occurred to him and he smiled wider. "Why didn't Raji just set you on the couch?"

Ross was funny. That was a thing she liked about him. "I quit smoking."

"Of course you did." He kissed her like he was chasing the taste of her last cigarette.

He helped her up, and they noticed Raji in the doorway. She asked if he could call to cancel her flight. Ross looked confused. "Your ankle?"

"Not that." She touched her stomach. "I want to take it easy."

A doctor saw her at the emergency clinic two hours later. The sprain was severe, but nothing rest and ibuprofen couldn't take care of. She left with a pair of crutches, a sonogram, and a reminder to schedule an appointment with her OB-GYN. The sonogram seemed like a promise that everything would be fine, despite the otherworldly glow surrounding the baby's head, the ominous black inside Barb's own body. They sat staring at it in the waiting room until her ankle began to throb. On their way home they picked up painkillers and prenatal vitamins, two large pizzas, and a piece of tiramisu for her birthday.

"You do this every year," she said to Ross as they turned into the driveway.

"Cold pizza's underrated as a breakfast food." He turned off the car, and she noticed her annoyance from the morning was gone. "You've been going to DC for, what, seven years?"

"Eight, yeah." She released her seatbelt.

"It's nice not having to fit your birthday in whenever." He touched her cheek and she leaned into it, suddenly thankful that Ross didn't keep secrets—except for Jason.

He smiled. "It'll be just like the time I fell off the ladder, but reversed."

"Plus pregnancy!" She chewed her lip. "We should donate the waffle iron."

He laughed. To him it was just an eccentric gift. "You need help with your crutches?"

In answer she pulled them from the back seat.

They were sitting in front of the TV, some late-night host's monologue on low, one pizza box open in front of them, the other in the fridge, when Barb asked, "Had you suspected?"

He tilted his head. "Aren't there rules about assuming someone's pregnant?"

She nudged his knee. "But you see me all the time."

He shrugged. "You've been sick in the morning." His eyes met hers. "Why not tell me?"

"I needed time." Her stomach tightened, speaking the same words to Ross she had to Declan a year ago.

But Ross didn't turn away. He took her hand. "It's a big adjustment."

She realized later that this was the night to tell him, not just about the baby—the night he would have forgiven everything.

―――――

The call came the next day. Barb crutched into the office and discovered a shimmery balloon that Raji had bought for the baby. She thanked him just as the phone rang: it was Declan from Dulles. She hobbled into the hall, pressed the receiver to her cheek, and cleared her throat.

"Miss your flight?" He sounded far away, further than three hundred miles.

She forced her voice calm. "This was my choice."

"Well then." He hung up.

She returned to the office. Raji studied her, like he was seeing something frantic in her fingers as they pressed the bridge of her nose. Surely he had deduced the caller's identity, becoming her spy more than he ever was Ross's.

In exchange for keeping her secret, Raji found her an ear for the ups and downs of his new relationship with Dez. It wasn't long before they were all four going out—to the Teppanyaki place on Fifth or for *prix fixe* Italian at Michael's. The next summer, Raji and Dez's wedding would be the only one to ever make Barb cry. Tears still threatened if she recalled the swell of circus music the Amins had exited to. She was never more thankful her advice had been ignored.

The solace of the sonogram leaked from her slowly, like the air from Raji's balloon. Its silver surface reminded Barb *It's a girl!* whenever a gust from the vent turned it toward her. The balloon lasted for three weeks, but when they returned the next Monday, it had drifted laughably close to the ground.

"Don't you usually wait for the birth to get a balloon like that?" Ross asked at lunch.

Barb admitted the etiquette of it was beyond her. "Like needing a baby shower."

"Margo will take care of that." Margo was the assistant pastor's wife. "Is it worth keeping? Like for a scrapbook?"

Raji shrugged. "It was fun at first, but now it's, well, a downer."

Barb stared at the balloon, its face lowered in shame. "We'll get more." The inevitability that the congregation would flood their room in the maternity ward with balloons and flowers, even miniature pink pinwheels, made her a little queasy.

"Trash it is." Ross clamped his fingers around the balloon, and the Mylar screeched before it popped. Raji jumped and made a noise like the thunk of a sandbag on cement. Ross apologized and quickly threw the balloon away. That night, as Barb tried to sleep, she couldn't help but recall the screech of the balloon and the thunk from Raji. They seemed to be portents.

Most nights, she and Ross fell asleep talking about the nursery, the grandparents, their list of names. *Abeba* interested Ross as soon as he learned what it meant.

"Flower. We could spell it Ababa, too, like the capital."

He was already sold.

During her fifth month, Barb's mood dipped, but some flutter in her chest, perhaps the fear that she'd be disposed of like the balloon, kept her smiling. On a day when Ross was out on house visits, Raji turned to her, his face as serious as it had been that day on the roof.

"About those papers I shredded. And the phone call." He glanced at her.

She felt a coolness settle on her shoulders. Why had he waited to bring it up? Perhaps he'd spoken with Dez, a woman who didn't hide behind half-truths. Barb willed sincerity into her voice, needing to convince herself as much as him. "It's done, Raji. Leave it."

And it was. Except for the emails.

They started after the phone call, never personalized or with a subject line, the messages just quotations. One week it was *my body is but the lees of my better being;* another, *we are all somehow dreadfully cracked about the head, and sadly need mending.* She didn't recognize the source until he sent *I am tormented with an everlasting itch for things remote.*

She remembered what came next: *I love to sail forbidden seas, and land on barbarous coasts.* When she had first read *Moby-Dick,* she had marked this passage as a defense for remaining in Welete. There was *barbarous,* too, from the same origin as her name, which felt more fateful at sixteen than it did at thirty-one.

Declan was quoting the book she had once read to him. It upset her equilibrium.

Then Abeba was suddenly there, among a forest of Mylar well-wishes—on Christmas Day, no less. Even the slew of visitors wasn't something worth crying about, visitors who called them blessed. (Ross still cringed if a syllable was out of place.) Perhaps, Barb thought, she hadn't been forsaken: there was a faceless benefactor watching over her from the clouds after all.

But in the weeks that followed, Abeba refused to suckle, to gain weight, to stop crying. Dr. Peters called it *difficulty latching on.* Barb imagined it was her fault—both because she had breasts difficult to latch onto and a daughter who was starving herself out of existence. Barb's nipples became cracked and raw. All she could do was endure the pain and correct the baby's grip. Even with this correction, the throbbing worsened. Ross often stayed awake with Abeba and purchased formula while Barb bit her lip to hold back tears.

The soreness of her nipples was an acute pain; the emptiness inside her, a dull one. It slowed her movements to an unbearable pace. She grew forgetful and worried something *had* irretrievably broken. Any moment she felt as if Abeba might turn to sand and fall through her fingers—a nightmare she'd had during her pregnancy and more often now. If Barb laughed, it came out as a dry rasp. If the sound happened around Abeba, the baby cried—crying that Barb feared because she couldn't stop it. No one really could, except for Ross.

Anticipation stretched this phase of their lives into forever.

Then, on a Tuesday morning in late January, Abeba latched onto a breast on her first try. Feeding times soon joined naptimes as predictable islands of peace in Barb's and Ross's days. She even had time to sneak a look at Declan's newest email: *Such is the endlessness, yea, the intolerableness of all earthly effort.*

Abeba started to crawl. She burbled nonsense so intently that Barb searched the syllables for meaning. When she laughed now, so did her daughter. This wasn't a sack of sand she was holding: Abeba was a *person*, something Ross had never doubted. Barb had mislabeled the emptiness she had felt after Abeba's birth: it was something new growing.

They were a family now. They even went to the shelter to adopt a dog, an older yellow lab used to being passed by, whose tail came to life as Ross crouched in front of her cage. Barb remembered Olly and how he had been an accomplice to Ross's marriage proposal. She remembered leaning into the dog's fur and saying yes, so she said yes again, this time to Gabi.

Marty made a crack about her not planning ahead—if Abeba had been born six months later, her grandparents would have been in the country. Barb knew her parents' retirement would affect their lives, but she never would have predicted the amount of God spam that arrived in her inbox that first year. Once Abeba adjusted to a sleep schedule and Barb had the energy to get annoyed, she wrote, *I love you, Dad! But can you please stop sending me forwards? :)*

"If only you'd signed my name, too," Ross said.

"Just send him the same thing."

Gabi scrambled onto Ross's lap. "Oof, you tub o' lard." The dog panted and Ross scratched her ears. "If I send one now, he'll think we're abandoning him."

"He totally will, but those forwards are awful." Abeba cooed and the dog yawned. "We're all in agreement."

"There's a certain niche that really loves those forwards. Your dad and, apparently, my mom."

"But your mom's are, like, flowers."

"Glittery flowers."

"Animated sentiment. There are worse things."

He sighed. "I'll put it on the calendar in four months. Then I'll ask your dad to stop."

"You're way too nice, dude."

Ross called Abeba "dude" for the next week to tease her and stopped only after Barb convinced him it would be her first word if he didn't.

Days passed and she didn't think of Welete. When she realized this, a pang hit her—she could never quite admit that life was easier when she forgot. Then, in May, Abeba said her real first word—"juice" (it came out *jooz*)—and a series of bombs hit Addis.

Six Ethiopian political parties had just met in the Netherlands for peace talks. None of them owned up to the bombs, but Barb cared only about the reports of casualties. She waited. She tried to get lost in Abeba's eyes. She clenched her teeth so hard at night that her jaw ached in the morning. Finally, another *no subject* appeared at the top of her inbox: *Real strength never impairs beauty or harmony, but it often bestows it; and in everything imposingly beautiful, strength has much to do with the magic.*

Then, three months later, there was flooding in Oromia. This time she emailed her dad to see what he knew, and Simeon responded with an emoticon of his own creation—was it a smiling clown?—meant to indicate that all was well. She turned from the screen and blew a raspberry on Abeba's arm.

When Abeba was almost two, Mengistu was convicted of genocide in absentia. The trial had lasted for twelve years. Barb expected to cry but got angry instead: the repercussions, like the scant coverage on CNN, felt too little, too late.

———

Barb · December 2007

Holly garlands and icicle lights decorate the Mathesons' house, as much for Abeba's birthday as for Christmas. It's the shortest day of the year and the guest list is small. Both sets of grandparents will arrive on Christmas Eve, heralded by the blowing up of air mattresses from the hall closet, but Barb prefers her own island of celebration with friends before holiday traditions press the joy out of her like whey from a cheesecloth. She leaves behind a little of herself every Christmas and spends all of January retrieving it.

Assistant Pastor Gary is the first to arrive, a widower since his wife's brain embolism in May—he's taken to calling it a "freak thing" and "something only God saw coming." His two teenagers, Dinah and Rich, are in tow, still willing to entertain a three-year-old (*"Almost three,"* Abeba says). Raji and Dez come late.

The last guest is unexpected. Barb's carrying a tray of assorted crackers and hummus into the living room when she sees the unfamiliar car parked across the street, framed by their picture window. She thinks the neighbors must be having their own holiday party, but then the driver's door opens and he emerges, a brown paper bag tucked under one arm like he's been out picking up ingredients for tuna salad at the store. Flowers sprout from his other hand.

She sets the tray on the coffee table and retreats to the kitchen, the safety of the house dispersing like a startled flock of birds. She grips the edge of the sink and fixes the chrome splashguard in her stare, blinking as the doorbell rings, then again at the sound of Declan's voice and at the surprise in Ross's. It's the obligatory confrontation between the members of her love triangle (every book she reads has one). Her regret for leaving Declan alone at Dulles had been buried, but laying eyes on him immediately unearths it.

Ross calls her name. She releases the sink. Her warped reflection in the splashguard stares back at her.

She turns into the foyer, where she sees Declan. The creases around his mouth and eyes have deepened. Whatever's in the bag looks like a bottle, not groceries. She must have imagined the bouquet.

Something clicks on. "What a surprise!" She leans in to kiss both of his cheeks as though they've rehearsed it. *Maybe,* she thinks suddenly, *everyone knows.* She sticks her head into the living room and makes Declan's introduction to their guests. "He was a pilot on the mission. We reconnected at the conference in DC, but I haven't seen Declan in . . ."

"Four years."

"He wrote to you once. Declan Kline?" Ross shakes his hand, and the pilot shifts the paper bag to get a firmer grip.

Declan's letter has squatted for seven years in Ross's memory, but she has no time to discern why.

"I saw the cars, so I picked something up." Declan reaches in the bag, its paper crinkling in protest, and pulls out a golden dessert wine. "Not quite *tej.*"

Barb wonders if Gary will be offended—she's never seen him in the same room as alcohol. "*Tej* is, um, an Ethiopian thing."

"That's generous," Ross says, and Raji offers to chill it.

Declan surrenders the bottle reluctantly, as if it's the only thing keeping him here.

"We're just celebrating our daughter's birthday. She's upstairs with Gary's kids." Barb hopes this mention of Abeba is explanation enough. "She'll be three on Christmas."

He looks at her face—her mouth, she notices—but directs his comment to Ross. "I shouldn't have come."

For a moment the three of them are statues. It's Ross who finally speaks.

"We'll go somewhere and talk." He leads Declan to the kitchen. Barb floats behind them like a specter, fortifying herself against the worst of her history. Declan starts in once they're alone.

"I didn't know you had a kid." And here it is, Barb's front-row seat to her own demise. But Declan isn't talking of the past; he's explaining that the mission is understaffed. "We need more bodies, particularly teachers."

"And you thought of us," Ross finishes.

Declan nods. "Barb always spoke of going back. My furlough year was up. Thought I'd stop in."

"To recruit us?"

"Yes, Mr. Matheson."

"Ross."

"We're trying to rebuild."

Barb watches them discuss details—staffing needs, Abeba's options for school—and reality sets in: she's getting away with it, the nights spent at the Renaissance Hotel no more mentioned than the dust in the air. Still, the longer Declan stays, the more she withdraws—shrinks away from her skin and curls up between her heart and lungs, everything else a remotely controlled appendage.

"The Eklunds' house is still empty. I'm the only one left from Barb's time. There's a Swedish couple whose English is as good as their Amharic." Declan half-smiles. "You'd need to learn the languages, Mr. Matheson, but that's easier once you get there. Barb's a good teacher, I imagine." They both turn to her, and she at least has the presence of mind to nod.

"I should mention the timetable," he goes on. "My return trip's May 15."

Barb sees the excitement in Ross's eyes. He offers to talk it over now if Declan will make excuses to their guests.

The pilot's features darken. "I should go."

Ross lays a hand on his shoulder, and Barb knows the power of that hand, the confidence it's instilled during her own moments of insecurity. Ross whispers something that makes both men smile, as if she'd imagined the shadow on Declan's face.

"What about Abeba?"

She and Ross have shut themselves into their room; she sits on the bed where the coats lie piled. What a surprise to hear Ross advocating for Welete, what a surprise that she's the one making excuses.

"Abeba's not much younger than you were," he says, as though she needs reminding.

"Too young."

He sits down and bumps her shoulder. "She would love it."

Would she? Barb still feels the effects of leaving Welete. Would they be dooming Abeba to the same future: dissatisfied with America, an outcast among Ethiopians? But she can't say this without admitting her own sadness. Ross's eyes dart as he thinks of the possibilities of Ethiopia. She dares not scuttle that hope.

"You're not thinking we could leave in May, are you? Pastor searches take years."

"Gary would step in as interim."

"If he agrees—"

"Well, it would mean a raise. And it's not the first time we've asked." He's referring to a residency in Chicago that Ross (unsuccessfully) applied for last year.

He touches his forehead to hers and takes a breath. There's something centering in it.

"Are there deacons in Welete?"

A smile tugs at her lips. "Course not."

"Then you know my answer." And he kisses her, a kiss she feels in the pit of her stomach, that unspools the curled ball of herself, spreading it back to her fingertips, her worries about Abeba and Declan silenced for now.

"It's not too fast?" She touches his chest.

"Of course it's too fast. That's the best part. Think of the fun Beba will have."

"Being called *ferengi*?"

"Look how good you turned out."

"That's one interpretation."

"Hey." He pulls away, and Barb thinks he's grown tired of defending her goodness. She's never convinced.

She waves dismissively. "I'll call Dr. Peters on Monday. We'll need vaccinations and visas. Abeba needs a passport. I think mine's expired."

"Mine should be good till 2013." He stands. "Let's tell him."

"Talk to Gary first?"

"You're right." He's about to leave, but pauses. "Is Declan a little off?"

"What do you mean?"

"He's quite intense."

She hesitates. "He hasn't had the easiest go of it. He went missing for months. We all thought he was dead."

Ross studies her face. There's a spark of surprise in his eyes, perhaps because she hasn't mentioned this sooner. Then he smooths his shirt, the surprise gone. "Wish me luck?"

"Break a leg."

He leaves to find Gary, she to check on her daughter.

Abeba and Dinah are playing with Ross's old Lincoln Logs. Rich is sprawled on the toddler bed, his nose in an issue of *Dark Horse Presents*. Barb clings to the doorframe as Abeba announces that they're making the tallest building in the world.

"I warned her about the Tower of Babel," Dinah says in a studied monotone.

Barb watches in silence. She came here to avoid Declan, but now she's subject to the opinions of two teenagers and her daughter. She can just imagine the conversation in Gary's car on the way home: "What's wrong with Mrs. Matheson? Why doesn't she *do* anything?" She relaxes only at the sound of Ross's footsteps on the stairs.

He touches her shoulder. "Gary's a 'yes.'" Her neck warms where his breath hits. She tries to appear relieved, but the news does the opposite. *It's happening,* she thinks, the *it* referring to any number of things, most of them ominous.

Abeba's face brightens when she spots Ross. "It's gonna be the highest tower, Daddy!" Dinah repeats her Tower of Babel comment, dissatisfied with Barb's silence.

"I wouldn't worry," he answers. Barb marvels again at the ease with which he addresses kids of all ages—something, she realizes with a pinch of guilt, he and Declan have in common. "We already speak different languages in this house."

He looks to Barb and she understands. They speak in unison, she in Amharic and he in Ancient Hebrew, the result a mix of languid vowels and throaty *chs*. Dinah looks horrified while Rich smirks behind his comic. Abeba laughs, hugging a Lincoln Log to her chest like it's Birdy, her most treasured stuffed animal.

Ross promises, "We'll be back, pumpkin." He tugs Barb's hand and leads her downstairs.

"What was the Hebrew?"

"Judges 11:35. The sermon's on Jephthah this week."

"Poor Jephthah's daughter." Barb remembers the story well: her death caused by her father's hubris—not surprising for the Book of Judges.

"We should give her a name," Ross says.

"One that means *I'm no one's sacrificial lamb.*"

He laughs. "I actually know this. Gabriela is *God's bravest woman.*"

"Good name for a dog." Barb's smiling again and feels foolish because of it. These easy moments between them come more often the further she gets from the Renaissance. Now she feels forced backward.

"Oh, Gabi." Ross covers his mouth with his hand. Gabi passed three months ago, when they thought she had more time. Barb remembered the joy of witnessing the subtle color change in her fur across the seasons—golden brown in summer and a cream in winter that Ross called her "white lab coat." Barb wonders how Gary must feel, missing Margo more intensely.

"We gave her a few good years," she says. Ross nods, but seems abstracted. She squeezes his arm as they reach the foot of the stairs. "You should talk to Declan." His brow furrows. "It's better if the decision comes from you."

He hesitates, but they part without a word. She locks herself into their room again, lying next to the coats. She fingers a yellow toggle on Dez's emerald anorak and breathes deeply, trying to dismiss the tightness in her chest. She spent the years between college and Abeba's birth believing that America was the blight on her reality and that a return to the mission would solve her most vexing problems—her distance from God and her displacement from those around her. Now she's started to believe Raji: she's changed too much for Welete. She might escape by pulling Ross aside and carefully revealing Declan's secrets, but part of her knows this won't matter. Ross hates passing judgment on others, calls it a waste of energy, though she's never tested that conviction by revealing her own secrets.

She's suddenly aware of the awkward way she's draped herself across the bed, hips half-twisted so her shoes avoid touching the guests' coats. The way she's contorted herself without thinking, all for the sake of some parkas, annoys her, but she withdraws from the thought like a dinner conversation she wants no part of. She leaves the room and makes her way as far as the kitchen when Declan finds her.

"That was easy," he says.

She starts washing dishes and placing them in the drying rack. He's smiling, a smile she'll have to deal with.

"The other families don't have children," he continues. "Abeba will have run of the place." Barb stiffens at his use of the name. His accent makes her homesick.

"You all right?" He reaches for her arm.

She steps back, pressing the wet plate to her chest without thinking. "You came to Ross and me as a couple."

For a moment he stares at her, a lost look in his eyes. Then his jaw clenches: "You think that's why I'm here." He sounds hurt and sad.

Raji suddenly appears in the doorway. "Anybody need help?"

Declan shifts his weight, as though recognizing Raji's voice from their two chance phone calls. She remembers the months preceding Raji's wedding: his eyes bloodshot most mornings after the umpteenth shouting match with his parents in India. How had he known what he wanted so clearly that even his own family seemed to be a necessary casualty?

"We're fine, Raji."

"Call if you need help." He adds, "With the dishes." She nods and sets the plate in the drying rack, just noticing the damp chill of her blouse.

Declan waits until Raji's gone. "You have a daughter," he says, like it's everything.

She suddenly wants to ask about the AWOL bouquet, to tell him about the copy of *Moby-Dick* on her nightstand, but he's already gone.

Other than the essentials—clothing, shoes, and books—they pack the only two items Ross refuses to part with: one set of Lincoln Logs and one of flannelgraphs, cutouts of biblical characters and settings affixed to a gray flannel board.

Their first summer together Ross sneaked Barb into a Sunday School room in Deerfield, set up an easel, and showed her the story of Daniel. He populated the board with cutouts, smoothing one before adding another, and changed out scenes with nimble fingers: a young Daniel praying on his balcony was surrounded by lions in a flash. Barb thrilled as MENE, MENE, TEKEL, UPHARSIN appeared on the banquet room's wall.

The memory seems too far away as Ross tucks the flannelgraphs among his clothes. His excitement has settled, but his skin still hums when he speaks of the future.

"What would *flannelgraphs* be in Amharic?" he asks.

"No idea." She pauses. "*Cherk tarikoch?* I'm just making it up."

"Raji and Dez are taking each of us out next week to say goodbye."

"I'll miss them most."

Ross shuts his suitcase. "You'll have Declan at least."

"Oh?"

"A friend there."

She relaxes. Ross isn't insinuating.

Raji and Dez treat her to lunch at a restaurant that sits on the Allegheny River, and Barb can't help but tell the story of how she fell down a riverbank when she was eleven.

"How was the water?" Raji asks, sipping his Coke.

"Hopefully you never found out." This from Dez. "For the crocodiles' sake."

"Never made it to the water. Daddy came to my rescue."

"Barbara, Barbara, Barbara." Dez takes one of her hands.

"Typical?"

Dez sighs and Raji squares his shoulders. The sudden movement makes Barb uneasy. Dez must sense her fear. "You know we both love you, right?"

Barb nods but feels like a child just before her parents announce they're splitting up. "Are you guys all right?"

"Peaches and cream." Dez smiles. "We want to talk about you."

It's obvious what she means.

"You're strong, Barb," Raji says.

"You are," Dez echoes, "and we want you to stay that way after you leave. No regrets."

Barb senses a threat in the words. The lunch, she realizes, is an intervention. "I'm fine here." Her voice is cold and even. "I'll be fine there."

Dez suddenly looks apologetic. "Oh. Barb, we weren't—"

"No no no," Raji says. "We're just sorry to see you go."

"We're saying the same thing to Ross on Wednesday—that we'll miss you both. We'll try to visit. We're just not sure when, with law school and my master's program."

Barb hugs Dez, partly to hide her relief and partly to save her from more explanation. "I'll miss you, too."

Raji smiles, still her secret-keeper. She worries she can't live without either of them, that she isn't as strong as they think.

———

Declan picks them up for the airport on the morning of their departure. It's clear they're the only recruits. Barb hoped they wouldn't be. Anything to divide Declan's attention.

It doesn't matter how diligently they prepared Abeba for the trip. She cries once they're on the plane, all four of them lined up in a middle row: Ross, Abeba, Barb, then Declan. Barb immediately regrets not bringing Birdy and wonders why Marty hadn't let her bring Oscar the cat. Surely Barb must have cried, too. How did Marty stand it? Ross plays a game of I Spy to no avail. Abeba's tears end only when Declan produces paper and colored pencils from his carry-on. Barb shuts her eyes as the two reach around her.

They're all ready to stretch their legs when the plane touches down in Amsterdam, but something—the signs in Dutch?—sets Abeba off again, as though each new leg of the trip reignites her sadness.

When the Jeep pulls through the mission gate, Ross announces, "We're home."

By the reverence on Abeba's face, she already knows.

"You're in the same house Barb was, but with electricity!" Declan says with exaggerated enthusiasm. He and his copilot, Arnold, had put in the wiring. "Ask Caj and Karin if you need anything. They're in the office." With that, he shoulders his duffle and turns toward the hangar.

"Huh," Ross says as they reach the porch of their new home and Barb's old one. "Thought he'd show us around."

"He's the pilot, Ross. He probably has to check in with Arnold." It's her first of many excuses.

———

Two

And some certain significance lurks in all things, else all things are little worth, and the round world itself but an empty cipher. . . .

Herman Melville, Moby-Dick, *chapter 99*

THE QUEEN OF SHEBA
AND THE FOUNTAIN

T HE MOMENT YOU HEAR OF THE WONDERS OF JERUSALEM you must see them. But when you meet Israel's king, you're more taken with the fountain in his courtyard, Solomon's face too boyish for your liking.

As you discuss lands and trade routes beyond your two kingdoms, you warm to him, but by then it's time to leave.

He orders a farewell feast. At the table, he leans in and calls you beautiful.

You accuse him of being obvious. He demurs and promises to take nothing from you. Not until you take something from him first.

He speaks in riddles, and there is witchcraft to this evening. The food tastes of heat and burns less like a kiss than a slap.

You lie awake that night remembering his promise. Surely he won't begrudge you a sip from his fountain, just as he won't begrudge you provisions for the trip home.

The fountain is more beautiful than you remember, worth getting punished for. You submerge your hands. The water is as soothing on your lips as the shade of a cedar tree.

There's a noise, sharp and quick, and you turn to behold the king's face, no longer boyish.

"It's only water," you say, a feeble defense.

"My most precious treasure."

He lifts his hand to your cheek. You see right through him.

The next day you leave with his son in your belly.

WELETE

Barb · May 2008

ALL OF THE MATHESONS REQUIRED TIME TO ADJUST TO life on the mission—pumping water, tending gardens and chickens, eating in a refectory instead of their home, walking outside for the bathroom, moving through spaces uncluttered by magazines and electronics—but Barb took the longest. Memories dogged her: there were her parents sitting next to her on the porch; there was Berhanu waving at her from the gatehouse or Makeda sprinting from the grove; there was Declan lying next to her in the Cessna, gripping her arm so tightly she felt it in the present. She couldn't help but see what had changed—not just the Internet in the office but the buildings themselves. Inside their bungalow Barb pushed back a dresser and discovered that the hole had been plastered over, probably by Declan when he refinished it. She'd come to this spot once before and been disappointed. Now she was angry at her willingness to hope.

The refectory seemed smaller, barely as large as a two-car garage, and the trees in the grove shorter, less majestic. Still, she brought her family there within a week of their arrival.

"I haven't been here since Makeda left. She was . . . a friend."

"What's this?" Abeba pointed at a beetle creeping along the grove floor. Barb crouched to examine it. The insect was green with yellow piping on its shell.

"A scarab. These are friendly, but watch out for snakes, honey."

Ross's lips pursed. "Are we sure about this?" It was his first sign of hesitation. She covered his hand with hers.

"It'll be safe. I'll teach you." He blinked in response, still uncertain, so she told them both to sit down; she was going to tell the story of Kaldi and the dancing goats.

"Is it like *Aladdin*?" Abeba asked.

"It has magic." It didn't matter that the magic was explicable. Abeba sat in rapt attention, and Ross's shoulders relaxed.

The mission still had the community's only school, but Welete itself had grown in Barb's absence, with its own café and market. Barb waited for her sense of God to expand as well. She used to see God everywhere, no separation between the birds she fed and the Bible she thumbed through. Marty would disagree—she lived by rules, and if Barb asked why she needed to follow those rules (innocently as a child and petulantly as a teen), her mother set her straight, end of discussion. But without discussion, Barb remained unconvinced. How could a pastor's wife—*missionary,* she corrected—lose faith? Faith required sentiment in large doses, and hers had withered with time. Saying any of this to Ross would make the doubt too real. Instead, she woke before dawn each morning, hauled a sack of feed from the shed, and trudged toward the chicken coop.

Within their first two months on the mission she spotted a viper, iridescent, coiled patiently against one of the coop's stilts. When she was a child, snakes' deaths must have occurred offstage at the hands of the Nilssons, the Bjornstads, her parents. Killing was part of the job. She could have chosen any veteran of the mission to teach her.

"Declan will know," Ross said from where he was reading, and she couldn't argue.

Five years had passed since the ultimatum, and she and Declan had spoken only at staff meetings. As she approached the hangar, the main doors ground open, the sound strident against the peace of morning. He stood inside, arms crossed and jaw set.

She told him about the snake. "I need to kill it."

He sucked on the side of his cheek before disappearing behind the Cessna, emerging with a shovel in one hand and a forked stick in the other. She vaguely remembered the tools had once leaned against her parents' doorjamb. He started toward the coop, but she protested. "I need to do it on my own."

He resigned himself to a demonstration of pinning an imaginary viper's head to the ground with the stick and decapitating it with the shovel. He held out the implements, but wouldn't look up until she took them. That old sadness was in his eyes, and Barb indulged it for a moment, laying a hand on his arm. Her fingers trembled.

"I'll see you through it this time," he said.

Her hand dropped. She was sweating more from the heat than from nerves, but the sensation was the same. She worried about losing her grip on the stick, of not cutting deeply enough with the shovel.

"I'm all jittery," she said as they approached the snake.

"Just keep the stick between you." He added, "I'll be here."

She extended the stick as she neared the coop. When she was within spitting distance, the snake sprang into attack form. She slid the shovel along the ground to her left, and the viper struck at its blade. She struck back, trapping the snake between the stick and the ground. The snake writhed, and Declan whispered, "Do it!" She brought the shovel down behind its head; the body seized as the head flopped free. Declan's hands were suddenly on her arms, pulling her back. He held her as they waited for the snake to stop twitching. She remembered those mornings in DC and felt warm.

"Hang garlic," he whispered. "Snakes hate garlic."

She managed to step out of his arms. "Like vampires?"

He smirked. He looked like he was about to kiss her. "No such thing."

"What about the stick and shovel?"

He shrugged, already walking backward in the direction of the hangar.

"Thanks, Dec."

He nodded again—"Bag the body for meat"—and jogged away like he was still in his twenties.

Declan called the mission understaffed, but there were more personnel now than when Mengistu was in power: Caj and Karin Thorn, who worked in the office; Aida and her adult son Roger, who worked in town; Declan and Arnold, who flew the Cessna; Ross and Barb, who ran the school and worship services; and Abeba. Ancillary jobs, as always, were staffed by locals.

Barb's first year on the mission passed too quickly, perhaps because she had tasks she'd been unaware of as a kid—killing snakes and planning lessons. On her best days, these were small prices to pay. On her worst, an emptiness slid between her ribs. It spread from the paperwork to her students and the other missionaries, even to her daughter. Abeba was relentless in her need for attention. She played with her schoolmates, but more often Barb alone was required to entertain her with a game, a language lesson, an afternoon in the garden, or something else that sapped strength.

Barb spent most nights enclosed in mosquito netting and staring out the window. Declan's light stayed on, making her wonder if the same emptiness was keeping him awake. She envied Ross's slack body next to her. Sometimes she felt as if he didn't need her.

She couldn't say the same of Declan.

One night she crept from the netting, slipped on her loafers, and wandered the mission the way she had as a child, this time within the halo of electric lights. She took another walk on the next night and the next, watching until the hangar's mouth was open. She passed by close enough for Declan to call out to her, but he was bent over the worktable, under three different lamps, wearing reading glasses now. Arnold was probably in his bungalow, asleep like everyone else.

She came to the edge of the grass and let her shoes touch the concrete lip of the floor, as close as she could get without stepping inside. She remembered herself as a child, perched on the back seat, still in the same place against the wall. She recognized most of the hanging tools. A few had been replaced.

"You should shut this. Keep the mosquitos out."

He stayed quiet, still facing the metallic alphabet.

"Just like old times." She couldn't hold back the disappointment in her voice.

"Not quite," he said finally.

She felt relieved. "I'm taller now."

"Among other things."

"You're working on the new plane?" She tugged at her sleeve, suddenly conscious of the scar on her shoulder. Sometimes she forgot it was from a cigarette, certain it had come from the *buda* instead. It was a mark Declan had never seen on her.

"It hasn't been new for more than a decade." He turned, and after seeing the look on his face, she wished he hadn't. "Why are you here, Barb?"

"We haven't really talked since—"

"It's easier if you stay away. Especially at night." He turned back to his work.

"Okay." Her voice sounded weak. "I'll go." But she stayed a moment longer, willing him to look again. His resolve was greater than hers, and she turned toward the constellations, studying them: stars light years apart that some ancients had grouped together, forcing a pattern where there wasn't one.

"We can be friends," she said to Sagittarius. "Right?"

She went straight home and slipped under the net next to Ross. He rolled away from her, as though sensing what was up.

———

Despite Declan's warning, she returned to the hangar the next afternoon, in the safety of daylight and with Abeba in tow. Declan's last meaningful interaction with Abeba had been on the plane from the States. She was four now and hid behind her mother's legs.

"You know Mr. Kline, Abeba."

The child nodded shyly, no different from how she would slink behind books at the back of Barb's classroom. Little more than edition numbers had changed between mother and daughter. Abeba also preferred running around without shoes, and Barb now understood Marty's concerns about hookworm. "Is Arnold here?"

Declan gestured to the far wall of the hangar. "Say hello, Arn!"

She saw a movement near the back workbench. "Hiya, Barb."

"And Abeba!" Declan called.

"And Abeba!" came the response.

Abeba cupped her mouth and cried, "Hello, Arn!"

Arnold's chuckle was followed by the sound of his work resuming. Declan avoided Barb's eyes as he squatted in front of Abeba and asked if she wanted to draw. She nodded, and he went to the table, found a sheet of drafting paper and some charcoal, and motioned for her to sit on the back seat. Barb crossed her arms and settled in to watch.

Declan leaned an elbow against the wall next to her. "She's much younger than you were."

"And my mother never escorted me." He looked down, and Barb's anger at the prejudice of her mother and the other missionaries rekindled. "They were small people, Declan."

"In all things." He smiled. "You remember the pilot before me, from when you were little?"

She could almost picture him, sitting across the table from her family when her feet still couldn't touch the floor. She swung them back and forth until Marty clamped a hand on her thigh. Barb searched for the pilot's name. "Jeff?"

"Know why he left?" She thought he had accepted a post somewhere in the north. She had always, for some reason, imagined him with the Sphinx in Egypt. Declan cleared his throat. "Nilsson had an affair with him."

"Mrs. Nilsson was hardly—"

"Not Mrs."

"Oh." The reverend's face materialized in front of her: his jutting brow and tightly trimmed hair, his square jaw and thin lips. She understood his stern look in a new way, as an anger he turned on others to avoid turning it on himself. She had been afraid of him. Now she found they shared common ground.

"Jeff and Nils, that was their business. Your parents—" Declan stopped, afraid to offend her. But what could he say that she hadn't already thought herself? She couldn't remember the last time she had agreed with a pronouncement of her mother's, usually because they *were* pronouncements. How could one thing be true in every circumstance?

Declan stretched his arms over his head, a sign that their conversation about the reverend was over, but Barb's mood had shifted—it was impossible to revisit her childhood without getting lost in those feelings of loneliness. This was what she really missed about Declan: their camaraderie in the face of adults.

"Remember when you told me your name meant 'extreme screw-up'?"
He looked confused. "The day you nicknamed me? Well, I looked it up.
Declan means 'full of goodness.'"

"Sounds like I missed the memo."

His tone made her chest hurt. She tried to remember—had she
said something similar about herself to Ross?

His face relaxed. "Should I show her the cockpit?"

She'd nearly forgotten Abeba, fingers blackened, working diligently with her charcoal. It was nice to forget her sometimes. "You
certainly should."

He sat next to her daughter and whispered something in her ear.
Abeba gasped and nodded before he lifted her into the copilot's seat.

Declan • *April* 2009

They couldn't be friends. The first time she came to him—about the snake—he'd been too quick to touch, and spent the next year punishing himself. It was like when she left for college and wrote him letters: wariness didn't just serve him well; his survival on the mission depended on it.

Barb and Abeba's visit to the hangar that afternoon had reminded him of all the things he might have had, if only. Tonight he turned off the hangar lights and locked the doors. He tossed his cap on the dresser, wiggled open its bottom panel, and retrieved the bottle of *araqe* stashed inside. It was a liquor the locals made him. He didn't bother with a glass as he crawled under the netting. He closed his eyes and saw Barb's face. The pull between them still felt primordial. He remembered the first time he had felt it—one afternoon when he was tuning the plane's engine and chatting with Nils, who had suddenly gone silent at the worktable. He was staring at the photograph Declan had shoved in the drawer.

Nils looked up, no attempt at an apology, no indication that he'd invaded Declan's privacy. "Who's she?"

"No one." The last thing Declan wanted to talk about was his dead sister. Surely Nils had read his file. He set the photo down and Declan resisted the urge to snatch it away.

"You all right, man?" It was a question he didn't like asking. He preferred to allow everyone their secrets, but Nils's face was tense. He was a formidable man. To see him anxious made the world feel upside down. He shrugged in answer and walked past Declan, rounding the tail of the Cessna and caressing its stressed skin. The movement looked too intimate.

"You're like the last pilot," Nils began. "So serious. So secretive. Though not with everyone." His tone held a threat. It took Declan back to Fulton, where threats needed to be dealt with swiftly.

He crossed his arms. "I spend time with you."

"Ah, but that doesn't speak well for your character. I am not, myself, without blemish."

Declan didn't understand. "None of us are. That's where salvation comes in."

Nils gave a few sarcastic claps. "So convincing. You should write this week's sermon."

"What's your problem?"

"It doesn't look good—you with that photo, spending your spare time with the only minor on the mission." Declan put his hands up, warding off the insinuation. "Not to mention your copilot, who's a sexual deviant."

Nils spat the final words. His disclosure invited Declan's own.

"She's my sister. The girl in the photo."

Nils gave no sign he'd heard. "Men and women shouldn't be alone unless they're married—no dinner, no conversation behind closed doors. Keeps them from temptation." He ran a hand over his thinning hair. "Women I can be trusted with."

It was clear what he meant, even before he reached for Declan's collar and tugged.

Declan had never felt a man's lips against his. He was from Georgia, where any rumor of queerness was met with a drawling "That's just not right." But he knew driving into midtown Atlanta flipped the script. Queerness became cause for celebration.

He put his hands on Nils's shoulders and nudged him back. The man's eyes were half-shut, as if it didn't matter who Declan was.

Nils sighed and stepped away. "It's Jeff I miss."

Declan remembered the reactions of the other missionaries whenever he spoke of Nils, as if they were bracing themselves for another scandal. Anger at the whole lot rose up inside him, at the assumptions that became truths because no one bothered to ask.

"What if the rules are wrong?" As he said it, he felt the truth deep in the pit of his stomach: given time, the rule could change—it *would*.

"Nice of you to say." Nils smiled sadly.

It was his last day as Declan's copilot. They never spoke of their confessions. Nils had given Declan enough to ponder—why he so preferred the company of a ten-year-old girl to that of his peers.

He didn't have an explanation, but when Barb went on furlough two years later, the mission grew unfriendly in her absence. If he hadn't been so good at his job, the other missionaries might have staged a coup like the one the EPRDF was planning for Mengistu. He wondered if Nils had been right to question what he had with Barb. It felt deeper, somehow, than friendship. No one else over the course of his adult life had bothered to understand him the way she had. She sat on the seats against the wall, the axis around which he turned. He'd look up from his work and find her staring. They'd smile and he'd ask if she was tired or wanted lunch. He hung on her every word, she on his. It was almost unbearable when those words were suddenly gone.

So once the Eklunds returned, he asked Simeon if Barb could be his unofficial copilot. Simeon agreed, but only after asking if Declan could sell her on the idea of college in America. "She trusts you," he said, and pride rushed into Declan's chest, tempered only by the onerous task of sending Barb away.

One moment she was reading him *Moby-Dick;* the next she was standing at the Cessna's cargo hold, saying a reluctant goodbye.

How could he not kiss her?

He hadn't realized that it happened in the same place where Nils had kissed him.

The fervor of Barb's letters from school sobered him. She still hadn't read his file, and he wasn't sure she'd want him once she had—like Marty, who never trusted him, except on the day he chauffeured her to Jimma on her pearl-trading errand; he returned there alone and bought the necklace back for Barb.

Instead of giving it to her as she climbed into the Cessna that summer, he told her to forget him.

She didn't. She came to him in the hangar, everything small and withdrawn, He worshipped her ever-present sensitivity and that tremulous pulsing in her fingertips as they touched. He felt more than that as they made love: her sadness, her betrayal, her exhaustion.

It took him months of indecision, but in October, as the Ethiopian government was settling with the creaks and groans of an old farmhouse, he requested a furlough. (He needed to visit Barb outside the mission's influence.) What happened instead was six months in a dirt-packed cell in Addis where nothing mattered, least of all the pearls squirreled away in his dresser, now just shiny pieces of sand.

The day the guard released him, he found his way to the Svenska office downtown. No one there knew what to say—how does one apologize for not yielding to ransom demands? Perhaps it was relief he saw in their faces when he walked in—despite the blood stiffening his shirt, the weight he'd lost, the stench—not guilt.

There was some guilt. They put him up in a hotel, flew Svenska's director down to see him, and let Declan choose between a severance package and a job anywhere in the organization. His mouth opened, but no answer came. He was still getting used to the feel of clean skin again.

In the hotel, he thought about those six months over and over, never in order, like a waking dream. How many times had he floated above himself in that cell, watching the guards' batons rain down? He'd thought the tether to his body—to the pain, to the blood and snot and piss—would snap. How he prayed it would. The real tragedy came every time he woke, corporeal again. Why had he survived? Why hadn't he just let go?

He had reemerged into a world where Eritrea had officially seceded; he had seceded, too, from whatever life he didn't deserve with Barb. He came face to face with this life one day in the market, when he recognized a woman in the crowd as Barb's friend from Welete.

He ducked away and kept to the hotel after that.

It became clear that to stay in Ethiopia was to live with that unpaid ransom hanging over his head, his past punishing his present. It surprised the director when he requested a transfer to their headquarters in Stockholm.

"Are you qualified for an office job?" he asked. "I'd hate to set you up for failure."

Declan shrugged. "It'll be new." He didn't add: *It has to be.*

Declan · September 1993

The anonymity of a new job, a new language, a new city made it easier to forget the cell with worms and roaches in the walls. He could close the door to his office (even if it felt too much like the cell), he could listen to the radio in Swedish, he could stop cracking jokes about ABBA, and he could ignore the change from summer to winter—the twenty-two-hour days preparing everyone for an age of darkness. He had never lived in a place with all four seasons. In Georgia he saw winter twice, having woken to the wonders of an ice storm in fifth grade and to eight inches of snow a decade later, when he was behind bars.

His first day he expected to walk into an office of idealists bent on making the world a better place, but he found narcissists and bigots and some, like himself, who needed religion to be good—a discovery that made him dread more than the waning daylight.

But he couldn't figure out the lawyer who consulted for human resources. She appeared only when employees were laid off—a grim reaper for the professional set. He heard two men in the restroom speaking about her so cruelly they reminded him of high school. They made a point to call her *Herr,* not *Fröken.* Declan imagined plucking the word from the air like an arrow and shooting it at their chests. Instead, he chastened them with his dead eyes. One man blinked and shut his mouth. The other didn't care. Assholes would be assholes, regardless.

He was surprised by how much he hated them.

Suddenly, a month after he was hired, the lawyer was sitting at a seminar table across from him. He could see the two men from the bathroom staring at them through the conference room's glass walls. Declan's breath shallowed.

She asked if he knew why he was here.

"Should I?"

She seemed to be smiling, but her mouth hadn't moved. "We sent you a letter."

He remembered seeing the Svenska insignia on an envelope last week. How could he tell her seeing it in his home recalled memories that made him sweat? He thought, *I'm no good at coordinating. I get lost between the paperwork and the computer. I'm strung between one world and another.* Instead, she was asking him not to take legal action against Svenska for failing to report his ransom to the proper authorities.

"We need you to promise, Mr. Kline, to let this go."

Declan suddenly saw Ellie, with a wooden caterpillar in her hand. It had been their most prized toy. They loved to pull its leash and watch each segment follow on tandem wheels. Someone had made it—their father? They were in the treehouse in the back yard. Declan had been crying. Ellie was leaving for summer camp, and he worried she wouldn't come back. She wrapped her free hand around his and smiled. "You need to let go of me, Dec. Just let go." She dropped his hand from hers and the caterpillar from the treehouse. It landed with a clatter. He imagined its segments cracked open on their lawn, but from a distance it looked intact. When they retrieved it later, Ellie said, "See? No harm."

Later, after she'd gone (not to camp, but to the stream), he noticed the crack along the caterpillar's last segment. It took a month for the toy to fall apart completely, and here this lawyer sat, asking him to forget that impossible-to-forget dirt cell. The scars reminded him whenever he changed clothes.

He shifted forward in his chair. "This isn't what you usually do."

Her smile showed this time. "But I'm perfectly capable."

"Not what I meant. You ask me in here, I think I'm getting fired."

"Not at all."

"You're wasting your time. I don't want to sue." He stuck his hand out for the papers. She stopped him.

He raised an eyebrow and she continued, her accent barely audible: "Understand, if you sign *these* papers, you agree not to sue—"

"I get it."

"You also waive your right to a settlement."

He leaned back. The last time he'd settled, he'd been facing a year. "I don't need a settlement, Ms. Nyman."

She slid another set of papers in front of him. "I understand your loyalty to Svenska Ministries, but I don't share it. As your advocate, Mr. Kline, I encourage you to sign *this.*"

He skimmed the new documents. The settlement sum was ten times his salary.

"I don't know what happened to you, Mr. Kline." The way she said it, he knew she was lying. She'd lived through something, too. "I do know this amount is not enough."

"But it's something?"

"We understand each other."

He shook his head. "Ms. Nyman, I don't have anyone who can use this money."

"Yourself."

"Not how I operate."

"Then do it because I say it's the right thing."

"You do make me nervous." He signed.

She put the papers in her briefcase with a quick movement. "I can see that."

He thought of her that night as he stumbled toward *Mariatorget* because he'd heard it was Stockholm's version of midtown Atlanta. He didn't know if she even liked bars, but that didn't keep him from wandering into one to search the patrons' faces and try something on tap. He imagined running into Nils here. If God had such a sense of humor.

He went to a different bar the next night. And the next. He wondered what would happen if anyone from work saw him. For some reason he felt untouchable.

Two weeks and fourteen bars later he'd made no progress, so he switched tacks, drafting a note: *Ms. Nyman, I'd be honored if you'd have a drink with me tonight at 6.—Mr. Kline.* He included the name of a bar near the office, tucked the note under his desk calendar, and waited until she showed up to reprimand another employee.

It took three days. She hung up her jacket at reception, and Declan slipped the note into its pocket. He returned to his office, smiling to himself for the first time in God knew how long.

He got to the bar early and sat facing the door. He spotted her, brow furrowed as she searched the crowd, and stared into the depths of his porter. It felt important that *she* notice *him.*

She sat on the next stool over. "If it isn't the nice missionary."

He kept his breath under control. She wore perfume that was just sweet enough. "That's not a privacy violation?"

"We both know you won't sue. But I don't want you nervous."

"Not nervous now." He waited for it to be true. She ordered a highball and he noticed that her makeup was different, her eyes and lips darker. "What should I call you?"

"Ms. Nyman isn't good enough?" The question would have been coy if not for the tension in her face. She looked ready to leave and he suddenly understood.

He placed a hand on her arm. "I just mean—"

The tension disappeared. "*Fröken* Tilde."

"So formal."

"Always a *Fröken,* never a *Fru.*" She waved a hand in front of her face. "Tilde."

Her highball arrived. He sipped his porter, struggling to find the next rung of conversation. "You must know what your name means in English."

"How wonderful to be a punctuation mark." She leaned in. It gave him hope.

"A shapely one though."

She laughed. "So undulating."

"Good word."

"You can say it *vågig* in Swedish."

He took another sip. He felt the need to pace himself.

"What about you, *Mr.* Kline?"

He swallowed. "Sometimes I go by Dec."

"Like our word for tire."

"*Däck.*"

"Ah, you're learning."

"Slowly."

"You poor *amerikan.*"

He smirked. "I haven't been there in a decade."

"Well, you can avoid it right here for another decade." She indicated the bar and twirled her stool. He wondered if this wasn't her first highball. It might explain the grand movements she cut through the air. Or maybe this was just her. "So long as you survive the winter."

"Something else that makes me nervous."

"You won't die," she promised. "The cold's too beautiful."

He knew they would fall together, had known since that first meeting when she had chosen him over Svenska. He made them dinner reservations that weekend in slow Swedish—"*Bord . . . för två . . . på sex*"—reservations they missed. When she answered his knock, she wore the most stylish dress he'd ever seen on a woman he liked. He'd never cared about fashion, but she would teach him to notice, to see a dress on her and imagine the fun of taking it off: asymmetrical straps, low backs, zippers, even though he hated them. He preferred slippery fabrics—so did she.

They were in her kitchen drinking merlot one moment and on her couch with their cheeks flushed and lips swollen the next. She pulled away, caught sight of the clock on the wall.

"We're late."

He held her face. "Bedroom?"

She led him down the hall and stopped, pulling her hand away. "There's something . . ."

That tension was in her face again. He kissed her forehead. "There's nothing."

". . . you should know."

He smiled and tucked her hair behind her ears. He watched her put the pieces together—the *there's nothing* with the look of hope on his face.

"You already . . . ?"

"I do."

She asked how. He looked down, ashamed.

"Some assholes at the office."

Her lips pursed. "I can imagine who."

"Maybe someday you'll get to fire them."

She snorted, but her posture was still uncertain.

"You should know," he inhaled, "I sort of shot my adoptive father." One of her eyebrows went up. "Then I did time in jail. It was a thing."

He spoke quickly, his gaze fixed just above her shoulder. When he looked at her again, the uncertainty was gone. Then she was pressing him against the wall, her mouth locked on his.

The morning after, he asked, "Do we need to report to human resources?"

She rolled to face him. "Hold your horses, cowboy."

"Don't be smug."

She shrugged. "We've just started."

He reached for her waist and kissed her shoulder. "I won't want to stop."

"You don't want to admit this. Have you read your contract?"

He lay back and rubbed his face with his hands. "Blackmail, then?"

She sat up and drew her knees to her chest; the sheet tightened across his torso. She stuck out her hand and mimed shaking his. "I'm *Fröken* Tilde. I will never judge what you do with your body." There was such seriousness—or was it anger?—in her face. He remembered their first meeting, when he'd seen something in her that he recognized. And last night, he had noticed her own scars—faint, on her thighs. She seemed to be the kind of person who would never explain what they meant.

"Come here," he said.

She leaned forward and kissed him. "You I'd like to keep."

He liked the softness in her voice. "If I can keep up."

"As long as you don't get fired, *Herr* Kline."

Where Declan had grown up, women were locked in houses. They emerged perfectly coifed—even debuted if they had money. Barb had loosened the dirt around these notions, but Tilde uprooted them.

They were in bed when he first told her about Barb. She had pulled back from his side, her expression clouded. "But she was just a child when you met."

It was like he was back in the hangar with Nils. "I can't explain it."

"Didn't you think?" She stopped.

"What?" His stomach dropped at her tone.

Tilde shook her head. "She didn't have a choice."

"I don't understand."

"She grew up isolated and you were . . ." Tilde waved a hand. "You were you."

"Her only option," he said after a beat. He knew he was right when Tilde relaxed.

He worked at reading her face. He learned that her lips disappeared when she was angry. (The first time he saw it a thrill ran through him.) He loved watching her performance dissolve as she returned home after work, the slight shift in her shoulders, the stiffness that vanished from her face. Her hair was always tied up, white-blonde with a mousy color underneath, but she let it down in the evening. He felt privileged every time he saw it.

He confessed, "You think there's no one for you. Then someone just pops up."

"This is how you feel about Barb, yeah?"

She looked uncertain and he wanted to say, *Not her. Not this time.*

Jesus, Tilde, he thought now and swigged from the bottle. Ever since that day at the stream he had felt the water closing in. He had learned not to speak—about Ellie, about his imprisonments, about the way he felt separate and inhuman.

On the first anniversary of their missed reservations, he led Tilde to bed and kissed her slowly, inching up her dress. She accused him of stalling.

This was when he told her everything.

He started with his sister: Hera's warning before they left the house, the burst of happiness when they discovered the stream, the adventure in Ellie's eyes as she skipped across the stones in the water, even as she fell. This was the awfulness of nature, he knew, the danger hidden in its majesty. As a child, he didn't understand what was happening, could only watch her black hair whorl in the water . . .

He looked down, ashamed, and Tilde lifted his chin.

He told her of the adoption, the gun, and the time he'd served. He hesitated at the six months in Addis, but Tilde had already seen his scars. As he described his sentence in that dirt cell, patches of his skin started to sweat and his arms and shoulders tensed. Somehow he finished. Tilde touched his hand.

He blinked. "Sorry. I don't know how long I've been talking."

She kissed him. "For days and days, *De.*"

He almost apologized again, but she was sliding her fingers up his thigh and lowering her mouth.

Tonight, the bottle in one hand, he used the other to touch himself, remembering.

Two weeks later Tilde told him she'd once been in a relationship that went spectacularly wrong. "We were in *gymnasium*—your high school—and *hjärtevänner*—best friends. Me now was me then, horribly curious. It's a fault."

"It's not."

"It really is." Declan shook his head. "So stubborn. Fine. In this story it is."

All she wanted then was to feel something good. Alcohol made her sick, drugs—uppers and downers—made her sad, but being able to press buttons on her body, to press those buttons on another person and create pleasure "out of nothing" was a wonderful discovery.

"My mother was home, but her *multipel skleros* kept her in her room. We started out simple." She blinked.

"*Te,* you don't have to."

"*Sötnos.*" She smiled sadly. "Let me say it."

As she told him about the assault, he closed his eyes, ashamed he couldn't stomach her story as she had his. He hadn't been—he could hardly think the word—*raped,* but he had heard it happening in other dirt cells. Why had he been spared? Because he was American? The thought invited a loathing so intense he could hardly breathe.

She noticed the change and kissed his temple.

"I should be taking care of you," he argued.

"Don't be nervous, *sötnos.* You do."

In the wake of these conversations he became the kind of person he didn't trust—someone who was (more often than not) happy.

He didn't mind it as much as he had expected.

Now, even in the safety of the hangar's back room, he still dreamt of the guards' batons. On supply runs he forced Arnold or Caj to walk the Addis streets while he lay in the back of the Jeep, trying to empty his mind. In Stockholm he would stop what he was doing, hit with some gruesome memory—an isolated moment that wouldn't leave him—and Tilde would hold him in the middle of the sidewalk or in her kitchen, wherever it happened, and whisper, "Breathe in, *sötnos. Andas in.*" Then, when he came back to himself: "What can I do?"

She was doing all she could.

"Is there something to say?" She pressed. "Like a safe word?"

But he remembered. "I survived jail by keeping my hands busy. Carving mostly."

She stared. "You *are* a cowboy."

He put on his best Georgia accent, geographically inaccurate, but it did the trick. "Thas right, ma'am."

The next day, she found him some balsa. He stared at the block in his hand. How she'd known what to get, he couldn't understand.

He said, "Let me take you flying."

"So you can keep your hands busy."

"Something like that."

When he took her up, she was so quiet he thought he'd finally succeeded at making her nervous. He landed early, afraid something had upset her. The look on her face as she climbed from the cockpit evinced a concentration reserved for her most perplexing problems at the law firm. On the drive from the airfield, he reached over the stick shift for her hand.

"I can't be here."

He couldn't argue with her tone. They were just outside Stockholm proper. She pointed at a sign for a hotel and they got off the E4. She held his hand through check-in and during the walk to their room. He couldn't read her profile. He couldn't let go of her either; she wouldn't let him. When the door to their room shut, she pressed him against the wall and kissed him hard, biting his lip. He followed her lead and a half hour later, they were on the floor, kissing again, despite their rug burns.

"*Te.*" He stopped her. "What is it?"

"Were you unimpressed?"

"How can you be silly?"

"It's in the timing."

Even as she joked, there was something heavy in her eyes. He laid a hand against her sternum because it settled her.

"You think you know a person." She waited for him to nod. "And when you see something new in them, it's such a surprise. You feel a part of their lives forever."

He smiled. "My flying."

"It was the most you I've seen you. It was like seeing you with your family—your real one, wherever they are."

It had felt so wonderful when she'd said it. Now it just made him sad.

"You couldn't say that an hour ago?" He kissed her neck.

"I had to wait for the words to come. It would be easier in Swedish. I could just call you *mitt hjärtegryn*." It meant *my heart-grain*. He thought of the *tef* fields surrounding Welete.

She said they shouldn't go up again. Once was a friendly gesture; twice would invite suspicion.

Her favorite American author was Melville, everything from *Omoo* to "Bartleby, the Scrivener." "So many words! So carefully positioned!" Melville reminded her of Bergman. Declan thought she meant Ingrid. "Dear *Gud, De,* you have to immediately watch *Det Sjunde Inseglet*. Bergman's as obsessed with God as you are." He gave her a look. "Don't deny it."

He held up his hands in surrender, and they rented five films.

"They'll be great for your Swedish," she said, before cuing up *The Seventh Seal*.

Barb's wonder made her glow, but Tilde's glow was contagious. If she was excited, it was Declan's breath that grew short. He read Melville for her, too, and barely recognized *Moby-Dick* from his flights with Barb.

They celebrated St. Lucia's Day in December because holidays were the one thing Tilde liked about religion. She cooked and told him stories of celebrating as a child, how she always wanted to wear lighted wreaths with the girls but could only watch her sister with envy. She made the memories sound very Swedish. Declan sat at the breakfast bar and played with the hem of his shirt.

"Hey." She tapped his foot with hers. "Today's about a martyr who lived in the fourth century, not now."

He almost smiled. "I don't know what I am. Irish or what." In Ethiopia being a *ferengi* was all that mattered, but listening to Tilde made him think he was missing something.

She took his chin in hand and studied his face. "You've always struck me as—what's the word? Swarthy, like *Medelhavs*." His brow furrowed at her answer. She let go of his chin. "It's just a guess. Nothing is fixed."

He said, "Nothing's ever fixed," though he hoped the two of them could be.

They went on like this for two more years, long enough for him to carve her a wolf, a moose, and the plane he flew her in (so different from when he'd done it for Barb). Tilde was with him, before him, beside him. She even managed his finances, investing the settlement from Svenska. Every crevice of Stockholm reminded him of her. So one night, lying in bed, chest pressed to her back, he asked, "Have you ever thought of children?"

She tensed in his arms. "Children?"

Her voice was small. She moved away, pulling the covers around her shoulders, before he could explain.

"Hey." He tugged the sheet until she turned toward him, her eyes sad.

"You don't know," she went on. "You said you knew, but you don't."

She couldn't have children. He knew that. He did. "There are ways. We could both—"

"*We* couldn't, *mitt hjärtegryn*."

"You know what a family means to me."

"Yes, and I've always known: no children."

"It's the only thing I've ever wanted." He watched her carefully. Her eyes ran along the mattress, along his chest and hips and legs, anywhere but his face.

"We could . . ." She closed her eyes and swallowed. "We could adopt?"

She was fighting for them, this woman with her Bergman and Melville and secularism. He wanted her to win, but not like this. "No."

"You're serious."

"How could I put anyone through that?"

"It doesn't send everyone into existential crisis—"

"You're the *queen* of existential crises."

Her eyes flashed. "Not everyone shoots someone."

He wondered how long she had wanted to say it. He tried to breathe. "No children. Right. Marry me then."

"Oh, no no no," she said too quickly. "I won't marry. You know this about me."

"'Always a *Fröken*, never a *Fru.*' I thought it was a Swedish saying."

"'Caught with your beard in a mailbox' is a Swedish saying. That was *my* saying." She sighed. "You can't even marry me, *De*. I'm not Christian."

"You could say you are."

She shook her head. "How could I possibly. You know what they believe."

"It's nothing like that. We'd know what's real."

"This is pointless." The words felt like a slap. "I'm not getting married. This is why I told you at the beginning."

He could see it then: the end of them—*nothing's ever fixed*. Still, he tried. "I want it to be the two of us, no end in sight."

"We can have that without marriage. We can go on and on like this. We can move in."

Even in his anger and confusion, he loved her for saying it. "Not with my job."

She rolled her eyes. "Eighty percent of Sweden could care less about religion, and you work for a company with a morality clause. A clause you break by being here."

"This is different. It's easy to hide."

She blinked at the word *hide*. He shook his head, willing her to know what he meant, not how it sounded. Her lips disappeared. Her anger wasn't wild. (It never was.)

"You stupid, stupid man."

Silence stretched between them and something permanent settled behind his sternum, something that would follow him for years, all the way to the Renaissance Hotel, where he would ask Barb for a family with the same result.

He stood and yanked on his shirt. "You're all-consuming, *Te*. You know that."

"Still, you need more." Her voice was dead now. It scared him.

He hovered in the doorway. She was always strong when they fought like this. She was the strongest person he knew. He doubted that would change.

So he left.

The next time he sat across the seminar table from her he wasn't nervous. She placed the papers for his transfer in front of him.

"It's your move, Antonius Block. Have you lost interest in our game?"

He knew the scene from *The Seventh Seal*. "Lost interest? On the contrary."

There was something new in her face. He couldn't help but ask what was wrong.

"I'm afraid I've turned you into the kind of person who will sue with impunity."

He was taken aback, so used to trusting her. "You still don't understand." He said it to give her solace, but his voice was bitter, as if he were trying to hurt her. She was Tilde, though, in masterful control of her face. He saw the effort it took to set his comment aside only because he'd been a diligent student of that face.

"Hey." He failed at a smile. "Those two assholes outlasted me."

"'Happiness comes, happiness leaves.' That's a Swedish saying, so you know. I wish you happiness, all the same."

He sighed. "I won't find it in Florida."

She reached for his hand. "*De*."

He stared at her cold fingers on his and found the name of the thing that had settled behind his sternum. "Don't you know? I'm cursed."

Her breath sounded too full. "Did you enjoy your reprieve?"

He was confused at first, but she was playing the part of Death again. "I did."

"I'm happy to hear that." She stood and grabbed her briefcase. "Now I'll be leaving you."

He didn't miss the Stockholm winter.

She was impossible to leave without consequence. Her brief light had let him hope again, and the dark plunge back into loneliness made him angrier, less flexible, more selfish. He'd felt as blessed as David in Stockholm; in Florida, he felt as cursed as Job. He couldn't even pick up a block of balsa without thinking of her, and every stroller in Florida reinforced his belief in the curse. Life was better in Welete, where mothers tied their babies close—they might as well be loaves of bread slung from their necks. He became (again) the coworker addressed only in memos. He sank (again) beneath the surface, water up to his chin, his mouth, his nose, just his dead eyes left peeking out. After a time he didn't notice the rising water. It offered him calm—*sensory deprivation,* they called it. Still there were days, hours, moments when the silence became a hum—loud, louder, too loud—moments when he needed to thrash and call for help, when isolation was the thing he had to shake free from.

There was no one to save him in Florida but the women he met in bars. (His first date with Tilde had been in a bar. He couldn't keep this thought from bobbing to the surface.) These were the girls he'd grown up with—the ones he'd stumbled through at the vo-tech. Now they were divorced or high on something. They gave him the excuse to stop flailing for just a moment—or to flail, but with a partner. (He learned this was worse.)

In the light of the morning, he remembered to be a good boy and reached out to his parents on a whim. He assumed they would want nothing to do with him, but Hera responded. He made the six-hour drive to see them every few months, so they could stare at each other from across the sitting room. He filled the time with old stories from the mission. Zeus listened between scoffs while Hera said he was so brave going to Africa like that.

He was a recruiter now, just like the ones who had found him. Once, he returned to Fulton County Jail. He recognized some of the jailers and remembered their names better than he did his current coworkers'. He wondered if this might be a sign of aging or something worse—that his memory was contingent on the number of threats he faced.

The Florida office had copies of everyone's files. He resisted the urge to page through them until one night when he saw—what did they call them in Atlanta?—two old queens in a bar. They made him think of Nils and Jeff. Declan pulled Nils's file the next day and found a packet documenting the *altercation* on the Welete mission. What a word for two consenting adults who had loved each other, however briefly. Perhaps this was always the way with love: those few moments Declan had had with Ellie, with Rod, with Barb, with Tilde. He couldn't explain his wish for a greater continuity, for someone beyond him—not just a god. Someone to touch.

According to the file, Nils had left Svenska on March 23, 1994, but Mrs. Nilsson had no termination date. One mystery solved: they had likely separated. Declan wanted to believe that Nils was retired, living however he wanted, but something derailed the thought. He saw Nils with a gun to his head, offering a last prayer and pulling the trigger, doing the thing Declan didn't have the courage for.

He dug up Jeff's file next. He'd had a termination date, too, three months after Nils's, and suddenly their lives crystallized in front of him: the reverend strolling arm in arm with the pilot through *Humlegården,* the park where Tilde had once pushed him off the path, making them miss dinner again. The likelihood that Nils and Jeff were together was infinitesimal, but Declan believed. Hope crept back into his eyes, enough for him to say yes to sharing his testimony at the annual conference when the director asked.

When Declan found Barb again, Tilde's revelation had plagued him—that Barb had chosen him only because he was there. But that was then. Now she stood in front of him, confessing that she had floundered without him. He said yes again. Because Barb would survive her floundering (even the Omo couldn't swallow her) whereas Ellie hadn't.

He had forgotten how Barb was—the way she threw her emotions around, was somewhat victim to them. (So different from Tilde.) Then she left him waiting in Dulles, searching for her at the baggage claim, calling her name into the women's lavatory.

He was grateful when he returned to the hangar and his back room. Twelve years had passed, but the bed and dresser were in the same place—not just a dresser, *the* dresser. He calculated the likelihood that the previous pilot had never discovered the panel. He reached behind it, and a moment later his fingers brushed the necklace.

Everything was coming together. For once.

But then he remembered he didn't have Barb anymore, and the pearls turned to plastic in his hands.

———

Declan was right. She needed to keep away from him. She stopped taking walks at night and began reading in bed with Ross. The mosquito net shut out all distractions, except for Abeba when she couldn't sleep. Once the child was tucked safely under the net in her own room, Barb laid her head on Ross's chest. With the anchor of his breath in her ear she could let her thoughts drift to the emptiness, poke it and prod it, as he ran his fingers through her hair or offered a litany of things he loved about her: he pointed to places on her body or spoke in abstractions. At first she had felt exposed and uncomfortable, but she squirmed less over time.

Something in her chest unclenched.

He would say, "You're the best part of me." She remained silent, thinking the opposite. His kindness felt so expansive that she let it envelop even the secrets she hadn't told.

"I could say the same to you, *redat.*" The word was Amharic for helper.

He didn't quite believe her. They were too alike in this way, a side effect, she suspected, of being raised on original sin. Everyone was born broken and needed God to put them back together, like Humpty Dumpty. She hoped Abeba wouldn't resemble them in this regard.

One night Ross asked, "What needs to change for you to be happy?"

The question surprised her. She hadn't thought she was so obvious. "I don't know."

"Be sure to tell me"—he kissed her forehead—"when you figure it out."

Barb moored herself to Ross—before she knew tautness could wear a mooring thin—and to her duties on the mission. It was hard to believe her greatest solace would be the prayer meetings. Once a week she met with Aida and Karin to pray for the school, the town, the political unrest in Ethiopia, and for Svenska. Attending these meetings as a child, Barb had been more abstracted than reverent. She didn't do much better as an adult. The pressure to ad-lib the perfect prayer—one insightful enough to make the others *mm-hmm*—made her live in dread. She had disjointed dreams about her failures, and upon waking struggled to convince herself they hadn't happened.

After *amens,* conversation sprouted, mostly between Aida and Karin. Barb always took more time to thaw. Once Karin said she had come to the mission to change the world, but without "disrupting the country's infrastructure." Aida had scoffed, "Good luck with that."

Barb stayed silent. Changing the world wasn't even among her top-ten reasons for coming back, but Karin's words stayed with her. She wondered how Karin would react to her own growing conviction that the mission's presence here was condescending at best, destructive at worst.

But the next week Karin was absent from prayer meeting.

"She's sick." Aida said it casually, though sickness on the mission was just as likely to mean malaria as the flu.

They prayed quickly and left, as though Karin had been their binding ingredient.

Barb asked Ross's advice in bed that night. "I don't know what to do."

He set his books on the nightstand: commentaries from the mission library, three shelves filled with everything from theology to children's stories. "Yeah, you do."

"I'm bad at friends." Her voice sounded too high. "Maybe she wants to be left alone."

"Take a breath. Do you know what's wrong?"

"It's just—it's like she dropped off the face of the earth."

"Okay. Have you ever done that?"

So many times, she thought, and remembered how she had isolated herself at Trinity and how that isolation had ended, when Ross goaded her into talking about Ethiopia.

"I love you."

He seemed surprised. "I love you, too."

She asked if he had ever dropped off the face of the earth.

"We all do at some point."

"When?" she pressed.

"Jason. Mostly after Jason."

She waited for something more—"I was in the car, too" was all he'd ever said—but he reached to turn off the light.

The next afternoon she and Abeba stopped at the office to visit Karin, but they found Caj alone. He asked how he could be of service.

"I was looking for Karin."

"Ah, she's sick."

"Right. But she's missing meals."

"I'm delivering them to her."

"Oh, good. I—does she?" Barb paused to breathe. "Would she like someone to talk to?"

He leaned back in his chair, appraising her. "She might."

Barb left Abeba with Caj—he insisted—and walked to the Thorns' bungalow. Her knock was tentative. She wasn't sure Karin had heard, but then her sunburnt face appeared in the window. There was a long pause before the door opened and Barb saw that the red on Karin's face was from tears, not the sun. Her own face grew soft. "What's wrong?"

"Just come in."

They sat across from each other at the circular table that all the bungalows had. The air around them hung heavy. Barb wondered if they would sit in silence until Caj returned home.

"I'm sorry." Karin's voice carried the correct inflection, but it sounded mechanical, and her shoulders crowded her clavicle. Her posture reminded Barb of Declan—his innate sadness, which she had always hoped to banish. It was the thing that most separated him from Ross, who was buoyant by comparison. She found herself wondering what Declan had done during those years in Florida without her.

But Karin was the one, now, stultified by sadness. Barb thought back to Ross's advice the night before. "Are we friends, Karin?"

"Of course. That's why you're here. To be a friend." Karin stared at the table, as though unconvinced.

"I mean *real* friends—able-to-say-anything friends."

Karin looked up. "Is that an American phrase? Like *hjärtevänner*?"

Barb started over. "I know what this place can do to you. It gets under your nails. Grinds into your skin." Karin's eyes were wide. *In judgment,* Barb thought.

Karin slowly opened her mouth. "When I came back from Sweden, it started again." There was a quiet noise—not a laugh. She was keeping herself from crying.

"We don't have to talk," Barb said quickly.

Karin reached across the table for Barb's hands. "I'm glad you're here and not Aida."

Barb understood. Aida was like Marty: she knew where she was headed and didn't have time for tears along the way. "Aida would call this visit *an indulgence.*"

"Yes, as bad as the ones Martin Luther fought."

Karin let go of Barb's hands, and Barb felt another wave of questions wash over her. But now wasn't the time. "So Caj isn't letting you starve."

Karin nodded, tears returning to her eyes. "I've been good for so long. There's so much sun here I thought it would be fine."

Barb knew the fear of the unnamed *it.* "Yeah."

"You have the look of someone who understands."

"What a horrible club to belong to."

Karin's laugh was sad.

"I shouldn't be nice," Barb said. "It's easier to keep the front up if no one smiles."

"Pity's worse." Karin glanced at her. "You had that look at the door, but it's gone now. I can't go outside for fear of that look. And inside I can't stop *thinking.*"

Barb remembered her first months after returning to Welete. "You're lost in a fog."

"It hurts more than it should."

"Don't be hard on yourself."

"But . . . I'm Swedish."

Barb smiled. Karin's thoughtfulness, her ability to joke without trying, was rare. But that same thoughtfulness was what invited the emptiness. What would Ross do? *Tell a story,* but not one about dancing goats or the gospel. Barb wondered if Karin, like Raji, could keep a secret.

"What I'm about to say is private."

Karin nodded gravely. "Like in therapy."

"Sure."

They spent three afternoons sitting across from each other in the hours between the end of school and Caj's return. Karin made tea with a hot pot, and Barb described her first fourteen years in Welete, the disappearance of Makeda, and her infatuation with Declan; then her arrival in the States, her years with Ross, and Abeba's birth. Over the course of the confession Karin's shoulders opened. She asked questions. She laughed at something unexpected, and Barb got more *mm-hmms* than she ever had at prayer meetings. She ended the story with the day Declan came to recruit them.

"Now I'm back here. Too late. But still." She stared at their mugs on the table, Karin's empty and hers untouched.

"Has anything happened since—with Declan?"

Barb shook her head. "I miss him though. It's strange when he's just in the hangar."

"Will you tell Ross?"

"No." The math no longer balanced out—Barb's need for forgiveness was outstripped by the pain it would cause. She feared, even now, that she'd shared too much and retribution would rain down. This was the way it worked in the Book of Judges. Mistakes, like Jephthah's, cost lives. The only retribution was Caj opening the door and putting an end to her visit.

"Should I come back?" she asked to avoid her real question: *Am I too dirty a thing?*

Karin looked at Caj. "I'll come to you, Barbara."

The two of them soon made a habit of volunteering in the garden. Sometimes Karin even helped with the chickens in the morning. Barb's confessions across the table had exorcised small talk, so they fell into secret sharing. Karin always had a response to Barb's doubts about mission work. Once, in the garden, Barb recalled how reading *Things Fall Apart* in college had sent a liquid terror through her limbs.

"That's the worst-case scenario," Karin was sure. "The missionaries *ransom* the village leaders. Mission work in the twenty-first century is more enlightened."

"There's barbed wire on our fence." Barb pulled up a weed and thought of Declan's ransom. "We come here, plaster a bunch of walls, and call it good."

"Aida and Roger don't. They help in town, but not with plaster. Not using plaster is part of the enlightenment. There's an American saying with fish or horses?"

Barb thought a moment. "You can lead a horse to water, but you can't make him drink?"

"Ah." Karin clapped the dirt from her gloves. "The horse is male."

"I think that's just the English."

Barb had done mission work most of her life, but Karin made her feel as if she were a strange mixture of professional and amateur, like the contestants on musical-competition shows. Maybe she belonged in the "raw talent" category.

Karin's own secrets had started when she got pregnant in high school. When her parents found out, they set up a doctor's appointment to end it, but Karin wouldn't consent. She took the baby to term with the support of the state and gave him up for adoption. "My 'rebellion' was finding religion. Then I met Caj." She hadn't told him. Barb nodded in solidarity. "But I want kids," she continued, "and we're having trouble. It feels like a punishment."

"Is that the kind of God you want to believe in?" Barb surprised herself with the question. It felt too wise, too well timed—what Ross might say.

Karin shook her head. "That's what Isaiah 55:8 is about. Our thinking isn't God's."

The statement unnerved Barb. It sounded like Karin was giving something up. "What about adoption? Be on the other end of things."

"It's come up."

"Declan's adopted." She must trust Karin if she was divulging his secrets, too.

"That gives me a little hope. When we first came here, he was so nice. He spoke Swedish to us."

"He learned Swedish for you?" This, too, seemed more like something Ross would do.

"Oh, he already knew it. From living in Stockholm."

Barb paused. "He was at the Florida office forever."

Karin shook her head. "He was in Stockholm first." She went on, describing a joke Declan had told. Barb turned her attention to getting another weed out, trying to ignore the feeling of betrayal creeping through her body. Of course Declan existed apart from her—she'd been acutely aware of this her whole life. That he'd been happy without her, able to make jokes, was the surprise. She wondered, suddenly, if her presence was what made him sad. Had she grown into some kind of symbol for him? The thing he could never have? She thought of the *Moby-Dick* quotes he used to send. But she couldn't treat her life like a passage of literature, turning it over and over, seeking a direct line of cause and effect. Or was that direct line God's Plan—the thing she always failed to see?

This gnarl in Declan's past brought back the old emptiness, too strong to ignore. That evening she lay with her back to Ross, her mind chasing the answer to his question: *What needs to change for you to be happy?* Karin seemed to be happier now. Perhaps Barb had been using Karin's unhappiness to distract from her own.

"I'm going for a walk."

She didn't wait for a response, just grabbed her hoodie from the dresser, slipped on shoes, and left, retracing her circuit among the mission buildings. Her return to the hangar felt as inevitable as another famine, and by the end of the week she made her approach.

The main doors were shut, so she rapped on the smaller front door, feeling just as desperate as she had when she stood before Declan's room at the Renaissance.

He opened the door and jerked his arms across his chest like he was embarrassed. "Christ, Barb." He looked down at his t-shirt and boxers, then yanked her over the threshold. They were alone. Arn was still on furlough. (Declan would go, along with the Mathesons, when he returned.) "Why are you here?"

"The light was on." But it was an excuse. The light was always on at this hour.

She was suddenly unsure if the emptiness or Ross's question had brought her here. Maybe they were different permutations of the same worry that had dogged her since college: that they were alone in the universe. Tears she'd avoided for years surfaced.

"Don't. You can't *do* that all the time." Whereas Ross indulged her, Declan treated her crying as the weakness it was. Still, he closed the distance between them.

"Oh, god," she sobbed into his shoulder, but stopped herself before saying how much she missed him, how much she thought of him during the day—she hadn't quite understood how much until he touched her. Even the thoughts that weren't about him had only been to keep thoughts of him at bay.

He pressed his nose to her hair. She wondered if he cared that she smelled of chickens and sweat and dirt. Perhaps she seemed more real now than she ever had between the hotel's starched sheets.

"Ross?" His question startled her.

"I love him, too." There was no use lying.

He lifted her chin and searched her face for something. When he found it, his eyes turned dark, but her thoughts moved too quickly, jumping forward.

"I- I won't get pregnant again."

He looked confused for a moment until his brow cleared. He led her to the worktable and shimmied a drawer open (the same drawer that had once held her drawings of Makeda and the rooster). He reached inside, and the wrapper's crackle brought back the guilt of their affair, like a child sneaking candy. She stared at the condom absently, as relieved as she was ashamed.

"Don't think—" He cleared his throat. "Don't think I haven't thought about it, too, about coming to find you."

She placed her hands on his face. "Kiss me, then."

He did.

———

When a door closed, God opened a window (or this was what her mother said).

They had barely made it to the seat pushed against the wall, but in the aftermath, Barb was unsettled by the realization that this was the place where her daughter had sat drawing. There was something illicit about the vinyl, the way it gripped her skin, its obscene noises as she peeled body parts from its slick surface. The seat was only wide enough for one, so she draped herself over Declan, her ear on his chest, the same way she had pressed close to Ross for years.

"Where'd you get this?" he asked, thumbing the cigarette burn on her arm.

"Long story." *A buda cursed me, I sprained my ankle, I said goodbye to you, and my daughter was born.* "Not interesting," she promised. "Not like yours anyway." She cast her eyes over his own scars and touched the one on his side, now faded with time.

"I still imagine what it would have been like," she said, "if you'd found me sooner."

They fell back into silence, but Declan started to fidget.

"Someone will be missing you." His words reverberated down her spine like a pronouncement from on high.

She sat up, the vinyl screeching in protest, and climbed over his naked body. He propped himself up, watching as she slipped on her clothes and shoes.

"There's a bag of clean rags under the table."

She wasn't sure what difference that would make—everyone on the mission was sweaty at this time of year, even after the sun went down—but she obeyed, peeking under the worktable. She hauled the bag forward, threw Declan one of the rags, and used another only after smelling it.

"Didn't believe me?" He smirked.

"Everyone has a different definition of 'clean,'" she said, annoyed at her own distrust.

But other things worried Declan. "What were you thinking?" he asked. It was a question she would often ask herself in the days ahead, searching for that direct line of cause and effect.

She forced a smile and shrugged before sneaking out the back.

Inside their bungalow, Ross stirred as she crawled into bed.

"Barbie Doll?" He sounded like he'd just woken from a nightmare.

"I'm here." She touched his back. He turned toward her, his face dark.

"Is this a good idea?"

Not at all. But he was only talking about the walks. "I have a flashlight."

"What good's a flashlight against a"—he searched for a threat serious enough—"a cobra?"

Her stomach tensed at the idiocy of what she was doing. "I'll bring a stick next time." Still, she was imagining a next time. She stared at the mosquito net, gathered to a black point where it hung from the ceiling. Ross remained silent so long, chastened by her quick responses, that it seemed as if he'd fallen asleep. But Barb sensed that he, too, was staring at the dark tangle above them.

"I'll only go out once," she offered. "Once a week."

"I know it's your only time away . . . when she sleeps."

"I love Abeba."

"But that doesn't mean it isn't hard." He took her hand, and Barb felt him remembering their conversations from before—how she never wanted kids. Now she wondered if she had just been waiting for Declan to turn up.

It was true. She was too dirty a thing.

Ross turned over, facing the wall between Abeba's room and theirs while Barb stared out the window at the hangar. Why had she let her old room become the one she now shared with her husband? How had she not foreseen the complication of memory—that every time she looked out the window she would feel the same rush she'd had as a teenager? *You love him,* she thought, over and over, meaning first her husband and then not her husband. *You love him. You love him.*

———

Ross · December 2010

Ross hated mentioning the walks. He worried whenever the bed was empty beside him, but tried to check that worry. Last night he had given in, something that pestered him all morning like a pulled muscle. He limped through his lessons and headed to the grove after dismissal, free of his students' faces until tomorrow, some bemused, some sour, some smiling, some missing teeth. He would never create unity among them. The same thing had been—and still was—true about his congregants on Sunday. That was something he missed about theatre. When the house lights were down, it was easy to presume the audience's acceptance; audible confirmation, like laughter, was a bonus.

The grove offered him sanctuary from the faces as he slumped against one of the eucalyptuses, pressing his spine to the trunk. He was relieved to be alone, without the worry from last night bubbling up inside him. He remembered to watch for snakes.

No one knew today was the thirtieth anniversary of Jason's accident. Ross hated that he ascribed meaning to the passage of decades. He envied his students, for whom time meant something different— even down to the Borana calendar.

Jason had been driving the two of them to his first playoff game with the varsity basketball team. Ross loved basketball. He'd received a book to log the team's statistics as an early Christmas present, and his plan was to secure a seat directly behind the bench before warmups. Jason had been talking about Kristy, a girl from youth group he liked. Ross was ten. All he knew was that Kristy's dad was Black and she wore the bluest eye shadow Ross had ever seen.

Their parents were experts at driving in bad weather, having been raised in the snow belt south of Lake Erie, but this was Jason's first try at winter driving. They were listening to the radio—that stupid radio—and when Jason reached for the dial at Ross's behest, the tires lost their grip.

Ross couldn't remember what song had come on. The mystery of it would send him to the library as a teenager, in search of the Top 40 from that week: songs by Stevie Wonder, Queen, the Police, and Devo. He hoped Jason hadn't reached to turn up "Whip It." (That would be tragic.) But here was the truth: a basketball game, the radio, and black ice added up to his brother's death.

———

Ross • December 1980

Ross remembered the swerve, but not the flip. He remembered hanging upside down as the seatbelt cut into his shoulder and seeing Jason's head flush with the roof of the car, neck bent at ninety degrees. Ross closed his eyes—he wouldn't open them again, he wouldn't. Then he did and regretted it.

He played this horrible game with himself until he heard the sirens.

The paramedics cut him loose. They told him this at the hospital because he couldn't remember. Had he passed out? Pain he hadn't noticed in the car throbbed to life under the harsh lights of the ER. But he was home in his bed by morning, a few butterfly stitches and bruises all he had to show. Each breath felt like a knife sunk into his chest.

He relived the wreck so often in the following weeks that he exhausted himself. To remember those moments was to be forced to eat the same plate of spaghetti over and over (like he did during recovery) until there was nothing to see but worms, nothing to feel but the sliminess as they wriggled down his throat. He would sit on the bus to school and wonder about the song, the slick road, his part in all of it.

His ribs couldn't heal fast enough. Once they did, he took off running when the memories became too much, sprinting through the neighborhood until his mind quieted. Just as his reaction was movement, his mom's was stillness. He was used to walking through the door and being greeted by the aroma of Sunday sauce burping or wedding soup simmering on the stove, of bread baking or chicken roasting. But lately Mom was just sinking into the recliner and staring at Jason's pictures on the mantel. He wondered if she was praying. His dad played along, even held one-sided conversations with her, but Ross couldn't be a good sport. After saying hello, he would retreat to Jason's room and shut himself into the closet.

Like the running, sitting in a pile of Jason's clothes quieted his thoughts. Sometimes he did his homework in the closet; mostly, he put on one of Jason's polos and looked at the Dr. J poster that Jason had promised him last summer. The two of them had always rooted for the Sixers, their dad for the Cavs. Dr. J made his dad nervous: "Too much above-the-rim play." But Ross wondered if this discomfort had more to do with some deep-seated fear in his father—the fear of change, even if that change made things more interesting. Ross would practice dunking on the hoop at the community pool, despite the likelihood of his becoming a below-the-rim shooting guard like his brother. The poster felt like his inheritance, as valuable as what other people kept in safe-deposit boxes.

Below the poster were two shelves stocked with shoeboxes. One held Jason's old caps, broken in and folded; ticket stubs to a few college games and R-rated movies; and the pin he had gotten for baseball last year. Another box, pushed to the back, was filled with homemade cassettes, most of the labels written by someone else—Joy Division's *Closer,* Queen's *Jazz,* the *Xanadu* soundtrack. The *is* in the Clash's *Sandinista* were dotted with hearts.

On the last day of school Ross returned home to his mom's empty recliner. He started calculating possibilities—her head in the oven—but when he turned the corner the oven clock blinked 12:00 to the empty kitchen. He moved to the pantry, the backyard, the basement, but met no signs of life or death. He wondered if the Rapture had come and he'd been "left behind," as in the Larry Norman song. But where were the clothes? In the movies he'd seen, the person's clothes lay neatly folded in the wake of a disappearance (because God was thoughtful like that). Ross ran upstairs to Jason's room, where he'd at least feel safe.

Instead, he found Mom tearing shirts from hangers, an (unfolded) pile growing in the center of the room. The Dr. J poster lay at his feet.

"Ross, help me!" To see her so off-kilter made him feel the same.

"Okay, but what are we doing?" He hated how high his voice was getting. It always seemed to crack when he was scared. At least he wasn't frightened enough to lose control of his face. She had reached that level of anxiety first.

"We're collecting everything that belonged to Jason!"

He nodded like this was news. "I'll check downstairs. Any idea when Dad's getting home?"

Mention of her husband gave her pause. "Oh, I don't need his help now that you're here."

Ross descended the stairs, overwhelmed by images of his dead mother.

Perhaps she *had* died. Perhaps the person upstairs was a stranger.

As he searched the living room for signs of Jason, he saw the basketball near the back door. Would that count? Communal objects shouldn't count. His stomach tightened as he realized what the purging meant—he would lose the Dr. J poster and each of the things he had clutched to his chest in the closet. If he managed to salvage something from the pile, his mom would recognize it. And basketball—not just the ball, but the game itself—was over for him. A pickup game with friends, sure, but he could never go out for the team—watch a game, even—without reminding Mom of her other son. His gaze lighted on the pictures on the mantel. He removed his brother's wallet-sized photo from its frame and stuck it in his back pocket.

The Erving poster, the basketball, the box of tapes, and everything else were dropped into a chute behind the Salvation Army. When they returned home, his father stood in the center of the living room, mouth open.

"Shelley, upstairs," he said in his outside voice. Ross felt his own insides shake.

Hours later his dad came down to the basement. Ross kept his eyes trained on an episode of *Taxi*. Dad sat next to him on the couch.

"You eat some tater tots?"

"Yup." Ross was bouncing his knee.

"I see she took the basketball."

"It'll make some kid happy." Ross's voice had finally settled. His dad placed a hand on his knee. Ross stopped bouncing and waited.

"This raid on Jay's belongings. It was just your mom's way of moving on. . . . It's not the way *I* would have done it."

"But it's the only way—for her."

His dad sighed. "See. You get it. She'll wake up tomorrow and everything will be back to normal."

"Normal?" Ross didn't know when the word had started offending him.

———

Dad was right. Mom returned to herself, all except for her smile, which had grown lopsided. Nothing—not a birthday cake or a Christmas present, a perfect attendance record or an A-plus—ever brought her real smile back.

Ross learned how to make life easy for his parents. He didn't lie, mostly because he didn't need to. He wasn't one to give in to peer pressure. His interests rarely overlapped with his classmates', and Jason's death had only widened the gap. The one time he yielded to the pleas of his friends and attended an eighth-grade dance, he just stood and marveled. Every boy wanted to slip a hand under some girl's shirt or deftly graze a boob. Ross was instantly bored.

When he came home, he hid himself in the basement and tried to forget the embarrassing way Jeremy Schulz had tried to grind on Leslie from math. That was when the Children's Fund commercial caught his attention.

Ross had seen it before, but this was the first time it mattered. The children onscreen reminded him of Randy Holmes, a classmate from kindergarten. One day a group of kids had been making fun of him for playing with Barbies; Ross joined the teasing and Randy, his timing impeccable, walked past the children with a look reserved for animals at the shelter. In the next hour, Ross became so ill that Mom had to pick him up.

That evening his parents crouched at his bedside and asked what was wrong. Ross shook his head and turned to face the wall. Of course Jason knew. He told them what had happened.

"I'm not a bully," Ross said.

Jason rolled his eyes. "You're so sensitive."

"Jay," Mom warned.

The thought of his brother getting in trouble on his behalf made Ross start to cry. He demanded that everyone leave and, in the darkness of his room, thought about what he'd done: first, he had accepted his classmates' ridicule of Randy without question; second, he had assumed playing with Barbies was something Randy couldn't do. But hadn't Sunday school taught him anything was possible with God? Ross was so stupid. Stupid and mean. He didn't want to be either thing ever again.

He made a vow to never be the cause of another person's sadness. The next morning he marched into kindergarten and apologized to Randy, who looked like he'd forgotten the whole thing.

Later, in an eastern religions class in college, he would learn that his vow was a common precept in India—the commitment to *ahimsa*. If the vow was broken, an individual worked toward greater self-awareness; but when Ross failed, he punished himself more than his parents ever could. Even Jason's death, in its own way, felt like a punishment for his inadequacy. It didn't matter whether the punishment fit the crime.

Now, at age thirteen, in the glow of the Children's Fund commercial, he felt a call—to keep that vow by becoming a missionary, like the ones who came and spoke to their church. Ross had always liked their stories.

News of this calling made Mom smile without reservation for the first time since Jason's death. Ross decided not to question it.

To bide his time until becoming a missionary, he kept busy. As a freshman, he joined cross country. The meets were nothing like basketball games; no one attended unless they were dating or related to one of the participants. He told his parents he didn't need them there. "I'll get a ride with Jeremy."

They didn't protest, despite their having been to all of Jason's games. They set a curfew for him, sure, but he wondered if they trusted him too much. It would have made more sense if they'd become overprotective after losing one of their sons. Instead, they seemed to be daring the universe, *Go ahead, take the other one.*

Ross joined the musical, too, because rehearsals didn't conflict with practice. He started singing show tunes and listening to rock operas begrudgingly approved by his parents, who preferred floating between rooms humming the praise songs from church (why Jason had hidden his secular cassettes in the first place). Ross was cast as Nicely-Nicely in *Guys and Dolls*—the one who sings "Sit Down, You're Rockin' the Boat." His evenings spent watching *Taxi* and *The Jeffersons* had been a master class on comedic timing. Making a person laugh, let alone an auditorium full of people, might not be harder than what missionaries did, but it seemed just as effective.

After each production was a cast party, which started with striking the set at school and ended at a student's house. Ross left these parties early and, at school the next week, heard all about the "crazy shit" that had gone down at 2 a.m. For theatre kids "crazy shit" usually meant singing karaoke and playing Spin the Bottle with the alumni. One of those alumni was Kristy—Jason's Kristy. She was twenty-one when Ross was a junior, the same year she volunteered as stage manager for *The Sound of Music*. (Ross played Max Detweiler.) He knew better than to pretend to know her. They had never spoken when she was in youth group, and he didn't remember if she had attended Jason's memorial. When he saw her backstage, she pretended not to notice him, no matter how small the space that they were occupying. He took the hint.

Things changed on closing night. Her blue eye shadow was back, and right before he went on for the Salzburg Festival scene, she grabbed his arm. "I hope you're coming to Chelsea's."

He took a moment to understand. "I have a midnight curfew."

"Right." He could tell she was disappointed. "Just come for a bit."

He nodded, and she pushed him onstage to announce the Von Trapp Family Singers.

At strike, Kristy stayed out of sight, and Ross almost skipped the after-party. But there had been too many possibilities suggested by her hand on his arm. If going meant he could make her laugh, he couldn't betray his vow. He arrived a quarter after eleven.

"You're here!" she said when he came down to the game room (where Chelsea's mom had assured him the rest of the kids were).

"I got lost."

"I know. There's, like, a turn and a turn and a dead end and *another* turn."

"Her driveway's forever long."

She bit the inside of her cheek. "We're playing Seven Minutes in Heaven."

"Upgraded from Spin the Bottle?" Ross didn't know why he was trying to sound like an expert. He'd never played either game and wasn't about to start.

"Tyler took Zach in there. I'm next."

"That's how it works?"

"Well, we changed the rules. I just pick someone to go in with."

"Oh." Part of him was relieved that Tyler had finally taken the plunge—the sexual tension between the two eldest Von Trapp brothers had been palpable onstage.

The other part of Ross wasn't relieved—it was acutely aware that he would be Kristy's pick. His chest clenched in anticipation as much as in terror. This was exactly why he had avoided prior cast parties. A moment later the sophomore who played Mother Superior knocked on the closet door, and out came Tyler and Zach to a smattering of applause, the former dipping the latter with a flourish, their cheeks flushed.

Mother Superior turned to Kristy, who grabbed Ross's hand. Someone was yelling his name and making that whooping sound reserved for live studio audiences, a sound suddenly muted by the closet door. Kristy fumbled for the light.

"Screw it." She felt for Ross and pulled him down to kiss her. He didn't know how to navigate the kiss: all he had to go on were stories from the locker room that always rang false with exaggeration and scenes from movies he had watched uncomfortably with his parents. He thought he was supposed to use tongue.

Kristy pulled away. "Whoa there. I thought you were a nice boy."

"No one's just 'nice'—" But she kissed him again. He was less concerned with enjoying it than in giving Kristy what she wanted. He thought about touching her face, but then her hands were on his chest, nudging him back.

His eyes had adjusted to the dark. He saw her disappointment, but it wasn't directed at him. "Hey. You're okay."

She scoffed. "I am so many shades of fucked up." She was silent for a moment, long enough to swallow her tears. "You probably don't even remember me."

He caught her hand. "I remember." He knew then: Kristy had been the one to dot the *is* on Jason's cassettes with hearts. Of course she had.

"Then you know. It's hard to explain. You have a person and then you don't." Her voice had a dreamy quality. She seemed caught between worlds—what people said about ghosts. "You blame yourself. You always blame yourself." He squeezed her hand to prove she was real. "I just, I kept looking at you hitting your marks and thinking if there was anyone that would understand . . ."

"It would be Max Detweiler."

"Sort of."

Ross half-laughed. "So you lock us in a closet."

His laughter brought her back. "Hey, this closet isn't so bad—if we could ever find the *light*." The way she said *light,* he thought one would turn on, powered by her annoyance. Then there was a knock and the sound of Mother Superior's voice. Kristy wiped her eyes. "Can we talk somewhere?"

"I have to make curfew."

"Shit."

It made him say, "I can be late."

"No, you go home. I'll follow."

Mother Superior knocked again and called Kristy's name. Ross touched her face. "We can't have you crying."

"That's where the acting comes in." She flashed a brilliant smile as she opened the door, marched past Mother Superior, and dragged Ross up the stairs and out of Chelsea's house. The smile dropped only when they reached his car.

"Do you need me to wait for you?"

She shook her head. "I know the way."

He got home with five minutes to spare. Olly rushed to greet him at the door, wagging his tail and making that wonderful snarfing sound. Ross was still thinking about the eyes of his classmates as he and Kristy marched past them. Maybe that would be the story they told at school on Monday. He found his parents half-asleep in front of the TV and made quick work of them.

"You coming to bed, honey?" his mom asked from partway up the stairs.

"Need to wind down. I'll be out on the porch with Olly."

"Don't forget tomorrow's church," his dad said, as though Ross had ever forgotten.

"I'll be up." But they were already gone.

He went to the kitchen and made hot chocolate in a Thermos, listening to Olly's toenails on the linoleum. He noticed something moving outside—Kristy walking up the drive. She already knew to keep out of range of the motion light. He slid the porch door open. Olly looked at her once and barked. Ross shushed him and the dog lowered his head.

Kristy bent down and patted her thighs. "Hey, you." Olly shoved his nose at her as she grabbed his ears.

"We've had Olly for a year."

The dog followed as they took their seats on two of the four deck chairs. Ross had sat at this table for countless summer afternoons, waiting for lunch to be served, noticing that fourth empty chair, tonguing its presence like a canker sore.

She caught sight of the Thermos. "You're already a better host than your brother was."

He blinked thoughts of the chair away and poured cocoa into the Thermos lid. She accepted it with an overstated carefulness.

"Jason was a good-enough host."

"It was a bit of an act. You have to act to be a smart ass; he was the other way around."

Ross pushed down the need to defend his brother and sipped from the Thermos. The cocoa was scalding, but he swallowed anyway.

Olly was lying between them, head on his paws. Ross petted him with a foot, unsure how to read Kristy's certainty. She was like one of his classmates who knew the answer to every question. Maybe she knew *better*. She'd been Jason's peer, he the kid brother Jason was tasked with humoring. If he were more like Jason, maybe he would lean in and kiss her properly instead of stewing in uncertainty.

"I'm not always nice."

"We'll have to agree to disagree."

Olly yawned, as though trying to change the subject. Ross did. "So . . . *Xanadu?*"

When Kristy worked out what he meant, she ducked her head. "Jason said he would hide those."

Ross assured her he had. "I spent some time in his closet."

She stared at her cocoa. "Do you still have them?"

He shook his head. "Mom raided his room. I don't have anything of his anymore."

"That's rough. Also, kinda crazy."

He shrugged. It was strange to say these things aloud, and to Kristy. He suffered alone because that was how it had always been. But here she was, placing a hand on his shoulder.

"Ross, you're not a rock. You can be angry. You can just be sad."

He didn't understand how she knew what he'd been waiting to hear—from his parents, his friends, the leaders at youth group. "I never—" But tears cut him off. He took her hand from his shoulder and cried silently. She waited. Olly waited, too. He'd only cried into the dog's fur once before, on his sixteenth birthday.

"Not sure how you did that," he said when his voice stopped trembling.

"I'm real good at making men cry." She was smiling. "I made your brother cry all the time."

"Really?"

"No. He only ever cried when he fought with your mom."

Suddenly Ross remembered coming home from school and hearing the two of them yelling, seeing Jason rush down the stairs and out the door, running (Ross now realized) to Kristy. He wondered if guilt, not grief, had chained his mom to the recliner. "I'd forgotten they didn't get along."

She shook her head. "I think about it all the time."

"The thing I think about? How I'm as old as he was when it happened. Last month I officially outlived him. I honestly didn't think I'd make it."

They grew quiet, holding hands, sipping cocoa, an idyllic scene, except for the death hanging like a scrim between them. Olly heaved a sigh.

"I should go." She set the empty lid on the table and tried to pull her hand away.

Ross held fast. "Can I kiss you again?"

She smiled, then tried to hide it. "Your parents . . ."

"We can figure that out later."

"I already snuck around with your brother."

Ross set down the Thermos. "So you can teach me." He couldn't shake the feeling that letting her go would be a mistake. She had secrets he needed to understand.

Her eyes met his. "Go on then."

This time he didn't use tongue.

———

Kristy did teach him how to keep from getting caught. His parents' laissez-faire attitude made that easy; and once school started, Kristy's job at the public library made it easier. Ross told his parents he was headed there to do homework. He would, before leaving his car in the lot while he and Kristy walked the neighborhood. There was a park five blocks away, where they would lie on a blanket he kept in his trunk.

Ross started changing. When he was sitting in class, part of him paid attention while the other part remembered Kristy's lips (her tongue, too), her hands on his back, her legs between his as they rolled together on the blanket. He didn't know how he had missed this before—the connection between a person and their body. He felt he had been horribly shortsighted at that eighth-grade dance.

"None of those boys cared about the person they were dancing with," Kristy said on one of their walks. "You knew that and didn't like it."

He nodded. "What are we going to do when it snows?"

Kristy was already wearing her winter coat. "You know. We'll park."

"Where?"

She half-smiled. "You're adorable. *Anywhere.*"

"And you're an exhibitionist." He grabbed her hand and kissed under her ear, a spot that made her legs go wobbly.

She pushed him back. "I'm not."

"Sorry." His stomach dropped.

"You have that horrible look on your face. It's fine. You're just new to this."

"We've been together six months."

"I was with your brother for two years. At our age, that's an eternity."

The comparison derailed Ross. That made Kristy twelve and Jason fourteen when they had gotten together. It came as a shock.

"How far did you and Jason go?" The question drifted through his mind whenever they kissed. (He hated the phrase *made out.*)

She shot him a look and started walking faster. "I can't believe you."

He didn't take long to catch up. "I shouldn't have asked."

She stopped and faced him. "But you still want to know."

"Sort of? You know I don't care about it."

"I *do* know that."

"Just forget it."

"You can't unask it. If I don't answer, my sex life with your brother will *haunt* us."

"Well, I know *now.*"

Kristy put a hand on his arm. "You *never* push me, Ross, and you're nicer than he was, remember?"

He held her then and let her cry.

They went on like this for the rest of his senior year: evenings spent in cars, telling each other what no one else would abide—if they fought, it was when Ross couldn't forget Jason—but the summer after graduation he followed in the footsteps of so many seniors, unable to square his feelings for Kristy with his leaving for college. Whatever was between them started to feel less like love and more like a bad after-school special.

They were walking to her car after a hike on Jakes Rocks when he asked, "Would we be together if not for Jason?" He had rehearsed the question silently all morning, but it came out stilted.

"Of course not." She settled behind the steering wheel. "But I could say that about most things. 'If not for Jason . . .'"

"I wish things were different." He slumped against his seat.

Kristy went rigid. "What do you mean?"

"I guess I'm at a point where I don't want to think about him anymore."

"I think you're just being Nice Ross again. Say what you mean."

He sighed. "Do I have to?"

"Oh, grow up."

"I worry—that if we stay together we'll ruin each other's lives. We won't ever crawl out from the accident."

"Like you did?"

"I guess."

"At least you were with him."

Ross scoffed. "You think I was lucky?"

"If I'd been there—" She cut herself off. The pause shook Ross out of his anger.

"Kris?"

But she was staring through the windshield. He couldn't read her face—didn't know if she was wishing herself dead or thinking how she'd lost both Matheson brothers to bad timing.

Wow, Ross, he thought, *arrogant much?*

But he had been using Kristy. For her secrets. His vow loomed in front of him, and he cursed himself for not foreseeing the inevitable.

"Whatever." She collected herself as though prepping for her next line onstage. "I've been waiting for you to say something. You've been thinking so *loud.*"

"You're not mad?"

She sighed. "I'm twenty-two and dating a high school senior. You deserve better than something this weird."

"It's not a bad weird."

"I just mean." She reached for his hand. "You should find someone who's nice back."

He watched her face for signs that her response was just an act; instead, he saw the beginning of someone who would go through life convinced that love didn't exist, at least not for her. He'd felt the same before they met. Now he couldn't believe in such an absolute—there were too many variables.

"Technically." He smirked. "I'm an incoming college freshman."

She punched him in the shoulder. "Do we make a clean break or prolong the agony?"

"Hmm. Wouldn't call it *agony*." He kissed her.

She pulled back and started the car. "You know it could have gone either way." He looked confused. "Your mood. It was either a breakup or a proposal."

When they parted at the end of the summer, his memories of Jason no longer pierced; they throbbed and entwined with those of Kristy. At college, he did his best to forget them both.

The theatre department was his salve; being anyone other than himself made the nights easier, even if he was too much in his own head to successfully inhabit someone else's.

Barb was a part of his life he didn't want Jason to haunt. Unlike with Kristy, he wasn't the lost one—she was. Now she walked the mission at night to quiet her thoughts, just as he used to race through the neighborhood to calm his.

He was ruining *her* life—he just didn't know how.

Barb • December 2010

The next morning Barb kept to her routine. Her exhaustion mattered less than avoiding suspicion.

She hadn't expected Karin to be the one to see through her.

They were collecting eggs when Karin faced her, eyes puffy from crying. "How do you feel about Ross?"

Barb's shoulders tensed. "Much the way you feel about Caj, I'm sure."

"I keep secrets from Caj."

Barb stared at the three eggs cradled in her shirt. She heard the insinuation. Karin, awake and crying, must have spotted her heading to the hangar last night.

She sighed and set the eggs in the basket. "Okay."

Karin wiped her hands on her trousers. "You like it—that Declan reminds you of before."

Her tone made Barb wonder if staying away from Declan had been an unspoken condition of their friendship. She shouldn't have been surprised. Most of her friendships had ended: with Makeda as a child, with Julie as a teenager, with Ann at the conference. But not Declan. Never him. She shook her head. "I don't know what I was thinking."

Karin shouldered the basket. "I think you do."

Barb considered following her, worried she might say something to Ross, but part of her wanted to be outed. She also knew Karin wouldn't do that.

She stood in the coop's entrance and stared at the hangar. Severing ties would result in a slow death, like an ear of corn snapped from its stalk and left to wither. Still, sever she must.

The thought plagued her as she taught lessons. After dismissal she headed to the hangar and found Declan running maintenance after his last flight out. All Barb had to do was lean against the wall for him to look up. He motioned her toward Arnold's empty workbench.

"Can't close the doors without drawing attention." He sat on the bench while she remained standing. There was an edge of panic in his voice.

She hugged her elbows. "I was wrong to come to you last night."

He stared at her, his face blank before settling into its usual mask. "You don't love me."

"Of course I love you." Even now she wanted to sit close to him, though she was afraid of losing momentum. "But I'm not who you need. And—" She hunched her shoulders. "I was a little terrified the day you came to recruit us."

"I was there. And you're easy to read."

That annoyed her, but also made things easier. "I make you miserable."

He spread his hands in front of him. "Don't you mean *I* make *you* miserable?"

She wavered. It wasn't her first time projecting her feelings onto someone. "Don't you think that what we're doing—that no good can come of it?"

"You sound like your mother."

She wanted to argue, but guilt pressed against her sternum and kept her on her heels, silent, waiting for the next assault. He stood and she backed away without thinking.

A dry laugh escaped from his throat. "This is my curse."

The despair in his voice worried her. It was too much like how she'd felt when she first found him at the conference. But that desperation had driven them together; this desperation was unpredictable. Maybe it was how he'd felt when he shot his father.

"What curse?" She thought of the *buda* in the grocery store and the cigarette burn, her own curse that had turned into a benediction with Ross and Abeba. Abeba would be seven at the end of the month. *Would it be so bad,* Barb suddenly thought, *to have another child?* She would have to give up caring for the chickens if she did.

"No parents, no sister," he listed, "no children, no family." She saw his resignation. "I shot that man, after all."

"It was an accident," she said. "He didn't even die."

"She did."

He must have misspoken, but Barb wondered if he *had* killed someone else. "You mean your father."

"I ruined the chance God gave me." He smiled, but the smile was joyless. She was spying into one of his darkest moments, and it looked remarkably like one of hers. Something inside her changed—she was already calculating a solution to his problem.

"I'm sorry," she said suddenly. "I'm sorry. I'm sorry."

The change caught him off guard. His smile dropped. "Barb?"

"It's not the end." She didn't know what to do with her hands anymore.

He caught her arm, the one with the scar. "What's wrong?"

"I should go." She was starting to see the solution more clearly, but she had to get out of the hangar and hide somewhere. *I'm losing it,* she thought. This is what it feels like—so close, on the precipice. "Don't follow me."

He let her go.

"It's fine. It's fine." Why was she repeating everything? She headed to the door.

"You're sure?" he called after her.

"It's nothing." Then louder, "Nothing!"

When she was out of sight, she ran to the garden and sat among the rows of corn, breathing deeply until she felt safe again.

Her thoughts lined themselves up like the stalks surrounding her.

Was this God's Plan?

The plan started with Karin. One day, when Caj was out of the office, she handed over Declan's file. Barb had thought it would be impossible to find—surely the mission no longer kept paper files—but there it sat in her hand.

Karin gave her a look that could only mean one thing: this was the last of Barb's secrets she would keep. *The days of your kingdom are numbered.*

"I need to know."

Karin raised her eyebrows. Barb ignored her and sat at Caj's desk to read: first, what she knew—the adoption, jail, the detention in

Addis—and then what she didn't know: that before Florida had been Stockholm. For a moment she felt relief at knowing that this was everything. Then her gaze landed on a scrawled note from Declan's last intake interview—*Won't speak of sister's death.*

But Declan didn't have a sister. Barb flipped through other notes until she found her name, *Elizabeth Kline;* her death date, August 3, 1969; and the word *Drowned.* She thought, *He hates water,* as though it explained everything. In some ways it did—that succession of cause and effect lining up behind her. He'd always seemed like he was working out a problem in his head, and here was the cosmic calculus, the root that stretched back through his entire life.

She remembered their last exchange. He hadn't misspoken when he said *she.* There had been the photo, too, the one he sometimes studied when he thought he was alone. She once saw a flash of it. *His sister.*

Barb was a hypocrite. She'd thought of the file as a last test before giving herself to Declan, but she hadn't expected to learn anything she hadn't already guessed. How naïve. Despite Declan's secrets, she had never hidden anything from him. Only now, when she was ready to have his child, had she gone out of her way to gain her own secret.

This is what's wrong with you, she knew.

Karin asked if she had found what she needed.

Barb nodded and left.

———

She told Ross that he'd been right about the danger of her walks at night. They would be out of her system soon.

"I don't need you to stop."

"I want to." She took his hand to show that she meant it. "I just need time to say goodbye." There was that request again, for time. "The walking, it's a way of avoiding reality. Does that make sense?" His nod was subtle. "And it wears me out." She smiled because she knew the power that smile held. (The sight was so rare.) "It'll be good to give it up."

Ross drew her against him, the movement so quick she had to catch her breath. "I don't care if you walk," he said into her hair, "just come back to me."

She knew the best day of her cycle to find Declan. (She still kept a meticulous calendar.)

She waited until dark, told Ross goodnight, and left with a snake stick and a flashlight. She made two circuits of the buildings, then stepped into the shadows beyond Arnold's bungalow and headed for the back of the hangar. On the door to Declan's apartment hung three dried ears of corn like the ornaments she had once made him. These memories of their younger selves were phantom limbs. She ignored the nostalgia and knocked.

The door opened. Something about the way he slumped against the jamb told her he was drinking—just another secret he'd stashed somewhere.

"You're back." His eyes were tired.

She let herself in and shut the door, setting down the flashlight and stick. "Get the light."

He followed her orders. "We need to talk, don't we?"

They did. She should confess that she'd finally done it—read his file—but that wasn't what tonight was for.

She kissed him in the dark. He was slow to respond. She had surprised him, something she was never good at, and a tingle of confidence ran along her scalp.

"Told you it's not over."

"Where?"

She was eighteen again, and he was pushing her against the fuselage. She was twenty-six, waiting at the threshold of his hotel room. It was a month ago and she was sticking to the Cessna's back seat.

"The plane. Where else?"

They picked up a blanket along the way and lay on it in the cargo hold, clothes off—the same place as her first time. Declan's mouth lingered at her neck.

"Hey," she said. "You here?"

"Yeah." He smiled. When was the last time she'd seen him like this, no trace of his defenses? "Just need a rubber." She stayed his arm. There was a question in his eyes.

"You want a family." Her voice sounded too small. It was meant to be certain.

He seemed sober for the first time. "You can't be serious."

"I'm here, aren't I?" She touched his face and tried to kiss him, but he pulled away.

"You're going to leave them?" His gaze flicked to hers.

"Dec." She closed her eyes.

"So, what, you have my kid and we just . . . pretend?"

"It's a little more complicated, but yeah."

"It's insane."

"O ye of little faith." She hadn't anticipated his protest. What if Declan, when faced with what he wanted, preferred unhappiness? *You're projecting again,* she thought, but she wasn't sure. "What if," she continued, "this is our chance?"

His eyes narrowed. She wondered if he felt like she had when he'd given her the ultimatum, caught between the present and what he'd wanted so deeply in the past.

"You deserve it." She didn't know if that was the right thing to say.

He blinked. "We won't be a real family."

"Pretty near it." She leaned forward to kiss the scars on his flank.

He sighed, as though in that moment he understood that he couldn't win. Ross had been her partner when Declan disappeared. There was no rewriting that.

She pulled back and his face softened. He looked younger as he kissed her. She felt relieved and weary at the same time.

It seemed to be the only way with them: a stolen string of nights. She felt the need to memorize the shape of his body. It had changed since their affair—small changes. His chest hair had grayed. He would never eat enough, she thought, to gain that middle-aged weight, but there were still pockets of flesh that were new to her—the ones right above his hips, the one under his belly button, as though his skin were slowly pulling away from his body. Then there was the way he moved against her, the speed of his breath on her skin, the taste of his mouth. She already missed these things and wondered if every time she looked at their child, she would feel this loss more than love.

She cleaned up as best she could. The next part of her plan required it. Declan's voice startled her as she dressed. "Remember the flight when I gave Abeba a pad and pencils?"

She smiled. "They were a godsend."

"They were for you." He hesitated. "I thought you could pick up drawing again." She looked down. The revelation pleased her, though she had no right to the feeling. "It's stupid, looking back. A kid thing to do."

She blinked. "What names do you like?"

He drew the blanket over his chest. "Don't know."

"The baby'll be born while we're on furlough—even you." She stared at her feet dangling over the lip of the plane's body, then sneaked a look at him over her shoulder.

"You have it all planned." He sounded strange—maybe a little afraid of her.

They were too aware of this being their last night. She dared to take his free hand, already feeling the distance growing between them. Neither of them looked up.

"Is this it?" he asked.

"I'll never be out of reach. But it'll be different."

He took his hand back and trained his eyes somewhere below her face. She saw an anger in his gaze that could burn for years. She should say something to help him forgive her, but it was better for him to stay angry.

She picked up her stick and flashlight and slipped out the back.

A light was on in her and Ross's room. On any other night after leaving the hangar, this would have been cause for panic, but tonight it made things easier. Ross was lying in bed when she came in. She placed her things on the dresser and asked if he was all right. He patted the bed next to him. She crawled under the mosquito net.

"I've been thinking," he started.

She took his hand as she had Declan's moments before. Ross almost smiled.

"I'm the reason you're unhappy."

She squeezed his hand. "You're not."

"I forced you back here."

"It wasn't like that."

"Just tell me." His eyes glowed wet in the lamplight. "What can I do?"

She looked down. Nearly all her choices since college had been meant to re-create that solid feeling she remembered: shielded by the leaves of the *buna-zaf,* listening to Makeda's stories. But as she passed between Ethiopia and America, the current had broken her apart. It was Ross who had put her back together, so carefully she hadn't even noticed the act of mending: with his plastic hippos, his rants, his box set of apocalypse films. Leaving Declan was hard, but leaving Ross felt impossible.

"I chose you over the mission."

He sighed. "Something has to change."

She pressed him close and whispered, "Let's make a baby."

He hesitated. "It was—difficult before. It'll be worse here."

"Furlough year's up, remember."

"Wait." He smiled as he understood. "You've thought about this."

She smiled, too, and he kissed her. *Ross,* she thought as they moved together. *It was fate I found you.*

When they rolled apart, breathing hard, he put on his glasses and propped his head up to study her. "We should try again tomorrow."

Something about this closeness felt new, but it didn't banish the worry. He placed his thumb against the center of her forehead and tried to smooth her brow.

She huffed. "You always know when something's wrong."

"And when not to mention it." He looked at her, a question in his eyes.

"I love you," she said, "I love you, I love you," and meant only him.

She waited a month to see if the plan had worked. She dug through the sex-ed supplies for a pregnancy test, without luck; Ross had to find one in Jimma. Declan was the next to know. She told him in the hangar. He held a hand over his mouth and looked down, the reaction so different from Ross's—he had jumped up and down.

She didn't know who the father was. That was part of the plan, too.

"We can be friends now," she said to Declan.

He lifted his head. "There's more love in you than in anyone I've ever met."

She hugged her arms to her chest. "I doubt that."

"Don't." His voice was firm, but the pain in his eyes was still there. She didn't understand why it hadn't changed.

As he turned away, she wondered, *Am I Declan's curse?*

———

HOME ASSIGNMENT

Barb · April 2011

T HIS FURLOUGH WAS UNLIKE THOSE BARB HAD EXPERI-
enced as a kid. She felt no fear of disappearances, just relief at
escaping the mission's too-familiar faces.

The month before they left was a long goodbye that started with
Declan flying Barb and Ross to a doctor's appointment in Addis. The
doctor reminded them of the higher risk involved at Barb's age, then
tasked them with building the baby's strength to guard against malaria.
Barb worried, reminded of Abeba's difficulty gaining weight. Ross
took her hand and promised, "If the baby's not strong enough—we'll
postpone our return." He was so sure that she wondered if he felt
God's Plan by proxy—weren't pastors meant to be this way?

Two weeks later the Mathesons' substitutes arrived, a younger
couple who haunted the school to learn its rhythms. A week later the
mission threw a baby-shower-turned-going-away-party that ended
with Abeba twirling in a paper tutu until she collapsed into Declan's
arms. He didn't even blink, and Barb barely hid her joy.

Then, suddenly, she was standing in their kitchen in Bethel, wiping
every available surface with Lysol. Already, Ross and Declan had gone
on to the fundraising circuit.

She wondered at the smoothness of it all.

"We had a dog?" Abeba was lifting one of Gabi's bowls out from
under the sink.

"We had Gabi until you were three." At Abeba's look, she added,
"There are pictures . . ." But she couldn't remember where.

Abeba stared at the hard plastic dish in her hands. "We're different
people here."

Barb knew better than to argue.

Abeba spent her days running around the overgrown backyard, reacquainting herself with the flora and fauna that didn't exist in Ethiopia—or that existed in a much altered form—while Barb reacquainted herself with the house she and Ross never spoke of selling. Raji and Dez kept them company in the evenings. Raji now ran himself ragged as a clerk for an old professor while Dez was completing supervised counseling hours at the YMCA. Barb cooked for them on a budget while still catering to her own cravings.

Abeba was the first to mutiny. "I've eaten so much fish it's coming out my gills!"

All of her jokes were like this now: so unfunny that they turned the corner and became funny.

"Oh! Are the gills a necklace you take on and off? Because I don't see them now." Barb made a show of looking around.

"Mo-om!" Nothing was more mortifying to Abeba than her mother's attempts at humor.

The next day Dez took Abeba to summer camp at the Y, and Barb met Raji downtown for coffee. He had never been able to shake his roots as a barista; and once they sat down, he started critiquing the server's form.

"The weight is nice." He lifted his cappuccino up and down. "But the one foaming the milk is too stationary with his arm. He needs to slide the pitcher down the wand." Raji demonstrated as he spoke. "It's a lost art here."

Barb just blew on her tea. Raji smiled, knowing he was being teased. He asked how the mission had changed, and she named the things that had surprised her—the first snake, for one, though she left out Declan. As a child she would have hunched her shoulders at the omission, her cheeks twitching. Of course, omissions were another way of admitting the truth.

Raji reached across the table and squeezed her hand. "I want you to know." His eyes were cautious. "It's okay."

"What is?" But part of her knew.

"You smile more now, but sometimes your face falls." He nodded at her stomach. "Is it Ross's?"

This man could still see things that those who knew her best had missed. "How?"

"I sat across the desk from you for years."

"And Dez—"

"You should be the one to tell her."

Barb wouldn't tell Dez, and maybe he knew this. She wondered if he also knew of her conviction that this was God's Plan. Ever since that day on the roof, she had marveled at Raji's strength of conviction. "Is it strange to ask . . . ?" He motioned for her to continue. "Why did you become Christian?"

"I've asked you worse questions." He winked. "There were things about Hinduism that always felt . . . off." She watched him try to put words to the inexplicable. "You know Ross. He made Christianity sound simple. It's a good story."

Barb mm-hmmed, which Raji recognized as the compliment it was. She wondered if familiarity with a religion bred contempt, no matter what. Raji had said, "You know Ross," but since college she and Ross hadn't spoken much about what they believed. Now they just assumed.

"You once said you never had a choice," he continued. "That you were always Christian."

"I was born into it." She shifted. "It's like my mother. She's Lakota, so I'm Lakota, but it's . . ." She stared into her empty mug. "It doesn't belong to me."

"For now. Maybe not always."

He had a way of making her shortcomings sound harmless. Ross did, too. Sometimes she hated that, but not now.

Raji smiled suddenly. "My family's speaking to me again."

"Seriously?"

"Might be because I graduated from law school. Might be they just forgave me. Well, not my father. The drama's all online. We unfollowed each other. Then my sisters unfollowed both of us in retaliation." He rolled his eyes.

"Have you seen them?"

"We've been using WhatsApp, but next year we're trying to go over for Onam. It's a—like a homecoming holiday? Dez hasn't seen India, and I haven't met my nieces." He stopped at the look on Barb's face.

"WhatsApp?"

He smiled and pulled out his phone. She soon found herself an unwitting student of tech developments from the past three years.

———

In the final months of her pregnancy with Abeba, Barb had made little progress accepting the state of her body. She had been overwhelmed by the letters from her mother, by the periodic calls from her mother-in-law, and by the emails from listservs, their titles written in strident caps: *Get READY for your THIRD TRIMESTER! We're in the HOMESTRETCH now! Baby coming SOON!* She'd dragged herself to doctors' appointments only because of reminders in the clinic's voicemails. Her body had moved slowly, as if she were wearing waterlogged overalls. Even the maternity jeans, built for comfort, had chafed. But the weight of her second pregnancy was never as bad. Whereas Abeba had squirmed and struggled, her second child sat like a stone, what Barb herself had once wished to be. Sometimes she pressed a hand gently on her stomach, waiting for an eternity until he answered with a kick or an elbow.

This time her mother-in-law told her, "The second pregnancy's easier." The remark was one of her rare confirmations that Ross hadn't been an only child.

"You carry him well," Dez said one day. Raji nodded, and Abeba squeezed Barb's arm. Their stateside doctor was also impressed, and a confidence Barb had never known took hold.

Svenska scheduled fundraising nearby—Pennsylvania, Ohio, New York, West Virginia—for the last month of the pregnancy, and Barb started counting down the days to her husband's return, using an old advent calendar Abeba had unearthed from the hall closet. Barb was surprised when Ross called to say Declan would be staying with them.

"We discussed it a few days ago on the road. What do you think?"

For a moment, she felt a familiar dread, but she paused. A chance like this would have seemed impossible in Welete, but here Declan could have the family he didn't believe he deserved, at least for a time. Circumstances were lining up without her having orchestrated them, as if confirming she'd done the right thing. "It's good," she said.

Ross exhaled. "I hate being away."

"Some days I wish this pregnancy were harder so I wouldn't notice you're not here."

He half-laughed. "You'll tempt fate."

"Oh, please." That confidence again. She no longer felt as if there were writing on the wall, or maybe the writing was just too blurry to decipher.

A week after Abeba started school, Ross and Declan pulled into the driveway as the sun set. Barb and Abeba stood at the foot of the porch waving furiously as the headlights blinded them. It took everything for Barb to make it off the porch as the van turned in. She wasn't sure what made her cry: her hormones or the sight of these two men emerging from the van with smiles. They were *laughing*. They had spent three months *getting along*. What an absurd, unexpected gift. She was so distracted by the sight that she forgot to stop waving. Abeba yanked her arm down with a superiority only a newly minted first grader could muster.

Ross jumped out and held Barb close. "Don't cry, Barbie Doll."

She closed her eyes and breathed him in. "Don't think I didn't catch that."

"Don't think I didn't miss your sass, your smell, your—"

"Gargantuan stomach," she finished.

Then Abeba was at their side, hands on hips. "Where's my hug?"

Ross released Barb and swung Abeba into his arms. He kissed her cheek with a *mwah*. "How's it hanging, pumpkin?"

"So many friends, Daddy. I have so many friends!"

Ross shared a glance with Barb. This was a new development from their conversation on the phone last night, when Abeba had told Ross she'd been stuck on the swings alone at lunch. Today, though, fourteen girls and boys had been enthralled by her stories about crocodiles. Abeba told Ross every detail as they headed inside.

Declan appeared, dragging two suitcases. Barb told him that Ross would come back for his own, but Declan shook his head. "He's got more precious cargo. Like you." He nodded at her stomach. He looked the same, but was she imagining this or had the last three months loosened his ligature? "You're still a sight, Barb Wire."

"I'm a sight, all right."

Dinner was pizza from Michael's. Ross sighed at her, "You just get me."

They shared stories as they ate. Ross talked about a woman in her eighties who was ready to propose to Declan, Barb did an impression of Raji obsessing over the perfect cappuccino, and Abeba shrieked in approval. Even Declan smiled, a smile that wilted as quickly as it bloomed.

Ross did the dishes while Barb gave Declan the tour. Abeba tagged along and spent too much time introducing him to Birdy, whose stuffing was so old it crinkled when Abeba hugged it. They soon lost her to a DVD of *Frozen,* and the tour ended in the guestroom, where Declan had already placed his suitcase. He sat on the edge of the bed and Barb closed the door.

Here they were, alone. She sat next to him and took his hand. He tensed.

"Shh," she said, as if he were a stray animal to win over. "It's okay." She placed his hand on her stomach. The change in his face was hardly noticeable: the way his eyes turned down. He had the same look of wonder when she'd told him she was pregnant. Then his face fell.

"I can't feel it."

She nodded. "He's very still—just the opposite of his sister. Sometimes after a garlicky meal, he kicks."

Declan shook his head and removed his hand. He still carried the curse with him.

"Be patient. You'll feel it." She rose slowly and went to the door. "Barb?" She turned back. "Ross is good."

She didn't know what to say to that. She nodded and left.

On weekends the men still fundraised nearby. On weekdays there were three years of house maintenance to make up for (though Ross's parents had done what they could). This was just one of the reasons why missionaries didn't own houses. Ross started with the overgrown back yard, raking debris, sawing through unkempt branches, weeding a bed of robust shrubbery. Barb toddled out with drinks when he was forty minutes in.

"Declan back from the store yet?" He tossed his work gloves onto the ground and took the lemonade Barb offered.

"Not yet. Sorry I can't help."

"What do you mean?" he deadpanned. "Hacking through my own lawn is fun." He sat on the deck steps and folded himself in half, stretching his hands toward the ground.

"We're getting old." She leaned on the railing. "This pregnancy is geriatric."

"I refuse to believe it." He gave her a playful look over his shoulder. "I've been meaning to ask—what was up with Karin before we left?"

"What do you mean?" She tried not to tense.

"You hardly spoke at the baby shower."

"I think we're just—growing apart."

Ross thumbed at his bottom lip. She wanted to kiss his concern away, but he was already saying, "You should let Declan know if you need anything. I think he misses the whole family thing."

"Oh?"

"I catch him watching us. It might be all in my head." He stood and twisted his torso from left to right. "Maybe we should sell."

"Or at least rent it out."

He leaned over to kiss her cheek.

Declan helped with the yard work but, per Ross's suggestion, spent more time looking after Barb: driving her to pick up Abeba from school, to buy groceries, even once or twice to see a movie. Sometimes the two of them were alone, so Barb could take Declan's hand and watch his smile bloom again. If they were going out with Ross, she took his hand only so he could feel the baby kick. That was something Declan never seemed comfortable with, as if her stomach had become as holy as the Ark of the Covenant, untouchable for fear of death. In every other aspect of the pregnancy he was more than involved: attentive to her slow movements, her winces and aches, and inquisitive about the prenatal checkups to which Ross invited him. While Abeba found the doctor's office torture, Declan treated it like an education.

So when the induction date arrived, they all piled into the car, with Declan driving.

———

Declan · September 2011

The TV in the hospital waiting room blared a live interview: a man with a yellow mullet describing his near-death experience. Declan envied Abeba doing sudoku puzzles next to him. Looking at them made his stomach turn, so he tallied typos in the TV's captions instead. He wondered if there was an honest-to-god person on the other end of those words or if it was just a computer. *Just a computer,* he was sure.

Abeba scooted closer, and he put an arm around her.

He looked at the phone that Ross had shoved into his hand before following Barb through the double doors. His instructions were to get hold of the grandparents and Raji and Dez, but Declan felt incapable, unused to people who wanted to keep tabs. He located each contact and managed a short text—*Regional general. He's coming.* (Figuring out the apostrophe had taken some time.) The message sounded like a line from a Stephen King trailer: *He's coming* in a ragged font reminiscent of dripping blood.

Declan looked up and saw the captions do something new. The cursor erased *Its an angle beside* and wrote *I had an angel by my side.* Proof of life. He wondered if it was a sign.

He struggled to read the signs correctly, like that day in Bethel when he brought flowers. He looked through the picture window and saw Barb turn from the sight of him. He had tossed the lilies under the porch and regretted coming at all, happy to leave the Mathesons to raise their daughter in the comfort of their two-story Craftsman. It was Ross who had stopped him. They were strangers, but Ross had leaned in to whisper, "Stay. Pocket your lunch per diem." Another man might have bragged about being able to talk his wife into anything. Zeus would have.

Declan had smiled without thinking.

Now Ross was no longer a stranger, and around him Declan felt the unwonted need to confess. He'd thought he was past that need, having long ago emptied himself to Tilde, but in Ross's presence every secret rushed to his throat. Ross reminded him of the lines from Melville: *Dissect him how I may . . . I know him not, and never will.*

When Ross had a certain light in his eyes, Declan knew to stay away.

He remembered the night he hadn't. They'd been in Clarksville, Tennessee, the closest they would get to Atlanta on this leg of the trip. As they loaded the van with their collapsible displays, projector, and laptop, Declan had stopped to look at the stars, visible despite the light pollution from Nashville, and felt a hand on his shoulder.

"You want a drink?" There was a giddiness in Ross's voice, even without alcohol. Declan shrugged. "Come on, Kline." Ross raised an eyebrow. "I won't tell if you won't."

"You? Keeping secrets?"

It was Ross's turn to shrug. "Don't we all?"

They hoofed it to a nearby dive bar that promised twenty chicken wings for five dollars and whatever was on tap for two. Ross sat cross-legged in their booth like a yogi. Declan slumped over his beer. Each sip brought a cascade of calm, silencing his doubts. There was a question he had always wanted to ask Ross. He stalled now, pouring salt on the table and dividing it into three small piles. Finally, he cleared his throat. "You think there are things God never forgives?"

Ross smiled. "You think there's a god?"

Declan smiled, too, though he didn't know why. Ross wasn't making sense, even though he was only half a beer in. Declan was on his second, but it felt like his fifth. "Don't know why I agreed to this. You and your goofy smile gonna steal all my secrets."

Ross reached into his pocket and produced his wallet, then positioned it on the table between them. "You too." Declan looked confused. Ross sighed. "We look into each other's wallets. For secrets, if that's what you want."

What simple logic. It made him *want* Ross to find out.

Declan flipped his wallet onto the table, marring his salt piles. Ross dusted the wallet off and actually held it to his nose before leafing through the billfold. Nothing of consequence there—he lifted out the condom and laughed. "Not going to ask!" He shoved it back where he'd found it. It was the only thing that could tie Declan to his wife.

Ross found the secret, though. Of course he did—a picture whose edges were curled white from sliding in and out of a pocket meant for credit cards. Ross laid it on the table so the photo's subject was staring Declan in the face. She was a girl in pigtails with a Band-Aid on her chin. She stood under two oak trees, arms akimbo, wearing a pair of green polyester shorts and a t-shirt from the Atlanta Zoo with zebras on it. She looked ready to tell off whoever had the camera. The photo cut off at her knees, but Declan knew she was barefoot underneath.

"Who's this?" Ross asked.

Declan swallowed. "My sister." He felt the memory crowding him, crushing his throat. "She was nine." He took another sip—was it his third glass? He was annoyed at how his eyes kept watering.

Ross's gaze was steady. "She died."

Declan nodded. "My fault." *We ran, she jumped, the stream . . .* but he didn't speak.

Ross could have asked anything and Declan would have answered. All he said was "My turn," and nodded at his wallet next to the salt. Declan expected to find nothing, Ross being Ross—someone you told secrets to, not someone who kept them. He opened it.

"My god." He lifted the photo from the billfold, just as worn as the one of Ellie, but this was a school portrait. *You have one, too.*

Ross nodded as though he'd heard. "My brother. I was ten and asked him to turn up the radio." Declan didn't know how long they sat staring at the table, knee-deep in each other's unmentionables. "Most men our age," Ross went on, "carry pictures of their kids."

His eyes were the kindest Declan had ever seen. For a moment, he wished he'd never met Barb and found her husband instead. He thought of Nils and Jeff and wondered what that kind of love felt like—if he wasn't already what Zeus would call queer.

Sitting in the waiting room next to Abeba, Declan tried to imagine himself in Ross's place, but he couldn't shake the feeling he didn't belong here. His child with Barb already felt impossible. It was only a matter of time before he would be abandoned to his fate, peering through the picture window from the outside.

He closed his eyes and saw Tilde, pale and sharp, saying goodbye in that seminar room fifteen years ago. The curse beat in his chest.

Abeba squirmed under his arm and asked if she could make an infinite sudoku. "Or at least a bigger one?"

He blinked himself back to the present. "They make 'em bigger. As for infinity . . ."

She sighed and turned to her next puzzle as he turned back to the news. The mulleted man had been replaced by an equally blonde woman analyzing the nation's unemployment rate. He stared at the captions, praying for his son to be born healthy and for the strength to look him in the eye.

———

Barb · September 2011

Barb woke to a room with fewer Mylar balloons than at Abeba's birth, just one that read, "IT'S A BOY!" from Raji and Dez, and flowers from both sets of grandparents. Declan and Abeba entered while Barb's hair was still matted to her forehead, but her son seemed to be fully recovered, swaddled and feeding without the pain his sister had caused in her first weeks. He had dark hair—Abeba was bald until her second month—and wider eyes than his sister, who had Ross's. At the sight of Barb nursing, Declan hung back, but Abeba ran at her brother. Ross whispered for her to be gentle. She made a big show of tiptoeing to the bedside.

"His hair!" She jazz-handed her fingers—something she'd picked up from her friends at school. "Did you name him Eli?"

"We did, pumpkin," Ross said.

Declan shifted his weight and Barb saw a familiar restlessness on his face.

"Good name." He nodded and backed out the door.

———

For four days they were all five together. Declan, when Eli was nearby, developed an uncharacteristic clumsiness. He no longer sought Barb out.

The night before the grandparents would arrive, when five would become nine, she woke before dawn to Eli's cries. She crept downstairs, cradling her son, only to be greeted by Declan's suitcase perched at the front door.

"Is this why you woke me?" she asked Eli, only partly joking. She found Declan in the breakfast nook, spooning a bowl of Chex into his mouth.

"What's going on?"

"I'm packed." He downed the leftover milk from the bowl.

"I can see that." She shifted Eli to her shoulder; he'd stopped crying.

"Overstayed my welcome." Declan stood and lifted his jacket from the back of his chair, avoiding her eyes.

"Dec." She slowly held Eli out to him. He shook his head, but she pressed the boy into his arms. "Behind the head." She guided his hands.

He stared down at Eli, their mouths set in the same serious line. Then Declan blinked, breaking the spell, and handed him back.

"Does Ross know you're leaving?"

He crossed his coat in his arms as though protecting himself from the memory of Eli. "I said there were still churches to visit. He told me to wait. I'm taking the van."

That was that. She wasn't about to fight his urge to run.

"Let me see you off at least." But by the time they were in the foyer, she couldn't stay silent. "Please look at me. If we're going to be friends, you need to look at me."

Instead he looked at his suitcase, then out the picture window— the same one she'd spotted him through four years ago. "Hurts to."

She stared at the swatch of black on Eli's head, two cowlicks already detectable on his crown, and sighed. As she unlocked the door, he reached for her.

The kiss was gentle, like it was their last.

Then he was out the door.

The rest of the furlough was spent visiting with grandparents, adjusting Abeba to the first grade (she was ahead in some subjects, behind in others), and trying to get Eli as healthy and well documented as possible. Ross was hurt by both Declan's sudden exit and the radio silence that followed. According to Svenska, he had taken over the rest of Ross's fundraising obligations.

"How's that even allowed?" he wondered while holding Eli.

"Declan's been with Svenska a long time. They trust him."

"He has them forwarding me his pay. Told them he didn't need it. It's too generous."

"Well, raising a newborn's a full-time job."

He looked up at her. "He didn't call, didn't leave a note. It's strange."

"*He's* strange." She wondered if the *Moby-Dick* quotes would start again.

"Touché."

"You could work on renting the house?"

Ross nodded and, in his best impersonation of Eli's voice—which sounded more like Groucho Marx—said, "Not a bad idea, darlin'."

On the day they headed back, Raji and Dez helped them load the airport shuttle. Dez wiped her sweaty hands on her shorts when they were finished.

"Well, we're in India this year, but hopefully we'll see you soon." Barb knew *soon* could mean years. Raji was still clerking while awaiting his bar-exam results and Dez was staying on at the Y. She liked her clientele, mostly veterans and WIC recipients. The Amins wouldn't default on their student loans, but they also wouldn't be going on another international trip any time soon.

Abeba hugged Dez's waist. "Can you bring Cora and Gregory when you visit?"

Dez groaned in sympathy. "Probably not, Beba honey."

She held Dez at arm's length. "Tell them Abby misses them?" This Dez could agree to. Barb promised Abeba she could email Cora and Gregory—maybe even use WhatsApp—from the mission office.

The Mathesons met up with Declan at Dulles. (He'd flown in from Atlanta.) Barb wanted to ask if he'd visited his mother, but they were stuck exchanging polite greetings. The fallout from his abrupt exit had affected everyone but Abeba, who described the dinosaurs she'd learned about in science class. Barb blamed herself. Marty would have accused her of playing God, trying to control Declan and Ross by leaving them in the dark about Eli. She was in the dark, too, but Marty would have still called it *blasphemy,* though it seemed just as likely to be something God had wanted. This was the problem with faith. It was up for interpretation. Hadn't Ross told her, though? All the best things had once been called blasphemy. She couldn't ignore the feeling simmering under her skin that promised her that every piece would fit—if not now, some day.

Eli turned out to be a miraculous flyer. His crying, the few times it occurred, was quickly resolved. At their layover in Amsterdam, Barb leaned toward Ross. "If Abeba had been like this, we might have had more."

He nodded absently, distracted by Declan, standing in line for sandwiches a few yards away. Barb saw in her husband the familiar desire to work out the pilot's mystery. Then Abeba was tapping his shoulder, asking, "Do you think they'll remember me?"

He knew who she meant. "Always. There was a boy I went to kindergarten with. We did everything together until he moved to Michigan. I still remember his name."

"What was it?"

"Randy Holmes," Barb said.

Ross looked surprised.

"Your dad's even told me stories about him, that's how well he remembers." What she didn't say was that Ross was the exception; most of his classmates were only reminded of Randy when they looked at old pictures, if they even knew where those pictures were. Still, Abeba sighed, placated for now. She had no way of knowing that Cora would meet her at the baggage claim on their next furlough or that Gregory would die of leukemia before the sixth grade.

Barb held fast to the peace of mind she had gained in the States, but even on the flight over the countryside she started to doubt herself. She suddenly missed Makeda. They would have laughed together, Barb knew, if they'd known each other as adults. There would have been an ease in her presence. Perhaps Makeda's leaving, not Declan's, had changed the course of her life. If she had remained, would Barb have ever been Declan's copilot? Would he have kissed her? As the hills surrounding the mission came into view, this backcasting did nothing to restore her peace.

She visited the hangar when Declan's afternoons allowed it, wanting him to see Eli start to toddle and babble. Abeba came with her, sometimes to draw, sometimes to examine the cockpit or chase butterflies on the runway while Eli crawled on a sheet spread on the floor. Today he pulled himself up using the back seat.

"It's a new thing he does," Barb said. "Not walking, but close, and he still seems healthy." She ruffled his hair. "Despite the DEET."

Declan leaned on the Cessna. "Good." It was as much as she could get out of him most days. She wasn't sure how she'd imagined him acting as a father, but it wasn't like this: sometimes regarding his son with sullen eyes and sometimes avoiding him altogether.

"You might as well accept it."

He sighed. "What we did wasn't right." It had become a refrain between them.

"It's too late to feel guilty." She hesitated. "I'm guessing this has to do with Ross."

He sucked in the side of his mouth. "Not just that."

She smiled at Eli, who reached for the collar of her shirt. Her voice switched to singsong. "What else could it be?" She lifted him onto her lap and wondered if everything she couldn't pin down about Declan had to do with his sister.

He shifted his weight. "I never told you where I went after I left you on furlough."

"Fundraising, I assumed."

"I got called home." She sensed what was coming. "He died in March."

"Why didn't you call? I could have—"

"You've done enough."

She drew back, scolded. Silence grew between them.

She changed the subject. "I heard Arnold's transferring."

"That was my doing."

She pulled Eli against her chest. "But you loved him."

Declan winced. "He knew."

"Oh."

She stared at the floor, eyes out of focus, as though she were looking beyond it, to the soil and worms and beetles underneath. She thought of her life—tethered to the soil of Welete, yes, but more to Declan and Ross. Her thoughts reminded her of the speech she had once given Ross over pizza—about Ethiopia, Eritrea, and Somalia, countries that, no matter the treaties or stalemates or embargoes, couldn't let go of each other.

These tethers felt like all she had. Eli's shriek in her ear was a strident counterargument.

When he started to speak, months later, his voice was more timid. It folded in on itself, his words half-swallowed. While his sister bubbled with information about a trip to town or to the Omo, he trickled. On their next furlough, this one without Declan, when Eli turned four and Abeba eleven, he followed his sister everywhere: she was almost cruel in the way she pushed him if he stood too close and answered his questions in exaggerated baby talk. Their behavior worried Barb, but reminded Ross of him and his brother. It grew less frequent when they returned to the mission, but the right confluence of events still set Abeba off. When Eli tired of her punishments, he shadowed his parents or visited the other missionaries' bungalows—never the hangar. He was more at home with adults than with the schoolchildren, who spoke incessantly and competed with each other; he'd rather play with Abeba's Lincoln Logs or make up stories with Ross's old flannelgraphs.

But then he found Takla. The Mathesons were on a picnic in the grove when they saw the striped grass mouse fall from a tree. It had landed awkwardly on one leg and lay there helpless. Eli, usually one to hang back, pushed past his sister. He started up a high-pitched undersong, like squirrels chittering in the States.

Ross placed a hand on his shoulder. "What do you think, *brehane?*" It meant *my light.*

"I think we can help it."

On cue, Barb removed a bandana from her pack and used it to scoop the mouse into her son's hands. None of them were sure how to care for it, but they all agreed to try. He named the mouse after the Ethiopian saint—Satan had cut off his leg for praying. Now Takla was able to balance on both feet, though he couldn't use them to run away. There was something so touching about the relationship between boy and mouse that Barb would find herself blinking away tears in their presence, at once charmed by what was in front of her and terrified of losing it.

———

Makeda · March 1989

What can be said of girls like me? We're adults before we're children. The games of *mancala,* the wooden toys, the pranks on the healer, the visits to the waterholes that pocked the landscape during the rainy season—all brought us moments of amnesia. But that amnesia soon yielded to the fundamental truth of our lives: no one can remain in the shade of the coffee grove forever. Hunger, disease, and death punctuate our stories. We must rip our luck from the jaws of the hyena.

When my aunt died I came to the capital because I needed a change. If there's one thing life in the hills prepared me for, it was the way of the city: do your job despite your disgust at the tasks required of you, none of which are legal, and someone might deem you worthy of a gift.

I lost my accent. Then I became a waitress because the restaurant's owner thought me beautiful. Being beautiful and keeping myself clean were more important than if I could count change. Our regulars included diplomats and government officials, even the president himself, and I needed to let them grab me. The restaurant wasn't just a restaurant, after all. I acted as the appetizer but refused to become the main course.

"Why?" Jalene asked. "The tips are better and you get your own room." She lived in a building out back where she entertained her clients. I told her I was content to make rent the honest way, and she scoffed. What she did was honest, too.

"But it's illegal," I argued. I didn't know then that sex work was as widespread in this world as water. Jalene looked at me like I was six instead of sixteen.

"The laws aren't enforced."

That shut me up.

Tourists at the restaurant were oblivious to its side business. They reminded me of the missionaries: the way they chopped up our capital, rich with history, into pieces. "Which parts are safe?" they asked. I was certain *unsafe* meant Ethiopian.

I wanted to reclaim my home, put it back together in front of them. They looked at me like I was the hyena, standing there without an answer. I laughed like the animal they thought me, my smile too wide. Then I went to the back, shoved a napkin in my mouth, and screamed.

Things changed when the president fled, leaving the women he frequented without a second thought. The anger of those women was set to explode with the power of all the Derg's grenades. But business in the back never lagged, even as the restaurant's revenue dwindled. I was worried about rent. One of the cooks (I always liked him) told me to speak to the owner about extra money. It was obvious what he meant.

The conversation was mortifying, the frank way the owner spoke of my earning potential and the fact that customers had already asked after me. (Why had I taken this as a compliment?) The inevitable change in regime didn't scare him. He was an institution, the brothel an indispensable part of Addis politics. No matter how the city changed, he would remain. This confidence (and Jalene) convinced me to split my responsibilities between waitressing and sex work. My one condition was prophylactics. The owner sighed, but agreed because he liked me. Because he wanted to be the first to hire me.

"For my son."

I had been with men, but this was a boy of eleven. That night I entered his room and found baubles spilled over every surface, a kind of liquid opulence. He said his name was Tony.

I suddenly knew. "Your mother's Italian?" He nodded. Another boy might have spit at me. "Do you know the language?"

"*Bella donna.*" He flung a hand toward me. "*Come si chiama?*"

I recognized the question, but wouldn't give my real name. My aunt was no longer alive to hear the gossip, but that wouldn't keep it from traveling over the hills to Welete. I would rather my family imagine me as an émigré, a secretary, a manager of a kiosk.

"*Mi chiamo* Barbara." Saying that felt like summoning a ghost.

"You're Oromo?"

I nodded. It seemed only fair that we should know this much about each other. He stood quietly in front of me, shifting. I promised we would do only what he wanted.

He looked at me thoughtfully. "What am I supposed to want?"

I asked him to lie in bed with me. Except for the fine sheets, it felt like sharing a bed with my brothers. I saw the terror in his stillness.

"We could stay like this, *il mio amore*. There's nothing else we need do." He nodded and we lay staring at the ceiling until his father pounded on the door and asked if it was done.

"It is!" Tony called. He gave me an uncertain look, and I left without a word.

Jalene was right about the money. I made three times what I did at just the restaurant, and being a waitress meant I could vet my clients. I felt a modicum of control.

Two months in, the owner sent me back to his son's room. The door locked behind me. Tony stood there, his lip split, his cheek purple. I recognized that kind of bruise. He still looked scared, but only for a moment.

"I know what I want now."

I gave a quick nod. My trick had been discovered—being with a woman was more than just lying under the covers. Tony wanted to see inside me. I asked what he meant.

He ordered me onto the bed. "Take off your clothes and spread your legs."

I did as I was told—he was just a boy, hurting. He did look inside me, carefully, like a kind doctor.

"Can I kiss you here?" he said from between my thighs.

We watched each other. I was nearly twice his age and hated his father's obsession with his son's virginity. It was an obsession that existed in most of the men I knew. I thought, *Maybe not this man,* and promised to let him do to me what his father had done to his mother—what he would one day do to his wife. He agreed as if we were conspirators in his future. He asked me questions, so many I didn't know the answers. I found myself saying, "Ask your father," as though I were married to the man. From the look on Tony's face, I knew his father wasn't someone to ask about anything.

"Can we do it again tomorrow? Can we do it other ways?"

"You can," I said, though I wasn't convinced his father would allow this. "But I'm old for you."

Tony sighed. The sound was both petulant and apocalyptic. I remembered that feeling of entitlement, but I'd grown out of it by his age. Melodrama was a luxury reserved for the very young and the very wealthy. He would always be at least one of those things.

"You'll see me in the restaurant."

He smiled and turned away as I put on my clothes.

Tony visited me for weeks afterward, trying to flirt, often badly. His father chased him away until he got a girlfriend and stopped visiting.

We wouldn't meet again until years later.

My clients were more often politicians or internationals. They assured me of their worldly success before crawling into bed, so I could feel the honor of being fucked by them. No clients were women, but I still wished for one. She might ask about me instead of rattling off her accomplishments. She might do more than assume that I had come. She might make it happen.

But this was a fantasy: for a woman to see me more clearly than the jetsetters, the businessmen, the locals (who would sweat more for fear of being seen). Some clients I recognized, like Little Wedu from my aunt's neighborhood, who came here for a government job. He chose me out of convenience, no hint of recognition in his small eyes.

Little Wedu was a quick lover. The transaction would have passed easily if not for the mirror: he smoothed his tie, looked at our reflection, and knew me. My chipped tooth and hair gave me away. He looked down and sneered—maybe I had always disgusted him: a girl playing with boys when she was old enough to be a wife. Or was it that he'd always wanted the piece of me he now had?

I saw, too, the missionary who flew around the country and had given me the toy hyena. I called to him in the streets, but he didn't speak.

I changed my hair the next day, picked out the dense rows until the parts along my scalp were invisible. It was time to leave behind Makeda, the Queen of Sheba, and become Barbara, the whore of Addis.

———

WELETE

Barb • July 2017

B ARB'S MORNING ROUTINE HAS VARIED LITTLE IN HER NINE years back on the mission. She pauses at Abeba and Eli's door, listening for two sets of breathing. She slides on her boots and retrieves a sack of feed from the shed on her way to the coop. (Karin stopped joining her long ago.) Barb prefers the chickens to the ibises—a reversal that has happened without her noticing. She's grown to hate the ibises' wattles poking from their necks like deflated red condoms and their calls teasing anyone within earshot—a cackle preceded by a disgusted snort. She's tried to explain this, but Ross and Abeba don't hear it. Eli alone gives any hint of dislike. When the ibises land on the mission, he skirts the flock like it's made of hyenas.

This morning Barb spots a viper five feet from the coop entrance. The hanging garlic must be old. She makes a mental note to replace it and ducks inside the coop, setting the sack next to the stick and shovel by the door. (Killing snakes is second nature now.) The chickens have been lucky—only two casualties in nine years: Xerxes to a snake and Aquila to a thief. Eli was too young to notice, but Abeba sobbed on both occasions. She was on their porch when a man named Negasi tucked Aquila under his arm and bolted for the fence. Barb stood petrified as Ross gathered Abeba to his chest and gently explained that Negasi needed the hen more than they did, that Aquila would be a gift to his family, and Barb felt the blood gradually return to her limbs.

Abeba discovered Xerxes on her own: his body stiff, his head enveloped in the jaws of a green mamba.

The Bible calls vipers subtle. To kill them isn't.

When the dirty work is done, she heads to breakfast, carrying a basket of eggs in one hand and the snake carcass, rolled in burlap, in the other. She climbs the refectory steps under the banner for her parents, a white sheet they used last year for the director's visit. Its greeting—*Welcome back Eklunds!* written in Oromo—seems muted despite the efforts of Barb's students. Maybe it's the colors: the red from coffee berries more maroon, the yellow from safflower more ochre, so unlike the harsh red and yellow of American fast-food signs. She wonders if the subdued palette diminishes the excitement of the visit: is it as muffled in Welete as it would be amplified in the States?

She slips off her boots and socks. Her parents have been here for three weeks; in that time, she's gone barefoot indoors more often, a protest against Marty's watchful eyes, though those eyes are usually fixed on Abeba and Eli. It's strange now to think that the problem of her mother was once something she hoped to solve (along with all her problems) by moving back to the mission. She was wrong, of course; life complicated with age. She asked her father a few days ago whether retirement had changed that. All he said was "My calendar's still booked." She wishes someone had warned her of this: that life gets the better of you no matter what, and by life, she thinks she means time.

But here are her children—those great buffers between her and Marty: Abeba finally a teenager and Eli almost six. They dutifully sit at the table awaiting breakfast. Eli's legs swing above the ground, as if he's nervous for Takla. He's learned to hide the mouse from his grandmother, who tells him animals shouldn't be fed at the table. (It doesn't matter that Eli hasn't.) This is one of the great tensions between Barb and her mother—Marty *assumes.*

As Barb arranges her boots at the door, she sees Marty speaking to Ross between the tables. He seems confused—nothing uncommon. Marty often bewilders him with offhand comments and stalwart positions. Simeon, seated next to his grandchildren, is a more fluid in-law. Still, Marty likes Ross and he likes her—in small doses.

He steps away from Marty and sees Barb. She waves the burlap in front of him and threatens snake stew. He doesn't smile.

"What's wrong?" She sets down her quarry, but doesn't crowd in close and take his hand like she wants to. She's never sure how much affection to show in front of the kids or her parents.

"Nothing," he lies. "I just need a break." He looks over his shoulder at Marty, and Barb understands. School's not in session, which means more free time. It also means fewer excuses to escape.

"I'll tell them you have to work on this week's message." She straightens his collar. Relief creeps into his face.

"I love you," he says, on his way out.

———

Marty · July 2017

Marty watches Barb and the children clear their plates and head out to the garden. Her gaze settles on Eli. He's always surprised her, with his immediate mop of hair as a baby and his pensive expressions. "An old soul," Simeon calls him. Barb was the same way, and Marty worries Eli will spend his childhood in a morose stupor—shy, lonely, stubborn—just like her.

At sixty-six, Marty prefers retrospection to looking ahead. She's closer to the end—to eternity—than a person likes to admit, even one who believes this life is but a means to that end. Why else had she given up her home to serve God? They've started to bleed together, as if the land and God are the same; if that's true, then everyone must be an agent of God's will.

Or maybe Marty is the only agent left.

Her duty as God's agent started with Simeon at the kitchen table and Declan in the hangar. It accompanied her to North Carolina, where retirees she barely knows seek her out, waiting for her to speak truth to them, as if she were reading Tarot or natal charts. There's a moment in *Agnes Grey* that argues happiness is simply "the power and the will to be useful," and Marty has been nothing but useful her entire adult life.

It wears on her, truth be told.

But her work is never done: Simeon, Declan, the retired missionaries, and now Ross, the man slated to keep Barb in the States. He had, but only until the pilot returned from the dead.

Marty's never loved anyone more easily than Ross. He's diligent where Barb is lax, smooth where she bristles, eager where she drags her feet. Barb's incapable even of a respectful back-and-forth over the phone. Not so with Ross, who always picks up and never asks Marty to call back later. He's also better at his job than Reverend Nilsson. Marty feels kissed by God after his sermons. It's like he's done the impossible—reconciled melismas and straight tones.

He's Marty's only ally in her war against Barb. It's a war she knows Barb has outgrown—knows she should outgrow, too. Barb's an adult. Marty should step away, love from a distance, but this is her daughter. She can't ignore Barb's melancholy any more than she can Simeon's. She knows where it leads—five days in hell and a life of not knowing where to go. She must return Barb to the path.

There are two truths to tell: the brutal and the subtle. She chose subtlety with Ross, a quick comment to raise doubt, but with Barb she can only be brutal.

Her daughter's a responsibility that licks up her limbs like the steam from a sweat. Marty hasn't discovered the secrets to the universe like her own father had (her father now dead, her brothers maybe, too). But her daughter's secrets she does know.

Barb certainly could have been at the hotel gym, could have met the pilot by chance, but of course she hadn't. Chance didn't exist. Not with Barb and not with him.

Sometimes Marty wishes she had died young like her mother, so she and her daughter could be free of each other. She used to pine for freedom, back when she was in the habit of pricing tickets to Standing Rock on her phone. She gave that up after the protests in '16, her heart breaking enough nearly two thousand miles away and, in this moment, nearly eight thousand.

Maybe Barb has enough of Simeon in her to listen. He's reading a book over breakfast, one he's carted around for the entire trip: fiction set in World War II. He so rarely reads that Marty wonders if it will take him the length of that war to finish; the receipt marking his place is still in the first third of the binding.

She says she's off to visit the grandkids in the garden, but as she stands he places a hand on her arm.

"Be nice." Something like a threat rests in his eyes.

Perhaps she hasn't given him enough credit over the years—has he done the math after all? She reconsiders the book, wonders if he uses it to observe her, if he's seen the sadness in her eyes, the ticket searches in her online history. No one would suspect the retiree behind an Oprah's Book Club sticker.

"I'm always nice."

She slips from his grip, but gently.

Barb · July 2017

Abeba, Eli, and Barb leave the Eklunds to finish their breakfast—one thing that does seem to slow with age is the speed at which her parents eat—and head to the garden. Abeba commences the requisite hemming and hawing.

"Why do we need to weed *today*? The river will be so clear."

"Because it's Monday."

"Let's wait till after lunch."

"You won't want to do it then either. The soil's hotter."

Abeba relents with a groan. Eli has already squatted next to the tomatoes and started ripping out dog's-tooth grass. They settle into the rhythm of tugging and pulling. Barb's picking sugar snap peas off the trellis when she spots Marty approaching through the cornstalks. The look on her face makes Barb uneasy; it's no surprise when Marty asks if they can have a word alone.

Barb unloads the peas into her bucket and removes her gloves, tossing them to mark her place. She reminds the kids to pick only what's ripe. Abeba should protest, but her grandmother's presence silences her; she promises to keep an eye on Eli.

"Let's walk." Marty's manner reminds Barb of Ross this morning, nervous and antsy, though none of it shows on her face.

"Not far." Barb nods to the children—her exit strategy.

"Of course, not far." This is no consolation. "I'll never understand how that boy looks nothing like his sister." The comment makes Barb pause, but Marty links their arms. "We should picnic on the river today. Would the kids like that?"

"Sure."

"Only if they keep both feet on the ground?"

"Come on. I was eleven."

"Mmm. Twelve, I'm pretty sure."

"Pretty sure I was eleven."

Marty shrugs, though this is usually when she presses her point. "You have it easy now. We never told you how bad it got while you were in college. There were raids on the village, but they stole from us, too."

Something lurks in her tone. Barb can't help but poke at it. "Like when they took Declan?" It's a test, after all these years.

A shadow crosses Marty's face. "He told you that?"

"Why shouldn't he?"

"They requisitioned more than one Jeep back then."

"Requisitioning Jeeps? They held him for ransom."

"A ransom we couldn't afford."

We, Marty says, like she's still a part of it. Barb crosses her arms, but this feels juvenile. She lets them drop. "You should have told me."

Marty scoffs. "I told you he disappeared."

"You lied!"

"It didn't matter." There's an edge to Marty's voice now, something emerging. "He's here and you're pleased as punch."

Barb's throat constricts. "He's just a friend."

"Who's lying now?"

She steels her voice. "Fine. I'm pleased as punch."

"And Eli's the evidence." Marty speaks quickly, without remorse, but it takes a moment for this comment and earlier ones to coalesce. *Marty knows*—has known for some time, perhaps since Eli was born.

Barb remembers the sick look on Ross's face this morning. Marty's told him something, and this conversation should be taking place anywhere but within view of her children.

"Declan was going on furlough that year to find you," Marty says with more force. "He was going to keep you here. Away from your home."

"My home?" It's Barb's turn to scoff. "When was that ever home?" Marty's eyes soften and Barb doesn't know why. No—it's that she doesn't care. "You hated Declan because of his past. You held it against him yet taught me forgiveness." Her hands are shaking now. "And it wasn't just him." She wants to yell, *I was a child!* "It was anyone you disagreed with."

"I kept you safe—"

"You sent me away. I didn't want that."

"Children don't know what they want."

The statement surprises Barb, but why should it? It's just another of Marty's pronouncements. "Of course they do."

"They don't, so you make them obey."

"Not obeying is just how kids grow up."

"Disobedience isn't growth." Marty puts a hand on her forehead, as though the conversation has brought on a headache. "I've failed as a parent if you don't know that."

Barb's never felt anger like this. She turns away, afraid of what she'll do, and Marty grabs her arm, like the *buda* in the grocery store, like Raji on the roof, like Declan in the hangar, her whole life spent retracing patterns.

This time she jerks away. "Let go!"

Marty blanches, but straightens quickly. "It's Declan's fault you're here!"

The anger beats behind Barb's eyes and she sees it all—the way Marty has hurt her and how best to hurt her in return.

"It's not him. It's America."

Marty scoffs. "Call it 'the States' if you can't call it home."

"I'm never going back."

For a moment Marty says nothing. "You don't mean that."

Barb shrugs. "I've felt that way longer than I haven't."

Marty's lips tremble. This has always been her mother's unspoken fear. It's one of the reasons Barb tried to make things work in Bethel, feigning belief until it could take root again. Sometimes it did, only to disappear without warning. The doubt taught her Marty's most constant lesson—that lies are a surprising kindness.

But Barb's tired of being kind. "America," she says, baring her palms, "is just so small."

Marty's face hardens. "And you're just so lost. You never knew where you belonged," she spits. "It's your spiritual gift."

Barb hears the words deep in her ribs.

Marty stalks off, nothing more to say.

———

If Ross suspected anything, it was the day Declan came to recruit them. There was a delay to the pilot's movements. He hesitated before speaking, studying Ross's reactions, and there was a tightness in Barb's face when she greeted him; it made her less human, more like one of those automatons that sang and danced at Hershey Park. Maybe she, with her concerns and dodged conversations, had been trying to warn Ross, trying to save herself or their marriage, but he had been so ready to take her back to the mission, to slough off their history of unhappiness in Bethel, that he plowed ahead.

There were moments, inexplicable before, that resurfaced with the added context of the affair, like the single letter Declan had sent her. Barb had taken out the trash and, with it, the letter. How had he known this detail would become a piece of the final picture? And there was the day Declan disappeared from the house after Eli was born, when Ross and Abeba had gone to pick up the grandparents from the airport. Abeba turned down *Performances Today* and looked at him.

"What's up, pumpkin?"

Her face tensed. "I woke up last night."

"Oh, yeah?"

"I saw Declan."

"Did you get to say goodbye?" Ross shifted in his seat, wondering if his daughter had some insight into why the pilot had left.

She shook her head and sat back. "Can we listen to *Frozen*?"

He told her to pop it in. During the opening riff of "Do You Want to Build a Snowman?" she asked, "Do Mom and Declan ever kiss?"

At the time, he hadn't linked these statements. There was no reason to. "They're old friends, Beba." And he remembered how Barb had greeted Declan, a kiss to each cheek, when he recruited them.

What had she seen? What worried her enough to bring it up?

And there was a day during their second furlough, while the Mathesons were staying with Ross's parents for Christmas. He had been sent to the store for delicacies that didn't exist in Welete, like blue cheese–stuffed olives. He found himself staring past the jar in his hand, to a woman down the aisle. He didn't know why. Then she looked up, and he saw her face: the color of her eye shadow hadn't changed in twenty-six years. He looked back at the olives, but it was too late; this older, more mature version of Kristy stepped toward him. She made a show of looking at shelves across the aisle and whispered, "It's you, isn't it?"

"Of course it's me."

They looked at each other. She had a wry expression that he'd forgotten, despite what the Matheson boys had done to her, despite—maybe because of—those intervening years. They made quick work of those years: Ross with his wife and two kids, Kristy with her ex-husband and daughter in college. He remembers pitying her—ha!—though he kept that pity from his face.

"I can't believe I haven't run into you before."

"I can. I'm a missionary. This is my first time back in three years."

"You know what this means, Ross. It's kismet."

He smiled, remembering her. "Kismet next to the olives."

"Kismet we should take advantage of."

She asked him to lunch. They did the rest of their shopping together, aisle by aisle, and ate in the deli. Across the table from him, Kristy described what she called her "little life." She kept horses, despite her daughter's tuition fees, and two golden retrievers. "I do some productions at the community theater, too."

When she found out about seminary, she wasn't surprised he hadn't stuck to acting. "You were never really . . . like that."

He asked what she meant. He had been so sure he would act for the rest of his life, until one day he wasn't.

"Us actors are high drama."

"I faked it for a while, with us."

"If that's as dramatic as you get, that's pretty damn good."

He smiled to himself. "I guess our drama was mostly subtext."

She raised her eyebrows. "The best kind."

Lunch with Kristy reminded him of how often they had laughed. Adulthood had ironed this out of him—not the need to laugh, just its constant possibility—but she'd preserved her levity. They exchanged numbers and emails; and as he drove back to his childhood home, he thought about the subtext of his own marriage. There had always been something unspoken between him and Barb; he'd assumed it was Jason. He hadn't entertained the idea that Barb had secrets of such magnitude.

There was the day after the Mathesons had returned from that same furlough. Ross had missed Declan on the road, though Abeba and Eli were forcible distractions. The three of them set off to visit the pilot, but Barb made an excuse not to go—said she'd already caught up with him at breakfast. Abeba punched Declan on the arm in greeting. Eli treated his sister like a shield. He nodded at Declan, but seemed to be murmuring to himself. He was only four. Abeba was eleven and pushed him outside.

"Stay in my sightline," Ross called. He turned back to the pilot. "What'd we miss?"

Declan shrugged. "Pretty busy."

"Tell me how to help. I can—hold things."

"Is that why you're here? To hold things?" There was a bitterness in Declan's voice Ross hadn't heard before. He sat on the back seat and looked out at the kids, unable to decide if they were playing tag or Simon Says or some hybrid of the two. Abeba was being nice to her brother, maybe showing off for Declan. Ross would take the victory.

"Just talk," he said. "Start anywhere."

Declan ducked his head. "I had something twenty years ago— with a woman in Sweden. Didn't work out, obviously." He paused. "I emailed her while you were gone."

Ross nodded, wondering if Kristy would ever do the same. They stayed silent, Declan at his worktable and Ross on the back seat, both thinking of women other than Barb. Now he wonders if they weren't. If the detail about the woman being Swedish was a red herring.

Then this morning Marty intercepted Ross on his way to breakfast. He didn't remember how the conversation started, just that she had said, "It's a waste, really. Like you and Barb."

He shifted his weight. "What's a waste there?"

"You love her more than she loves you."

She spoke calmly. His instinct was to dismiss the comment as confabulation. He found he couldn't.

"Lots of marriages are like that." Marty smiled. "Take me and Simeon."

What bothers him most is that they were happy: in Deerfield, in Bethel, in Welete. No matter how sad Barb seemed, there was always enough of the opposite.

Or so he'd thought.

———

Barb · July 2017

There's only one person left to speak to, but first she needs to make excuses to her children. They're almost done picking vegetables.

She wills her voice steady. "Beba, I need you and your brother to take the food to the kitchen and go help with lunch."

"But it's not *our day.*"

Barb opens her mouth to argue, but Eli speaks first: "You and Gram fought."

She stares at her son, his bright brown eyes that always seem to hide a secret. She's seen those eyes so many times before. She used to think they were hers. Now she knows better.

"Sometimes families fight, Eli."

He looks down at his knees, capped with soil. "You and Dad never do."

She tries to smile but can't.

"Fine," Abeba says. "See you at lunch. We'll be the ones *serving it.*" There's venom in her voice. Barb just takes it.

She walks to the bungalow, hugging her arms, trying to keep herself from flying to pieces. She suddenly misses the States, that time when she felt free, before Declan and Ross knew each other, when Abeba was so small. There was something about the limits of that life that had straightened her out even as it had clamped her into place.

Ross lies on their mattress, crosshatched by the mosquito net. His chest rises and falls evenly, like he's asleep. But as she draws even with the foot of the mattress, she sees that his eyes are open, his stare blank. He's been crying, and Barb knows what about. She inhales and tells him what she's avoided for twenty years: the truth.

The air shrinks as soon as she's done.

"Oh," Ross says, impassive. "I know."

Barb shifts her weight. She can feel her shoulders crowding her neck, as if she's assumed the posture of an ashamed animal—a dog, a turtle, a chicken. "My mother?"

"She dropped a hint."

Barb hesitates. "I'm sorry."

"I figured that, too."

Normally she can read his voice, the shape of his eyes and mouth, but his face barely moves. Her body feels like it's collapsing in on itself.

"I knew there was always something making you unhappy." He laughs, dry and harsh. "I thought it was depression."

"That was part of it."

"The other part." Ross sits up, cross-legged on the bed. "The other part was me."

"Let me explain."

"Just what I was hoping for." He steeples his hands under his chin.

His sarcasm puts her off. "I was with him when I was a teenager. Before he disappeared."

Ross rolls his eyes like Eli sometimes does when Barb helps him with math—help he never needs. "I know you were friends."

She shakes her head. "Not just friends."

"What are you saying?"

"I—we." She shakes her head. "He was my first."

Ross's eyes are suddenly dark. "How old?"

"Eighteen, god. I was eighteen." Her chest tightens.

"And this—" He laughs again, a quick hiccup. "It wasn't worth mentioning?"

She closes her eyes and sees herself accusing her mother of the same thing moments before. "I'm a bad person."

Ross points at her. "Usually I would argue, but—" He shrugs.

She still can't move. Reality presses her into the ground: she'd ruined their marriage before it even started. When they were still in school, every time she mentioned Welete, a black hole appeared where Declan had been. Words curved around him in a way that convinced her he had never existed. Her stupidity is a thing she can taste in her mouth. She feels her lies like electricity in her ribs and gives a short cry, the *crrrk* of the ibises. It stirs something in Ross. He flips the net behind him so they're face to face.

"I didn't hide things from you, Barb. Not when we were first together, not during our marriage."

Not true. "Jason."

His face hardens. "What about him?"

"I still don't know what happened."

"You never asked."

"Then what happened, if it's not a secret?"

Ross's lips purse. "You're changing the subject."

"Or you're afraid to admit the truth."

"Yes!" Their eyes meet. "Because you're not someone I trust anymore."

She can feel the ugliness of her face. Everything presses to the center as she tries to keep from crying. "It doesn't matter. Your secrets would be normal, just like you."

"No one's normal, Barb."

"Compared to this?" She indicates the room, the mission, with her hand.

His eyes flick back and forth. "I didn't get why Declan took that special trip to recruit us. I hadn't realized the context I was missing." He closes his eyes. "Why did you do it?"

There's no right answer. She might be able to defend herself; but as she once told Karin, she doesn't always know why.

"All this time, I thought you were sacrificing to be with me," he goes on. "You were so sad. I started to think we didn't belong here, but it's you who never belonged. It's like you're incapable."

"Don't say that." Her voice sounds small. It's what her mother has said, too, and she can't believe it. She can't. She can't.

"I'm not leaving here and I'm not living with you."

"Ross, let me explain."

"Jesus, there's more."

Something rises up inside of her—she needs to protect her place on the mission, in this house, in their bed. "I haven't been with Declan since Eli."

"Not since Eli what?"

With any forethought, she could have saved Ross from this.

"Since I got pregnant."

He sits without speaking for she isn't sure how long. Then, "Are you sure?"

"Pretty sure."

"But we never stopped having sex."

"I had a feeling. I knew with Abeba, too." Barb is sick, paralyzed with fear, not of Ross, but of what she's done to him. It takes all her will to remain standing.

"You're not making sense." He pauses. "Do Raji and Dez know?"

She hesitates.

He scoots forward, takes her hands, and squeezes them hard. "*Don't* lie. Don't *ever* lie again."

"Raji . . . figured it out." She feels what Ross must, not just her betrayal, but the betrayal of his closest friends—of Raji and of Declan, whom he loves in his own way.

He lets go of her. "I didn't follow you to the conference because I wanted to give you something of your own. You were always sad afterward. You'd drift for weeks. I didn't think you were . . ."

"I know."

"*Ever.*" He stares at his knees. "We came all this way, didn't we? Just so you two—"

"Ross."

"But you asked to have a second child." Then something clicks. "It was during the walks. That's what you did while you took walks."

"Not always!"

"Did you get a paternity test?"

"How could I possibly?"

He scoffs. "Clearly your capacity for dishonesty is greater than I once imagined."

"My mom's convinced Eli's his. She knew just by looking."

"Well, she never saw me as a kid."

Barb sees her way out. "I'll get a test if you want. Maybe you're right. There are days when I look at Eli and he's only yours."

Ross meets her gaze. "Meaning there are days when he's not."

She squeezes her eyes shut. "We came because it was a better place."

He holds up a hand. "I remember." But the memories don't console him. "I loved you."

"I'm sorry."

"You have to go."

"I know."

She stumbles to the dresser and starts pulling out clothes. She packs a shirt from the Bethel YMCA and thinks of the Amins. They'd planned to visit in December, a stopover on their way to India.

Ross seems to read her mind. "I'll take care of Raji and Dez."

She clenches a blouse in her fist. "And what will you do about Declan?"

He flinches. "I don't know."

"Don't punish him."

"Okay."

"The kids?"

"We'll work it out later." For a moment, his words give her hope.

"Do you think—" Her voice breaks. "Do you think I'll ever come back?"

He lies down without answering.

———

Declan · July 2017

A mixture of regret and the bottle of *araqe* made Declan email the first Melville quotation to Tilde a year ago: a blind lob into the darkness, a way of proving that no one was listening. Because he threw Tilde away for the possibility of children—people who didn't even exist. Because it didn't matter how many families crumbled over time, he still wanted one.

Three months ago her name greeted him at the top of his inbox. Now he prints her emails in the office and hides them in the dresser between his liquor and the pearls. She quotes Bergman or tells stories, an amalgam of nostalgia and annoyance and vivacity. Her closings are tender:

> *Your skolnit, Tilde*
>
> *Your punctuation mark, Tilde*
>
> Sometimes just ~

Beneath sits her phone number. It's auto-populated; she hasn't wasted thought on it. Still, it feels like an invitation. He wonders if he should add his own number to his signoff. Would she even notice? Would it make him look desperate? (Because he's thought about calling her. Oh, he has.)

Tilde isn't the only one he abandoned. He left the Mathesons behind when Eli was born to drift among churches, promoting the mission across the States. Declan preferred the road, where there was always the promise of a bar at the next exit. Once he found a girl in middle-of-nowhere Montana and stared at her so intently in bed that she looked away. He woke the next morning knowing he wouldn't do it again—not without a shared history with the person, that desire for continuity rising in his chest.

In Nebraska Declan got the call from Svenska that Zeus was dying. He had refused dialysis and fluid was filling his lungs, his health not just taking a turn but jerking the wheel into oncoming traffic. *Let him die,* Declan thought, but not without wondering if revisiting the past might grant him some peace. Maybe he could dig up Ellie's memory, or at least loosen the dirt around it.

Svenska rearranged his schedule for the next month and he wondered, as he often did, if a special addendum to his file—*Endured six months of torture*—greenlit all his requests.

He returned to greater Atlanta and slept on the Klines' pullout couch. Hera's eyes warmed as she fixed him a sandwich. She squeezed his shoulder with surprising strength for someone who requested his help in opening the pickle jar. That night he lay awake trying to forgive himself for the years he'd assumed she was her husband's accomplice.

He couldn't bring himself to ask her about Ellie. The next day he drove to child services, but they had expunged their records. The '60s were long gone. Ellie's file had vanished, just as she had.

He tried the town archives next and, amid old newspapers, found the impossible: their birth parents, long dead.

Their father had set their mother on fire. It was strange how frightened he was by something he should already know.

The house had been engulfed in twenty minutes. Every microfiche article used the phrase *sins of the father,* but there was no mention of how he and Ellie had escaped.

He searched their parents' obituaries, hoping for some taste of their lives. Their father had been an unemployed welder named John Smith (Declan laughed aloud at that), but the obituary for their mother read *née Hernandez* and the ground shifted under his feet.

He thought of Rod Granger's comment over lunch and of Tilde calling him *Medelhavs.* He remembered offering a girl in his sophomore class a cigarette. Her hair was strawberry blond, her skin freckled. She had glared and whispered, "You're dirty." At the time he thought she meant his hands, but she hadn't said that.

One moment he was staring at his mother's maiden name on the microfiche and the next he was in the archive's bathroom, watching his face in the mirror, trying to see it anew, to glimpse what Tilde had. He had a fleeting thought, *I've been checking the wrong box on surveys,* but he didn't know if it mattered.

He stood too long searching for answers, feeling just as he had when he'd grabbed Zeus' gun.

He went to a bar.

There were thoughts, generic to start—*It was a lie. You're living a lie.* He could keep them hazy by reaching for a bottle. Only when the thoughts dove into the clouds and came out at a lower altitude, closer to the truth, did he falter.

Kline had misled him, convinced him of a privilege that wasn't real. (Which of his other beliefs were false?) As a Hernandez, his jail sentence would have turned into a prison sentence, and the beatings in that Addis cell would have certainly killed him. The guards had thought he was their white savior—no, that was wrong. *He* had thought it, when life on the mission was as simple as flying supplies to Oromo villages—but he had just been playing a part.

Was he lucky? Was this luck? It felt wrong to call it that.

He ordered another bottle.

If *Hernandez* was his heritage, he didn't know how to claim it.

He had this in common with Barb, though he'd only found out a few months ago. They were watching a *Twilight* movie, of all things, and she joked about being a werewolf like the Quileute. Then she made a face at herself. He waited for her to explain.

She hadn't meant to pass. It just happened. Then there was Tilde, who had worked her whole life to pass in a different way. Tilde, who knew his life was a lie just by looking at him.

She was right. He was a stupid, stupid man, destined to repeat his mistakes.

He wrote it in his last email, *I found out my mother's from Mexico.* But he couldn't expound. His knowledge began and ended with that obituary.

She hadn't emailed since.

It didn't matter. It doesn't. Life goes on. There's always another lie to believe.

He thinks about the pearls in his dresser and wants to tear the string apart, just to rid himself of the awful truth that whatever he tries fails.

But he can't destroy them. He and Barb are a family of two (and Eli makes three) that oceans and dictators and decades have forged. He's as sure of this as he is of his status as a fuck-up, so sure that, when Arn asked, "How long's that been going on?," he sighed and said, "A good while."

He put in the paperwork for Arn's transfer that same evening.

So when Barb comes to the hangar today, no Eli in tow, Declan expects she wants to start up again.

And, God Almighty, he can't hide his smile.

Tilde becomes a mere footnote in a life where Barb is the theme. Even if he started as Barb's only option, it's not true anymore.

But then she speaks, her voice like dried leaves. "Take me to Addis."

"You okay?" He steps forward, she backward, as if it's choreographed.

"Don't touch me, Dec. Just fly me to Addis."

"I don't have permission." Her suitcase registers. "Is it an emergency? Is it Eli?"

She clenches her free hand. The movement's small, but he feels the force of it. "Just drive me then."

"Barb—"

She drops the suitcase and throws her fists down to her sides, looking too much like herself at eighteen. "Why did you have to kiss me? We could have been friends!"

Three

. . . see how elastic our stiff prejudices grow
when love once comes to bend them.

Herman Melville, Moby-Dick, *chapter 11*

SAINT TAKLA AND THE CAVE

IT MADE SENSE WHEN THE MIRACLES STARTED. THE Archangel, after all, had foretold your birth.

Once, as a boy, you touched staples in the pantry—flour and honey and oil. After that they never ran out.

As a man you have a reputation for chasing demons and smashing idols. On one occasion you goaded a tree into fighting the Devil. (No wonder he stole your leg.) On another you belayed down a mountain; and when the rope snapped, you sprouted wings and flew away.

Anything, it turns out, is possible with an Archangel on your side.

But all that was long ago. The Archangel has left you, as have the miracles.

Then one morning you wake to a vision of a cave.

You don't question the vision. You depart on the same day, with a crutch on one side and your pack on the other.

You arrive, look around, and find only detritus: hollowed gourds and fossilized ibises. You try not to be disappointed.

Then you discover something in the cracks of the wall: the face of the Virgin.

You stand on one leg and pray.

The Archangel, you realize, has brought you here to die.

Time expands until what's left of your body lifts as though on wings.

———

AFTER WELETE

Declan · July 2017

D ECLAN WATCHED BARB RELAX, FIRST HER TURTLED NECK,
then her shoulders, then her fists. He sensed she was here out
of desperation, something she confirmed as they headed to the Jeep.

"You were the only one I could ask."

He did as he was told, but something had changed between them,
and he felt asea. That sensation kept them silent on the five-hour drive.
By the time they neared the city limits it was dark.

"You'll need a place to stay."

"Just drop me at a hostel." She trained her gaze out her window.

He took her to the Monarch, a hotel near the Edna Mall. The
director stayed there on visits, so the purchase was likely to be ignored
by Svenska's accountants. Declan ordered the room in Amharic while
Barb and her suitcase stood behind him. He thought for a moment of
Tilde in that motel off the E4, standing silent, hand clasped in his.
He'd felt just as out of sorts, but Barb wasn't Tilde; she had passed
the breaking point.

The concierge, thinking they were a couple, asked if they wanted
a bottle of something.

"Some *tej.*"

He led Barb, keycard brandished, to their room. It was hard not
to picture the hotel in DC—*their* hotel—to feel its textured wall-
paper under his fingers. Once inside the room he was unsure where
to put himself. Barb sat on the edge of the twin bed, suitcase drawn
between her knees. She put her head in her hands and two quick sobs
came out. He expected her to crumble then, but when she looked
up, her eyes were calm.

"You've pieced together what happened?" He nodded slowly. Ross knew—about Barb's affair, about him. "Then you know you can't stay here. It'll just confirm suspicions."

Anger rose in his chest. Suspicions had been confirmed the moment she got into the Jeep with him, but he collected himself. "I'm not leaving you alone."

"You should." She chewed her lip and spun her wedding ring around her finger.

"You're a mess."

"I'm allowed to be a mess. My marriage is over."

He felt a quick hope. Barb saw it in his face and blanched. Reading each other had become too easy. He tucked the hope away, somewhere she couldn't find. "You'll need help getting on your feet."

"I don't need help." He had primed her to argue. "You need to let go."

Declan thought of Ellie holding the toy caterpillar and pleading, "You need to let go of me, Dec. Just let go." It hadn't mattered—the toy had fallen apart anyway.

He said, "I won't let go. Not of you."

Her gaze softened. She stood and took his shoulders in her hands. "Find someone else, Dec."

He scoffed. "I'm fifty-four."

"It's not impossible." There was something strong in her grip that reminded him of Tilde pressing him against a wall.

He said, "When I met Ross, your choice made sense."

"Ross isn't the only person out there." She seemed to speak for the both of them.

"What about you?"

She released him and rubbed her brow. "I need to learn to live without him."

"Are you happy?"

Her hands dropped to her sides, dead weight. He took that as an answer.

"I'm staying," he said. "Best not to drive at night anyway." She didn't argue this time.

They ate dinner in silence—room service from the restaurant in the lobby and cupcakes from a bakery down the street. Even during that quick walk, something had crouched on Declan's shoulder, waiting to drag him back to his cell. He ran the few blocks back to the Monarch, the cupcakes cradled to his chest. He'd bought them to cheer her up, but now they sat on the dresser like two uninvited partygoers.

He poured himself another glass of wine and watched, expectant, as she took a cupcake and teased away the liner to reveal a moist, airy, charcoal-colored crumb. Then she hesitated, returned the cupcake to the dresser, and slumped against her chair. He wanted to tell her to go ahead, but she was too stubborn to eat just to ease his conscience.

"You know we missed the DC cupcake craze by about a year," she said. She was looking at the ceiling, head tilted back, neck exposed.

"Didn't know there was one."

She nodded, picked up the cupcake again, and twirled it between her fingers as if inspecting the facets of a diamond. "A few shops absolutely blew up. A show, too. I watched it in Bethel."

Finally she yielded and sank her teeth into the cake. He actually sighed in relief.

She said, "You know the summer Eli was born? When you lived with us?"

That decapitated cupcake. Neither of them could look away from it. "Of course."

"That was my happiest."

He didn't respond, just sat still and wondered if he was understanding Barb more in this moment than he ever had.

She got ready for bed and lay curled toward the wall. Declan followed suit, crawling under the covers on the other side of the mattress and facing her back, something that used to seem soft and inviting.

He couldn't help but rest a hand on her waist. She turned suddenly, pressing her forehead to his shoulder. He held tight until she fell asleep.

By morning one of his arms dangled empty over his side of the bed. She was facing the wall again. Her breath told him she was awake.

"Morning," she said without moving.

"Morning."

He grimaced. This wasn't going how he hoped.

"I missed you, you know." He said it to her back. "Those three years I served on the mission without you—it felt wrong."

She flexed and relaxed her feet. "I missed you, too."

Maybe her refusal to look at him proved not that they were over, but that they *weren't*. He slipped from the sheets, circled the foot of the bed, and crouched against the wall in front of her.

He smiled. She did, too, but hers fell flat.

"Barb Wire. Know why I gave you that name?"

"It's a pun."

"It's ironic. Barbed wire keeps people away. You weren't like that with me."

"But I kept away everyone else. I can count my friends on two hands."

"How nice. I can count mine on two fingers."

She went silent, chastised. He wished he'd grabbed the pearl necklace from his dresser so that he could inject this moment with importance.

"I'd leave the mission." He stopped, reversed, started again, like an unsuccessful parking attempt. "You know I'll marry you."

She nodded, slowly enough so that he understood her answer. He rocked back on his heels until the wall caught him. Everything he said was wrong, ill timed.

He sighed. "What'll you do now?"

"Go to the embassy to check my visa—make sure no one can revoke it."

He placed a hand on the wall and slowly pushed himself upright. "Stay in the room as long as you like. They already have the card on file."

She said, "Okay," but he knew she would check out as soon as he left. Now was the perfect opportunity for her to disappear.

"You know," she continued, "the curse is something you made up. I made one up, too. It isn't real."

"It isn't unreal either."

"It's a trap." She stared at the spot on the wall where he had been leaning. "The kind that makes you lose a leg."

"Can I see you again?"

She sat up and wiped her eyes in two resolute movements. "I don't know, Dec. I'm so lost."

"You don't have to cry."

"Promise me." She looked at him. "You'll find someone else."

He nodded without meaning it. Something really was changing in her; he couldn't stomach not knowing what.

He tossed his keycard on the desk and walked away.

Declan called Caj to say he would be back at the mission in six hours and stopped for a pint off the main road. He downed a glass of *tella* and nursed a platter of *injera* while exchanging pleasantries with the shop owner. He caught himself thinking of Barb as a child, when he'd given her the news that Makeda was gone. She had begged him not to disappear. Later he'd broken that promise more than once. Now he wanted nothing more than to keep it.

He left the shop quickly, afraid the owner could read the sadness in his slack mouth. He was surprised by how normal his reflection looked in the Jeep's rearview mirror.

His stop had only delayed the inevitable. He would return to the mission to face the man he'd betrayed, the only person there who knew about Ellie.

Ross had a panoramic view of him, and Declan had given him every reason to shield his eyes against it.

———

Ross had spoken to the kids the night before, prying himself from the mattress long after Barb had left with Declan in the Jeep.

"Your mother's gone now." He couldn't tell if he'd chosen to remove the emotion from his voice or if it had left on its own. He was about to keep talking, but Eli looked up from the cloth napkin he was folding. The three were sitting around the table, the fourth chair empty. The sight drove Ross's thoughts back to the chair on the patio of his parents' deck.

"She had a fight with Gram," said Eli.

"She did?"

"We saw her leave," Abeba added. "Do you know when she'll be back?"

A fight with Marty. So that was all they knew. There was the chair. He kept looking at it. "I don't know. She was—broken up when she left." He winced at his choice of words. "We'll be in a holding pattern while we figure it out." His mind skipped from *holding pattern* to *planes* to *Declan*. Everything Ross said could be traced to what he wasn't telling them.

Eli went back to his fabric origami, but Abeba rose—two empty chairs now—and hugged Ross. He took a moment before closing his arms around her. He felt the sting of tears as she whispered, "Love you, Dad."

He pressed his ear against hers. "I love you, too, pumpkin."

She let go of him, smiling. "I used to think you called me that because I *looked* like a pumpkin." Her face fell when she saw his eyes.

He wiped the tears from his cheeks. "When did you figure it out?"

"Maybe the first furlough. When I heard some other kid get called the same thing."

"I wasn't very original."

"'S okay. My name is."

"Your mom's doing." There was the chair again. "I was rooting for Gabi."

"Abby's pretty close."

"Yeah." He managed a smile. Abeba told Eli to get ready for bed.

The next day she dragged her brother outside, knowing Ross needed time alone. She was only twelve, but as good as an adult in some ways. He took a moment to be thankful for her.

The morning was full of questions from Marty and Simeon. Ross told them he didn't know what Barb's departure meant. Marty looked at him with disapproval; but as he stood on his newly disrupted foundation, he could see the guilt behind that disapproval. He'd seen it on more faces than he could count. Being a pastor meant being a symbol of his congregants' guilt. They'd spot him in a crowd, and any trace of a smile would drop from their faces, his presence reminding them of some sin they'd committed. They would rewrite his identity in a moment, though Ross had never been punitive. So many times he'd wanted to shake them by the shoulders and plead, "Look at *me*." But they couldn't help it—the church demanded he be God's stand-in. They forgot he was a person—some days he did, too.

The guilt on Marty's face was different, though: it was personal. She had done something to *him*. He could imagine what.

He didn't need to report Barb's disappearance. Everyone had known from the moment the Jeep had driven through the gate. Still, Ross visited Caj and Karin in the office to make her exit official. It turned out there'd been precedent. "We've had runaways before," Caj said, as though this would be a comfort. "We terminate in two weeks, sooner if she leaves the country. It's all in the contract."

"I doubt I'll be able to come up with a sermon this week." The Ross of two days ago would never have let the mission down. He barely flinched now.

"We'll do a music service instead." Caj grimaced. "Heard from Declan. He's on his way back."

"Oh." Ross tried to hide his surprise. He'd assumed Declan was a runaway, too.

Knowing he wasn't didn't change anything.

Ross crawled back into bed after lunch and remembered the feeling of Barb lying next to him, too hot and sticky after making love. He'd never complained.

Time grew intractable.

He heard a knock and ignored it, but then he heard a voice. Karin's. She was already bringing Abeba and Eli back home.

He opened the door, and the kids slipped past him into their room. Abeba didn't look at him, but Eli did. With Declan's eyes? With Jason's? Ross couldn't tell anymore. He invited Karin in, then stood as she took a seat—in Barb's chair. He didn't want to sit beside it. He didn't want to sit at the table ever again.

There went time again. Karin was speaking and he was staring at the table as if something on it had curdled.

"She told me years ago." *About what?* he wondered, then felt stupid. There was only one option anymore. "When it happened again, I stopped speaking to her."

He gave a curt nod, as though Karin's news was of grave importance. She was confessing, and he was her pastor. It was almost a relief now not to be a person but a receptacle for her regret, what some called a *sin eater*. He couldn't tell if she wanted his approval, but Karin's act of ending her friendship with Barb was too punitive for him to bless it. He'd known—forever, it seemed—that the worst thing to do to someone who disappointed you was to abandon them. Then you doomed yourself to miss their moment of change—when they about-faced, "came to Jesus," had the a-ha moment, got woke, whatever phrase people used now.

"I'm sorry, Ross." He wasn't sure what she was apologizing for.

"I appreciate your honesty." His response was rote, which meant safe.

She nodded, the conversation ended, and she left. It was dark out. The kids were quiet in their room, and he lay in bed again, as still as he could make himself, thoughts hovering around the empty chair before they drifted back to Barb in her mid-twenties, when she'd had difficulty getting out of bed herself. Of course, she'd also had the energy to carry on an affair.

He remembered how difficult it had been to furnish their home on the mission. As they unpacked Barb would pause mid-movement in the act of arranging shelves or making beds, the work less a settling in than an emptying out. Around that time Declan had helped her kill the snake. Ross had watched from the window as they'd leaned into each other. He'd thought he'd imagined it. He wished he had.

The Jeep's engine sounded in the distance, a sound he'd been waiting for without knowing. Something deep inside him roared to life, almost like he was on autopilot. He got up and left the bungalow, following the same path his wife had taken so many times.

He hid behind the hangar and watched Declan approach. The stubble on the pilot's chin was gray, the skin around his eyes dark. He looked used up in a way Ross had never seen, the signs of a rough day—or night.

Ross stepped into the light, and Declan looked straight through him.

"What do you know?" Ross meant the question to sound confident. It came out strangled.

"She's in Addis." Declan adjusted his cap. "Not sure for how long."

Ross wanted to ask whether he had spent the night with her, but something held him back—maybe a whiff of freedom. There was nothing he could do now about Barb's happiness. He liked the feeling.

But news of Barb wasn't the only reason he had gotten out of bed. "About Eli." He hesitated. "I know you may be his father."

Declan kicked at the ground. "I mean no disrespect, but he's my son."

"There's a chance," Ross returned, "he isn't."

Declan's eyes flicked up. Ross saw confusion there, not disappointment. His study of Declan had taught him that the pilot found solace in the uncertainty of *maybe*. Being a parent was the kind of situation he would want to wriggle out of, like he'd wriggled out of saying goodbye to Ross on their furlough. Ross was banking on Declan's attachment to his own freedom—something as familiar to the pilot as pulling back on the throttle.

Ross knew that a paternity test would be just like that awful game he'd played the night of the accident, hanging from his seatbelt next to Jason: closing his eyes until some grotesque urge took over and forced him to look. He would make the right choice this time and keep his eyes firmly shut. "I have a proposal," he said.

Declan shifted his weight. "I'm listening."

"We don't tell Eli what we don't know, I never keep him from you, and we make you his guardian should anything happen."

Declan's eyes widened, barely detectable in the dark. "I can't——"

"You *can*."

Declan pressed his lips together and nodded.

Instead of relief, Ross felt as if he had swum to shore and left his friend treading water in the deep. The feeling didn't bother him as it should have.

Declan sighed. "If you don't mind, I'm worn out."

Ross wondered if Barb was responsible for Declan's exhaustion. He pushed the thought aside.

He returned to the bungalow, pausing at Abeba and Eli's room. In the days after Jason's death, he had known he would have kids, felt it like a prophecy: he would protect them in ways he hadn't protected his brother and, in doing so, would achieve some sort of karmic balance. Now he felt that balance shifting, dissolving. His children had done nothing to warrant Barb's disappearance. What other tragedy would they inherit without knowing?

He returned to his room and pulled out one of Barb's drawers, filled with more things she'd walked away from. He expected to find her wedding ring among them. The fact that he didn't was a snarl that would take too long to unravel.

He shut his own ring inside the drawer and stared out the window at the hangar.

Declan's light was already dark.

———

Barb · July 2017

She wanted to forget Declan the moment he left the hotel, but he knew how to stay in her thoughts: the cupcake sat like a pearl in its plastic clamshell on the desk. She considered abandoning it with the note *Eat me* à la *Alice's Adventures in Wonderland,* but the cake seemed almost lonely.

She took it with her.

When she found her way to the U.S. Embassy, clamshell in hand and suitcase rolling behind her, she discovered that her visa wouldn't expire for six months. Otherwise, it would last for as long as she stayed married. She should have been relieved at the news.

The cupcake seemed to be watching her, so she carried it against her hip, out of sight. She wondered if Declan was watching her, too, as he had always seemed to be. She made a sweep of the lobby. Nothing. No one even hiding behind a magazine. All of the faces went about their business and none of them were his.

She tried to focus on the desk attendant, who was answering her questions about neighborhoods in Addis. Suddenly there was a map in front of her and a typed list of Internet cafés. She asked where the nearest ATM was. In the next moment, she was beyond the double-glass doors, walking down the street, getting money from the machine. She pocketed the receipt (the start of her tab) and hailed a taxi, the cupcake raised heavenward. The car smelled of leather and sweat. She hesitated when the driver asked her in English where she wanted to go.

She looked at the map, the list, her ring, the cupcake. "The airport?"

But as she faced the entrance to Bole, she realized she had nowhere to go. The house in Bethel had renters, her parents were still at the mission, and she might never talk to her mother again. She could find Raji and Dez, but there were people here she wanted to stay close to. The best decision—God's Plan?—wasn't clear. Marty had called her lost, and she'd been right.

But what if Addis was the place to find herself?

She stared at her suitcase, waiting for a moment of clarity.

When it came, she moved quickly, opening the clamshell and biting. She wasn't hungry so much as compelled to swallow this final reminder of Declan.

She wiped frosting from the tip of her nose and hailed another taxi.

———

It took her a month to find temp work as a receptionist at Amanuel, a hospital near the *mercato*. In that month, she used her single credit card to purchase a phone plan and rent a sparsely furnished apartment on the city's west side. Her landlord was fair, though inattentive, which seemed appropriate at this stage in her life—to be abandoned to leaky faucets and subpar plumbers. There was a great satisfaction in fixing things outside of herself.

She was broken; it hurt to no longer hear Abeba's snark at meals or Eli's explanation of his latest origami project. She walked to work, a forty-minute trip both ways, and searched the faces of passersby. Declan had once seen Makeda on these streets. Barb hoped to be so lucky. The thought was a distraction from the guilt that growled in her ribcage.

She refused to think of Ross.

He contacted her two months later, in an email she opened at an Internet café. (Her phone wasn't smart.) It requested her number and address, like a scam would. When he called, he restricted their conversation to one topic: the kids' monthly visits to Addis. She agreed with everything he said, but that only made him suspicious.

"You don't have to see them. I can make excuses."

"I want to." But she sounded uncertain.

He exhaled. "I'm sending you some papers to sign."

"Divorce—"

"For a change in guardianship." His voice was firm. "They'll make sense when you see them. Are you trying for a permanent job?"

"Yeah."

"We should stay married until you get something that qualifies you for a visa."

A lightness slid onto her shoulders. "Hopefully I won't need to worry about that."

"The chickens are good."

It took her a moment—how had she already forgotten the chickens? Ross cleared his throat. "Do you want to speak to the kids?"

"They're not in class?"

"It's still summer."

"Oh. Sure."

She heard him instruct Abeba and Eli to keep it quick.

In three more weeks she returned from the hospital to find Declan sitting on her stoop, ballcap in hand, his back pressed against a water stain on the wall.

A quick love rose into her chest at the sight of him, like muscle memory, even as she considered bolting back across the street.

He spotted her. She noticed that, thirty-five years older than when they'd first met, he was using the wall to help him stand up. Something else was different, too—as if he were the naïve teenager, she the pilot ready to set their course.

He cleared his throat. "May I come up?"

She remembered the blank look on Ross's face when she'd left the bungalow. "How'd you find me?"

"The embassy." Suddenly she saw that he had a tell—a slight grimace. "Anyone with you?" she asked.

"Caj. We're heading home in an hour, but . . ." *That depends on me,* she thought, and crossed her arms. He knew what the posture meant. "Look," he said, "I'm not here for anything—like that." His hesitation highlighted the strangeness of their relationship: the falling together that had been inevitable. She'd said no on her first night in Addis, and her answer had stuck. For now.

"I just." He carded a hand through his hair. "How are you?"

She blinked at the question. His tone seemed to hold none of the usual heat that would pass between them. She wondered if he were trying to be friends.

"I guess I'm fine," she said.

He furrowed his brow.

"Okay." She almost smiled. "It's really, truly shit. But . . ."

"You're alive?"

"I'm that."

He smirked, and that was the best kind of familiar. "I have something I've been hanging on to for you."

Declan reached toward his pocket and, in that movement, the possibility of their friendship dimmed. Her mind flitted to his sort-of proposal on the morning after she'd left Ross. It was happening again. She panicked, searching for words that would push him away.

"I read your file," she said.

His hand never made it to his pocket. "Since when?"

She steadied her voice. "Before Eli."

His eyes shone as if he were about to cry. He didn't, of course. "That long?"

Her chest hurt, a bloom of guilt growing too fast, crowding her lungs. "I needed to know, and you weren't going to tell me."

He made a fist.

She should stop talking—he was already angry—but she didn't. Because they *couldn't* be friends. Because she wanted that impossible friendship so intensely.

"You were right," she said. "What we did was wrong."

His face hardened into something unreadable. "Other side of the window then."

She didn't know what he meant, but that didn't matter. He left her shivering in the alley.

———

Ross • August 2017

Ross lay in the darkness listening to Abeba and Eli talk in their room. He listened only when they spoke of Barb. Right now they were talking about taking their first visit to Addis. Barb had needed another month to make the apartment habitable for three—or that was the excuse she had given.

Once he overheard Eli say, "Mom's like a scab on my elbow." That meant nothing to Ross until he took a tumble, driving his knee into the corner of the porch. The skin broke. A scab formed. Over the next week, the bruising and stiffness lessened, but the scab sat there unchanging. It started to pull away eventually, and Ross had flicked it off into the dirt, the skin underneath bright and new.

That was the moment he understood. Eli always picked his scabs. One on his kneecap he could stop picking when he saw it scar, but one on his elbow he was doomed to pick until the scars became permanent.

Abeba hadn't even admitted to missing Barb aloud. Ross knew this was a bluff. Even when she wasn't talking about Barb, loss was written on her face. He was no better. He had counseled congregants about the choice to separate. Divorce had always seemed inevitable, no matter his efforts. Of course an ending was sometimes required for renewal—a burn in the woods that made way for new shoots. Fires swarmed without conscience and couldn't be blamed because they did their job. He tried to think of the separation in the same way—neither good nor bad, but something beyond.

Abeba and Eli were quiet by the time the Jeep drove back through the gate. Ross slipped on his shoes and headed outside.

He had been worried. No, not worried. Curious. But he couldn't check up on Barb without giving the kids (or himself) false hope. So Declan had agreed to go, probably too easily. "Unfinished business," he'd said, and trained his eyes on his dresser.

Now Ross was slinking behind the hangar, just as Declan was shutting the door to the Jeep. His gaze flicked onto Ross.

"I didn't get inside," he said.

"But?" Surely there was more.

Declan shoved his hands into his pockets. "She's still wearing your ring."

Ross looked at his own empty finger. "It's probably a safety thing. Smart."

"She knows about Ellie." Declan huffed. "I didn't . . . I thought she didn't."

Ross had already discovered this truth. During his nightly stupors he'd made the connection, from Ellie to Eli. He remembered Barb nudging him toward the name every time they spoke of child number two. Now all her nudging glowed, fluorescent.

Betrayal had settled onto Declan's face. Ross understood that *this* was the moment when Declan was seeing Barb for what she was, though it was more like seeing how she saw herself: as the main manipulator of her relationships. She didn't believe in a person who could love her without that manipulation, which only meant she hadn't looked at Ross closely enough.

Declan would have to make his peace with this—would have to forget her; and if the pilot could manage that, well, Ross envied him.

He set a hand on Declan's shoulder. "I'm sorry." It felt strange to comfort him, but Ross was used to strange.

"It's over." Declan shrugged off the hand and pushed past him, wedging the door of his room shut. Like most doors, it needed coaxing when the air grew wet and heavy. The door to Jason's room had been the same. The door to the guestroom at their house in Bethel, too—door after door wiggled shut or open. None of them mated well enough to their frames. Was there a way to go around the doors, Ross wondered, a way to move beyond the maze laid out for a person? Or did the exit of one maze just lead to the entrance of another, like a kind of afterlife?

He supposed it didn't matter. Not while he was still breathing. But it had mattered for Jason, who had been forced into the next maze, whether it existed or not.

———

Barb • October 2017

Barb's receptionist position lasted as long as the original employee's pilgrimage to the Himalayas, and she spent those four months submitting her résumé to nonprofits in the city. She wanted to replace the list of her sins with a list of others' needs. But five weeks after the temp position dissolved, so did her money. She refused to go into debt and pull Ross down with her. That night she emailed Simeon about admitting defeat and moving back to the States.

When she checked her email at the café the next morning, a request for an interview sat at the top of her inbox. She couldn't rescind her surrender to Simeon quickly enough. Three days later she was hired as the live-in administrator at a halfway house for women. (Ross would have called the timing *kismet*.) She celebrated by opening her own checking account and giving her landlord notice. She sent Ross the news and waited for a response that never came.

The halfway house was east of her old apartment. The previous owner of the building had gone bankrupt starting a gym, so the house was furnished with free weights and benches, and Barb created a workout area for residents from these odds and ends. The living quarters reminded her of a college dorm—a communal bathroom surrounded by bedrooms. The other side of the building held the kitchen, dining, and rec areas, along with three classrooms, one with six heavily used sewing machines. Barb's room and office were in the basement next to one of the lounges, an oasis in the hot humidity. She cleared out the storage closet and lugged in two cots for the kids.

Her favorite part of the building's five stories was the back patio. It was a straggling rectangle of grass with metal chairs scattered around a few tables, bolted to the ground and decorated with ashtrays and half-smoked cigarettes. But the patio provided a view of the lawn and mansion of an Ethiopian dignitary. There were topiaries and bonsais, banana and coffee trees. Barb hadn't seen ibises in the city, but two peafowl strutted from a coop—one male in his many-eyed glory, and a peahen that was all white fluff. Colobus monkeys, the kind sold in cages, littered the yard. A wrought-iron fence, topped with barbed wire, kept the animals in.

Barb still missed her chickens and made a note to ask the building owners if the tenants might benefit from pets—maybe one of the stray cats she saw on her walks to the *mercato*. The owners were Kevin Beringer, a professor somewhere in Canada, and Zubeda Fekede, a social worker who had finally realized her dream of starting a program for women in transition. Barb was just relieved to be hired by people who would allow Abeba and Eli to visit.

The house also employed cooks, teachers, counselors, and Alma, Barb's assistant. At full capacity it held thirty-five tenants who were working their way through a two-year program. They were the abused, the prostituted, the abandoned—women and some girls who had to lie about their age on the intake forms. No one minded; they had all lied to meet their needs at some point. Each tenant received a physical upon admittance, conducted by Dr. Fekede, Zubeda's brother. Their days were then packed with activities that encouraged routine: group meetings, games, one-on-ones, and classes about everything from childcare to accounting.

Most tenants were Oromo, but fights still broke out with those who weren't. Though Alma knew how to end them with a shout, the conflicts made Barb feel breathless and out of her depth. She didn't understand the intricacies of being born Oromo, Tigrayan, Gurage. She wasn't even sure she should be included in the conversation.

Perhaps her mother had been right. Barb didn't belong here either.

Raji and Dez kept their promise to visit in December but were in Addis for only a week. They stayed at a hotel; and while Dez could help at the house, Raji had to wait until visiting hours. (The only exceptions to the gender rule were Dr. Beringer, Dr. Fekede, the security guard, and Eli.) The Amins had spent the previous week on the mission with Ross, and Barb eventually broke her silence and asked about it. The three were in the basement lounge, waiting for visiting hours to end before heading to dinner downtown.

"There are some new missionaries—both women," Dez whispered, as if the news would make Barb jealous. "Ross looks good."

They said he was talking to hospitals about sending doctors and students to the mission. This was something Ross had mentioned before—as a pipe dream. To know he was actually doing it made her warm with satisfaction. Of course, setting up relationships with hospitals meant he had been to Addis without acknowledging her.

"You should go back and visit," Dez said. "They've just approved a new building."

Raji cleared his throat. "Maybe it's best if she didn't."

Barb hesitated. Raji was probably right, but her stomach still swooped at the comment. "It's fine," she said, then realized, "I don't want to go back. I don't really believe in it anymore."

Dez tilted her chin. "Meaning?"

"Raji probably knows."

"About religion?" he asked.

Barb nodded. "About the mission. About God. I don't know."

Dez looked angry for a moment—but not at Barb. "Is *that* why you think she shouldn't go back?" Raji stared at her, unspoken words passing between them. Dez turned to Barb. "You know we don't care."

She blinked. "I do now."

"Raji pulls that mind-reading shit with me all the time."

He leaned back, satisfied. Dez tickled his armpit.

Amid their laughter, Barb felt the prognosis of her old life fall away—no longer missionary nor pastor's wife nor Christian. She was something yet undiscovered.

———

The kids wasted no time settling in. They papered the walls of their closet-turned-bedroom with pages from the tenants' magazines, accented with ticket stubs from their excursions. Barb kept them busy. One month they toured the National Museum, another they climbed Entoto Hill. They skipped the Red Terror Martyrs' Memorial Museum. Barb went alone and cried as a docent told his story of being a prisoner of the EPRDF. It was impossible not to think of Declan.

Their least successful outing occurred at the Addis Lion Park, which boasted that its inhabitants were descended from Haile Selassie's own lions. The kids had never been to a zoo. Abeba tugged Barb's hand and nodded at Eli, who hung back from the cages, squeezing and releasing his elbows.

They abandoned the zoo for the stone Lion of Judah near the National Theatre, the one that Selassie had commissioned from French sculptor Maurice Calka. Eli petted the imbricated scales of its mane, and Barb imagined him patting Takla's shivering body in the same way, as the mouse was dying last month. She made a note to take them to the other Lion of Judah at Arat Kilo.

So many Christian symbols, and still Svenska was bent on saving the country.

She loaded their schedules until Abeba pointed out that they would be fine if they just stayed at the house and played games with the tenants.

"Maybe a movie now and then," she said, not letting Barb entirely off the hook. It felt nice to be chastened by her daughter for trying too hard.

This wasn't the last time that Abeba put Barb in her place. One day at the *mercato,* when Eli had stayed back at the house with Alma, Abeba blurted, "You left because of Mr. Kline, right?"

Barb stopped walking. Abeba slowed, waiting, and Barb felt caught, unsure how to answer without accusing Ross of telling her secret. "Does your brother know?"

Abeba shook her head. "I just needed you to know that I do."

Barb searched her eyes and found them sincere. "I love you, Beba." The words came more easily for Barb now that the two of them spent time apart. "You know that?"

Abeba nodded and began talking about something else, leaving Barb in momentary awe of her.

While the kids visited, Barb suspected that Ross lurked somewhere in Addis—at one of the hospitals or at the Svenska office. He'd avoided her for five months before he spoke to her again, on Christmas. Barb had called to wish Abeba a happy birthday and to push down her guilt at not being with them, but then Eli had said, "Stay on for Dad." She barely had time to compose herself.

"Merry Christmas," he said.

"You, too." She swallowed, her mouth suddenly dry.

He immediately reminded her of their impending furlough. For a moment, she thought he would invite her along, but of course he didn't. He knew she couldn't take a year off from the nonprofit and expect the job to be there when she returned. "But I have a proposal," he said, and a familiar relief settled across her shoulders. Ross fell naturally into making big decisions; comparative analysis gave him solace. It was likely how he'd started his pitch for the mission's contract with the hospitals. *I have a proposal . . .*

"You take the kids on a real vacation for the first month. Just the three of you." Her heart sank at his words, but she should have known. That was the way with them now. "I was thinking a tour of Europe," he went on. "The rail system would make it easy."

"Sounds like you've thought it through. Why not come?" She heard the neediness in her voice, but hoped he wouldn't.

He was silent. She imagined him closing his eyes and taking a breath.

"Ross, I made a mess—"

"I need to go." His voice trembled. "Figure out your work situation. I'll call next week."

The pleading of the dial tone mocked her.

Still, she did what Ross suggested, oscillating between excitement and apathy as she studied maps and timetables.

Simeon surprised her by visiting Addis in the weeks leading up to the furlough, though Marty stayed at the mission, having chosen sides.

Her father's visit was the most time they'd spent alone since Barb had become an adult. He had a gift for putting her at ease. As they sat on the patio drinking "a *real* Coke!" (it tasted different in the States, more metallic), their conversation turned serious without effort: the separation, the grandkids, the mission, the feelings of uselessness draping Simeon in his retirement. He volunteered at the community garden alongside student athletes and church youth groups. Their presence kept him young.

His patience tilled Barb's words—he waited and, in that space, her confessions bloomed. He admitted he hadn't always been this gentle, which she found hard to believe.

"I'll take that as a compliment," he said.

He swiped a hand over his whiskers, and a shadow crossed his face. She bumped his shoulder, an invitation to speak.

He hesitated. Then, "Was it us? Are your mother and I the reason you . . . ?"

He didn't finish, but she understood. "There's no one thing," she told him.

She spoke of Makeda's disappearance, of Declan's, of the mission's hierarchy and the inflexibility of her mother—Marty's quick accusations that grew into arguments.

"She's so severe." Even as Barb said these words she worried that her perceptions were distorted, like reflections on a teakettle. "She hated Declan from the moment she read his file."

"What file?"

"You know. We all had them in the office with our history and, like, psych evaluations."

He shook his head. "All we knew was that Declan had come from the recruitment program."

Barb paused. Simeon had no reason to lie, which meant Declan had always held the keys to his own prison. It also meant that *she* had been the only one to read his file. The revelation was so absurd that she laughed.

Simeon shifted in his chair. "Your mother always struggled with living here. Being away from her people." Barb didn't know what to make of his words—did he mean Marty's friends, her family, her tribe? He continued: "It's easier for you and me."

"Is it? She has so little attachment to things. Like the necklace—"

"She's not detached." He sighed. "You live with her, you learn her moods. But she'll never tell you. If she tells you, something's really wrong."

"She can't expect people to read her mind."

Simeon shrugged, but Barb knew: that's what she herself had expected of Ross in her unhappiness—that she would never have to explain herself. In this moment, she felt too close to Marty.

Simeon took a swig of Coke, and the shadow returned to his face. "You know your mother wants Beba and Eli to go to school in the States."

Barb blinked. "It wasn't enough to do it to me?"

"I mean grade school."

Her entire body—from her neck to her calves—tensed. "That's not her decision."

"No," he agreed. "It's Ross's."

She huffed, "Sure." And then she remembered: "We filed some paperwork. Declan's, um, he's the kids' guardian now."

Simeon rubbed his chin. A smile tugged at his mouth, but it seemed rueful. "And what did he do to earn the honor?"

She looked down. "That was Ross's decision, too."

Silence drifted between them until Simeon said, "I have something to say." He took her hand and squeezed so hard that her knuckles crowded together.

"Not about Mom," she said.

He nodded and let go. "I'm getting a stent put in when we fly back to the States. We wanted to wait till after the trip since flying can . . . mess with the surgery."

Barb couldn't help the fear that shot through her body.

"It's nothing," he assured her. "I'm healthy otherwise."

"Did you wait to tell me just so you could eat *sambusas?*" She smirked. "And drink pop?"

He winced. "It's soda, Barb. I can't die with you saying 'pop.'"

Part of her registered the word *die,* but she buried her worry and countered, "I spent too many years near Pittsburgh for you to break me of that."

"Yeah," he conceded. Then he said, "Ross called you Barbie Doll, right?"

"Mostly in college." His question was a testament to how little her parents had seen them as newlyweds. Simeon was grasping at a distant memory—their rehearsal dinner, perhaps, when Ross used the nickname in a toast.

Simeon chuckled now. "That boy. He thought he was being funny."

Barb smiled. He wasn't vying for her to reconcile with Ross, something even Raji and Dez had struggled with. He just missed Ross, and since Barb did too, she said, "He was."

———

Ross · *April* 2019

Ross tried not to storm out of places—from rooms, from the house, from a game of kickball. His mom had always warned him, "Don't leave the room angry. Someday you'll regret it." Her words were just a reworking of the admonition in Ephesians: "Do not let the sun go down on your anger." Ross, already in a huff, would rail against her platitude. But that was before his dad had spent an entire week storming from rooms after being laid off at work. "That's no excuse," Mom had said, but Dad hadn't listened, and Ross had lived in fear every time he heard his father's footfalls. (Jason had just rolled his eyes.) Eventually, Dad took to reading the classifieds and updating his résumé, but by then Ross had resolved never to storm out of anywhere—it caused harm, after all—and he'd stuck to that vow.

Until now.

Marty sat across from him in the refectory. She'd been his shadow in the week since she'd arrived on the mission. Simeon was in Addis with Barb, and Marty without Simeon was a sight to behold. She had summoned Ross here, alone, to talk. Anticipation mounted as, with knife and fork, she delicately folded her *injera* around a mouthful of stew.

He had his own bite in hand—no utensils necessary—when Marty spoke the unthinkable: "The children might do better at school in the States."

He put down his bite and flattened his hands on the table. "I'm not leaving the mission, Marty," which was what he thought she'd meant.

"You don't have to. Simeon and I would take care of them. There's a wonderful school in our district."

He cleared his throat. "Barb's here. I'm here." He thought of Declan and his status as guardian. "And the kids want to stay."

She sighed. "So did their mother, and look how she turned out."

Ross felt the water level rise inside him, felt warning lights flash. It took everything not to point out that Barb hadn't had any trouble until after leaving Ethiopia. *No trouble,* he thought, *until she met me.*

He stood and pushed his plate away. (He would apologize to the staff later for not bussing his dishes.) Marty was startled. Good. "Let's agree to disagree," he said. He locked eyes with her and saw her guilt again. She still felt responsible.

He should have gone to see Karin. It was Saturday, and the mission personnel rotated who watched Eli (Abeba was swimming with kids from the school) while Ross prepped his sermon. Of course, the same initiative was never taken when Barb was here. (This wasn't the first double standard to reveal itself after she left.) He walked past the Thorns' bungalow and saw Eli at the window.

Ross forced a smile and waved. There was only one person he wanted to see now.

Inside, the hangar seemed too cavernous, even with the Cessna filling it. He went around back and found Declan's door partially ajar. He knocked and nudged it open.

Declan lay on his bed, the mosquito net thrown to one side, a hand-rolled cigarette between his lips. Ross wasn't sure what he'd expected—shock to flit across Declan's face? disgust? Declan had been avoiding him, and Ross wasn't sure what parts of their friendship remained.

He nodded at the cigarette. "Got any other contraband?"

The corners of Declan's mouth twitched. "What'd you have in mind?"

"Something strong."

Declan rose and ground the cigarette out on the floor. He knelt in front of the dresser, removed a panel at the bottom, and pulled out a bottle of something clear that he poured into a glass from the refectory.

"Make it a double."

Declan hesitated. "You sure?" But he poured anyway. Ross downed the liquor in one swig. It tasted of licorice. The burn traced the plumbing of his body and settled in his stomach.

Declan raised his eyebrows, took the glass, and poured his own. "Cheers," he said, and tipped his down, too. "What brings you here?" He cached the bottle.

Ross plopped onto the bed—there were no chairs. "Need a break from the mother-in-law."

Declan sat next to him, carefully, unused to sharing the room and the bed. "This is probably the safest place then."

"That's a bullet you dodged."

Declan scoffed, and Ross wondered what Declan's life would have been if Marty hadn't taken Barb from him. Then the pilot said, "I think she likes you," and it was Ross's turn to scoff.

"She *tries*."

"If this is what we're talking about . . ." Declan rose, made quick work of the panel, and poured more from the bottle. Ross declined. He needed to finish his sermon.

"There must have been a time before—" He was about to say *Barb* but stopped himself. "When Marty was nice to you."

Declan shook his head and returned to the bed. "There was never a time when she hadn't read my file."

"I imagine she played it off. Unsuccessfully."

"She does that."

"Barb's the same," Ross said without thinking.

The mood shifted in the silence that followed. Declan began: "I was wrong to—"

"Dec." Ross didn't want to hear this. Not now.

"Barb was young."

"She said she was eighteen."

"She was." Declan sounded uncertain. "But it was—she didn't have any other choices. I was just . . . easy."

"Have you *met* Barb?" He fixed his gaze on Declan. "Has she ever in her life picked something because it was easy?"

The comment silenced them both. Declan had needed to speak, but Ross couldn't bear being turned into a confessional. Not now. He sensed the mix of anger, sadness, and frustration from the pilot. He felt the same things in himself, but was too tired to nurse a grudge. The more he learned about what the mission had been like when Barb was a child, about Marty, the more he understood. It didn't take long for empathy to grow.

He sighed. "How's your mom?"

"Still in Baton Rouge."

"You ever think about joining her?"

"Not yet." Declan looked at him sideways. "Would *you?*"

Ross shrugged. "Don't know how much longer I can last here." He hadn't admitted this to anyone else.

"You're the best thing to happen to this place."

"After you."

Declan mimed tipping his hat. "There are other places hiring. Hell, Svenska has an office in Addis. Right next to your wife."

Ross winced. "Too soon."

"I can lend you money."

"I know you're swimming in dividends, but no thank you."

"I want to—not lend, but—give you something." He hesitated. "For Abeba. For Eli."

Ross's eyes fell on Declan's dresser. On it sat an origami crane. "Should we ever tell him?"

"No way."

Ross blinked. "Well, that's settled."

Declan played with his lip, lost in thought. "Just don't tell him on a special day." He dropped his hand. "Tell him—I don't know."

"We'd do it together." Ross tilted his head. "I promise not to have a cabinet of guns handy."

Declan stared into his glass. "As long as he knows he's not losing something."

Ross nodded and slouched back. He closed his eyes, listening to the pilot's breathing, until he couldn't put off his sermon any longer.

———

Declan • May 2019

The mission felt empty without the Mathesons. Declan got used to change when other missionaries left on furlough, but he couldn't stop looking for Abeba out on the runway or Ross on his porch. Eli he pictured in the open hangar, where he had stood the day after Declan returned from visiting Barb in Addis. The boy had asked how she was, and Declan hadn't known what to say.

In the silence Eli reached into his pocket. The mouse—Takla—popped out his head. Declan remembered Caj taking care of the mouse while the Mathesons were on their last furlough. Eli nudged Takla back into his pocket and pulled out a crumpled paper crane.

Declan fell into a smile. "I used to do the same thing, but with wood."

"Whittling," Eli volunteered, overenunciating the *whuh*. He tugged the crane's tail and beak so it appeared to fly. "You can have it."

Declan wiped a hand down his chin, pulling his mouth into a more somber shape. "I shouldn't."

Eli held it out. "My sister crushes them."

Declan found himself opening his hand, as he always did when help was offered, no matter how earnestly he tried to go it alone.

Eli set the crane in his palm. "It'll be safe here."

Declan sighed against the tightening in his chest. "Your mother's fine."

Eli drew his hand back as if he'd been burned. "Is she coming back?"

"She's not going to disappear."

"It's like she already did."

Declan couldn't disagree, so he stayed silent. Then Eli glanced up. "You're tall."

Declan paused. "You might be too one day," he chanced. "Taller than your sister even."

Eli's face screwed up like he didn't believe it.

The Mathesons weren't the only ghosts Declan couldn't shake. There were days when he pictured Ellie in the hangar, as if his mind were searching for a sign that a nine-year-old could fake her own death.

Tilde had written in her last email that she hoped he no longer tortured himself about Ellie. *My sister wouldn't stand for me having such guilt. Not even if she died in my house. You've forgotten Ellie would forgive you.* Tilde meant well, trying to shake him free of his past. But she was also playing with him, stranding him on the island of her latest email without hope of rescue.

Let go. Let go. Let go.

He couldn't let go of Ellie—neither her short life nor her death, a moment that had birthed him more fully than his actual birth to John Smith and Julia Hernandez. Tilde didn't understand how his guilt had compounded and solidified over the years. He had sat in bar after bar, questions tangling inside him like a fishing line it was better to cut than unsnarl. He couldn't cast a single thought without an accompanying judgment—thought, judgment, thought, judgment, ad infinitum.

The judgments made him desperate and, eight years ago, had chased him to Zeus' deathbed.

The TV blared *The Price Is Right* as Zeus, tubes in his nose, refused to look at him. For a moment Declan felt something like respect. It took courage to die as stubbornly as you had lived.

"How are you?" he tried.

Drew Carey instructed a contestant to spin the big wheel. It chirped as each number flew past. Zeus didn't take his eyes off the TV as he answered, pointing to a pain in his shoulder—the same place the bullet had pierced him.

Declan blinked the guilt away and broke the unspoken rule. "Did Ellie leave anything behind?"

Zeus' face hardened. "The family Bible." The book sat on the mantel and was never opened except to read the Christmas story. "I burned everything else."

Fire. Of course. It was what had brought the children to the Klines in the first place.

Declan found the drawing stuck somewhere between Jonah being swallowed by the whale and Micah's prophecy of melting mountains. The picture itself seemed of little consequence; the once-wet marker lines had puckered: a face with butterflies for eyes, a shrub for the nose, a flower for the mouth, a briar patch for hair. It could have been a landscape except for the rosy blush of its cheeks. Declan was reminded of an exhibit he'd seen with Barb in DC of Giuseppe Arcimboldo's work: faces composed of food or animals. He wondered what Zeus had seen in the drawing that had made him spare it.

To Declan it was just odd.

He kept it with him anyway, even as Zeus took his last breath a week later.

After the funeral Hera leaned in to his side. "I'm moving in with my sister in Baton Rouge." She didn't want him to worry.

He wished he *were* someone she wanted to worry, wished he had let himself be her son.

He reached for her and they both cried silently, not for the death they'd just witnessed but for the one that had surprised them so many years ago.

He spent the rest of his furlough pulling Ellie's drawing from his pocket and searching it for meaning. In the airport he wanted to talk to Ross about it, but Ross's face shuttered whenever Declan got too close. (He deserved it.) He considered showing the picture to Abeba to gain some insight, but in the end he just crumpled it around his half-eaten sandwich and tossed it into the trash. The paper expanded like an inhale. He remembered watching Ellie's chest grow inert, the curl of her lips smooth.

He imagined her saving him from the fire that had taken their parents' lives: lifting him from his crib, singing to him as he cried, and picking her way barefoot among the flames.

Five years later, she would skip from stone to stone in the moments before she died. He had been six. What else could he remember from that year? The face of his kindergarten teacher? The scooter he rode around the neighborhood?

The stream—only, always, the stream.

The game was: hop from rock to rock and don't get wet. She was so much better at it! Her legs were longer! So how had she slipped? What was she thinking in those moments as she jumped, neither foot on the ground? Did she think of the violence springing from their father's hands, the flames eating up their house without remorse? What good, in Ellie's short life, had she been allowed? What had God given her? A baby brother who cared too much? She had shepherded him without complaint.

Because he didn't remember the fire, but she couldn't forget it.

For the first time he wondered whether she had fallen into the creek or jumped.

He had been the only witness: the one who saw her foot slide from the rock, who heard the sickening crack of her head; who splashed to her, sure it was a joke; who saw the terror in her eyes and how her jaw moved like a monster's; who was sure a demon had found its way inside her; who hadn't gone for help; who just stood there and watched the light go out; who found his voice too late (*Mom! Mom! Mom!*) and ran so fast he tripped.

Who had been sure it had been an accident until he wasn't. He felt suddenly small, at once a shriveled old man and a scared boy lying under a mosquito net. He tucked his knees to his chest and tried to sleep, but his breath was too loud. His eyes landed on the origami crane, perched on his dresser. He wondered if Eli would ever be kept awake with thoughts that were too large.

Declan had spent his whole life tracking people down, though he'd always found a way to leave them behind, often when they needed him most. He imagined telling Tilde, *The guilt's there because it keeps me safe!*

Ellie had saved him from the evil of his birth, but Declan had found it anyway. Still, there were years, as a teenager, when he was far enough removed from her death on one end and jail on the other to feel the freedom of skipping between rocks without getting wet. She had done this for him, but the freedom hadn't been his. It was an awkward piece of clothing, like a hair shirt. He'd sought roughness without knowing. That roughness had made him open Zeus' display case, made him fall in love with the first person who reminded him of his sister, made him run away from the strongest woman he knew. He didn't believe he could hurt someone in a way that mattered because hurt was unavoidable. Without it, his heart would cease to beat— metaphorically? literally? It didn't matter.

Ross once said that Abeba and Eli were his chance to prove his own goodness. This was exactly why Declan had hoped for his own children. He knew, suddenly and deeply, that he would have been a parent who wouldn't have let go. Because that was the part you kept close, so close that words weren't necessary. It was the engine turning over. It was the spark the moment before, the crux of all things, a continuity.

Something shook loose inside him—the detritus of his self-loathing—and now he hurt to move, to think, to breathe. He wasn't used to this awareness; he was used to shutting the door on things he cared about. This was how he'd survived, each trauma a crossroads.

He dug into his wallet for the photo of Ellie. Looking at it was a familiar pain. To separate from that pain meant becoming something he wouldn't recognize.

The last time he'd risked everything, he met Tilde. He remembered her hope and, as he had done to the drawing, crushed the photo in his hand.

———

Ellie · August 1969

It's over in a flash.

There's something in the freefalling I can't describe. A bottom dropping out.

I guess I can describe it. I just don't have time.

But I do. Because I see it. All of it at once. I see his eyes, always angry. I see Ma trying her hardest—she was always trying.

Except when he broke the rules and set them both alight.

Dónde hay humo, hay fuego.

I hated him. Still do. Everything about him was pinched. His heart was as shriveled as a raisin. I remember watching the Grinch one Christmas with the Klines—Dad cut himself out of the story too early. His heart could've grown back. Just add water.

Ma watered him every day, even when his ears were closed, even when he'd rather shake her by the shoulders until her neck was sore. Sometimes she spoke to him in Spanish—blessings that sounded like curses.

Sometimes I sang them to you—*hoy por ti, mañana por mí*—but not after the fire.

I love the Klines. I never knew a family could be like this. The lights in their eyes. I think it's because they have all the Coke they can drink.

I used to beg Ma for Coke. Now I don't even have to ask. It's always in the fridge. I blow into the bottle tops, and the Klines laugh, the corners of their eyes crinkling.

I guess I won't see their eyes anymore. I can't see anything (not while I'm seeing everything).

I see you. Not now, but as you will be. I see your brambly hair and your butterfly eyes and your daisy mouth. Your face is sad.

I did that. Part of it anyway. Because I always felt that pulsing gloom under my skin.

I didn't mind it. Do you?

I wonder what you'll become. I wonder whose life you'll change.

Hoy por ti. Mañana por ti tambien.

There's so much love in your eyes.

Did I do that, too?

———

Ross • May 2019

The cowboy hat cinched Ross's forehead, even as it kept the sweat from his eyes. His only previous riding experience consisted of three weeks at a summer camp in middle school, enough for him to know how sore his sit bones would be for the next forty-eight hours.

Kristy, on her own horse, glided along the trail, one that cut through the back thirty of her property (*Her ranch?* he wondered). Her two retrievers bolted past, tired of nosing rabbit holes. Compared to Welete, there was a lavishness to Kristy's life that confounded him. She'd given him a cowboy hat less to sop the sweat (so much sweat that he wondered if she regretted the loan) and more so he'd look the part.

The kids had been gone for a week, and he hadn't heard from them since yesterday. They were in Europe with Barb, the longest he'd trusted her with them since the separation. He was both hoping and not hoping for a text.

At Bole, in the line for security, he'd texted Kristy to say he'd be staying with his parents for the rest of May. He waffled before mentioning the separation but, if anyone would understand, it would be her. The text slipped from his mind, once he'd boarded the plane. Her response surprised him as he sank into his parents' couch that evening—*Call and I'll take you riding.*—*Kristy.* Under her name were three sparkling emojis: a shooting star between two hearts. He wasn't sure if the emojis or the American food were making his stomach flip.

Now Kristy turned her horse and settled in alongside him. "You really want pizza for dinner? I can make something." She squinted at him from under the brim of her hat.

"A whole pizza, please. I'll pay." He tried not to sound winded.

"You ready for a canter?"

"Lord, no."

"But we'll get back sooner, which means we'll eat sooner." Then she sing-songed, "I'll draw you a ba-ath."

He couldn't tell if this was a joke. "Okay!"

"Alfred will follow Bruce and me."

Kristy cantered away and Alfred did follow, jerking Ross back in the saddle.

———

She had been serious about the bath.

"Epsom salts." She handed him a towel and a change of clothes— her ex's, he assumed. "You'll thank me in the morning."

Ross slipped into water up to his ears, grateful for the quiet. On the mission, baths were never soaks, and a tub was what a person saw in a period film: a barrel you curled up in. The water unraveled Ross's muscles but his mind still raced. He couldn't believe he was naked in Kristy's house (*her mansion?*). His separation from Barb lent an awful undercurrent to the visit—anything seemed possible. He pictured Kristy, the straight line of her back on a horse, and all of his teenaged feelings flooded his chest, including the shame at his hard-on.

He heard the muffled sound of the dogs' barking and Kristy's "Shut up!" Then she called through the door, "Pizza's here!"

After getting dressed, he passed under two crystal chandeliers on the staircase. He had left money for the pizza on the table in the foyer, but it lay there, untouched.

"I said I'd pay."

Kristy was setting the two pizza boxes and their plates on a dining-room table large enough for eight. "I know, hon, but you're my guest." She was wearing a simple sundress, but the avant-garde shape of her earrings made Ross question the polo shirt and gym shorts she'd given him. "Need anything?"

He shook his head, dismissing his errant thoughts. They sat across from each other. He took a slice from each box, pizza being the one American food he was happy to risk the consequences of. He would run it off tomorrow (if he wasn't too sore from the ride). "Where are the dogs?" They were a safeguard between him and Kristy that he was already missing.

She rolled her eyes. "I put them out back. They can't handle food on the table. Oh, the salad." She retreated to the kitchen and, in that moment, Ross imagined Barb sitting in her place. He felt the shift from Kristy's energy to hers, the safety there. But there was nothing wrong with taking risks. Kristy set down a salad bowl, tongs, and a cruet of homemade dressing.

He used the tongs on a tomato.

"You need to talk about her?" Kristy asked.

He lost his grip and the tomato skipped off his plate. She rescued it and put it onto her own.

"I don't know. You're the one who's been here before."

She shrugged. "Talking might help."

"It's been almost two years." His brow furrowed. "But it's still raw."

"Like a death?"

He stopped lifting salad onto his plate. "I don't want to talk about her."

"Then." Kristy smiled. "Let me distract you."

Ross heard the excitement in her voice. She had either missed him like crazy or missed being with anyone lucky enough to escape Pennsylvania. He understood the allure of getting up and leaving. The only reason he and Barb had settled three hours away in Bethel was his job. But he had to stop thinking of Barb. He listened to stories about Kristy's daughter, Jubilee, and told his own about Abeba and Eli. He asked about empty nest syndrome, which Kristy was staving off with her animals, by acting, sometimes by directing.

After Ross made good on his promise to eat a whole pizza, they moved to the living room, each with a glass of dark red, and sat on the couch. Kristy's shoulder nestled against his. Ross put his arm around her.

"Here we are, high school sweethearts," she said.

"I hate to be indelicate . . ."

"Yeah, yeah. I was a cradle robber."

"You don't prefer cougar?"

She scoffed. "We never even had sex." She set down her wine, then turned to him.

He took a moment to understand. "What, *now?*"

She laughed. "It would be fun."

"You're unbelievable."

"Come on. You're so sad, Ross."

She placed a hand on his chest. He tried to remember the silence of the bath as she took his glass and set it down. She was right. The sadness was pressing him into the couch, leaving a permanent dent. He usually looked to the kids for guidance when he didn't know what to do, but now they were gone.

He let Kristy kiss him, even held her waist as she climbed onto his lap. *It's the wine,* he thought, but the sadness made his thoughts sluggish. He didn't know if anything he did this month would matter. Then eighth-grade Ross surfaced. Did he even know Kristy? Had he ever?

But he said, "We should go upstairs."

They were used to back seats and blankets at the park—a park that wasn't even there anymore. Ross had driven by a Starbucks standing in its place. In bed now, he lost his shirt, she her dress with a timidity that belied their ages. They toed the same line they had when they were younger. He touched her breast and kissed that spot behind her ear. She touched him through his shorts. He bent his head and kissed the stretchmarks on her stomach, always his favorite part of Barb.

He paused, filled with the memory of his wife.

Kristy saw the anguish in his face. "What's wrong?"

He shook his head, unable to say it. She sat up, took one of his hands, and put it back on her stomach. She kissed him and Ross closed his eyes. She was Kristy. He'd thought of her like this far more times than he could count. Hadn't he thought of it since reading her text, seeing her sparkling emojis—the ride, the bath, the pizza, the wine all meant to ensure they ended up in her bed without guilt? They undressed the rest of the way, and Ross crawled under the sheet.

"So modest," she teased. He kissed her to keep from answering. Her hand found him under the covers. He could feel the polish on her nails, the perfect way she had shaved, and everything felt awful. He'd first kissed her in a closet because she wanted him to. But too much had changed. Fucking would make them both feel better, but it wouldn't be enough.

He pulled away and sat on the edge of the bed, quieting his breath, willing his erection down.

Kristy rubbed his back. "It's okay to move on," she said.

As on that night with the hot chocolate, she'd known just what to say.

"Not for me," he answered.

"But you want to."

"I can't." How could he explain to her his pathetic empathy for his wife and her lover? The problem was he'd already forgiven them both. He understood their infidelity too well.

She pulled her hand away. "Why?" She sounded angry—an age-old anger. "Because we'd 'ruin each other's lives'?" He didn't miss the sarcasm this time.

"I'm sorry about that. Always have been."

"You know that day could have been ours."

He didn't know what was wrong with him. He hadn't thought of Kristy's own pain; he'd been too distracted by the possibility of Barb's. "You thought I would marry you."

"Stupid Kristy. So naive at twenty-two." She half-laughed. "Now at fifty-three."

"Kris, don't."

"We would have been happy. We'd be happy here."

For how long, he wondered. He'd always feared that Kristy really wanted Jason: she had called them *high school sweethearts,* conflating him with his brother. Maybe he was Kristy's missed opportunity. Maybe she was his. He'd spent his whole life piling his regrets into a closet. Maybe one day he would open its door and sit inside as he had after Jason died.

"You were nice then." Kristy stared at him.

"Nice," he repeated with surprising venom. "So nice I deserved this." He indicated his nakedness and the bed. Kristy didn't understand: how he was nice to balance out the tragedy—of Jason, of his marriage, of the world. "Love is more than nice. Sometimes they aren't even the same thing." He stopped, afraid of what he might admit.

Kristy was tricked by his façade. So were his parents. Staying with them was unbearable at times; they saw only what they needed to, and he let them. He would always let people see his best—that was the thing that had made him a good, not a great, actor. What he needed was someone to see past the performance.

Barb had. She'd told him the truth so specifically it had inspired his trust—on their first date, when she proofed his sermons, as they packed for Welete—even if he wasn't ready for the truth.

He thought back to Kristy and the day on Jakes Rocks when she had all but wished she'd died with Jason. He wondered if this was the thing that had forced them into bed: the belief, somehow, that they could finally leave Jason's death behind.

He took her hand. She watched him as if the moment were happening to someone else. It had become clear that, despite their new lives, those days when Jason was their whole world would always be there. Ross almost crawled back under the covers.

Kristy withdrew her hand. "You should go."

I did ruin your life, he thought as he slipped on the shorts and shirt that weren't his. He descended the stairs, carrying his riding clothes, as his phone buzzed in his jeans. A text from Barb had come through— *All's safe in bles-sed Amsterdam.* He coughed out a laugh. What timing. It was almost enough to convince someone that, why, yes, God does exist. He looked up at the chandelier in the foyer, each light bulb shining with unexpected promise.

He stepped out of Kristy's (*definitely*) mansion, wearing her ex's shorts despite the crisp spring evening.

Makeda · February 1999

Every sex worker has regulars who make promises. "It's a play for a discount," Jalene told us.

One of my regulars (I dare not write his name) sat at the same table each night, like clockwork. His eyes were dark, his arms tawny, his voice like gauze against my skin. He made promises—to take me out to dinner, to an art show, to a film; to let me move in; to fly me to Italy on business trips. What made his promises special was that he kept them.

Love, as it does, made me feel different. I shared his house before long and quit my trade. Here, I thought, was luck: a wealthy man who loved me. A good man. A man who split me open with his tongue to my ear, with his fingers at the backs of my knees, with a word whispered against my breastbone. I first experienced women with him. We invited them into our home, even Jalene once. Everything came clear as I explored their bodies, wondering which would last and which would expire too soon.

He had three children, whom I tried to mother when they visited on holidays, fishing for money, but to them I was impermanent. I once asked for my own child, but he told me there was no way now. He used the word *vasectomy*. It didn't matter. I had mostly asked out of obligation. This man and the women who visited us—they were enough.

That time didn't last. Nothing does.

On the last night of his life, the men wrenched us from the car and pushed us to our knees in the alley. They recited a litany of his crimes—none of them real—before pressing a gun to his skull and pulling the trigger. I cried out, an anguished birdsong. An elbow bruised my cheek, and my face whipped to the ground. His brain was suddenly on the pavement in front of me. *So that's how we look on the inside,* I thought.

They yanked my hair like a leash and placed the tip of the gun to my forehead. It was still warm from the shot that had killed my lover.

I took to the skies—flew back to Welete, into my mother's embrace—and woke alone, huddled on my side in the alley, a croak the only sound in my throat.

Later, when I told this story to Lelo, she said this was my luck—that witnesses never survive. I don't know why I'm alive now (especially when Jalene isn't), just that the men saw something that kept me safe—perhaps the hyena that shone out of me. Sometimes I wonder if the assassin was Little Wedu or someone else from my past lives.

I couldn't return to our house, where they would have surely found me, so I went back to the restaurant. I hadn't been there for sixteen years. The kitchen staff said the owner was new, but when I went to the office I found Tony. He seemed small, even as a man. He didn't laugh at me, tail tucked between my legs, like I thought he would. It was enough that I'd come back.

He asked if I would manage the girls. "You can teach them," he said, "the way you taught me." And he wanted me to find new girls on the streets—those I could clean up.

"I can clean up anyone," I promised, and spent a week letting Tony use my body. I was still impressive in my forties, or this is what he told me. "I use condoms," I said. He refused one for himself, but I made sure the girls had them. I cared for them in all the ways I hadn't been.

I introduced myself as one of them.

"So was Jalene," someone spat. She sounded like she was from the north.

"What happened to Jalene?" I asked without thinking.

Another girl turned to me, pity on her face. "A curse." She touched her abdomen.

"It was an ectopic pregnancy," the girl from the north said. I wondered if she was a nursing student, paying her way through school.

In time, the girls took to me. I found others, too, whose families treated them like property, and pitched them on the idea of a new life: the job was easy—just remember the names of clients, the number of condoms needed, and the signs of disease too serious to treat with a night off. Some called me *imama,* the same ones who clung to me crying if a client left bruises, but this life was still better than the ones I'd saved them from. We told stories of our scars. We healed each other.

At first, Tony hired me out to clients who required a certain expertise, but eventually he kept me to himself. The way we carried on, I wondered if he loved me more than he did his wife and children. He told me secrets—about how he'd failed his grandmother, who had always wanted him to leave the country. He cried in front of me, still that tremulous teenaged boy asking what he should want. I coddled him, drew him to my breast as my mother had me. A tenderness grew, though I knew he was using me, like my parents had used the mission.

My life started to slip away.

Like Jalene before me, there came a day when I couldn't get out of bed. A pain crept from between my legs and wrapped around my abdomen, clamping down with giant talons, unlike any cramps I'd ever felt. Tony sat beside me, lines worrying his brow. But we weren't family; we weren't even in love. I was a favorite toy he couldn't part with.

Besides, I wasn't seeing clients. *He* had done this to me, and he knew it.

After a week, he told me to get back to work or leave.

The pain made me bold. "You'd have me on the streets?"

But the streets didn't feel like a threat anymore. I used what cash I had to buy a knife and worked to become dirty for the first time since coming to the city. Girls I had found on the streets now walked past me with their clients. More often than not, they found a way to slip me *birr*. I thought of the real Barbara. Where was she now? What had her skin and money and god gotten her that I had been denied?

Then one day she found me. Our meeting was like something out of the healer's fables.

It didn't matter, suddenly, that she had what I didn't. We'd both had the shelter of the grove, the roll of the hills, the laugh of the hyenas. For a moment, I felt some of the amnesia she'd once given me, something that let me forget these past three decades and fall into bed asleep.

———

HALFWAY

Barb · July 2019

During Barb's month in Europe with the kids, she'd dutifully ignored her doubts—about Ross, about her father, about the future. Now she took walks in the morning and let them run loose through the Addis streets. At the *mercato* she turned over vendors' wares, searching for a fossil under a rock, some sign she had landed in the right place.

She wasn't sure how she recognized Makeda, curled next to a stack of crates, a knife in her shaking hand. Barb always had an eye out for recruits, but at the moment the house was full, with a waitlist. There was no reason to look down into those eyes, glazed with the exhaustion that came from being all things to all people.

They both hesitated, unsure the other person was real.

Barb crouched and Makeda spoke. "It's you?"

Barb nodded and reached out her hand. Makeda stared at it, blinking, long enough for Barb to think she should withdraw. But then Makeda clutched her fingers.

They stood together and made their way slowly, silently, back to the house. Makeda scoffed when she stepped over the threshold.

"Where are we?"

"It's a shelter."

"You're in charge?"

"Sort of."

Makeda's only request was a shower. Barb took the knife away and placed it in the safe in her office. Then she scoured their inventory for extra clothes. Makeda's return felt like the most important coincidence of her life, and she let herself believe, for a moment, in the divine order of the universe. She didn't know if that order was the laws of physics or an unmovable mover, just that there was something, beyond. The moment expanded until she felt herself fade into the scenery, a blurring of edges, the blouse in her hand indistinguishable from the rest of her.

Transcendence landed on her shoulders, then scattered like the ibises when the Cessna's engine started. The moment passed.

To talk herself back down after such a moment was the true act of faith.

She twisted one of the buttons on the blouse. "It's Makeda," she said, and her eyes watered.

Makeda slept that night on Eli's cot. The next day, when Dr. Fekede examined her, he found symptoms of malnutrition and an advanced case of gonorrhea, but things were backed up in the lab and her bloodwork wouldn't be back for weeks.

"You're overbooked, too," he told Barb in English, the language he slipped into when talking business, as though it offered them anonymity. Most of the tenants already spoke it or were learning.

"I'm paying out of pocket."

He grunted, possibly in disapproval, and said, "I'll charge the NGO rate if I can." He pulled a sample of doxycycline from his briefcase. "It's a start." He would phone in a prescription for better antibiotics.

Barb thanked him, stunned by this kindness.

"She's in a lot of pain," he went on. "I need to take her for a sonogram."

Barb's shoulders crowded her neck. She forced them to relax. "How much will it cost?"

The doctor was quiet a moment. "We won't know until—"

"We can't—I can't talk about this. Not without . . ." Barb searched for the phrase. "A release of records."

"I'll leave the form with Alma." He hesitated.

"What?"

"You've never taken such interest in a tenant."

"We knew each other as children."

He sighed as if he understood what that meant.

Later she and Makeda were sitting on the couch in the basement, sipping tea and waiting for their nerves to settle. Barb still wasn't sure if God had brought Makeda here, and she had grown skeptical of her skepticism. She refused to be caught up in assumptions of God's Plan.

Makeda cleared her throat. "Did you get your book?"

It took Barb a moment to remember. "*Anne of Green Gables.* Yeah." She didn't bother asking if Makeda had read it. The request seemed foolish now.

"It's unexpected." Makeda shook her head. "Your still being in the country."

Barb looked into her tea. "For a long time I wasn't. But . . . I didn't belong in the States."

Makeda watched Barb's face, as though examining her faults. "No, I imagine you don't."

Conversation tripped awkwardly between them. More often they sat in silence, but each day Makeda grew more solid. This was something Barb had observed in other tenants: like their bones were settling. Sipping red tea in the lounge became their ritual, a last act before attempting to sleep in the warping heat of the city. The tea, sweetened with honey and smoothed with goat's milk from the market, became as sacred now as their coffee berries had been.

Barb noticed the pain Dr. Fekede had mentioned. Makeda moved slowly, as though she'd aged sixty years in thirty, and Barb gradually pieced together what had passed in their time apart. Makeda had come to Addis after her aunt's death. She had managed a brothel. She mentioned a man named Taye who sounded sometimes like her banker, sometimes like her lover.

One night, as they spoke of the past, Barb mentioned the stories Makeda had told in the grove. "There was magic in them."

"Magic." The word sounded like an insult. "Those stories weren't mine. They were my brothers' or the healer's." She hesitated. "No one at your mission liked the healer—said he did witchcraft."

Barb blanched at the *your*—the mission hadn't felt like hers in a long time—but Makeda meant the reverend's sermons, the ones that had called the healer's talismans "idols." To Barb they had seemed no different from the rosary beads Mrs. Bjornstad twined around her fingers.

She blinked away the memories. "I question what good we did there."

Makeda looked uncertain. "There was good. The school, the food, toiletries even. But you want the truth." Barb nodded. "My mother was thankful. But she wasn't proud to take the mission handouts."

Barb pictured the mission walls crowned with barbed wire. "We existed at a remove."

"*They* did." Makeda held her gaze.

Barb stared back. "You left and I never fit after that."

Makeda wiped at her eyes, and Barb wanted to say the right thing, to pluck it from the sky and present it to her, like one of the clouds they'd discussed at length as children, but there was nothing so concrete at this stage of their acquaintance.

Barb waited for Dr. Fekede to return with Makeda's bloodwork, but suddenly, nine days later, there was an open bed (something that made Barb wonder, again, at the possibility of God). The bed was provisional at first: Gondar, who'd left in the middle of the night in what her roommates described as a "bad news Land Cruiser," was allowed a week's grace before her space was forfeited. The week came and went, and with the sadness of losing Gondar came the relief of Makeda's acceptance into the program.

"What about the waitlist?" Alma asked from her desk.

Barb sighed. "It's the good kind of nepotism." If her privilege allowed her to give Makeda the bed, she would. She didn't care if it was right.

The next day Dr. Fekede whisked Makeda away to the hospital for the sonogram. They returned three hours later with Makeda in greater pain than when she left. After tucking Makeda into her bunk, Barb rebuked the doctor.

"What did you do to her?"

He didn't waver. "There are abscesses in her abdomen." He advised surgery and Barb saw that he had planned it all out, probably in conjunction with his sister. The surgery was set for the end of the week, with the best surgeon he knew, and suddenly Makeda was being loaded into the car again.

This time she was gone three days. On her return Dr. Fekede carried her from the car to her bunk, drawing stares from the other tenants. He handed Barb a bottle of painkillers before disappearing again.

Makeda used a wheelchair for her first two weeks in the program but continued their evening tea ritual as soon as she could use the stairs. One night she pressed a hand to her forehead, the spitting image of Declan with an unsolvable problem. Barb asked what was wrong.

Makeda looked as though she'd been startled awake. "It's you," she said, just as she had in the *mercato*. This time there was an anger—no, a bitterness—that Barb hadn't expected.

"I've done something."

Makeda shook her head. "It's my girls." The bitterness had gone, but Barb still worried.

"You mean at the restaurant." She couldn't bring herself to say *brothel.*

Makeda inhaled. "I thought bringing them in was the right thing. But there are many right things."

Barb leaned forward and rested a hand on her shoulder. The gesture was stiff—she was so used to hiding behind her barricade of books—but Makeda didn't notice.

"We have to save my girls." Makeda's tone was fierce. "Here they could write their own stories."

In a moment Barb's mind started racing with thoughts of the waitlist, of overbooking, of whether the women could sleep two to a bed. "Can you convince them to come here?"

Makeda nodded. "I've done it before."

She returned to the restaurant the next weekend. Barb tried to distract herself as she waited, but that meant thinking of her children, which meant thinking of Ross, then of Declan.

"Go for gelato," Alma said, "or you'll drive everyone crazy."

"Do you want some?"

"Surprise me." She waved Barb away.

Barb didn't go to the ice cream parlor. Instead she walked the length of the park near the National Palace, then backtracked until she found herself heading in the direction of her old apartment. Someone across the street called to her.

"*Ferengi!*"

She sped up and kept her head down. She felt safe in the halfway house's neighborhood, among her tenuous connections with shopkeepers and kids riding down the streets two or three to a bicycle. Here she was just another foreigner, likely an Italian left over from the occupation. She had that feeling, again, of blurring with her surroundings, of insignificance, this time coupled with a terror deep in her stomach.

Then she was standing in the spot where Declan had once crouched on her stoop, where they had talked about the end of things. But life moved on, further down the river. Her grip on the past released slowly; her fingers flexed and circulation returned, but she didn't let go—not entirely.

By the time she returned to the house, she'd forgotten the gelato, and Alma had fear in her eyes.

"What?" Barb felt an electricity in her chest, worse than being called *ferengi*.

"Makeda's back. She was jumped."

Shit. "The doctor?"

"He's in there with her."

Barb pressed her palms together in thanks before heading to the room used for exams. Dr. Fekede opened the door on her first knock.

"What were you thinking?" he hissed. "She's still recovering." He had never spoken so sharply. She knew he was right to. He moved aside and Barb could see Makeda wasn't alone. A woman in her thirties held her hand—the one not in a sling.

Barb tensed. "Who did it?"

It was the woman who answered—*werobeloch,* hired muscle for the restaurant. Barb looked back at Makeda. The left side of her face was barely held together with butterfly stitches. Where Barb only had calls of *ferengi* to fear, Makeda had fists. The mission walls surrounded her, even here.

She grew angry—at herself, at the mission, at the whole system—but the anger was more a bridge than a wall.

Makeda spoke from one side of her mouth, her words labored. "I got in. To see my girls."

Barb exhaled. "How many did you convince?"

Makeda squeezed the other woman's hand and looked at the ground. "Just Lelo."

Barb the administrator was relieved—no need for two to a bed— and then she remembered Makeda hadn't returned alone.

She turned to the doctor. "Did you start the intake exam?"

He hesitated.

"We're overbooked," she said. "I'm making a habit of it."

"I'll grab another release of records. If Lelo agrees."

Barb went to Makeda's side. Lelo helped her up, but not without giving away her fear of being left alone with the doctor. Barb spoke in Amharic and promised he was a good man. "You saw how he treated Makeda?" Lelo nodded. "He's always like that." Barb noticed both discomfort at the compliment and pride in the doctor's face.

Makeda leaned on Barb as they moved down the hall to her room. "I told Tony," she said, "the only reason this city doesn't collapse is because my girls were on their knees for the diplomats." She paused and coughed. "I shouldn't have gloated."

"It's not your fault." Barb lifted Makeda's legs onto the mattress and moved to get another pillow to support her arm.

"Tony laughed like he owned me."

Barb shook her head. "He just didn't know what to do with you. Because you're something new." She didn't know why she sounded so sure. Maybe it was the anger simmering under her skin. "Get some sleep."

Makeda closed her eyes. Barb felt the need to pronounce some sort of blessing on her, on this room, on the house.

When she returned to the front desk, Lelo was talking with Alma about where she would sleep. Dr. Fekede sat alone in the makeshift exam room doing paperwork.

"I'm postdating these," he said without looking up. "You're doing the right thing."

"Your sister would think so?"

"Of course." He waved his hand. "But I'll never tell her."

She felt herself smiling. "*Ameseginalehu.*"

"You have a good accent for an American."

She hesitated, uncertain if his question bore its own prejudice. "I grew up here, in the south."

He looked at her as though for the first time. "I wasn't always a good man. But it's smart you said that to Lelo."

Barb shrugged. "You're good when you're here. That's all that matters."

They held each other's gazes, then the doctor shut the folder on his paperwork. Barb watched him leave, wondering what had passed between them.

———

Lelo took up residence on Eli's cot while the kids were still on furlough. She also joined Makeda and Barb for their evening tea, where Barb learned that she had spent a decade of her life at the brothel. She was thirty-four now.

Lelo had that same unsettled feeling as the other tenants when they first arrived. But sometimes Makeda shifted on the couch so that their arms touched, and Barb watched the tension drain from Lelo's face.

One evening she hid her mouth with her tea and gave a distressed sigh. Makeda nodded, urging her on.

"I got the feeling I been dying."

Her tone made Barb's stomach tighten. *God has numbered the days of your kingdom.*

"I was sick before," Lelo went on. "I can't do what I used to." She sipped her tea. Barb wondered if it hurt to swallow.

"The flu?" It was supposed to be bad this year. Dr. Fekede had warned them.

"It feels like a curse."

No. No more curses. Barb prayed silently, her own ultimatum thrown heavenward, though she already knew the curtain would close on it. Ultimatums were no way to get a god's attention. Lelo's bloodwork would give them an answer, but Barb didn't say this. Setting a deadline would rush the curtain closed.

The only solace she could offer was Eli's bed and another mug of tea.

———

Barb · October 2019

It wasn't the flu. It was seroconversion.

Dr. Fekede told them in Barb's office. The NGO partnered with in-patient facilities if Lelo ever needed them. He brought a stack of pamphlets, and Barb was reminded of the tracts in the Cessna's cargo hold.

He promised Lelo, "You can stay healthy for a long time on antiretrovirals."

She looked lost at the news. Makeda put a hand on her arm and told her to go rest. Barb recognized Makeda's tone; Ross had used it on her the first months after Abeba had been born.

Lelo went to lie down on Eli's cot, the room only ten feet away so she could still eavesdrop. Makeda turned to the doctor.

"We don't have enough."

He knew what she meant. "The treatment's more affordable than it was."

Regret was written on Makeda's face. "You can help?"

"I can offer my services."

She turned to Barb. "It's you, then. You need to fix it."

Barb opened her mouth, but no sound came. *I'm just a missionary,* she thought, but that wasn't even true anymore.

Ross. Ross had medical connections now and had always been kind—if she hadn't pressed that kindness out of him.

"I'll find a way."

"You always could." Then Makeda followed after Lelo.

Barb slumped behind her desk. She'd just vowed to petition the person she'd hurt most to save the life of someone he'd never met. *That's what Ross does,* she reminded herself, though at the airport in May, he'd grimaced at the sight of her.

Dr. Fekede shifted his weight, and she remembered where she was. "This is the wrong time to ask." He tugged his shirt away from his chest. "St. Gabriel's—the hospital—is holding a fundraiser at the Sheraton this Saturday."

It took Barb a moment to understand. She took a breath. "I'm separated." She indicated her wedding ring.

"I'm divorced."

"I have kids," she countered.

He turned his palms up. "Me, too."

I'm too dirty a thing, she thought, but remembered the way this man had fought in the trenches alongside her. "All right, Doctor."

"Yonas," he corrected.

Yonas Fekede. She liked the rhythm of his full name as it flicked across her tongue.

(Not that he made her think of her tongue.)

It wasn't until the morning of the fundraiser that she realized she had nothing to wear. Everything was too *frumpy*—this she heard from tenant Kima. (Barb had to teach her the word, her insults were so severe.) Barb laughed at the teasing even as it sent shocks of anxiety through her. Help was upstairs in Kima's closet, and Barb's new dilemma became matching the extravagance of the event without baring too much. She chose a backless blue dress and a silver shawl.

At the thought of her mother's lost pearls, she left her neck bare. She found herself staring down at her wedding ring, considering if it was time. *If not now, when?*

She slipped the ring off her left hand and onto her right, a compromise.

Lelo had been taken to the Sheraton by her clients, so Barb was primed for opulence as she walked through the lobby on Yonas's arm, but the lavish fountains, the flowers, and the banquet of hors d'oeuvres were lost on her. She already missed her basement lounge.

There wasn't an open bar, except for Yonas, who'd set the leg of one of the bartenders. When he asked what she wanted, Barb said, "What could I even handle?"

He returned with a martini for himself and a ruby-orange drink for her. Garnishing her glass were a cherry, an orange slice, and a tiny umbrella.

"Sex on the Beach," he announced.

The tang of the drink made her glad he had picked for her. "I can't thank you enough. For Makeda's surgery, for her arm, for helping Lelo . . ."

Yonas shook his head. "No talk of work tonight." He leaned in to whisper. "Besides, I'm not the only one looking out for them."

She still hadn't contacted Ross. Every time she thought of doing so, too many questions stopped her. Should she wait until after the furlough to reach out? Should she—?

Yonas tucked her hair behind her ear. He was right. No work tonight.

She hadn't expected the fundraiser to include dancing. That wasn't something a Baptist pastor's wife usually did, but with Yonas's hand on her waist and his instructions whispered in her ear, she faked her way through the steps. She needed no guidance to sway back and forth, her cheek pressed to his lapel when the music slowed. She'd done this much with Ross at home, before Abeba.

The conversation danced around in its own way—first an innocuous comment about the food, then Barb's longwinded answer to the question "Where are you really from?" and Yonas's rushed tirade against the administration of the hospital where he used to work. His rant reminded her of Ross.

When they were back at a corner table under low light, Yonas brought her another Sex on the Beach. He had switched to IPAs.

"I like you, Barb."

She nodded. "Feeling's mutual."

"More important, I trust you." He smiled and leaned forward again, placing a hand under her chin. She let him pull her forward until their lips met. For a brief moment, the kiss felt awkward, but then something lit inside her. With her hand on his neck, she eased the tongue that liked saying his name into his mouth. By the time she pulled away, Yonas's hand was on her thigh.

She took a breath. "Must be the Sex on the Beach."

He started to chuckle. Barb wasn't sure if the kiss had set him off. He touched her hand. "That's the fruit juice talking." He snickered again.

She understood, then blushed. She had all but admitted to being a lightweight. Of course he would get her a virgin drink. "Placebo effect?"

"You are perfect, Barbara. I'm the one who's had too many." He slouched against his chair and loosened his tie. It was her turn to lean forward and touch his hand.

"I'll get you something greasy from the buffet, right?"

"Good plan." There was something in his look that made her stop wondering what the kiss meant. They were friends now—that was what mattered.

That night, after changing into worn shorts and a shirt, she plopped down at her desk and opened a new email to Ross. The cursor blinked at her. She wished she had a cocktail as she typed:

Sorry to reach out like this. I hope the furlough's going well. I think of you all, to the point of distraction.

But one of the women here tested positive for HIV. We need help getting her on antiretrovirals. It feels like I'm breaking a rule just by asking, but I promised someone.

Because if anyone knows how to make this work, it's you.

She hit send and stared at her left hand, the indents from her ring visible but faint.

She spent four days dreading Ross's response before it appeared, beneath an offer for cheaper flights to Las Vegas. The first line was just three words: *Consider it done.*

Her pulse quickened. The words felt as much an end as a beginning.

The email closed with questions: who was the doctor, the hospital, the patient? *I'll take care of the rest,* he wrote.

Barb found Lelo with Makeda in the kitchen and told them the news.

Makeda squeezed Barb's arm. "It's what you promised."

"It's a step closer."

"We were meant to find each other again."

Barb hoped this was true.

—

Ross · May 2020

The mission gate was closed. The Cessna was grounded. Ross woke each day hoping things would change, and by bedtime that belief had shattered.

What he felt now wasn't that different from what he'd felt before COVID-19, when he was teaching, preaching, and liaising between hospitals, but now the feeling of uselessness wasn't just a distraction. It was an unalterable truth.

There was nothing he could do. No change he could galvanize. No new proposal to begin.

Svenska Ministries' pandemic plan had frozen his fundraising in February, when he was somewhere outside Tulsa. The moment had been surreal: taking calls and emails about a virus that had barely broken the news cycle in the States. The director presented Ross with the choice to stay there or return early to Ethiopia. He didn't even consider staying, much to the chagrin of his parents and in-laws. He wanted the kids in the same country as their mother.

He, Abeba, and Eli flew into Addis on March 16, the day that the city's schools closed. The kids spent the next forty-eight hours with Barb while he stocked up on supplies for the mission. Declan arrived to fly them back, with the kids stacked between crates. The next day Ethiopian Airlines suspended flights to thirty countries; by the end of the month the mission had shut down, and his decision to bring the kids back to the same country as Barb was suddenly moot. They did their best with WhatsApp. At least the mission and the halfway house had Internet.

Ross hated teaching Abeba and Eli without their classmates. Abeba hated it, too, though Eli hardly noticed. The three of them made masks from old clothes and kept track of the cases in Oromia as Ross steadily drove himself crazy. Sometimes he left Abeba in charge and walked outside to clear his head.

Today he ended up lying on top of Declan's bed. He was three sheets to the wind. It was becoming a habit.

The pilot slumped next to him, sipping from the bottle whose level never seemed to go down, as if he were keeping it full with magic.

Declan raised his glass. "'All my means are sane, my motive and my object mad.'"

Ross recognized the impulse, but this wasn't about him. "You have it backwards," he said.

"It's just *Moby-Dick*," Declan replied.

"*Your* means? They're anything but sane."

"Excuse me?"

"You slept with someone else's wife to start a family." Ross only said this because he was drunk. No, that was wrong. He would have said it sober, too.

"Her idea, actually."

Ross rolled his eyes. "Splitting hairs."

Declan took a sip. "You talk about it so casual-like."

"Pastoral training. I've heard too many awful things from congregants."

"The human race." Declan tipped his glass in acknowledgment.

"You should spend more time with Eli." Ross knew this was bad form, reminding Declan of his avoidance. "It restores your faith in things, knowing he's going to outlive you." He thought of Jason and took another drink. "If not him, someone like him."

Declan nodded. "That's why people have children—to make sure someone's there when they die."

"Oh, is *that* why?"

"I only meant—"

"I know what you meant." Declan didn't have anyone obligated by blood or paperwork to be there in the end, but Ross had never wanted that—the obligation soured the act.

He changed the subject. "Still getting those emails from your Stockholm sweetheart?"

"Mm-hmm."

"So she's real." Declan nodded. "I thought she might be . . ."

Declan blinked, understanding. "I wouldn't have—"

"Forget it." Confinement really was getting to him. It was probably worse for Declan, who was used to flying. Ross just missed having an audience. (Sometimes the kids pretended for him.) "Tell me about her."

Declan chewed his lip. "There's nothing to say. I miss her."

"Eli would do well in Stockholm."

Declan blinked again. "Nothing's going to happen to you and Barb."

"Something might."

"Something might happen to *me*."

Ross bumped his leg against Declan's. "Only if you forget to wear your mask."

"When this is over . . ." Declan drifted off, as though scared to predict the future.

Ross didn't share that fear. "You could try for a commercial pilot's license."

"I'm too old."

"That's just your inner critic."

"Tilde will never take me back. She shouldn't."

"Never say never. On furlough I had a date with my high school sweetheart."

"Pfft."

"Almost did something we'd regret." Ross didn't need to elaborate. A threat rose in Declan's eyes. "Don't worry. I still have a Barb Eklund . . . What's the word? Not *fixation*." He was doing this more often, missing English words when he remembered the Amharic.

"You once told me to go to Addis." Declan half-smiled. "Take your own advice, pastor."

Ross stared at his empty glass. Everything was slick and sliding. He shut his eyes, just for a moment. "You say that, but we could be stuck here for months. Years."

"The first word out of your mouth wasn't *no*."

Ross hummed, annoyed at himself. Declan nudged Ross's head with his glass.

"What?"

"We. Don't. Belong. Here." He tapped Ross's brow with each word.

"You mean we, Ross and Declan, or we, Americans—the West—in general?"

Declan shrugged and sipped his *araqe*. Ross nodded as though he'd spoken.

The pilot stood. "I have another secret for you." He crouched like he was reaching for the bottle again, but his arm disappeared further under the dresser and pulled out a packet. "Barb ever tell you about the pearls her mother used to wear?"

Ross nodded. "She hates jewelry, but I would catch her pausing in front of store displays. Always pearl necklaces. She thought she was being stealthy." He half-laughed.

Declan unwrapped the package slowly, revealing the necklace.

"No—"

"Don't doubt." It was a reprimand, followed by Declan's account of the pearls' history. Then he stepped forward and held the necklace out to Ross.

"Dec." Ross couldn't believe what he was about to say. "You should be the one."

The pilot watched him, eyes intent. "But I'm *not*."

Something had changed. Declan never spoke of the future—of getting a change of scenery—but here were the pearls in Ross's palm. He didn't care, suddenly, that he was separated, that he didn't know who Eli's father was. He was just grateful—for Declan and for the marvel of his gift.

Ross looked at the necklace, waiting for it to transmute, to shift into a bird and fly away.

"*Affliction,*" he finally said. "Barb Eklund *affliction.*"

———

Barb · June 2020

As threat of the pandemic grew, visiting hours and new intakes at the house ceased. Everyone stayed indoors, trying to slow the spread and flatten the curve, aware of what was happening in Italy. Yonas's work at the hospital made him a rare sight. Still, on his few days off, he visited the patio at the back of the house. He refused to come inside, but he sipped Fanta and smoked cigars with Barb and Alma, each of them at a separate table.

Barb began unstacking her barricade of books in his company, personal detail by personal detail. Maybe it was the pandemic, maybe it was the kiss, or maybe it was that he, too, had been told by the person he most loved to leave. And separation had been worse for him; his ex had tried to keep the kids to herself.

"She was right to," he admitted. "I was a shit father. Young and stupid." He'd since changed the trajectory of his life. After the divorce, he quit using cold medicine to get through shifts at the ER and cut back his time at the hospital in favor of work at nonprofits. He even volunteered in Liberia during the Ebola outbreak of 2014, something akin to but altogether different from what the world was experiencing now in 2020.

"I can do very little," he said, "but that very little is important to me."

Barb liked that he admitted this. There was a selfishness in her need to help others. Sometimes she felt guilty about enjoying it, but that was just the specter of the mission's strict morality. God punished you for being proud, so she trained herself not to take credit. She sometimes wondered if this was why she had stopped foreseeing the consequences of her actions—if she had no agency, whom could she hurt?

One day she stole sketch paper and pencils from the house's art supplies and spent the afternoon on the patio drawing the dignitary's peafowl as Yonas and Alma looked on. She had to keep shaking out her hand, she was so rusty.

Yonas cleared his throat and she looked up. "Ross called me at work to check on Lelo's regimen."

There was a buzzing in Barb's skull, like the news had shaken something loose. "Oh?"

"Don't take this wrong." He sipped his Fanta. "But he's wonderful."

Ross struck everyone this way. The difference was that his first impression lasted. Barb felt she grew wearisome after six months. First, Raji and Dez had stuck it out, then Yonas and Alma—the very same Yonas and Alma who had started sharing glances when they thought she wasn't looking.

"He's passionate," Yonas went on. "It's contagious."

"You barely mention him." This from Alma.

Barb thought of her glimpses of Ross on WhatsApp, always off to the side or in a quick flash as he ended the call and waved, tight-lipped. She remembered what it was like to rest her arm on the center of their bed and brush his hip with her hand, to see the vestiges of his morning around the bungalow after she cared for the chickens. Now they would need to quarantine for days just to end up in the same room, and Ross didn't want that anyway.

She crossed her arms, trying to quiet the tingling in her head. "We barely speak."

Yonas nodded and puffed at his cigar. It smelled like roasted chicory and gravitas. She tried to remember her last cigarette—had it been before Abeba? What a strange thing to forget.

This was when Yonas suggested she start a journal. The act of writing had helped him get through his own divorce.

The next morning Barb found a forgotten notebook in her office and started to fill its yellowed pages.

Her words came in fits and starts: *Did we ever see each other clearly? There was a density to both of us—I had no idea.* Then, *Why did you help me? Why do you always manage to help me even when I don't deserve it?* She confessed, *I don't know if I believe in God anymore. I wish I could come home.* She asked, *Was there a time when you knew that, whatever I ended up, it wouldn't change how you felt? Because I'm starting to realize, I loved whatever I saw of you.*

She didn't mean to write *to* Ross. It just happened.

Sometimes she illustrated the margins of the notebook with Abeba's eyes or Eli's hands. It took weeks before the words came more smoothly, as if she had finally learned how to slowly release the clutch and let her pen run across the page. She sustained paragraphs and pages. She wrote about Makeda's recruiting trip—*It's what brought us Lelo*—and Yonas's role in it:

> *I wonder what you think of Yonas now that you've spoken to him. He's been indispensable to me. He's also the reason I started writing.*
>
> *He's a friend. I say this despite the conviction that I've gotten friendship wrong my whole life. It's a craft, like drawing or whittling or origami. The work it takes is subtler than I imagined. I used to measure it by grand gestures, but those only sparkle for a moment. I think you taught me this, though I'm not sure how or when.*

She rambled on about the mundanity of her days—the menagerie in the dignitary's back yard, her favorite teas, her visit to the Martyrs' Museum, how she missed Raji and Dez—for months before venturing into the past.

> *I started to keep Welete a secret in college. No matter how I explained, no one understood my connection to it—first to the people, then to the red soil, the landscape of hills, the lapping of the Omo River—and the birds and insects and snakes and trees.*

She wrote about growing up with Declan: the way he looked after her, fascinated her, nicknamed her. She even wrote of three years ago, when he had come to find her in Addis—*Did you know? I always suspected he got my address from you.*

She detailed her last argument with Marty and how Simeon had been peacekeeper, not just among the missionaries but between his wife and daughter. Any time she wanted to hold something back, she wrote it down. Keeping secrets had served her poorly, so she fought the instinct as best she could.

She wrote of Makeda—how they had lost and found each other and about how Makeda's laughter had started to fill the house. Barb studied that laughter, memorized it, tried to distill it to its purest form on paper: *Her laugh is nothing like a bird's. It has a full body, like red wine without the bitterness.*

No no no, she second-guessed. *I'm being reductive. Makeda's laughs are multitudinous. The wine is one of my favorites, but a wonderful thing happens when a laugh bursts forth mid-sentence: part duck quack and part sneeze—shk-choo.*

But between laughs, worry still creased Makeda's brow. Lelo's treatments came with side effects—fatigue and nausea—and Makeda lingered by her side. Barb noticed the same thing growing between them as between Yonas and Alma—gradual looks that added up to forever.

It took more time for Barb to write about God. When she did, the words sank below and above the lines in her notebook. Nothing felt firm.

I lost God in the States. It was my belief in Welete that grew—so large it became an absurd thing. But Welete is just a place. I can grow into and out of my beliefs anywhere. Like here. I blunder from task to task, sometimes convinced that there's no God and other times that God is sitting right next to me, bumping my shoulder.

She filled the notebook for as long as Addis was under quarantine, letting her words take her where she needed to go—to the past and to her uncertain future, to the height of her hope and the nadir of her regret—until one day she woke without the burden to reveal herself.

She didn't mind the emptiness. It almost felt like peace.

But something still caught in her throat. She wrote her final secret:

I love you, Ross. I love you with the part of me that fell for the mission pilot, the part that wore ugly skirts on principle, and the parts that are Barbara and Barbie Doll and Barb Wire.

She went back and added a *d* to the end of *love,* then regretted it.

Still, she kept the feeling in the past.

She fanned the notebook's pages, and a lifetime of secrets and symbols flipped by. They had felt so precious until she spelled them out.

But her life wasn't just the words. It was the spaces between them—where she used to get lost in her mother's letters.

She wondered what Ross would make of those spaces.

She stuffed the journal in a manila envelope, addressed it to the mission, and placed it with the outgoing mail on Alma's desk.

She didn't need a record of her secrets. She hadn't written it just for her anyway.

That night, with the warm scent of rooibos still in the air, Makeda hung back after Lelo had gone to bed. Her jaw was tense.

"What is it?" Barb didn't bother to keep the concern from her voice.

Makeda's graduation from the program was getting closer and, despite the pandemic, her mentors were encouraging her to think ahead.

"I've never made plans for the future. Or I did, but only in Welete." She turned to Barb. "How do you do this to me? Is it a gift you have?"

Barb didn't smile. To look to the future set Makeda apart from those around her; it was as isolating as it was hopeful. Barb wondered if it was a curse, not a gift, but then a voice inside her (a voice like God and not like God) said, *It's curse and gift.*

Time expanded and contracted. "What plans?"

Makeda paused. "School. In business. Maybe accounting." There was a flash of something in her face that reminded Barb of when they had traded languages in the grove. "Addis University has special interest in supporting women. It makes me hope."

Barb thought the conversation was over, but Makeda looked down, her mouth open. "I also . . . I've thought of writing a book. Not about finance. But—my life? I have these memories that feel trapped."

Barb nodded. She had felt that way with the journal. "You should. You definitely should." Then she surprised herself by asking, "Would you ever take over here?" She had once posed the question to Alma, who had looked at Barb as if she were out of her mind. "Take over after university, I mean."

Makeda stared at the ceiling. "The only time I returned someplace, my shoulder was dislocated. Is it always like that?"

"Maybe."

"It depends." Makeda sounded certain, and Barb stared at the ceiling, too, following for the thousandth time a crack in the paint that stretched the width of the basement. *What persistence,* she thought, then teased herself for believing something like a crack could be alive.

But maybe she was wrong. A crack had as much right to persist as a person—to survive and to hope, even, in its own way.

Barb · February 2021

With an unfamiliar peace in her chest, Barb found it easy to forget the journal. It seemed more likely to be lost in the mail than to be read by Ross.

(*If* he bothered to read it.)

She certainly hadn't expected him to write back.

The envelope stuck out from the pile of mail. Alma had always been considerate, but Kima wasted no time, teasing, "What do you have? From Dr. Fekede, yes?"

Barb shook her head. "My husband." Her shock bordered on fear. She was a child in the hangar again, staring at the alphabet of tools, enough possibilities to swallow her whole.

She waited until lights-out to open it and smoothed the pages so slowly she chastised herself. The worst he could say was *I never loved you.* Though the thought paralyzed her, she forced herself to read anyway.

He started with *Barb*—not *Dear Barb,* just her name—and a perfunctory paragraph describing how his function on the mission had changed during the pandemic. It took time for the Ross she knew to bleed through, like the ink from his pen when he pressed too hard:

For what it's worth, I wish we'd come to Welete sooner. Because I see what you saw as a child, the largeness here. I spent years going on those mission trips trying to capture that largeness, but it was all wrong.

I'd been told a story in seminary—one where I was going to change the world for the better, no matter the cost.

Now I'm just tired.

It's hard being around people on the mission who never admit their doubts. Like the way our parents believe in God—it's hardly faith, they're so sure. They just blink the doubt away.

The university in Jimma might need a language instructor, but I don't know.

I'm happy to hear that you think less of me. *of me less often. I've noticed the same thing in myself. It's easier to take walks, to visit the hangar, and not be reminded of the day I asked you to leave, of my naïveté and disappointment—the things I'd like to forget.*

There was a space, and a change in pen.

You wrote that you used to measure friendship in grand gestures. I knew this about you. I think I even used it to my advantage.

Another space, another change.

I told you about Kristy, my other serious relationship. I reached out to her, and while you took the kids to Europe, she took me on a horseback ride, and, yes, I was sore for a week, but I'm stalling.
    After the ride, we started something that we didn't finish—just like when we were teenagers. Some days I wish we would have finished.

Barb thought she had left the pain in her ribs in the States, but here it was, flaring up as she discovered she'd lost something. She pushed herself away from the letter, went upstairs to the bathroom, and sat in a stall deciding whether she was nauseous or something worse—angry? jealous? disgusted? She had been the last person to share a bed with Ross until, suddenly, she wasn't. She imagined Abeba and Eli calling Kristy *Mom* and knew someday it would happen—if not with Kristy, then with someone else. She felt powerless at the inevitability.

But the story also made her wonder if Ross, too, was giving away his secrets.

By the time she retrieved the letter from her desk, she'd shaken free of the nausea. She crawled into bed with the pages, counted to ten, and read to the end.

Do you remember Ralph Wheaton? I keep thinking of him. I don't even know—is he still alive? On house visits I'd always find him in his old recliner. It was pink and gave massages, but it broke down and his disability checks weren't enough to get a new one. I thought about taking a collection at the church, but he refused. He lived in that chair, sleeping, eating, watching talk shows . . .

One day I came into his trailer with his groceries, and the chair was empty. He was sobbing on that filthy floor—he'd never let me sweep it. He'd seen a story about an ex-girlfriend on the news. She was missing and he got up to call the police or I don't remember, but his back gave out. I called an ambulance, though he begged me not to. He just lay there, sobbing and moaning the name "Jennifer" and then just "jenjenjenjenjen." I put away the groceries and tried to think of something to say.

Sometimes there's nothing to say or do. (That's the lesson.)

When the ambulance came, they helped him get comfortable and left. (There's no bill that way.) In the car later, I stared at the dashboard and couldn't stop hearing the pain in his voice or thinking of the pain he felt every day. I thought of the game the deacons were playing with me, how they didn't want the truth of human experience—they didn't want to feel Ralph's pain or even admit its existence.

Because that God scared them.

Sometime later I was reading the Nicene Creed and felt even this I couldn't believe. Not one word had changed, but I had. I looked at Christians—the loudest ones, anyway, equal parts entitlement and insecurity—and I knew they didn't want me.

So I stopped using the word, and people just assumed, like they assumed sending "missionaries to Africa" was a good thing—like I'd assumed for so long.

It was like a decoupling. An unfollowing. I don't know.

I still believe, but there's no word for it.

Barb flipped the page over and found Ross's signature, followed by a P.S.

The first question you wrote was "Did we ever see each other clearly?" I don't know if you were looking for an answer, but I loved whatever you let me see. I believe I would have loved even what you hadn't.

(I always knew you wouldn't be the one to ruin things.)

———

Barb · June 2021

A month after the halfway house reopened to new clients and visitors, Abeba and Eli arrived in Addis. Barb had spent the morning washing sheets and handing out masks to tenants. Usually Caj would drop the kids off at noon, but today noon came and went. By the time visiting hours began, at two, Barb wasn't sure who to call or where to go. She was reminded of a moment in Vienna during their month in Europe, when she'd stood shouting on the steps of the *Donnerbrunnen,* thinking she'd lost them, until she spotted Abeba's pink windbreaker.

Alma whispered, "They're here," and Barb turned to find her children, smiling under their masks. She left reception and squeezed them hard, but neither Abeba nor Eli was fazed by their tardiness. They stared, gauging her reaction. Barb wasn't sure why until she saw the man in the doorway: her husband, dressed in a suit she'd picked out from a Nordstrom in Pittsburgh. It was too big now. He held a soft portfolio in his hands.

"You got new glasses," she said. They were all she could see of his face.

His hand went to the rims self-consciously. "Sorry for being late. The kids told me I had to wait for visiting hours."

"Right." She exhaled. "It's good to see you."

He nodded and rocked onto his toes. She asked the kids if they would keep Alma company while she talked to Dad.

"Of course," Eli piped up, uncharacteristically. Abeba just kept smiling.

"Do you want the tour?" Barb asked. "To meet Lelo?"

Ross's gaze cut to the ground, then back to her face. "Talk first."

She walked him down to the basement, as if reversing their roles on the night he'd proposed at his parents' house. Two tenants played cards in the lounge: Kima and Totit, who was new. Their masks hung unused around their necks.

"Escaping the desperation." Kima gestured above her, where most of the tenants waited for someone. Kima never had visitors, and Totit hadn't notified anyone of her whereabouts.

Barb was thankful her mask hid the desperation on her own face. She led Ross to her office. He surveyed the stacks of papers, the bookshelves filled with haphazard volumes, the general clutter of her office. "Not much privacy." He tightened his grip on the portfolio.

Barb looked at her bedroom. "It's that or the kids' room."

He followed her inside and sat on the edge of her bed. "Cozy."

Lonely, she thought, and remained standing, afraid to close the distance between them, not just because it was the responsible thing to do after a pandemic—she'd hugged the kids without thinking. She still didn't know why Ross was here.

He touched his mask and raised his eyebrows. She nodded and he slipped it off.

She folded hers into one of her back pockets. "It's good to see you. To be able to thank you in person for what you did for Lelo."

"It was nothing."

Barb wasn't sure if this was false modesty. "The kids seem happy."

"They're hopeful—nothing we can do," he replied matter-of-factly, and Barb understood.

"What's in the folder, Ross?"

"I had a lawyer draw up papers." He opened the portfolio and there they were. To think she'd locked away a similar sheaf in her desk at Mount Olive, ready to ruin them both.

"Thing is," he went on, "you might not need me for my visa anymore, but I need you."

A half hour later, they'd come to a decision: to hold off signing until Ross had found a new job.

"You wouldn't move the kids back to the States?" she asked.

He looked annoyed. "You can still trust me, Barb."

"It's a divorce, Ross."

"Not yet." He sounded ready to fight for her, but already looked defeated. He patted the spot next to him on the bed.

She sat without thinking. "How are the kids? It's been so long since . . . I can't get a bead on them anymore, and Abeba's almost ready for college."

"It must be hard." He sounded far away.

"Isolation was hard for everyone."

He shook his head. "I'm sorry. I'm just—I'm glad we're all safe."

She was used to the Ross who blustered and amazed. She had forgotten this one—quiet and contemplative, who held more empathy in a moment than she sometimes felt capable of in a lifetime. If she were to say this aloud, he would probably argue with her, call her shortsighted.

He straightened up, pulling his shoulders back. "Abeba and I actually talked about doing her senior year at an international school in Addis."

"Really?" Barb wondered if that would mean seeing more or less of her.

"She wants your blessing."

Barb scoffed. "She's never needed my approval."

"You don't know?" Ross looked surprised. "It's not Abby anymore. She prefers Beba, the name closer to yours."

Barb smiled. "You should have been the lit major."

"I have textual evidence for my claim." He looked at her sidewise. "It's good you can make jokes—that's not a criticism. It's just there were long stretches when you didn't."

"Well, I learned to be funny from you."

"That's why it took so long." He paused. "You know the kids adjusted sooner than I did."

Her stomach warmed. "You look like you're doing just fine from where I'm sitting."

"But you're not sitting very close—not as close as you used to."

"Pandemic."

"Don't care."

She scooted in until their shoulders touched, and the tension eased. "You're a little thin for that suit."

"I didn't believe Declan, but." He pointed at her right hand. "You still wear it."

She made a fist, the ring biting into her skin. "You don't."

He shrugged. "You left."

"You asked me to."

"I have something." His brow furrowed as he reached into his breast pocket. It was a folded piece of parchment tied with twine. He handed it to her.

"What's today?" she asked.

"It's not an occasion."

Satisfied, she opened the packet quickly. Inside was a necklace—no, *the* necklace, slithering on her palm like a house snake. She looked at Ross, a little frightened, because he'd made her wish come true. Life was a fairy tale after all, or at least something written by L. M. Montgomery.

"How?" she breathed.

"It was Declan. He went back and bought it. He, uh, tried to give it to you."

"But I wouldn't let him." She unclasped the necklace and reached behind her. Her hands were clumsy and, without a word, Ross swept her hair away and fastened the clasp. His hands lingered. One traveled down her back. She laughed. "I could have used these for the hospital fundraiser."

His smile didn't reach his eyes. "The one at the Sheraton? When you went with Yonas?"

"Did he . . . tell you that?"

Ross shrugged again. He wasn't about to betray Yonas's confidence. She just wondered why Yonas hadn't warned her.

"We kissed," she said. "It didn't . . ." She stopped. She didn't want to justify herself. Not anymore and not to Ross. It was just another futile attempt to scramble up the banks of the Omo.

"You quarantined together, right?"

She didn't hear Ross's question, but the question under it. "Yes, but it isn't—"

"I'm not here to blame you." He took her hands and squeezed gently. He wasn't angry. He was scared and trying not to show it. "There's no high ground here. I was almost with Kristy. If you're with him, you can tell me—you can . . . write it down."

She hadn't written about the kiss because she hadn't needed to. "Yonas is my friend."

Ross rubbed his thumb against her hand. The movement calmed her more than words could. She wondered if she had kissed Yonas only because she missed kissing Ross. To sit close to him again, to have his hands on hers—she'd wanted to remember.

He let go. "I should head out." He stood and started toward the hall. "No tour?"

He turned and held her gaze for one beat, then another.

"It was too much work before. I can't go back to that."

He donned his mask and ducked out the door. She felt the loss like it was her last day on the mission.

―――

Declan • August 2021

The pandemic has overstayed its welcome in Addis. Passersby may be fewer, may be wearing masks, but their bright clothing still snags Declan's eye.

He doesn't speak in the car to Bole. He barely recognizes the neighborhood where the Derg kept him. The thought is as fleeting as his glance.

He thanks his driver as they arrive, and shoulders his backpack. There's next to nothing inside: a few changes of clothes, extra masks, his vaccination card and IDs, the crane from Eli. His flight number sits on a slip of paper in his wallet.

He's starting over.

Leaving the hangar's back room had been harder than he thought it would be. The place had been privy to a lifetime of secrets. There he said goodbye to Ross, who shook his hand and said, "You beat me out of here."

Declan smiled, though it was strange to smile about this, stranger still to pull Ross into an embrace. The wetness on his shoulder told him they were both crying because—why had it been so hard to admit?—they were brothers now.

He pressed a wooden figure into Ross's hands, a mouse standing on its hind legs. He didn't have to say who it was for.

Ross just raised an eyebrow. "I'll get the kids up there whether you like it or not."

Declan shook his head because he felt the tears again. "Just—come in the summer."

Ross slapped his back in answer, which cracked both of their façades, the action being so uncharacteristic of Ross and so characteristic of Declan.

They waved as he disappeared from the mission.

The moment felt different from his other disappearances.

Two months earlier he'd sat in the mission office, the last person awake, and signed into WhatsApp. Tilde's avatar greeted him, he enabled video, and suddenly there they both were. The picture was pixelated, and her hair was gray—such little difference between that shade and blonde. She wore it down. He commented on it.

"You used to like it this way."

"Still do."

She smiled. "The wolf and moose you gave me—they're in my bedroom."

"Not the plane."

She blinked slowly. "I hid it."

"The stain held up?"

She shrugged. She was quieter than he'd remembered. Maybe it was the connection.

"We're finally here," he said to break the silence.

"It could have been sooner." She coughed and he felt a surge of fear.

"Are you . . . ?"

"No. It's not that."

She told him she'd had his email address taped to her desk for so long that it would get covered in debriefings. She'd unearth it and say, "Tomorrow."

"Then you started with your Melville and still I thought, *i morgon*."

He wanted to say he'd never stopped thinking of her either. "What changed your mind?"

"The truck. It made me think of death."

She meant the hijacked truck that had killed five people on *Drottninggatan* in 2017, the same year Declan had lost himself to his spiraling thoughts and too much *araqe*. Tilde's emails had spiraled too, pirouetting between topics without landing, larded with quotations and accusations and memories.

He told this pixelated version of her the story of how he'd gotten back to Ethiopia, how he no longer trembled when walking the streets of Addis. He mentioned Barb and Eli.

"What aren't you saying?" she asked, like they'd spent no time apart.

"She was married."

"Was?"

"They're separated. My fault."

"Oh." Her face tensed. He didn't know what that meant.

Declan looked down at his hands, surprised at how creased they were. Talking to Tilde made him feel as if he were thirty again, but a softer thirty than he had been. Everything sat closer to the surface. He had spent so many moments regretting his exit from Stockholm and just as many being thankful for it. Their history together had expanded with regret in his memory; he'd never imagined she felt those three years just as deeply.

He said, "I was selfish when I left."

Silence. Then she offered, "I couldn't give you what you wanted."

It wasn't an apology, but he didn't want one. "Your turn."

She was a partner at the firm. Her family consisted of her sister in Stockholm and her niece, who'd run away to Canada when she was seventeen in a spectacular display of shouting and fists; Tilde had earned a bruise on her chest.

She liked to travel, too, though not to Canada. "I've been to Australia, to Mexico. Florida and Georgia, too."

He wondered if she'd traveled there in search of him, but that was too romantic a notion. "Now there's something you're not telling."

She placed a finger on her nose and pointed, as if they were playing a game of charades.

Her sister had been diagnosed with multiple sclerosis, just as their mother had.

"It's one of those diseases," she said, "where you know the future. Like the punctuation mark, she'll be up-down, up-down, good days and bad."

Declan had grown so used to the certainty of the past—the fixed nature of a photograph—that the changes in her life felt extraordinary.

"You'll stay with her?" he asked, without knowing why.

She scoffed. "Of course I'll stay."

He reached out and touched nothing but a computer. "On your own?"

"You expected an invitation?"

She sounded playful, but her face was serious; he'd forgotten how much weight it added to her words, so much weight he didn't know how she could speak.

———

Declan winds his way through the terminal, leaving airport security behind—along with the mission and the back room, his secrets and regrets. He takes more time to find his gate than he should, but he always takes the long way round.

This disappearance feels different because it's his last.

Because he had stared at Tilde's image and promised, "I'll be there."

———

Four

I promise nothing complete; because any human thing supposed to be complete, must for that very reason infallibly be faulty. . . .

Herman Melville, Moby-Dick, *chapter 32*

THE FIRST COFFIN

THE LAND OF YOUR BIRTH, THOUGH YOU DON'T REMEMBER being born, is flat and red. It offers you little shelter from the wind that cuts across the dirt. The food you eat grows close to the ground and sparkles like blood. You cross the terrain hoping someday it will change.

Waaq steps down from the clouds and brings you gifts—a fruit called a lemon, a leaf as red as the soil, a ball to kick around. Sometimes you and Waaq play a game with it.

You always lose.

Today Waaq bears not gifts but an invitation to build your own coffin.

"It'll be fun," Waaq says, as if this is another game. "I'll put you to sleep."

"But I'll wake too soon." You always do. You wake when the light is still gone.

Waaq has never punished you before, but as you build the coffin out of baobab branches, you can't help but wonder if a god can change.

Once it's done, you ask why you have to sleep.

Waaq shrugs. "It's a surprise."

This isn't an answer, and Waaq knows it. Another game. You lie in the coffin and wonder if you had any choice.

But you're already asleep.

You wake one day and see what Waaq has made you—hills and mountains, a companion and a people, a place to belong.

You never see Waaq again.

———

ADDIS

Barb · April 2022

B ARB SITS AT ALMA'S DESK, AS STILL AS A ROCK, IMMOBILE at the river's mouth, watching pedestrians drift past the open doors. This weekend the halfway house is deserted—all but a few tenants are on a retreat, where they'll come to epiphanies and cry on each other's shoulders, much like Ross's congregants did when they returned from their mission trips. All it takes for a person's life to change is different scenery and the absence of familiar pressures.

The retreat is necessary. Tensions have run high among the tenants since the Tigray War started more than a year ago.

A cat, a black tuxedo, jumps on the desk, landing near Barb's discarded mask, and mewls. He's nothing like Gabi, who would shove her wet nose and tongue into her humans' faces. The cat appears just off to the side; he's been Barb's shadow since the funeral. In the moments before she starts to cry, the cat tends to find her, slips into her office or scratches at her bedroom door.

She's staffing the desk because Yonas has taken Alma on a hike to the church on Entoto Hill. He promised to have her back before the kids arrive, but he wouldn't look Barb in the eye. It was strange, granting two adults permission to go on a date. She hasn't even done that for the kids. Even with their more frequent visits, certain firsts escape her.

Abeba texts to say they're on their way.

Oh and dad's coming

For a moment, Barb thinks of her own father, but of course that's not what Abeba means.

She's getting ready to graduate from a high school in the city, the same school where Eli skipped a grade this year. The grandparents help with tuition, and Abeba plans to take a gap year, intern at one of the embassies, and live with Ross and Eli while applying to universities.

"Maybe Georgetown," she said when Barb asked. "Or Duke."

It's no surprise Ross is coming, but the news still makes her nervous. He tags along with the kids often enough that it makes her question what they're really doing with each other. She goes downstairs to retrieve the divorce papers from her bedroom, determined to make a decision about them, if not today, then soon. She and Ross don't need each other's visas anymore. They haven't in a while.

He started adjuncting at Addis Ababa University eight months ago. He hasn't had Makeda in class, not yet. She and Lelo moved in together as soon as they both completed the house's program, and Makeda keeps threatening to fill out Lelo's own university application. Lelo's viral load has been undetectable since January, but every decision about the future still feels like an act of faith.

Last month Makeda sent Barb the first pages of her memoir. Really, Ross should be the one critiquing it. Barb's too close to the subject, as the first line demonstrates: *One day long ago the white people came. . . .* Barb appreciates the images Makeda uses from her childhood, from Barb's childhood, too.

It's not all they've talked about. There are days Barb wants to lift her anchor, to place it in Makeda's hands, should she be willing to accept it.

Alma's desk is a mix of phone messages and work orders. Barb starts in on a request for new toilet seats, but that's a mistake. The divorce papers were the last thing in front of her, and her half-signed name makes her stomach lurch.

She shoves the papers into an unmarked folder.

The cat must sense her unease. He lands on the arm of the chair and licks her shoulder, where the cigarette burn has faded. A moment later he jumps to the ground and pads toward the entrance, as Alma and Yonas appear.

"Look who we found." Yonas flashes Barb a smile as Abeba and Eli duck past him. He and Alma must have been waiting outside, stretching out their last moments of privacy. It's what she would have done.

She hugs the kids as the cat nuzzles Eli's feet and lets out a threatening *mrowr*. Eli shows Barb Kaldi, the new mouse he found outside of Ross's apartment, now perched in his shirt pocket, its fur darker than the wooden figure Declan had made.

"I can't say no to pets," Ross says from behind them, always managing to catch Barb unaware.

Yonas scoops up the cat and carries him outside, away from the mouse, but not before sharing a look with Ross, who ruffles Eli's hair and tells the kids to put away their bags. "Then Yonas can take you to Igloo."

Barb hesitates. The kids used to love Igloo, Eli more for its décor of smiling penguins than for the gelato. It's been years since they showed interest, but the shop is more than a mile away, which will give their parents time to talk.

Her thoughts flit to the divorce papers. She picks up the folder and follows the kids downstairs. They disappear into their room, she and Ross into her office. She tosses the folder onto her desk, and the papers fan out. He hesitates, then straightens them. She wonders if he recognizes what they are.

He turns to her. "You okay?"

"Why shouldn't I be?"

He shakes his head, and Barb sees her obfuscation through his eyes. Abeba pops into the doorway to announce they're off.

"Will Bennie be there?" Ross nods at the phone in her hand.

She shrugs. "You know. Possibly."

"Bennie?" Barb raises an eyebrow. She relishes acting like a parent in a sitcom. She so rarely gets the chance.

"We're both going for internships next year." It's a rehearsed explanation. Maybe Barb will get more out of her later, maybe not.

"Be careful," she says, because that's what's expected. When the kids' voices disappear up the stairs, she turns back to Ross. "It's hard. Better since the funeral."

"I'm still thinking of the service. It was beautiful. In the best sense of the word."

Barb knows what he means. Simeon's funeral had been a fitting celebration of her father's life—which was more complicated than she'd ever understood. Getting all four Mathesons there had been surreal. She had just started feeling financially secure, and here was the cost of their trip to the States suddenly unsettling her. Of course the cost wasn't the only thing. Ross got the kids vaccinated and took care of their flights, Alma and Yonas managed the house in Barb's absence, but even a week seemed too long to spend in such close proximity to her mother.

On the plane Barb's tears were silent. They made her mask damp and stopped only when she'd exhausted herself enough to fall asleep. She woke with her head on Ross's shoulder and jostled him awake without meaning to.

"Barb?" He noted her red eyes—barely faded from her nap. Her tears started again. He wiped them away with his thumb.

"My mother," she said. "I can't speak to her."

Ross nodded. Marty knew this, too. She'd called him with the news about Simeon, sticking to their mother-daughter vow of silence even in this. On Barb's worst days, she stalked Marty's profile on Facebook. It was part God-spam, part activism, but no personal insights. Sort of like Marty in real life. She hadn't posted since Simeon's death.

"We'll make it through the week without any casualties." Ross smiled behind his mask. "Promise."

"How?"

"By assigning Beba and Eli to you at all times."

"What about the bathroom? She'll find me in the bathroom."

He took a moment to hear the joke. "Then the bathroom will be the site of your mutually assured destruction." His face fell. "I booked you a hotel. Just in case."

She looked down. Of course he had. Because Ross was thoughtful and, possibly, trying to keep his distance. "Can we afford to?"

"Hey." It was his old warning—maybe at her cavalier use of *we*. She kept doing that, and this week would only make the habit harder to break.

She took the hotel room. Abeba wanted to stay, too, so they made the most of it—loading up on made-for-TV movies that weren't available in Ethiopia. Barb half-watched as she finalized what she would say at the service. She missed Ross and Eli, but she was glad to see Abeba in such a state of comfort—sprawled on the bed, crunching loudly on tortilla chips, the loose hem of her shirt riding up. It let Barb believe in the bubble of safety Ross had promised.

Marty found her anyway, at the house during the reception. She pulled Barb away from the children and into the mudroom. Barb braced herself, already depleted from fielding compliments on her eulogy.

Marty didn't look at her, but just past her shoulder. "I need you to know." She exhaled. "I'm selling the house."

She sounded certain, even as one hand worried her skirt.

"Where will you go?" Barb wished she'd asked out of concern, but there was fear, too—she was the only family Marty had now.

"To North Dakota."

Barb wanted to ask why they had never visited there, not in all their homestays on furloughs, but she said, "Will it just be—will you be alone?"

"One of my brothers lives there with his family." Marty tightened the grip on her skirt.

Barb wondered how that would feel—to go back home, to have a place that was one. She looked at Marty's dark eyes, which dazzled. When had Barb stopped seeing them?

"Mom."

Marty returned her gaze and suddenly there were a hundred things to say. Her mother didn't even know about the pearls.

But there was only one thing that mattered.

"You know, right? That we love you?"

The words weren't perfect, too hesitant, nothing like Marty's pronouncements. They were part-lie, too—she shouldn't have spoken for the kids or Ross—and Marty didn't smile like Barb had hoped. She nodded instead.

Now, when Ross calls the service "beautiful," Marty's nod—certain and new and strange—is all Barb can think of.

"I'm tired," she tells him. "Slowly catching up." There's that kindness in his eyes again. She shies from it.

He clears his throat. "I have news. About Declan."

At the name, she makes her face stony, hoping the rest of her body follows suit. She's so concerned with hiding her reaction she's not even sure what it is.

"We should go outside."

The patio's deserted, like the rest of the building. The peahen scours the dignitary's lawn for crickets while her mate perches atop the coop, his head sparkling like an emerald. Barb hears the monkeys but doesn't see them. She points out the new fountain the dignitary has installed—it somehow stays clean despite the animals' daily baths.

Ross starts in. "Have you heard from him?"

Her brow furrows. "You know we don't talk." It's been almost a year since Declan disappeared north—disappeared from her. He talks to Ross, over email and WhatsApp, for more reasons than to keep in touch with Eli.

The mission itself hasn't looked for another pilot. Their focus has shifted. New teachers at the school are from nearby towns, and there's a Jeep with a trailer to bring in kids from farther away. The Thorns are no longer there. Caj took a job offer in England, and he and Karin plan to adopt.

Meanwhile Dez has just learned that she's pregnant. She and Raji have been so focused on India since the pandemic started that the news has taken them by surprise. One of Raji's nieces had COVID last fall, but she recovered without infecting the rest of the household. Raji's parents and sisters have been lucky. Mumbai has fared better with the virus than New Delhi has.

Despite these changes, both global and local, there are still days when Declan is all Barb can think of. She's the one sending emails now, quotations from whatever book she's reading. They go unanswered.

"One day he might be ready," Ross says.

"How's Tilde?" she asks, and tries not to be jealous as her husband tells her about the lawyer who once saved Declan.

"Declan's happy. Really. He's doing that thing. Looking up his blood relatives." Ross stops, like he's said too much.

Her tears come suddenly. "Sorry." She presses a hand to her forehead until they stop. Ross shifts in his chair. She says, "I used to think we were only broken until the right person fixed us. I always thought I would be that for him."

"You can't fix everything."

"But it's my job." She gestures at the house behind her.

He looks at his hands. She wonders if he's resisting his own urge to fix her. It's unfair of her to think it, to expect it.

She inhales shakily. "Who's Bennie?"

Ross's shoulders relax. "Full name Biniyam. Good kid. Polite. It's the first time she's really shown interest in someone. They both want to major in the same thing."

"Is it still political science?"

"International relations."

"I always mix them up."

"Our daughter: stepping into the global future. I'm just glad I get her for another year."

"What about Eli?"

"He's the saddest ten-year-old I've ever seen. He tells me that's just his thinking face."

Barb gives a quick laugh. "Sounds like him."

"He, uh, he's had some problems at school. Socially, I mean—he aces his work."

The news surprises her. It contradicts the changes she's seen—the way he no longer shrinks from the tenants, has them doting on him instead. It's more proof that she's missing pieces of her children's lives—pieces she doesn't even know exist. "If you want, I can take him for longer."

"Another change might not be the best thing. The grade skip was what started it." Ross pauses. "We can think about it."

We, she thinks. "How's work?"

"Grading. Lectures. Meetings." He shrugs. "You ever get around to wearing those pearls?"

She huffs. "Who has the time?"

He reaches out, carefully. She isn't sure why until he touches the ring, still on her right hand. For a moment, everything stops.

He clears his throat. "Yonas hasn't . . . ?"

"Ross."

He shrinks back and refuses to look at her. He still doesn't understand.

"Coffee and churches."

He raises his eyebrows. "What?"

"That thing Raji said."

"Right. And you still think it's true."

"No one's life is just coffee and churches." She sits on her hands to hide the ring from both of them. "But I'm almost fifty, and it's taken me this long to find a place for myself."

"It took Declan till he was sixty."

"But I still don't belong."

"What does that even *mean*?"

"It means some days I get the urge to pack up and leave this place to Makeda." *Some days it's more than an urge,* she thinks, but she doesn't say it.

"Then why don't you?" He sounds annoyed.

"It's not like I have anywhere else to go."

"Barb."

His tone stills her. *Kindness,* she thinks, before realizing it's something else entirely. Kindness isn't reading an entire notebook of broken confessions. It isn't booking a hotel room without being asked.

In an instant the divorce papers feel like a joke, the separation a play they acted out for the sake of an inscrutable audience. Because she has somewhere to go. She has a place—with *him*—if she chooses.

He says, "You can leave any time."

"Tomorrow?" She breathes in and out. "Can we . . . ?"

He ducks his head, banishing her hope.

She collects herself, packing away all of her half-sketched ideas. "Where would you go? If you had the choice."

He chews his lip. "Stockholm. Maybe. We're hoping to get up there this summer."

The *we* doesn't include her this time. "I keep thinking about him—my dad, I mean. Not Declan."

"You mean you keep thinking about death."

He knows. Of course he does. "If God's not real, if our parents aren't right, then . . . 'Where lies the final harbor, whence we unmoor no more?'"

"What's that?"

"Ishmael." Ross looks nonplussed. "*Moby-Dick.*"

"*Moby-Dick.*" He smirks, like he's remembering something. Then he straightens in his chair. "Heaven should be in the horsehead nebula. I've always liked the horsehead nebula."

"Heaven always terrified me."

"Seriously."

"It's forever. What can you do forever, swimming around in perfection?"

"No wonder Eve ate the apple."

"Right?"

"Barb."

"I know. I *know.*"

"The story we tell ourselves about the end is more important than the end."

Oh, she thinks, because he's put to words the unnamable thing sitting behind her breastbone.

"And we don't know which story's true." He pulls his wallet from his pocket, turning it over and over. "Your dad, it's . . . He's your first death. Your first close one."

There had been Declan's death, but only for a time. Besides, Simeon's cuts closer to the bone.

"There's something that starts growing in you." Ross reaches into the wallet for an old photo. She sees the crease-covered face of his brother. "Jason's been dead for more than forty years and sometimes I forget him. I'll be streaming a Sixers game without a passing thought, and when I remember, I can't—" His brow furrows. "I just want to hurt myself."

The comment sits in silence for as long as it takes the peacock to descend from the coop and strut toward the fountain.

Ross tucks the photo away. "This is the way I've always been. When I broke up with Kristy I told her we'd ruin each other's lives."

"Smooth."

"So smooth." He leans in, their faces close. "The point is, being lost is what we're good at."

"Yeah, but I'd medal."

He shakes his head. "You've changed. There's something new." He touches the space between her eyes. "Just there."

She wonders if the something new will tip the scales and send Ross away.

He leans back. "You know it was my fault we were in Bethel so long."

"Blame me."

He looks at the ground. "Tried that."

It shouldn't surprise her, but it does. "I was too serious."

She means those years she was impossible to reach, but he still tried—with his dramatic readings of her mother's letters, his wrought PowerPoints on foreign countries, his cold pizza for breakfast. If Barb turns these memories over in her mind, she finds lightness and cynicism in unexpected places. Out of the corner of her eye, she recognizes it as love.

She takes a moment to return from a thought that large.

Ross is fidgeting. "How long do we have?"

The question used to be Declan's. "A while, I think."

She tucks her hair behind her ear. Suddenly he catches her hand in the air and places it on his knee. The act sends warmth shooting up her arm.

"I." She inhales. "I half-signed the divorce papers."

He squeezes her hand. "Okay."

"It was a mistake."

"Was it?" He looks away and back again.

"I thought it was a work order for the toilets."

He starts to smile—one she either hasn't seen before or doesn't remember—and like everything he does it's contagious.

"So." His eyes dazzle, too, when he puts his mind to it. "Should we shred them?"

She could answer, without thinking, but she looks up to find the family of monkeys, sitting under the coffee tree and eating its berries.

She points. "See the monkeys under the *buna-zaf*?"

"What are they doing?"

His hand in hers feels so light.

"Just wait," she says. "They might start dancing."

———

Acknowledgments

Thank you to Gabriel Bump, who chose *Unfollowers* for the Juniper Prize and whose own work abounds with humor, candor, and kindness.

Thank you to everyone at the University of Massachusetts Press—not least Dawn Potter, who rounded off all my sharp corners.

Thank you to my sensitivity readers: Vince Bantu, Kelly Silk, Linnéa Byers, and Lisa Eriksson.

Thank you to Nega Mezelekia, David C. Pollack, Ruth E. Van Reken, Tim Bascom, John Cumbers, Wolf Leslau, Claudia Rankine, and the Racial Imaginary Institute. These thinkers have broadened and deepened my understanding of the world.

This novel started as a writing exercise when I had just completed my MFA and was still slinging coffee in Washington, DC, so I must thank my cohort at school and my crew at Borders Café. You know who you are.

Countless others have inspired me along the way: my teachers Pam Whitmore, Kent L. Gramm, Nicole Mazzarella, Murad Kalam, and Maud Casey; my colleagues and friends at Great Falls College; the coffee adepts and trivia connoisseurs at Miss Kitty's; my cheerleaders Sarah B. Winchester, Laura Deffley, Paul Yount, and Kristi Voboril; my aunt Marty, who showed me how bright the world looked through kaleidoscopes; my aunts Arlene, Alice, and Belva, who showed me that literature was something you could love as much as people; my aunt Carol, who vetted this book's chronology; my father, who built tin can cars with me for Chuck Arnold's science class; and my mother, who still considers me her miracle child.

Most of all, I'm indebted to my partner, who has been with me for as long as I have been with this novel. This is not a coincidence.

JUNIPER
JUNIPER PRIZE FOR FICTION

This volume is the twenty-second recipient
of the Juniper Prize for Fiction,
established in 2004 by the
University of Massachusetts Press
in collaboration with the
UMass Amherst MFA Program
for Poets and Writers, to be
presented annually for an outstanding
work of literary fiction. Like its sister award,
the Juniper Prize for Poetry established
in 1976, the prize is named in honor
of Robert Francis (1901–1987),
who lived for many years at
Fort Juniper, Amherst, Massachusetts.